Other books by Karen McQuestion

For Adults
A Scattered Life
Easily Amused
The Long Way Home

For Teens
Favorite
Life on Hold
Edgewood (Book One)
Wanderlust (Book Two)

For Kids
Celia and the Fairies
Secrets of the Magic Ring

ABSOLUTION

BOOK 3
EDGEWOOD SERIES

Karen McQuestion

For Michelle Schrubbe

CHAPTER ONE

—————•◦●◦•—————

NADIA

I was glad our flight from Lima, Peru to Miami was more than five hours long because it gave me plenty of time to spend with Russ. The moments we'd had alone on this trip had been filled with real love. I knew that, I *felt* that, but I wanted more than just a happy memory. What I wanted was a lasting relationship. It was okay with me if it started off as a whirlwind romance, as long as it led to a lifetime of love. I knew that was a lot to ask, but the universe had dealt me a pretty crappy hand for the first sixteen years of my life. The way I looked at it, I was due for a lot of good things to come my way.

I made the mistake of lagging behind the rest of the group, and in those few moments, Mallory had already grabbed Russ and pulled him into a seat next to her. As I passed them in the aisle, she raised her eyebrows the way girls do to show they've got something on you. She acted like it was a joke, but I didn't think it was funny. Russ wasn't even looking in my direction. His eyes were only on her.

I walked by and found a seat a few rows back and dropped my bag at my feet. When we'd left for Peru more than a week earlier, all of us, four students and our three chaperones, had buzzed with excitement. This time around, going in the opposite direction, things were a lot quieter. Except for Mallory's constant talking and the sound of a video clip on her iPad, all was quiet. Once the plane was up in the air, I leaned over to rummage through my bag, searching until I found the plastic bag with the few sleeping pills I'd filched from my mother's medicine cabinet. There was no way I could stand to listen to Mallory and Russ talk all the way across the ocean. Better to be unconscious. I swallowed one of the pills and followed it with a swig of water. When I didn't feel the effects after ten minutes or so, I took another one. This time it worked. Everything got pleasantly woozy and even Mallory's nonstop chatter faded into the distance. For now, I let my worry about Mallory stealing Russ slip away, saving it for later.

Going back to my bag, I felt around the bottom, until I found what I was looking for—the Lucky Man I'd been given by one of the vendors in the market. Smaller than a Barbie doll, it was a pottery figure of a mustached man holding an armload of stuff—money, medicine, a heart. All of it symbolic. Getting a Lucky Man as a gift, I was told, brought the recipient luck. Specific luck in the form of money, health, and love. I was okay for money. It was the health and heart that interested me. I stroked it tentatively with one finger and thought about how Russ had assured me he'd heal the scars on my face once we returned. I could still see the earnest look in his eyes, when he spoke the words. *First thing, once we get back. I promise.*

Would it work, I wondered? Would the damaged skin that covered one side of my face respond to his touch, regenerating skin cells and making my face new? I longed for it to happen just that way. I yearned to be pretty, but if that was asking too much, I would settle for normal. I was sick of being the girl with the messed up face, the one with the disfigurement that scared small children and caused people to talk in hushed tones whenever I went out in public. I was ready to be transformed. It was time.

I fell asleep with the Lucky Man in my hand and the vision of a perfect, unscarred face. If only.

CHAPTER TWO

———••●•••———

RUSS

I kept glancing back behind us, but I was never able to catch
Nadia's eye. Every time I turned around she was bent over
looking at something by her feet or staring out the window.
And then eventually, she leaned back against the seat and
closed her eyes. Meanwhile I was stuck listening to Mallory
going on and on about the drama between the girls on her
soccer team. When I'd had about all I could take, I told her I
had something to do and I got up from my seat.

"You're coming back though, right Russ?" Mallory said,
her voice rising in concern.

I didn't answer. I wasn't sure how to answer, because I
was consumed with thoughts of getting back to Nadia. When
I got to her row, I lingered in the aisle for just a second.
Sitting next to the window with her head tipped back and
eyes closed, she looked like she didn't want to be disturbed.
She held a pottery figure I'd never seen before—a mustached
Peruvian man carrying a bunch of different stuff—a stack of
money, a heart, a tiny bottle. Something she must have gotten at the Mercado. I'd seen a lot of those kinds of things,
some were made into candle holders and stuff like that, but

it all looked like junk to me. She obviously didn't feel the same way because her hands were curled around this pottery man like she was afraid someone would take it away from her. I sat down in the empty seat next to her and looked at her face. There was an almost perfect delineation between the part that had been burned and the rest of her skin. Like a make-up artist had created a scarred mask from jars of colored putty. I knew from our long discussions driving through Peru that she would have loved it if that was all there was to it. If it were make-up, she would have washed it off in an instant. I couldn't remove the damage that way, but I might be able to restore her skin to the way it was before the crazy man on the bus threw the acid up in the air, ruining her face and her life.

I placed my hand over her cheek and eye, just barely making contact. My touch didn't wake her. I'd done this before, but it felt more important this time. Personal, for me and for her. I concentrated hard, trying to direct energy and love from my hand into her skin. I wanted life to be better for her, and this was a good start. She was going to be so surprised when she woke up.

Mrs. Whitehouse leaned across the aisle. "What are you doing there, Russ?" She was such a pain, always poking her nose where it didn't belong. Now she sounded accusatory, like maybe I was molesting Nadia or something.

I couldn't allow myself to be distracted so I didn't turn away from what I was doing. But I did answer. "Keeping a promise," I said. I kept at it, my hands hovering over her face in a stroking motion, expecting her to wake up but she was completely out of it. The plane must have hit an air pocket because it moved like a bus going over a bump. In front of me, Jameson said, "Whoa," in an exaggerated way, and I saw the candy bar he'd bought at the airport jump up over the top of his seat, like it had been knocked out of his hand. Instead of falling back down, though, he used his telekinesis to make it hover over Mallory's head in a slow circle. When she noticed it and made a grab, he had it move just out of her reach. "Hey!" she said, laughing.

I went back to Nadia, pouring everything I had into her face, especially the part around her eye, which she'd been told would be hard to fix even with plastic surgery. I heard Mrs. Whitehouse turning in her seat to see what I was doing, but my back blocked her view. Up front I noticed Jameson had switched seats so he was next to Mallory now. Good. She wouldn't ask me to come back.

When I finished, I shook out my hands. It was an odd feeling, knowing I'd done all I could do. Like pouring water out of a pitcher and knowing it was empty without having to check. I was through, and I didn't have any more to give. Now I was able to really look at Nadia's face and I was disappointed at what I saw. Her scars looked better, much better in fact, but they weren't completely gone. The color had faded and the ridge above her eye, the one she thought looked like a protruding earthworm, was flatter against her skin, but it was still there. The line between the damaged and unaffected skin was blurred.

What a letdown. I'd healed bullet wounds and cured a baby who failed to thrive because of a digestive problem. I'd brought a woman back from near death. I'd been so sure I could fix Nadia's face. I felt like I'd let her down. I'd done as much as I could, but it wasn't enough.

Using my healing powers always took a lot out of me and

I suddenly felt tired. I reclined the seat, and taking my cue from Nadia, put my head back and closed my eyes. After our time in Peru, worrying about being killed by the Associates, it felt good to relax. Unless something happened to the plane, we were safe for now.

CHAPTER THREE

―•◦●◦•―

RUSS

Four days later, I was one of hundreds of people sitting in my high school auditorium paying tribute to my science teacher, Mr. Specter, who'd died while we were in Peru. He was well liked, so there was a good turnout of students, past and present, and a ton of people from the community too. I overheard people in the crowd talking about him before it started. Everyone seemed to know him and everyone had a story about something he'd taught them or done for them. "Nice guy," was the phrase I kept hearing. I understood where they were coming from. I used to think Mr. Specter was a nice guy too.

On the other side of the auditorium I saw Mallory walk in with Jameson, but I didn't see Nadia anywhere. I hadn't talked to her since we'd been home. At the airport, her mother had come to pick her up. She didn't make a scene but angrily yanked on Nadia's arm and dragged her away from our group. Nadia hadn't even protested. It was like she was being taken prisoner. After that, I waited to see if she'd astral project to me at night the way she used to, but so far, nothing. I didn't think she'd be allowed to come to this memorial service, but I still looked for her. I hadn't told her about what I'd done to her face when we were on the plane because I wanted it to be a surprise. Since I hadn't heard back from her since, I could only imagine that she was disappointed it hadn't been completely healed.

On the auditorium stage, Kevin Adams, Mrs. Whitehouse, Dr. Anton, and Rosie from Rosie's Diner sat on chairs on one side of the podium. In the program they were listed as friends of Mr. Specter's who would be speaking. All four of them were members of the secret organization, the Praetorian Guard. Of the four, two of them—Kevin and Mrs. Whitehouse—had been on the trip with us. It was a little surprising to see all of them lined up in public.

I sat with my parents, my sister Carly, and my nephew Frank. I was glad to be on the aisle next to Carly, where my mother couldn't reach me. Mom had an awkward habit of giving people reassuring pats when she thought they needed emotional support. Earlier at home, when I was getting dressed and having some trouble with my tie, my mother had tried to get me to cry or have a breakdown or something. "It must have been terrible witnessing Mr. Specter's heart attack like that," she said.

"Um, yeah." I looped the fabric back behind the tie and pushed it through the circle and down again just the way I'd been taught. In theory it should have worked, so why did it look so bulgy?

She leaned against the doorframe, watching my face in the mirror. "Sometimes these kinds of things hit you later, when you least expect it. You think you're fine and then…"

There was a long awkward pause. I looked up. "It hits you later?"

She looked relieved. "Yes, exactly like that. Would you like to start seeing Dr. Anton again? You always liked him."

"We'll probably see him at the funeral. Don't you think?" I pulled the whole thing apart and started over. She meant well, but her talking was a huge distraction.

"Yes, probably." She spoke in measured tones. "But I meant seeing him in a professional sense. For grief counseling."

"Doesn't he specialize in stress-related sleep disorders?" I said, even though I knew the answer. I'd gone to see him for that very problem. Chronic insomnia. It turned out not to be stress-related, but I hadn't known that at the time.

"Well, it's not like he couldn't handle other problems too. And he knows you, which I thought would make things more comfortable."

"I appreciate it, Mom, but I'm fine, really. People die. I get it." From the shocked look on her face I knew that I'd taken it too far in the other direction. Now I looked heartless and cruel. She was probably going to Google the definition of 'sociopath' the next time she was online. "I mean, it's a terrible loss, and I have my moments like anyone else." I scrambled for just the right thing to say. "But it's not like it would be if something happened to you or Dad. Then I'd be a complete wreck."

That seemed to do it. "Okay," she said, seemingly relieved. "Well if you change your mind, let me know. It's an open offer."

I nodded. Downstairs I heard the unmistakable sound of Frank and Carly arriving. My sister was fairly quiet, but Frank was a presence. He had this nervous energy that kept him from crossing the room like a normal person. He bounded, he stomped, he jumped. For a ten-year-old kid he consumed a lot of everything: air, space, quiet. When he was around, it was exhausting. But then, after he left, everything seemed dull and boring. No one was like Frank. Now I heard him calling out, "Grandma, Grandma, where are you?"

"I better go see what he wants," Mom said, reluctantly pulling away. "Don't take too long. We need to leave in ten minutes." And then thankfully, she was gone. I heard her pass Carly on the stairs; Carly's steps energetic and light, my mother trudging downward, their voices exchanging greetings. Carly was telling Mom she wanted to give me money she owed me.

I went back to my tie, wanting to strangle whoever came up with the concept of knotting fabric around your neck for serious social events. "Hey Russell." Carly leaned in the doorway the same as my mother had. They were more alike than either of them knew. "How's it going?"

I raised an eyebrow in her direction. "You owe me money?"

"Yeah, you wish." She laughed. "That was just my excuse for coming up to talk to you alone."

"Okay." We'd already talked since I'd returned from South America. I'd given her the lowdown on almost every detail except one: I'd honored my promise to David Hofstetter, her former high school boyfriend and love of her life, and hadn't revealed that he did not, as commonly believed, die in a car crash sixteen years before. That, in fact, he'd faked his death to shake the Associates and join the Praetorian Guard doing work that would ultimately make the world a better place.

We'd found him in Peru working in a lab, doing what he called valuable scientific research. Valuable and top secret. Carly would have been overjoyed to know he was still alive, but I couldn't tell her. It killed me to have to lie to her, but David made it sound like it was a matter of life and death. Oh wait, there was another detail I hadn't told her, something that she should have known, but apparently didn't, that David, long presumed dead, was actually Frank's father.

She watched me fighting with the tie and waited, as if I'd say more. When I didn't, she said, "I just want to get this straight. Two weeks ago you went on a trip to Peru sponsored by the Praetorian Guard thinking you had proof that David was still alive."

I nodded, not taking my eyes off the mirror.

"It was you, Nadia, Mallory, and Jameson, all pretending to be students going to an academic decathlon in Miami, chaperoned by Kevin Adams, Mrs. Whitehouse, and Mr. Specter." Carly ticked off on her fingers as she said the names. "You went, you checked it out, you had a good time. Somewhere in there, Nadia became your girlfriend. And then, to top it all off, Mr. Specter dropped dead from a heart attack, and you brought him back in a body bag."

"Actually, an urn. His body was cremated there."

Her fingers tapped against the doorframe. "How convenient. So you didn't see David or learn anything about him while you were there?"

"I think we covered this already, Carly. Why won't you believe me?" I avoided looking at her. She'd been a huge troublemaker in high school, putting my parents through hell with one thing after another—flunking classes, sneaking out at night, getting drunk, smoking pot, wrecking the car. Out of necessity she'd become good at covering her tracks, while I was just a beginner in this area. She'd see right through me if I wasn't careful.

She stepped in front of me. "Let me do that." Taking hold of the tie she expertly looped it around and tucked it in, then adjusted the knot and smoothed the front. I tried not to look into her eyes, which was nearly impossible to do. She stood so close that I could smell the gum on her breath. "It's not that hard, Russ. Keep practicing, you'll get it."

I took a step back. "Yeah, I don't know if I really need to practice. I don't wear a tie that often."

"I'm not talking about the tie. I'm talking about lying. You need some practice." She put one hand on her hip. "You are one terrible liar. Your body shifts awkwardly, your eyes move back and forth. There are kindergartners caught stealing candy bars who tell more convincing stories."

"I don't know what you mean." I kept my voice steady, but my protest sounded lame even to me. "It all happened just the way I said."

"Just the way *they* said you should say it happened." Carly practically spat out the word. She had nothing but contempt for the Praetorian Guard. "Don't listen to them, Russ. They've got you brainwashed."

"I guess I'm not going to convince you," I said, my arms hanging loosely by my side. "We'll have to agree to disagree." I'd gotten that line from my dad. He used it often when arguing with Mom.

Carly jabbed a finger into the center of the tie she'd just so neatly arranged. "I'm going to be watching you, Russ. I know there's more going on than what you're telling me."

"If that were true," I said, considering my words. "I mean, if there's something I'm not being straight about, it would only be because I'm looking out for you. You know that, right?"

She sighed. "I can look out for myself, Russ. I've been doing it since before you were born."

"Yeah, I know, but…" I hated it when I couldn't come up with a quick answer. "If there's something else, I promise I will tell you eventually. Just not now. But as soon as I can. Okay?" I hoped it was okay. I'd already said more than I should have.

"I am going to get it out of you," Carly said, arms crossed. "I know all your weaknesses, Russ. I'm not giving up on this. By the time I'm done you're going to crack like an egg."

From the bottom of the stairs my mom called out, "Come on, you two! We're going to be late."

Carly muttered, "We're not going to be late. She always leaves too early."

She was right, our mother always did leave way too early, but I didn't mind this time because I was glad for the interruption. I just said, "We'd better get going."

Now all five of us sat in a row in the auditorium, watching the memorial service as a family. Around me came the sounds of sniffling, mostly girls and some of the moms. I heard someone say, "He was so young." Forty-eight-years-old wasn't all that young, but I guess it was young to be dead.

The principal and vice principal both spoke of Mr. Specter's record as a teacher. Behind them, a slide show silently flashed images from the school yearbook: a giant shot of Mr. Specter's head, like he was Oz the great and powerful, and then photos of him doing science experiments, taking kids on field trips, things like that. In every one he had on his trademark sweater vest and wire-rimmed glasses. His receding hairline made his forehead look extra large. I hadn't noticed that in real life, but in the photos it was prominent.

No personal pictures and no mention of his family, which was odd. I knew he wasn't married and I assumed there were no kids, but still, you'd think there would be other family members. As if to answer my question, Vice Principal Ehlers solemnly said, "He always said this school was his family." Ms. Ehlers was trim with blond hair and a friendly smile, which fooled the parents, but not the kids who'd had the experience of being called into her office. If you crossed her she could make your life miserable. "And that his students were his kids." She wiped away a tear. "Samuel Specter went over and above in his teaching career. He loved science and he loved getting kids excited about science. No one will be able to replace him."

Next to me Carly made a derisive snort and then quickly coughed to cover it up. My mom fumbled in her purse and handed her a tissue, then patted her arm reassuringly.

When the principal and vice principal were done speaking, Ms. Ehlers said, "I'd like to turn the floor over to some of Mr. Specter's friends, every one of them prominent members of the community. All of them first met here more than thirty years ago as students in this very high school. Each of them has a few words they'd like to share about their good friend and former classmate, Sam Specter."

She gestured to Kevin Adams, who lumbered up to the podium, hands in his pockets. His jet-black hair was slicked back as usual, but he wore a button-down shirt rather than his usual T-shirt. He cleared his throat nervously before starting. "Most of you know me as the owner of Power House Comics. Over the years Sam helped me out when I needed an extra hand at the store, so you probably already know that we were friends. He was a true friend, the best kind of friend. I met him when I was fifteen, younger than most of you, and at the time I had no idea the impact he'd have on my life. It was an honor to be with him at the end. His death is a loss for me and a loss for the world." He paused and looked around the room. "Don't let people tell you that the friends you make in high school aren't important. In my experience they're the only ones who count." He shuffled a little bit, and started to walk away, then returned and lowered his mouth to the microphone. "Thank you very much."

A few people, unsure, clapped. When Rosie reached the podium, they stopped. I always liked Rosie. She owned the local diner and waitressed there too. She had a motherly persona and remembered everyone who walked through the diner doors. I didn't get the impression that she and Mr. Specter had been close, but since they'd all had superpowers as teenagers and were part of the Guard, they'd had an uncommon bond that lasted more than thirty years. Secrets drew people together. I'd learned that already.

Rosie was more composed than Kevin. She mentioned his sweater vest, and that she'd been to blame for it becoming a staple of his wardrobe, since she'd given him one for a gift once. He liked it so well that she gave him one for his birthday every year. "He was an intense man," she said. "But a good friend, the kind who just shows up when you need him most." She nodded and looked upward as if remembering. "The night my mother died I drove back from the hospital in tears and wound up putting my car in the ditch on Highway 23. It was February, bitter cold, and I was in the middle of nowhere. That was before cell phones," Rosie said. "I was trying to rock the car back and forth to get it out of the ditch, but it wasn't working. I couldn't believe my bad luck. On the same night my mother dies, I'm stuck on a country highway, sure I was going to freeze to death. I was getting low on gas too, to make it even worse. It was awful. I closed my eyes and put my head against the steering wheel and prayed. I prayed harder than I ever had before. And what do you think happened then?" She had the crowd in her grip. Hundreds of people were in the room, but it was dead quiet.

Finally one girl's voice came out from the crowd. "What happened?"

Rosie smiled. "I heard a truck coming from the other direction. It stopped alongside me and I could see it was a tow truck. Sam Specter jumped out of the passenger side and came over to my window. I rolled it down and he said, "I had a feeling you might need some help.""

The crowd murmured in disbelief. Rosie raised her hand, palm outward. "I swear on my mother's grave that this story is true. Sam Specter was a miracle man. He just had a knack for knowing when a friend needed his help. He was a gift to everyone who knew him, and I am going to miss him more than I can say."

She walked away from the microphone. This time the crowd didn't hold back, but erupted in applause. Rosie sat down, ladylike, and didn't object when Kevin Adams took her hand. I wondered if this was what it was going to be like for me, Mallory, Jameson, and Nadia in thirty years. We were building relationships around secrets. We were special. Blessed with superpowers and cursed with everything that came with those powers. I knew that Sam Specter's superpower had been seeing the future, so it was a safe guess that he'd known ahead of time that Rosie's car would break down that night. It wasn't magic. But for people who didn't know better, it sure seemed that way.

Dr. Anton strode up to the podium like a man on a mission. He looked exactly like he had when I'd been his patient: snappy bow tie, goatee, impeccably dressed in a pressed shirt and dark suit coat. He introduced himself and talked about how he'd met Sam in study hall their freshman year. They'd hit it off right away due to their love of all things *Star Trek*. "I don't think anyone yet has mentioned Sam Specter's extraordinary mind. He was, in a word, a genius. He could read something once and recite it months later verbatim. He immediately understood complex scientific concepts that someone like me would have trouble grasping, even with much study. Talking to him was a joy. He was never boring and that's saying a lot." He looked around the auditorium. "When I heard that Sam died of a heart attack in Miami, I was horrified and saddened, like all of you here today. But I also thought, how fitting that he died while chaperoning a group of students who were competing in an academic decathlon. How like him to be a champion of education until the very end. I was especially heartened, but not surprised, to hear that those students took first place in their division."

Carly poked me with her elbow and I had all I could do to keep a straight face.

Dr. Anton continued. "His devotion to his students was unparalleled. His life was not in vain, but serves as an inspiration to us all."

A few students whooped and the rest of the auditorium broke out in loud applause. The clapping continued long after Dr. Anton reached his seat, and only stopped when he held up a hand for silence.

Mrs. Whitehouse was next. Although all four of them were the exact same age, she seemed the oldest of the bunch, walking hunched over in a slow shuffling gait. She'd been our high school lunch lady since forever so we all knew who she was, but she wasn't well liked by the students. Not to be mean, but she was weird. Talking to her was always awkward because she tried too hard to be friends with the kids. I noticed that the clothing she wore now wasn't too different from her lunch duty garb—shapeless matching polyester pieces. Navy blue today instead of her usual pastel colors. She grabbed hold of the microphone and lowered her mouth until we heard her lips bump against it. "Can everyone hear me?" she asked and then tapped the microphone repeatedly. When the crowd murmured affirmatively, she continued. "I will keep this short. In my whole life, Sam Specter was the only man who ever treated me decent. I don't want to betray a confidence, especially now that he's dead, but I can tell you that Sam and I were closer than we let on." Mrs. Whitehouse raised her eyebrows waiting for a reaction. When she didn't get one she said, "We were lovers. He was the light of my life and he felt the same way about me. I will never know love like that again and I can tell you this—" She paused dramatically. " Without him around, I will never be the same."

Mrs. Whitehouse trudged back to her seat and the stunned audience didn't react at all. Applause didn't seem appropriate. Mrs. Whitehouse had managed to be awkward and weird on a large scale, and somehow tarnish Mr. Specter's image at the same time. She also managed to take a man's death and make it all about her. I doubted that they were ever in love, and judging from the looks of the others on the stage, they felt the same, but really what did any of us know? Few people knew that Sam Specter, beloved science teacher and member in good standing, had acquired superpowers as a teenager and was a member of a secret society called the Praetorian Guard. Fewer still knew that he'd actually been a traitor, pretending to be on the side of the Guard while working undercover for the Associates, a group we'd been told wanted to come to power at any cost.

I'd seen the brutality of the Associates firsthand when they'd kidnapped my nephew Frank and forced me to do a series of challenges to get him back. I could still feel the pain of being jolted with electricity by two Associate thugs. We weren't formally introduced but I'd never forget the leers on their faces as they tortured me. The one with a snake tattooed on his neck was particularly nasty. If those two were the minions, I could imagine what kind of person led the organization.

And Mr. Specter, it turned out, was on their side. Right now the auditorium was filled with people who believed he died of a heart attack, when in fact he was killed in an explosion. Really, what did any of this matter now? Mr. Specter was gone and he wasn't coming back.

CHAPTER FOUR

RUSS

Afterward there was a social in the school cafeteria. Frank made a dive through the crowd and went right for the dessert table. He loaded a plate with cookies and brownies, then cracked open a Mountain Dew before Carly had a chance to stop him. It was a safe bet that he'd be bouncing around for hours after this. And good luck getting him to sleep later. The kid was a human pogo stick.

I took off my tie and stuck it in my pocket. My mom had been wrong. Very few of the guys were wearing button-down shirts and ties. I felt like an overdressed freak until Mallory came through the crowd and ran a hand over my sleeve. She turned back to Jameson who lingered behind her looking uncomfortable. He was wearing a polo shirt buttoned to the top so it looked like it was choking him. "Russ, you look so handsome!" she said. "Doesn't he look handsome, Jameson?"

Jameson grunted something I didn't catch. Meanwhile my mother, who'd planted herself next to me, beamed upon hearing Mallory's compliment. I could almost hear her thinking, *I told you so.* Mallory's mom made her way to us, and she and my mother greeted each other like old friends. They'd only met at the airport, but they'd bonded over the fact that their kids were academic decathlon winners.

While they talked, I asked Mallory, "Did Nadia come?" I glanced around the room as if saying her name would conjure her up.

"Didn't you hear?" Mallory said conspiratorially.

"No, what?"

Jameson stepped between us. "Nadia is under house arrest. Her mother is furious that her dad let her go on the trip without her permission. She has her under lock and key." He seemed happy to know something I didn't.

Mallory nodded vigorously. "I stopped over and she answered the door and said her mother has added all kinds of restrictions. She can't do anything anymore. Can't talk on the phone, can't go online. Her mother installed alarms on the doors, if you can believe it. They never ever let her be alone. She can't even sit on the front porch unless her mother is with her. It broke my heart to see her looking so sad."

"Did you see her face?"

"Well, not really." Mallory stopped to think. "She had her hood up, like she does, you know. I could tell she was crying though. We only talked for a minute and then her mother came charging up and basically slammed the door in my face."

"Wow." I thought Nadia had it bad before, but it sounded like her mother was in prison guard mode. Poor Nadia. I knew her mom would be mad, but I had no idea it would be this bad.

"So you didn't know any of this?" Jameson said.

I hated to give him the upper hand. "No, I haven't heard from Nadia at all. She hasn't projected to me either."

"Doesn't keeping her locked up like that sound like child abuse?" Mallory said. "I mean, that can't even be legal."

"I guess." I stuck my hands in my pockets. "Maybe her mom will get over it and loosen up after a while."

"Maybe," Mallory said. But she sounded doubtful.

Before this, my biggest worry had been the effects of the trip on Mallory. Mr. Specter had conducted a session with Mallory using his invention, a Deleo, a goggle-like device that strapped to a person's head and could be used to change memories and essentially brainwash them. This was before we realized he was working for the Associates of course. After Mallory had finished with her turn with the Deleo she came out of the room dazed like a zombie and I had big fears as to what had happened to her mind.

But Jameson and I had spent an afternoon questioning her after we'd returned home and all her memories seemed intact. Her personality hadn't been affected either. She was the same as always—personable, outgoing, smart, and still a total flirt. Maybe the Deleo hadn't worked or maybe it had worked but the effects had worn off. The Deleo had been a new invention, after all, just a prototype. It looked like Mallory had lucked out and it hadn't changed her at all.

So I'd been worried about Mallory getting her memories altered and her brain fried, but she seemed fine. Now my concern shifted to Nadia. How could her own mother treat her that way? Nadia was so good too. It's not like she was the kind of girl who needed constant supervision. All she wanted was a little bit of freedom. And to be like everyone else.

When Nadia and I had been dodging explosions in Peru

I was hoping we'd get out of there alive. I'd thought ahead to our return home to Edgewood. Maybe for a while we could be normal teenagers and do regular teenage things—go to a movie, eat fast food together, make out in a car. I looked forward to getting my driver's license so I could pick her up and we could do anything we wanted. Now it looked like I might not be able to see her at all.

Mallory broke into my thoughts. "I've been meaning to ask you about something, Russ."

"Yeah?" I said.

She tilted her head to one side. "It's about Nadia. Something she said on the trip. About you."

I noticed that girls did this kind of thing a lot. They say things in bits and pieces to catch your interest and then watched for your reaction. Why they can't just say what's on their mind, I don't know. Anyway, I played it cool, just nodded and waited. Jameson looked interested too. He shifted forward to hear what she was going to say. Suddenly the three of us were a tight little triangle in the middle of the crowd.

"Well, it's just… Nadia is under the impression that the two of you are in love." She gave a little half-laugh to show how ridiculous the idea was. "I tried to explain to her that you can be super close to someone, and go through a traumatic time together, but it's not the same as being in love, but she just wouldn't hear it. She really jumped all over me. I think you're going to have to talk to her about this, Russ." She ran a finger up and down my sleeve. "Maybe let her down easy? You'll have to do it carefully. She's pretty delicate."

"She said she's in love with me?" I asked, pleased. Mallory's words were bringing back a buried memory. Something Nadia had said to me when my brain was muddled and I'd

26

been really out of it in Peru. It was all coming back into focus now. Nadia and I had been running away from the convent hand in hand, trying to escape from the horror of Mr. Specter's Deleo. We were almost to the gate when Nadia had said, *You know, I really love you Russ.* Even though the memory was a little blurry, it rang true, and I knew in my heart it had really happened. The realization hit me in a good way. I felt like a guy who'd dreamt of winning an Olympic medal and then woke in the morning to find it hanging off his headboard. Puzzled to find out it was real, but definitely happy about it.

"Well, yeah, that's what she thinks," Mallory said, shaking her head.

But even as Mallory couldn't wrap her brain around the idea, Jameson caught on. He studied my face for an instant and then crowed, "I think Nadia speaks the truth. These two beautiful young people *are* in love. Isn't that right, Russell?" He slapped me on the back so hard he probably left a hand print.

I stumbled forward involuntarily, then when I got my bearings, turned around and gave him a forceful shove. "Stop it," I said, my voice nearly a growl.

"Dude, take it easy," Jameson said, throwing his hands up in surrender. "What's your problem?

"Keep your hands off me or there's going to be a problem."

From behind me, I heard my mother's worried voice. "Boys? Is everything okay?"

I ran a hand through my hair and smoothed the front of my shirt. "Everything's fine, Mom."

"Sorry to upset you, Russ," Jameson said. "Jeez, someone's a little touchy."

Mallory took hold of my arm and leaned in close. Her eyebrows furrowed in disbelief. "So it's true about you and Nadia? What she said—that's true?"

A few months ago I would have loved being in this scenario—Mallory up against me, her eyes imploring—but now it didn't mean a thing. "Yes, it's true about me and Nadia."

She let go and her gaze dropped to the floor. "Wow, I didn't see that one coming. Well, good for you guys. I guess I owe Nadia an apology." She glanced back up, but this time she looked at Jameson. "I'm really happy for them, aren't you, Jameson?"

"Ecstatic," he said, his voice tinged with sarcasm. "I hope they name their first son after me."

"Trust me, I wouldn't do that to a kid," I said.

Jameson opened his mouth to respond, but Mallory suddenly announced we were going to the refreshments table, which turned out to be a good distraction. All three of us grabbed cans of soda—diet for Mallory, not that she needed it.

On either side of the room, easels displayed photos of Mr. Specter. People clustered around taking a look. For the most part, though, the conversations I overheard had nothing to do with Mr. Specter. It was like people had forgotten we were at a memorial service. My friends Justin and Mick saw me across the room, called out and made their way to where we stood, which meant I was forced to introduce them to Jameson. He held out his hand stiffly, and said, "Nice to meet you." Mick smirked before shaking his hand.

It was one of those situations where worlds collided. I could see that Mick and Justin thought Jameson was a pompous jerk and that Jameson thought they were idiots. He looked at me standing next to them like we were the three Stooges. Frankly, neither of them got an accurate first impression. Mick and Justin were good guys. A little immature, but fun to hang out with and loyal like you wouldn't believe. And yes, Jameson was full of himself, but we had some history now, so it was getting easier to look past his prickly, in-your-face, I'm-smarter-than-you attitude. And if Jameson had actually invented the kind of surveillance system he'd claimed to have designed, then some of this smug genius act was deserved. It was entirely possible that someday all of us would be bragging about how we knew him before he became famous. Of course, he could just be making up crap to impress people too, but time would tell.

"How bizarre about old man Specter dying," Justin said. He raised a finger and pointed. "And all three of you guys were there."

I nodded. We'd been briefed on what to say, but I didn't trust myself with Justin and Mick. They knew me too well. Luckily, being a girl, Mallory was happy to fill in the gaps.

"It was terrible, just terrible," she began. She told the whole story, just as we'd been instructed, and threw in some embellishments of her own. "As soon as he collapsed, we all just automatically knew what to do. Russ helped Mr. Specter get to a chair and I got him a drink of water. And then Jameson ran to call 911." Her eyes filled with tears. How could she do that so convincingly? "The ambulance came within twenty minutes. The paramedics did everything they could, but even as they were working on him I could tell they were too late." She shook her head. "And this is the saddest part. He had just been telling me about a trip to Italy he was planning to take next year. I guess it just goes to show you that you never know how much time you have."

"Well yeah," Mick said. "But he was getting up there too. It's not like he was really young or anything."

"So what's the story about him and Mrs. Whitehouse being lovers?" Justin asked. "I was like—whoa! Does Mr. Whitehouse know?"

"That's the thing," Mallory said, giving his arm a squeeze and leaning in like she was telling him a secret. "There is no Mr. Whitehouse. Turns out she's never been married. She just calls herself that."

"Why?" Mick asked.

"No one knows," Mallory said.

"She's just weird," I said. "I don't think they were lovers and I don't think there's a good reason she goes by Mrs. Whitehouse. She's just a sad, lonely woman who makes stuff up. A cat woman who reads young adult novels and pretends she's still young."

"I guess that answers that," Justin said, punching me on the shoulder. "You seem to know a lot about Mrs. Whitehouse, Russ. How close did the two of you get on this trip?" And then he and Mick laughed uproariously, like jackals on crack, and high-fived each other. Jameson shook his head and gave me a look that said, *your friends are morons.* At that moment, I had to agree.

Mallory steered the conversation to more neutral territory: what everyone was doing now that we were on summer vacation, and how great our upcoming junior year was going to be. Justin had recently gotten a job at the popcorn kiosk at the mall and he told Mallory that if she stopped by when he was working the popcorn would be free. "We have all kinds too," he said. "Cheesy popcorn, caramel corn, and regular."

"All kinds," Jameson said dryly. "Three."

"Wow, that's great," Mallory said. "I'll have to come by and visit you."

"Bring a friend," Justin said. "I mean it."

"I know you do," she said.

Somehow it came up that Mick and I would each be getting our driver's license soon. I'd be driving one of my parent's cars when they weren't using it, but Mick's parents were buying him a car just for him to drive. He made it sound like he had a choice, and was going to pick something fast, but I knew his family. Chances were good it would be a used car and probably something practical with good gas mileage. Mallory acted impressed, but I think she would have acted that way no matter what he told her. She was good like that.

We talked until Carly came by to say Frank was hitting his limit, which my mom took as a cue that we should leave. I said good-bye to everyone. Mallory gave me a big hug, which caught me a little off guard, but I definitely was cool with it, especially when I saw the look on Jameson's face. Mick and Justin noticed too. Not a bad thing at all.

The crowd had dwindled considerably. As we headed out to the parking lot, I saw lots of other people leaving at the same time. Frank, impatient as always, charged ahead to where the car was parked, while my parents, Carly, and I walked behind. "That Mrs. Nassif is so nice, Russ," my mom said, referring to Mallory's mom. "I'm glad you're getting in with a nice group of kids."

"Unlike me and *my* high school friends, who were all big losers." Carly's voice was tinged with bitterness. "The scum of the earth."

"That's not what I meant, Carly," Mom said, weary like she didn't want to start up with this again.

"Mallory is nice," I agreed. I wasn't thinking about Mallory though. I was thinking about Nadia and how I was going to manage to see her. And I *was* going to see her. If the Associates couldn't kill us, a middle-aged woman wasn't going to keep us apart. Somehow, no matter what, I was going to find my way back to her.

CHAPTER FIVE

·•◉•·

RUSS

On Saturday afternoon, when I was alone in my room, I tried to reach Nadia by calling her parents' phone. It rang four times before someone answered. There was a long pause and then her mother's voice: "Hello?" The word was long and drawn out. She sounded suspicious and on edge, like she was ready to hang up at the slightest sign of trouble.

"Hi," I said, walking around my bed and looking out the window. "This is Russ Becker. I was one of the students who competed with Nadia at the Miami Academic Decathlon."

"I know who you are," she said stiffly.

"I was hoping I could speak with Nadia?"

The response came out in a short burst. "No. Nadia will not be taking phone calls."

Whoa, she sounded super angry. Enraged even. "Oh." I had to come up with something quick and Carly's lie was the first thing that came to mind. "It's just that she lent me some money on the trip. I wanted to pay her back."

"How much do you owe her?"

"Twenty dollars?" Shoot. Carly was right. I was a terrible liar.

"You aren't sure?"

"No. It's twenty dollars," I said quickly, putting my palm against the glass. "She gave me a twenty dollar bill and I really want to get it back to her. And thank her, too." Outside on the street, some neighbor kids were setting up a rail to do skateboarding tricks. It was a gorgeous summer day, breezy and almost hot, but not quite. The kind of weather Wisconsinites wait for all winter long. And here Nadia was trapped inside unable to enjoy it.

I could hear Nadia's mother breathing, but she didn't answer.

"So when would be a good time to stop by to give her the money?" I asked. "I could come over now, if that's convenient."

"You can leave it in an envelope in our mailbox anytime," she said.

"Okay, but I was hoping to stop in and talk to Nadia," I said. "Just for a few minutes. To thank her."

"I will tell her thank you for you." There was a click, and then nothing but silence. What a waste. I was no closer to seeing Nadia and because I felt obligated to follow through with my lie, I was going to be out twenty dollars.

I put a twenty dollar bill in an envelope and wrote Nadia's name on the outside. I thought about writing her a note, but decided against it. Her mother would read it and I was pretty sure she'd never pass it on to Nadia.

It took half an hour to walk to Nadia's house and once I got there I spent another minute debating what to do.

The house itself looked fine, just the way I remembered it. A two-story Colonial, with brick on the bottom, white siding on the top, and black shutters on either side of the windows. A generic suburban home. Nothing menacing about it except that the place was all closed up like the family was on vacation.

I could knock on the door and hope that Nadia would answer, like she had on the day Mallory stopped over. Then I could see her, at least for a minute or two. But my phone call had probably given her mother the heads up that I was coming. Chances were good she'd be the one to open the door and I was not looking forward to talking to her in person. The mailbox at the curb was the standard black metal box mounted atop a pole. It was slightly askew, like a snow plow had bumped it at one point. If I wanted to, I could leave the money there and try to reach Nadia another time, but that would be the coward's way of doing things. I was here now, I needed to see her, and knocking on the door would be a start anyway. Even if her mother turned me away, Nadia would know I tried.

I was halfway up the concrete walkway when some movement at the second-story window above the front porch caught my eye. A moment before I could have sworn that the blinds at that particular window were down, but now they were raised and I saw Nadia behind the glass. She wasn't wearing her usual dark-colored sweatshirt with the hood over her head. Instead, she wore a white tank top revealing her narrow shoulders and thin arms. Her hair was tucked behind her ears. From below, I couldn't see any sign of the scars on her face. To anyone else she would look like a regular teenage girl, nothing about her the least bit outstanding, but I knew better. She was different—special. In my universe she was the sun around which everything revolved. I lifted a hand to wave and she grinned, then pointed.

I shook my head unsure of what she wanted. Nadia walked her fingers across the sill and waved her arm around, again pointing to the corner of the house. Still not understanding, I followed her gesture and when she nodded, I knew I'd gotten it right. After I crossed the lawn to the side of the house I figured it out. Her bedroom had two windows and she had directed me to the one overlooking the side yard. Thick hedges growing along the property line blocked the view from the neighboring house. Presumably, I was now also out of the sight line of people passing by on the street.

I watched as Nadia frantically unlatched and lifted the window and then pressed her face as close to the screen as possible. "You came!" she said, the joy in her voice raining down over me.

"I would have come sooner," I said, apologetically. "I mean, I would have come over or called you, but your mom seemed so pissed off at the airport that I thought I'd give it some time. And then I was waiting for you to project to me and then when you didn't, I wasn't sure what was going on."

"I wanted to, really. I just couldn't. She's with me like almost every second." Nadia glanced back over her shoulder before continuing. "When I go to bed she checks on me every few minutes and I never get into a trance long enough to project. And then eventually I fall asleep. It's so eerie the way she's always hovering over me. It's like she knows."

"Do you think she does know something?" I asked.

Nadia shook her head. "No, it's just her being who she is.

Crazy. Controlling." Her voice sounded more sad and frustrated than angry. It was heartbreaking.

"I'm sorry," I said. I was sorry for what she was going through and sorry that we were apart. It was maddening that I could see her and hear her voice, but I couldn't touch her or even look directly into her eyes. And the window screen was one more thing keeping us apart. They never had screens in the movies; people popped their heads out of open windows all the time. "I'm really sorry."

"It's not your fault," she said, and sighed. "But I can tell you one thing, as soon as I'm eighteen I'm out of here."

She meant it, I could tell. I said, "I'll go with you, Nadia."

"Where?"

"Wherever it is you're going when you're eighteen. I'll go with you."

"But you'll still be seventeen on my eighteenth birthday. I'll get in trouble for contributing to the delinquency of a minor," she teased.

"That's only if they catch us. And they'll never catch us." I reached my hands up and shot a very small arc of electricity so it fell just short of the window. It was the closest I could get to touching her even if it was overly theatric. Even in the daylight the stream of sparks were impressive. "I'll blast anyone who tries to come near."

She laughed and gave a few slow claps of approval and for a minute it felt like it had before, when it was just the two of us together driving down a country road in Peru. Like we were the last people left in the entire world. I let the sparks fizzle down to nothing. "It's not the same without you, Nadia," I said.

"What's not the same?" she asked.

"Everything. Life. It feels empty without you."

From the other side of the hedge I heard a door open, followed by a dog barking, and the splashing of kids jumping into what had to be a large pool. A woman's voice yelled for someone named Matthew to put on his water wings. So much for being the last two people in the world.

"I know," Nadia said. "I've been feeling really lost too."

"You missed Mr. Specter's memorial service. There was a really big crowd. Mrs. Whitehouse was one of the speakers and she announced that they were lovers."

"Who were lovers?"

"She and Mr. Specter."

"She said that?" Nadia said, incredulously.

"To everyone there. Hundreds of people."

"Wow." She shook her head. "Bizarre. What else did I miss?"

I put my hand up to shield my eyes from the sun. "According to Jameson you and I are in love."

Her mouth widened into a huge smile. "Really."

"Really. That's what he said."

"And what do you say?"

"Well, you know how much it kills me to agree with Jameson, but—"

I'd lost her attention. She glanced back over her shoulder and returned with a worried look on her face. "Look Russ, I hear my mom coming up the stairs, so we don't have much time. Just so you know, my parents aren't letting me go on the next Praetorian Guard trip and I can't go to the meeting either."

"What trip? What meeting?"

"I thought you knew. Anyway, you'll hear about it soon," she said, waving my question away. She spoke more quickly now. "My mom put alarms on all the outside doors so I can't sneak out at night anymore. I can't make phone calls or send emails or write letters. I don't know when I'll be able to talk to you or see you again. Maybe not until I turn eighteen. Don't forget about me, okay?"

"We'll think of something," I said. "Maybe if I—"

"No," she said, "you don't understand. It's gotten really bad again. This could go on forever. Last time she was like this it went on for two years." She wiped at her eyes with the tips of her fingers. "Just promise that you won't forget about me."

"I couldn't forget about you. How could I forget about you?"

"Promise. You need to promise."

"Of course," I said. "I promise. I'll never forget about you. I couldn't forget about you."

"I'll keep trying to astral project to you," she said. "That's all I'll be able to do for now." She tucked her hair behind her ear, reminding me of something I'd meant to say.

"Nadia!"

She looked behind her and left the window. I could tell from the noises drifting down that her mother was in the room with her. I heard Nadia's voice, soft and subdued in contrast with her mother, who sounded furious. I didn't want this to be the end for us, today or any day. How could her

Mom be mad at her when I was the one who'd come to the house? Nadia hadn't even left her room. "Nadia!" I called out again.

She came back to the window, her mother behind her. Even one story up and from behind a screen I could feel the woman's wrath. Her face was contorted in anger, making her look gargoylesque. "I have to go, Russ," Nadia said. I could see that she was fighting to get the words out and even to stay near the window. Her mother had a grip on her and was pulling her back.

"Your face!" I said. "I forgot to tell you that you look really beautiful."

Nadia put a hand to her cheek and smiled, and that's all I saw before she was jerked from my sight. Nadia's mother filled the window, her anger spilling out. "You!" she yelled, pointing a finger. "I thought I told you to stay away."

"We were just talking, ma'am," I said.

"Sneaking around so I couldn't see you." She hit the screen with the flat of her hand and it rattled in the frame. "I'm giving you to the count of five to get off my property, you hear me?" She was shrieking now, and the world suddenly got quiet. Even the neighbor kids playing in the pool next door seemed to have stopped to listen. "And if I see you here again I'm calling the cops and having you arrested."

"Mom!" I heard Nadia's voice behind her. "Don't talk to him like that."

"I'll talk to him any way I like!" she said. "This is my house, young lady. And don't you forget it." She looked back down at me, and said, "What are you, brain-damaged? I said to go, now go."

"Yes, ma'am, but could you tell Nadia something for me?"

"No, I will not."

"Tell her—" Now I was the one raising my voice—yelling actually—for Nadia's benefit, "—that Jameson got it right this time."

CHAPTER SIX

RUSS

Nadia's mother never did count to five, but after she'd slammed the window shut, I went anyway. There was no point in staying, especially after she'd threatened to have me arrested. I left with mixed feelings, happy to have connected with Nadia, but sick to know how she was being treated. If I could have switched places with her, I would have. Her mother had to be mentally ill. No normal person acted like that. When I got to the street I glanced up at the window one last time, but the blinds were down again so there was nothing to see. Somewhere in that typical suburban house a teenage girl was being held prisoner, but you'd never know it from the outside. If Mallory was right, and this was considered abuse, it would be hard to prove.

I didn't feel like going straight home, so I wandered around town after that, taking my old insomnia route through the industrial park, past the strip mall, and ending up at the abandoned train station on the outskirts of town. The field adjacent to the tracks looked unremarkable. I remembered watching the light particles—the lux spiral—falling from the sky into a giant luminous swirl on the ground, and recalled how it felt to walk to the center and be surrounded by glowing, glittering fragments. Now, months later, there was no sign that anything like that had happened. If it weren't for the fact that I could sense electricity in the walls, shoot lightning bolts out of my palms, and heal people, even I might think I'd imagined it. I kicked at a few pebbles before walking around the boarded up building. This was where my sister Carly and her boyfriend, David Hofstetter, used to meet sixteen years ago to make out and smoke pot. Now it looked ready for the wrecking ball.

After that there wasn't much more to see. It was nearly dinnertime when I got back to my house. Carly's car was in the driveway and Frank was sitting on the front porch, a ball and glove at his feet. When he saw me he bounded to his feet and yelled through the door. "He's here, Grandma! Russ is back!"

That was the first sign something was up. The crepe paper and balloons in the kitchen clued me in even more. Turned out we were belatedly celebrating my birthday with a family dinner, but no one had bothered to tell me.

"I thought it would be a nice surprise," my mom said when we were all finally seated around the table. My dad had grilled steaks, while Mom had prepared a salad and rolls. A decorated cake and several wrapped presents sat waiting on the kitchen counter.

"Yeah, and then you ruined it by disappearing," Frank grumbled. "I thought we could play catch while Grandpa was grilling. I wanted to call you, but Mom wouldn't let me."

"My birthday was more than a week ago," I pointed out. "And I didn't disappear. I had no idea you were doing this."

"Yes, I'm well aware that your birthday was more than a

week ago." Mom passed the salt to my dad. "I was there for your first one, if you recall. But you were in Miami so we didn't get a chance to celebrate it."

"Okay, well thanks."

The meal was almost ruined when Carly mentioned that she'd lost her job earlier that week. This was a fairly common occurrence for her, but it still upset my mother. "What are you going to do?" Mom asked, worried.

Carly speared a chunk of steak and dipped it into sauce. "What I always do. I'll get another job. Hopefully a better one. That one sucked. I was just about ready to quit when they eliminated my position. How lucky was that?" She laughed and shook her head. "They saved me the trouble of giving two weeks' notice."

My mother's lips pressed together the way they did when she was about to lay it all out there. "Carly, aren't you getting a little old to be flitting from job to job? I mean—"

My dad held out his hand to make Mom stop. "I'm quite sure," he said firmly, "that Carly will be just fine. She's a big girl and has been supporting herself and Frank for a long time. Let's just have a nice dinner, okay? Russ's birthday, remember?"

My mom closed her mouth, but it was clear to me that she still had a lot to say. My dad had been slipping Carly money since Frank was born, and we all knew it. But talking about it wasn't going to change things.

It was after I'd opened the presents (a lot of gift cards, clothes from Mom, and a stack of comic books from Frank) and we'd eaten cake that the doorbell rang. My mother, who was clearing plates from the table said, "Russ, why don't you get that?" She and Dad exchanged a sly look that told me they were in on something. I raised my eyebrows questioningly at Carly who shrugged. Whatever was going on, she wasn't part of it.

My dad diplomatically herded Frank up to my room to play games. Frank bounded up the stairs eager to decimate his grandfather. This was the one area where Frank could come out ahead against my dad. He was so happy to have one-on-one time that he didn't even seem to realize that he was being banished upstairs to get him out of the way.

One minute later, Mallory, her mother, Jameson and his dad stood in my front entryway as if they'd been invited, which I guess they were. Mallory threw her arms around me and then wished me a happy birthday. "What's going on?" I asked her.

"Haven't a clue," she whispered. "My mom just said we had to come over to your house." All four parents exchanged pleasantries about the weather as if this were a normal social occasion. My mom directed everyone to sit in the living room and when I asked what was up, she answered with a mysterious, "Just wait. You'll see."

And then it hit me. This was the meeting Nadia had mentioned, the one she wouldn't be able to attend. Something about this said Praetorian Guard to me. Carly had a stricken look on her face, making me think she'd figured out the same thing. She opened her mouth and I knew she was just about to question my mom when the doorbell rang again. "Carly?" Mom said. "Would you lend a hand and get that?"

I could tell Carly's heart wasn't in it, but she did as asked, and when she returned she was accompanied by two men I'd never seen before. Following in their wake was Rosie, everyone's favorite from the local diner. The men in their dark

pants, white dress shirts, and diagonal-striped ties were a little overdressed for a teenager's birthday party, but they were
perfectly attired for a Praetorian Guard convention. One of
them held onto the handle of a large leather case almost as
big as a card table. I held my breath and looked at Carly,
whose stony expression told me she was clearly thinking the
same thing. "Happy birthday, Russ!" Rosie said with a wide
smile. "Sixteen, huh? What a great age. Enjoy it, the years go
by fast."

"Thanks," I said, looking at the two men expectantly.
Everyone in the room was quiet until Jameson stood up and
extended his hand. "I don't think we've met."

"Will Patterson," said the first man, the younger of the
two. "Mitch Gilbert," said the other one. Each one had the
good looks of a film actor, but there was nothing distinctive about either of them. If they left the room and I had to
describe them I'd have to say one was a white guy and the
other one was African American. They were both clean-cut,
of average height and build. And that would be it. Nothing
stood out.

Jameson was a pro at this, giving his name and then
introducing his father. Everybody except Carly joined in the
round of introductions and then my mother, unable to contain herself any longer, blurted out, "This is a big surprise
for all of you kids. Wait until you hear. You're going to be so
excited." She gestured for Rosie to sit down, and then joined
her on the couch. "Okay guys, take it away."

Mitch and Will stood across from the rest of us and set to
work as if they'd done this dozens of times. The black leather
case held a collapsible stand and a screen almost as big as our
television. When everything was in place, the two men stood

on either side of the screen with self-satisfied smiles on their faces. Their expressions reminded me of the guys who sell the specialty knives in the tent at the State Fair—the knives that can slice through anything. A person could get so caught up in the hype that they'd wind up buying a knife like that and be all the way home before they realized they'd probably never have a need to slice through tin cans.

"First of all," Mitch said, "we want to thank all of you for gathering here today. We appreciate your time and attention."

"And happy birthday to Russ, too," Will added with a nod of his head.

"Yes, happy birthday, Russ! Turning sixteen, that's awesome. I predict you're going to have a memorable year," Mitch said, grinning broadly in my direction. "Now to get down to business. I'd like to start by saying we represent the National High School Student Initiative, one of the most prestigious organizations in the United States. We've been in existence for decades honoring top students and giving them very special opportunities, the kind few young people ever get to experience. If you'd bear with us for a few minutes, we'd like to show you a short video."

Will leaned over and adjusted something on a remote and the room filled with the sounds of a choir singing God Bless America. A second later, the screen displayed an American flag. From there, the video launched into the history of the NHSSI, followed by explanations of the service projects and internships they'd sponsored as well as scholarships they'd funded. We were told that high school students associated with the organization went on to be awarded full-ride scholarships to prominent schools. Names like Harvard and Princeton were mixed in with names of universities located overseas. Former high school students who had benefitted from the organization included senators, esteemed scientists, Supreme Court Justices, famed mathematicians, *New York Times* bestselling authors, and one Pulitzer Prize Winner.

Various scenes of kids who appeared to be about our age flashed on the screen. All of them were good-looking and self-assured. No lack of confidence here. According to this clip, these teenagers helped to engineer and install water purification systems in Guatemala, tutored disadvantaged kids in Chicago, and assisted researchers doing important work in top secret medical facilities. They learned to program software for NASA, and joined expeditions working to recover sunken ships. In short, there was nothing these kids couldn't do.

Across the room, my mother leaned forward in her seat, eyes shining with excitement. In contrast, Carly, leaning back with crossed arms, couldn't have looked less enthused. The look on her face was like she'd just bitten into something nasty.

When the video was over, Mitch switched off the power and turned to face us. "What does this have to do with the three of you?" he asked, flashing a cheesy grin. "Well, I'll tell you. The kids you saw in the video, the ones who were chosen to take part in these incredible opportunities and then went on to be awarded full-ride scholarships? Soon, the three of you will be joining their ranks."

I could tell from everybody's stunned expressions that Mom was the only one who knew this was coming. She leaned forward and beamed at the other parents. "Can you believe it? Aren't you proud of our kids?"

Mitch continued. "Yes, I'm talking about you, Mallory,

Russ, and Jameson. The NHSSI has been very impressed with your test scores, grades, and performance at the Miami academic decathlon. We only select students who test well enough to be considered geniuses, and the three of you are no exception. I extend my personal congratulations to all of you. Being chosen is a great honor and believe me when I say it's an honor for me to give you this good news. I'm proud to be able to say I know you."

There was a moment of silence before Mallory said, "What does this mean for us, exactly?"

Mitch rubbed his hands together. "I'm so glad you asked, Mallory! As a member of our organization, you'll be invited to participate in exciting projects geared for your specific talents and strengths. Besides the wonderful experiences you'll have, you'll also gain valuable contacts. Your mentors will be instrumental in writing recommendations for your college applications and the scholarships you'll be receiving."

"That's it?" Jameson said. "We don't get a pony or anything?"

Will didn't seem to catch Jameson's sarcasm. "I like to think of it as a chain of success, Jameson. People often think that those who achieve great things get there through hard work and talent, but that's not entirely true. Connections are essential for becoming successful, and we're giving you a chance to connect in a big way."

Mitch said, "We're excited to tell you, Russ, Mallory, and Jameson, that the three of you have been chosen to spend five days in Washington D.C. as student ambassadors. The program we have set up is very much like the internships that university students participate in. You'll have access to areas not open to the public and get a real feel for how our federal government is run. I think you'll find this to be the opportunity of a lifetime."

"One of the functions you'll be attending will be the Presidential Black Tie Bash," Will said. His wide smile easily matched Mitch's. They were the perfect salesmen to give this pitch.

Mallory's hand flew over her mouth. "The Presidential Bash?" She couldn't contain her excitement. "We'll get to go?"

"So you've heard of it?" Mitch teased.

Duh. Everyone knew about the Presidential Black Tie Bash. It was like the Academy Awards of the White House. Only four hundred or so people were invited, which made it large enough to be exciting, but small enough to be exclusive. All the biggest celebrities went, as well as the most important people in government and business, and even though security was tight, the celebrity shows always had footage of the guests coming and going from the event.

"Of course I've heard of it!" Mallory said, grinning. "Last year I heard that Kyle Sternhagen got totally drunk and was dancing on top of the bar." In middle school all the girls watched a cable show starring Kyle Sternhagen and they talked about him all the time. Personally, I never saw it, but I wasn't the show's target audience.

Mitch continued. "As usual, the Bash will also be a celebration of the president's daughter's birthday. As you may know, Layla will turn nineteen this year."

Mallory's eyes lit up and her hand shot up. "Are we going to get to meet Layla?" she asked.

Layla Bernstein was as skinny as a model, and known for

her clothes, which were all designer this and one-of-a-kind that. Two years ago, there was some kind of big ruckus about her nose. All of the magazines had before and after photos, saying she'd had a nose job. For weeks, the gossip magazines went on and on about it, printing unofficial statements from "a good friend who would like to remain anonymous," saying that Layla had hated her nose and the surgery was a birthday present from her parents. The official statement from the White House was that she'd had surgery for a medical condition—a deviated septum.

The clothes and the nose. That's basically all I knew about Layla Bernstein, although there were girls in my school who knew every detail of the girl's life. Some thought she was stuck-up, even though she was often photographed visiting kids in hospitals and doing other charity work that involved smiling and accepting bouquets of flowers. Me, I didn't have an opinion one way or the other. Layla Bernstein's world might as well be Planet Neptune for all it had to do with me.

"Yes, you will meet Layla," Will said. "In fact, all three of you will be sitting with her as her personal guests."

"Isn't this incredible?" my mother said, looking around the room. "What an opportunity!" Mallory looked like she was ready to pack now, and even Jameson looked impressed.

"So, what do you think?" Mitch asked. "Is everyone on board?"

Jameson's father stood up and crossed his arms. He hadn't said much since arriving at my house, but I saw now that the guy didn't need to say much. He was as tall as Jameson but his shoulders were twice as wide. The man was a presence. "What commitment is required on our end? Will there be some kind of fee involved?"

"No sir," Mitch said. "No financial commitment is required from the families. We'd be honored to have your son involved in our program at no cost to you."

Knowing he didn't have to pay for it seemed to be enough for Jameson's dad. He nodded and sat back down.

"So who does pay for all this?" Mrs. Nassif put a protective arm around Mallory's shoulder. "The money has to come from somewhere."

"Our programs are completely funded by private donations. Many of our donors are past recipients who simply want to pay it forward."

"So am I right in assuming the kids would miss out on a week of school?" Mrs. Nassif asked. "I'm not so sure about that."

"I can assure you they won't have to make up any work. We have an understanding with your daughter's school. Both she and Russ will receive A's for all the assigned work and tests given during their absence. The school agrees with us that this trip will be far more educational than any classroom work ever could be. Sitting at a desk listening to a lecture just can't compare to real life experience." Will said this with a knowing smile.

"Remember, your achievements reflect well on your school too," Mitch added. "They're happy to help make this happen for you. It's a point of pride for them."

"I'm homeschooled," Jameson observed. "Can I just give myself A's too?"

"If you'd like," Mitch said, smiling. These guys really didn't get Jameson's sarcasm. "What the heck. Give yourself an A plus if you want. You deserve it."

"Maybe I'll make it A plus plus," Jameson said. "Why not? I deserve it."

My mom got up off the couch with an excited little leap. "I know it's a lot to take in, but I think this is an excellent opportunity for our kids. I know that I'm very proud of Russ. In my opinion he was always in the top one percent, but it's nice to hear that other people see it too."

Through all of this I kept sneaking glances at my sister Carly. When the guys first started talking she just looked wary, and then her expression evolved from wary to outright irritation. Now she looked like an explosion waiting to happen. Her face had that pissed off look that I remembered from her fights with my parents years ago. As a little kid I used to hide in my room at the first signs of trouble. I hadn't seen her like this in years, but I could tell she was right on the edge of losing it.

"Let me get this straight," she said, her tone icy. "You match these genius students with the right projects based on their specific talents and strengths, is that right?"

Mitch gave her a forced smile, while Will found something fascinating to look at down by his toes. Mitch said, "That's correct."

"So can I assume that since all three of them are going to be taking the same trip—" She pointed at Mallory, Jameson, and me. "—that all of them have the same talents and strengths?"

He cleared his throat. "That's right."

"And what would those talents and strengths be?"

My mother said hurriedly, "Carly, I think you're putting these gentlemen on the spot. There's no need to be rude."

"No, it's okay, Mrs. Becker," Mitch assured my mother. "We welcome questions." He took a step closer to Carly. "In this case, all three of these students demonstrated talents for quick thinking, logic skills, and discretion. The last one is imperative for this project because they may be working near classified material and we need to know that they can be trusted not to divulge private information."

Now Carly was the one moving closer. "So you can trust them, but can we trust you? Can you guarantee their safety? After your five days, will my brother come home exactly the same person he is now?" Everyone in the room felt her anger. To the parents it must have seemed kind of random.

I had almost forgotten Rosie was in the room until she spoke up. "I know where you're coming from, Carly, I really do. It's always a concern when loved ones are away, particularly when we're talking about teenagers. The world can be a scary place. But I promise you, all three of these young people will be surrounded by security at all times. And I myself will be serving as a chaperone for this trip. I give you my personal guarantee that Russ will be safe."

Carly turned to her, hands on hips. "*You're* going to be a chaperone? How did that happen?"

Will stepped forward and held up a hand. "If you'd let us finish our presentation, we can take questions afterward." He was clearly trying to gain control of the situation. "As it turns out, the subject of chaperones was next on our list. The NHSSI feels strongly about ensuring the safety of our students. To this end, we select members of the community to serve as chaperones. We find that it makes the families feel more secure and the students more comfortable when they have a history with the adult who is accompanying the group.

The obvious choice, parents, are never allowed to serve as chaperones because we find that the kids need distance from home to maximize their potential."

"How many chaperones will be going with the kids?" Mrs. Nassif asked.

"Good question!" Will said brightly. "We have a ratio of one chaperone per student, so there will be three on this trip."

Carly pointed to Rosie. "So that would be her and who else?"

"Dr. Anton, a very distinguished child psychiatrist who lives and works in this area has agreed to take time away from his very busy schedule to accompany the students on this trip. We're thrilled to have him on board. I understand that he's already met some of you." Will looked right at me when he said this. I dropped my gaze to the floor, uncomfortable. Who wants to be known as the kid who saw the psychiatrist? I mean, I wasn't crazy or anything, I just used to have trouble sleeping. And as it turned out, that didn't have anything to do with me. "And we're still filling the third spot. As soon as we have a candidate, we'll let you know."

"I'll do it." Carly got the words out before he'd barely finished the sentence.

"Pardon me?"

"I said I'll do it. Put me down as your third chaperone."

Will and Mitch exchanged an awkward look. Even without speaking it was clear they were trying to decide who would handle this. Mitch finally took charge. "I think you heard Will mention that we never allow family members to serve as chaperones because—"

"What Will actually said—" Carly's voice was now loud enough for the neighbors to hear. "—was that *parents* couldn't be chaperones, because you find that the kids need distance from home to maximize their potential. I am not Russ's parent, I don't live with him, and I don't think my presence will inhibit him in any way. Also, he's not going without me. That's the deal. You want Russ, you're getting me too."

"Carly!" Mom said. "What are you saying? It's not up to you."

Carly ignored her. "My brother is not going on any of your trips without me, regardless of what my parents say. I go as a chaperone, or no dice."

The two men exchanged another glance; Mitch shrugged. "It's not up to us, but I'll be happy to pass on your request to the committee members who will be making the final decision."

Carly said, "You do that," at the same time my mother was sputtering an apology for her daughter's rudeness. I could tell that she thought Carly was going to screw up my chances to go. The rest of the room just looked uncomfortable.

Finally Rosie spoke up, her gentle voice calm but firm. "I love seeing the family dynamics at work here. Russ, it must feel good to have a sister who loves you so much."

Carly's look dared me to say something contradictory. My sister wasn't one who was easily shocked, but I think I actually did it this time when I stood up and said, "Yeah, it does feel good and I feel the same way about her. And just for the record? I won't go on the trip unless she's a chaperone."

Mitch shrugged and then extended a hand to Carly. "Congratulations, you're a chaperone."

CHAPTER SEVEN

RUSS

You know how during the school year you dream about summer vacation and in your mind, those three months seem like they'll go on *forever,* but actually the time whips by before you know it? Well, multiply that speed by ten and you'll know how fast the rest of the summer went for me.

Now that I was sixteen, I could get a job, something I'd looked forward to since I'd started high school. A job meant an hourly wage. Money. Having more cash would solve a lot of problems, believe me. I filled out applications online and even had an interview at one of the fast food places in the mall food court, but no one hired me, which turned out to be just as well, because getting my driver's license and going to the Praetorian Guard practice sessions chewed up my time way more than I thought it would.

Of course, my parents didn't know they were PG practice sessions. They knew them as National High School Student Initiative preparation meetings. They never even questioned why I had to go four nights a week and every Saturday morning for weeks on end.

The first meeting came within days of the presentation at my house. Mallory, Jameson and I went, of course, along with our chaperones: Carly, Rosie, and Dr. Anton. That night, Carly came to pick me up after dinner. After getting Frank situated in front of the TV and making small talk with my parents, the two of us drove to a manufacturing firm in the industrial park on the edge of town. The sign said: Riverside Burial Vault Company. I'd looked them up ahead of time and found out that burial vaults, these large concrete boxes, were required by law in Wisconsin if you wanted to be buried in a cemetery. They lowered the vaults into the ground to hold the coffin. It kept the ground from sinking as the coffin deteriorated. The owner of the factory was a Guard member so it was a safe meeting place.

Carly and I crossed the asphalt parking lot to the building. "You don't have to do this, you know," she said. "You can change your mind at any time."

"I know," I said. "But I'm not going to change my mind."

She sighed. "I had a feeling you'd say that."

Once inside, we were greeted by Will and Mitch, the guys who'd given the presentation at my house. Apparently, the earlier formalities were only for the benefit of the parents, because now they were dressed casually in jeans and T-shirts, and I noticed they also dispensed with the handshakes. Mitch picked up a large plastic container and guided us through an office space where two women sat at computers. "Tiffany and Allison," he said, gesturing with a tilt of his head. We said hello and continued on until we reached a door that led into a warehouse half-filled with stacks of concrete burial vaults and car stops. Rosie and Dr. Anton were already there. A few minutes after we walked in, Will showed up, followed by Jameson and Mallory.

I'm not someone who usually notices clothes, but a guy would have to be completely blind to miss what Mallory had on—a sheer tank top and short skirt, the kind cheerleaders wear. She gave me a big smile like we had a secret and flipped her ponytail at me. My sister caught all this and nudged me with a sly grin. "Focus, Russ. Don't get distracted."

A second later, Rosie made the rounds, giving out hugs and saying she was glad to see us. There was the usual chatter about the weather and what everyone had been doing, but once we had quieted down and lined up, Mitch rested one foot on the plastic container and said, "Okay guys, before we start with the training does anyone have any questions?"

"I have a question," I said, raising my hand. "It's about Nadia. Have you tried to get her parents to let her come?"

Mitch shook his head. "At this point in time, it doesn't look like Nadia will be able to join us. To be honest with you, Russ, we've never had a parent turn down one of our opportunities. Nadia's mother is a tough nut to crack. We've offered financial incentives and scholarships, but she won't even listen, which is making it difficult."

Mallory crossed her arms. "How about using mind control?" she asked.

"We're working on getting one of our operatives into the home under some other guise, but so far we've been denied access. As I said, she's one tough lady."

I said, "How about just taking Nadia by force? There has to be a way to get her out of the house." When we were in Peru, David Hofstetter had said that Nadia and I would be essential to this mission because of our specialized skills, notably her astral projection. Having someone who could travel anywhere on a moment's notice and stay absolutely invisible was like having the perfect spy on your side. If this trip was so important, wouldn't she be invaluable?

There was dead silence for a second before Mitch said, "Believe me, we're exploring every option. If it can be done, it will. That's not my job, however. My job is to prepare the three of you, and *your* job is to listen and learn. I will require your complete attention during these sessions. I can't stress how important this mission is."

His partner, Will, said, "Any other questions?'

"I have one," Carly said. "What exactly is this mission?"

"It's a trip to Washington D.C. Our objective is to thwart a known threat by the organization known as the Associates."

"Yeah, yeah, so you said." Carly waved a hand dismissively. "What I'm asking about are the specifics of the plan. What threat are we talking about and how are they supposed to thwart it?" She put finger quotes around the word thwart.

"That will be covered later."

"You're asking each of these kids to put their life on the line, and you can't tell them what this is about?" Carly's voice echoed in the cavernous space.

Dr. Anton, who hadn't said a word up until this point, only nodding when we first walked in, held up a hand. Even though it was summer, he had on a suit coat over a button-down shirt and creased trousers. The bow tie he wore today was polka-dotted, a fun accessory to a serious outfit. "Carly, I understand your reservations, especially in light of what happened to David Hofstetter. I have my concerns as well, but I have an inkling of what this is about, and I can assure you they will be safe. I spoke to someone at the top just last week and this mission involves national security. I was told that there is a major threat to the office of the president."

Carly's mouth made a grim line. "And that threat would be?"

Dr. Anton said, "The Praetorian Guard has reason to believe that an assassination attempt will be made at the Presidential Black Tie Bash. The target is most likely the president, but may include her daughter, Layla, as well."

"So you're sending these kids right into the middle of something deadly? For crying out loud." Carly spat out the words. "What's wrong with the Secret Service? Are they on vacation or something?"

Mitch said, "The Secret Service will be doing their usual exemplary job. We're not worried about weaponry brought into the Bash; that's impossible given the safeguards in place. The kinds of things we're worried about involve superpowers and that's where these three come in. Any superpowers utilized by the Associates can't match what these three can do. Having them there is an added security measure. We very much hope that their skills aren't needed."

"I have a bad feeling about this," Carly said, sighing.

Will said, "Carly, I know you mentioned being unemployed. We wanted to let you know that if you get a job in the interim, we have a substitute available to take your place on the trip. While we think it's admirable that you want to be with your brother, we don't want you to miss out on any opportunities."

Carly's laugh came out in one quick, explosive burst. "Yeah right." She gave him a withering look. "Well, I have to tell you that while I think it's admirable that you're thinking about *me* and *my* opportunities, I *will* be on this trip so there will be no need for a substitute. Thanks for mentioning it, though. I appreciate your concern." I knew that Carly had been working for a temp agency—her solution to making some money between now and the end of summer. It was an agency she'd worked for before. This time around she was doing office work for a manufacturing firm that distributed fishing lures and hunting supplies. She hated it, but it was, as she said, better than nothing.

Will nodded. I had the feeling he knew it would go this way.

"Moving on. You will be fully briefed at a later date," Mitch said hurriedly. "Until then they don't want to disclose too much for security reasons."

Before Carly could object again, Will launched into what we'd be doing during these meetings. "We have two goals," he said. "Number one concerns fine-tuning your powers, and increasing them if possible, and the second involves the logistics of the mission." Each session at the warehouse would be considered training, he told us. We'd be practicing anything we might encounter on the trip. "This includes protocol for a formal event, ballroom dancing, understanding event security, and using your powers as needed. We want you to be over-prepared, if possible, so that you can handle anything you encounter."

"We'll begin by working with your powers," Mitch said. "Who wants to go first?"

Jameson stepped forward, both hands in his pockets, like he was one cool guy. "No point in saving the best for last. You might as well start with me."

Mitch reached down, opened the plastic container at his

feet, and pulled out a red rubber ball. Will then pulled out an electronic tablet, and started fiddling with the keyboard.

"We're playing dodgeball?" Jameson asked, his voice all snark. He pointed at Will. "And he's keeping score?"

"Not exactly." Mitch walked toward the pallets stacked with burial vaults on the far side of the room. He stopped thirty feet away from us and set the ball on the concrete floor. He called out, "We want to test the power of your telekinesis, both for distance and force. Do you think you can make the ball roll from where you're currently standing?"

Jameson sighed, the same way he did when he thought someone was being stupid. I'd been the target of that sigh more than once. "Yeah, I think maybe I can."

"Okay then!" Mitch rubbed his hands together eagerly. "Let's see what you can do."

Jameson rubbed his palms back and forth, mimicking Mitch, then wiped his hands on the front of his jeans. He held an arm out like he had Harry Potter's wand. "Move that ball!" he yelled.

In the past, I'd seen Jameson make a salt shaker slide across a table, lasso a man with a leather cord, make a cell phone float in the air, and get pieces of paper to levitate in a circle, so I knew he had the power to move objects with his mind. But being tested on it was different. How was he going to do under pressure? The group's eyes locked on the ball as we all watched for movement. Slowly, very slowly, it inched forward in a jerky, almost imperceptible motion. Mitch's face fell; he was hoping for more. Just then, I glanced Jameson's way and saw a glint in his eye; and that's when I knew he'd been holding back. A second later the ball picked up speed, barreling toward us as if it had been kicked. Mallory shielded her face when the ball approached, but it stopped right before it hit her, changed direction and headed for the ceiling. It zigzagged up and down and then circled around us, going so fast that the air whistled as it went past.

Mitch's eyes widened in amazement. And then the ball went straight toward him, struck him in the head and knocked him unconscious.

CHAPTER EIGHT

·•●•·

RUSS

Mitch's head hitting the floor made a loud thunk, amplified when the sound echoed off the high ceiling. "Oh my word!" Rosie said. Instinctively, we all rushed forward.

"I can't believe you hit him that hard," Mallory said to Jameson, as we stared down at Mitch who lay face up on the floor, his eyes closed.

"I thought he'd duck." Jameson's words made him sound uncaring, but judging from the look on his face he was a little shaken up. I don't think he had as much control over the ball as he wanted us to think.

Dr. Anton knelt next to Mitch and checked his pulse, then searched his head for injuries. "I don't believe that the ball was the problem. It was hitting the floor that did him in," he observed dryly. "His breathing is fine." Mitch's eyes fluttered and he attempted to sit up. "Easy now," Dr. Anton said, guiding him back down. "Why don't you just lie still for a few minutes?"

"I have an idea," Will said. With all the commotion, I hadn't noticed that he'd held back and was frantically typing into his keyboard. "Why don't we have Russ use his powers of healing to bring Mitch back up to speed?"

"Russ?" Dr. Anton said.

I shrugged. "I can try." I saw Jameson's smug look and immediately regretted not sounding more confident. Once again, he was going to turn this into a competition. Well, if that's the way he wanted it. "I mean, of course I can do it."

I knelt down across from Dr. Anton and let my hands hover over Mitch's upper body to assess his condition. "The pain and injury are limited to the back of his head. It doesn't feel serious."

"Probably just a concussion," Dr. Anton said thoughtfully.

I held my hands over the top of Mitch's head and closed my eyes. I had done this before, but usually it was for far more serious injuries and I didn't have my sister watching. Having her there made it feel weird.

"Man, it hurts," Mitch said, probably to give me a nudge to hurry up. It had the opposite effect though. Knowing that they were all waiting for me made me nervous. I willed myself to shut the world out and concentrated on pouring all my energy and concern into Mitch's head. I ignored the sound of Jameson clearing his throat and Will's tapping on the keyboard. In a few minutes, something inside me shook loose and I knew it was working. Such a relief.

Mitch felt it too because he sighed and said, "I can feel the heat coming off his hands."

When I'd finished, I opened my eyes and shook my fingers. "That's it," I said. I hoped it was enough.

"Mitch?" Will said.

Mitch sat up. He shook off Dr. Anton's offer of help

and got to his feet on his own. "That was remarkable." He smoothed his hair and adjusted his T-shirt. "Two minutes ago my head hurt like hell, there was ringing in my ears, and I was seeing stars. Now I feel just fine."

Mallory gave me a slow clap and even Carly smiled. "Not too bad," Will said, going back to the tablet. "Not bad at all."

Mallory's turn was less harrowing, but still impressive. Mitch and Will brought in five different Praetorian Guard volunteers, two men and three women, all of them looking to be in their forties, and had them sit in folding chairs arranged in a straight row. Mallory was instructed to stand behind them, rest her hands on their shoulders and wordlessly exert mind control over them, one at a time. Will showed her the instructions on his tablet as she went to each volunteer. It was eerily silent. Just one teenage girl in a really short skirt, walking behind a row of middle-aged people, resting her hands on their shoulders as she went. Like a weird game of Duck, Duck, Goose without the chase. When she finished with the last one, she nodded to Will, who took over from there.

"Volunteers," he said. "Do you have something you want to share with us?"

And just like that, all five of them popped out of their chairs and started acting like freaking lunatics. One of the men meowed like a cat, while the second one spun in circles. One woman flapped her arms, another sang the Star Spangled Banner, and the third made growling noises. It was so unexpected and ridiculous that I couldn't help laughing. And I wasn't the only one. Rosie and my sister couldn't help giggling either. "It's like a Las Vegas hypnosis act," Carly said, her voice rising to be heard over the singing and growling.

"That's why I'd never volunteer for those things," Rosie said, shaking her head.

"Like hypnosis," Jameson said to me. "Except she didn't say anything out loud. Way to go Mallory!"

The five continued until Mallory said, "Enough!" She pointed to the chairs. "I want you back in your seats, eyes closed, and quiet." Like trained German Shepherds, they obeyed immediately, sitting straight-backed in their assigned chairs, eyes shut, completely silent. Will nodded at Mallory, who went down the line, touching each one in turn. "Now open your eyes," she said.

The five blinked and looked around like they'd fallen asleep on a long bus trip and been jolted awake at their destination. One woman actually stretched and yawned.

"How do you feel?" Mitch asked. In unison they all said they felt great! "Never better," one man said.

"Excellent," Mitch said, rubbing his hands together. "Thank you all for volunteering tonight. If you go back to the office, Tiffany will have a questionnaire she'd like you to fill out before you go."

"Thanks folks!" Will said, as the group made their way to the door. "Much appreciated."

"Will they remember what they did?" Jameson asked once the door clicked shut.

Will turned to Mallory. "What do you think?"

"No." She shook her head. "They won't remember any of it. They think they took part in a new form of meditation. They woke up feeling refreshed and full of energy. I gave them instructions for when they get home. One woman is going to go home and clean her refrigerator, another will call a friend or relative she hasn't talked to in years." She started to tick them off on her fingers. "The third woman will decide she needs to redecorate her bedroom. One of the guys is going to start volunteering at a homeless shelter and the other one is going to subscribe to the *New York Times*."

"You've got to be kidding me." Carly's words were a whisper but I was close enough to hear. "Unbelievable."

Mitch said, "We wanted to vary the post-session suggestions so that some were long term, like the volunteering and the redecorating, and some were immediate, like the refrigerator. We're going to have them fill out questionnaires every week and see if they followed through on the suggestions." He gave Mallory an approving look. "Next week we'll try subjects who are resistant. Once we have that data we'll know how far we can take this."

"How will they be resistant?" Carly asked. "Are you gonna drag them in off the street?"

"Oh no, nothing like that," Will assured her. "The participants will still be volunteers, but they'll be told ahead of time that someone is going to try to assert mind control on them, and that they should attempt to resist."

Mitch came up and put his hand on my shoulder. "If you're up for it, Russ, next I'd like to have you show us how you expel electricity."

"I'm up for it," I said. "Definitely up for it." Out of the corner of my eye I saw Jameson giving me one of his looks. He was loving this.

"Great!" Will said, with an excessive amount of enthusiasm. "Don't start until we give you instructions." He strode over, picked up the ball, and juggled it back and forth between his hands. "I'm going to throw the ball up in the air, and I'd like to see if you can hit it while it's in motion. Wait until it's not anywhere near me, so you don't accidentally electrocute me."

"I wouldn't do that," I assured him.

Will laughed. "Well, after what happened to Mitch with the ball..."

"That was Jameson," I said. "He has control issues."

"Hey!" Jameson said.

"Okay then," Will said, taking a few steps back. "Remember to wait until it's far away from me."

I nodded. "Got it." I held my palms out, like Spiderman shooting a web.

Will swung the ball back and whipped it into the air. It sailed up, almost reaching the ceiling, picking up speed as it came down. Somewhere in there, Jameson cleared his throat, but I ignored him. Timing was everything. When the ball was halfway to the floor, I let loose. Electricity shot out of my hands in a blinding blast. I aimed my lightning bolt at the ball, instinctively allowing for the speed of the descent and I hit it straight on. My aim was perfect, but I miscalculated and put out more than was necessary: the stream of electricity obliterated the ball and kept going, hitting the stack of burial vaults behind it. Almost instantly, they crumbled and fell in a violent heap of concrete dust and rubble. The smell of burning rubber filled the air. The spectators had varying reactions, but all of them were amazed.

"Oh my word," Rosie said, putting her hand over her mouth. "Very impressive."

Mallory clapped. "Awesome, Russ!"

"Show-off." Jameson punched my shoulder. He sounded

a little proud actually, which surprised me. Man, he was a hard guy to figure out.

"I think we should all retire to the office area until the dust settles," Mitch said, waving a hand in front of his face. "I hope this doesn't trigger my asthma."

Will hoisted the plastic container onto his shoulder and ushered us toward the door. As we walked I heard Dr. Anton say, "Good grief, I haven't seen anything that impressive since David Hofstetter."

Carly spoke up, "David could do that without even trying, and look where it got him." I knew where she was coming from. She thought he'd perished in a fiery car accident, but the truth of what actually happened was almost as bad. David Hofstetter got stuck working in a laboratory for sixteen years while his friends and family assumed he was dead, and while his son was growing up without him. He left a big hole behind. Tragic, really.

But nothing like that was going to happen to me.

CHAPTER NINE

RUSS

For weeks on end we continued these sessions, fine-tuning our powers and taking tests, some of which didn't seem relevant to anything at all, but Dr. Anton assured us that everything was important. Some of the tests reminded me of standard IQ tests; others required us to memorize schematics of the building where the Bash would be held. We were also instructed in etiquette, table manners, and ballroom dancing. All of us had to complete questionnaires asking what we'd eaten that day, how we slept the night before, and how energetic we felt on a scale of one to ten. Over and over again they stressed keeping a low profile so that we didn't cause a panic. "People get trampled when a mob rushes to the exits," Mitch said. "We don't want a riot."

During one of the practice sessions they had me shoot electricity from my palms down into the concrete floor to see what would happen. "Start out slow and easy," Mitch said. "You can always crank it up later."

I held my hands out and gave one short blast on each side, but instead of the electricity pushing into the floor, the opposite happened: I was propelled off my feet and forward. "Whoa," I said, coming down hard. I gave the two instructors an irritated look. "Did you know that would happen?"

Both of them grinned like idiots. "We had an idea it might."

"It would have been nice to know ahead of time," I grumbled, thinking how close I'd come to falling on my face. Luckily Jameson was on the other side of the room practicing with a lasso or he'd have given me grief about it.

Mitch said, "Sorry about that. We didn't want to say anything that might affect the outcome." Neither he or Will thought this particular talent had a practical outcome, but it didn't matter to me. Boosting myself in the air by shooting lightning bolts out of my palms was the coolest thing ever. I practiced over and over again until I could rise as high as twenty feet and as far as the length of the warehouse. Mallory applauded when she saw me and even Jameson looked impressed. Only Carly had a worried look on her face.

The testing for my healing abilities was not as exciting. The started me off with some easy cases. Initially, they had me heal a man with cuts on his arm, and fix a dog with a problem hip. Skippy was the dog's name. He looked like a beagle mix, all ears, long body, and short legs. When he came in his head was down and his tail drooped. By the time I was done, his tail was wagging and he had a smile on his face. A proud moment for me.

Another test involved using my curative powers on mystery substances inside several different Petri dishes. It was hard for me to connect in those cases and I never found out the results.

There were about a dozen patients in all. After a while

they stopped telling me the problem and wanted to see if I could figure it out. I think I did pretty well right from the start. The first time they brought in an elderly woman with a mystery ailment. She was seriously old with white hair and skin like aged leather. I scanned her body with my hands, letting them hover from head to toe, and determined that the problem was in her midsection, close to her heart. I did the best I could to infuse my energy into that area. She looked better by the time I was finished but they wouldn't tell me if it worked.

My favorite training sessions involved the ballroom dance lessons. A tiny woman named (and I'm not making this up) Prima Donna came in lugging an ancient record player and a stack of vinyl albums. Her hair was dyed jet black and she carried a fan which she opened with the snap of her hand. "Like a flamenco dancer," she said. She was easily seventy years old, but she could dance like nobody's business. "You've heard of the Prima Donna Dance Studio, yes?" Most of her sentences ended with the word yes. She had a slight accent that I couldn't place. We all reluctantly confessed to not having heard of her dance studio and she was appalled. "For shame," she scolded. "The Prima Donna Dance Studio very famous. I train all the big names back in the day. Anyway, we begin, yes?" From the start Jameson stood out as the worst in the group. Mallory took to it right away, and I was, Prima Donna said, "somewhat trainable." But Jameson's long legs couldn't stick to the rhythm, not even to save his rapidly drooping ego.

"Tell your smart brain to talk to your legs," I said. "See if they can work something out." Mallory and I were paired up for a waltz and having an easy time of it, while Jameson looked like he wanted to dismember me and make my body parts dance using telekinesis.

Prima Donna came half a dozen times in all. After the first three times Mallory and I didn't need any instruction at all. We just danced. But Jameson never got any better. If anything he got worse, anticipating how Prima Donna would hit him with her fan when he'd make a misstep. I almost felt sorry for him.

Some of the other sessions involved learning facts about the government. In those cases, they gave us handouts to take home and memorize. Jameson was especially insulted when they asked us to memorize a sheet describing how the federal government worked. He looked down at the page and read aloud, "The federal government is made up of three branches: the executive, the judicial, and the legislative." He looked up, irate. "What is this, third grade?"

"Just read it. I think you'll find it has a new spin on the topic," Will said.

As we were leaving that evening, Jameson crumpled up his sheet and tossed it in a wastebasket. When Mitch raised his eyebrows, Jameson tapped his forehead. "Trust me, I've got it. It's all up here."

Later lessons included topics such as security protocol at our nation's capital, personal information about the presidential family, and the layout of the banquet hall where the event would be held. Carly sarcastically commented that I would be ready for a life as a politician or a party planner if the whole superhero thing didn't work out.

The tests that measured our powers—how far, fast, and accurately Jameson could move objects, or how much electric current I could generate in one go, seemed to fascinate the

Praetorian Guard officials the most. A larger group attended these tests, mostly men in their forties and fifties, armed with devices which measured and recorded our efforts. On those days, Jameson and I got super competitive, spurring each other on to greater heights. Just seeing Jameson's smug grin made me want to totally bring it, and I think I had the same effect on him.

At some point, Mitch and Will noticed us trying to one up each other, and it bothered them so they set up a different kind of test. "This time," Mitch said, "we're going in a different direction." He rested a hand on my shoulder. "You and Jameson are going to be working together." The exercise, he said, would involve Jameson moving an object through the air, and me obliterating it while it was moving. "Teamwork," Mitch said. "Like a relay race, Jameson. You *want* Russ to be able to hit it."

We started with a large beach ball, and when that proved to be too easy, switched to smaller and faster objects. The day Jameson shot a paperclip at top speed across the warehouse and I zapped it from thirty feet away was a proud day for both of us. Without even thinking about it, I found myself high-fiving Jameson. Somehow, we'd turned a corner. He could still be a jerk, but now we were on the same side.

At the same time we were double-teaming, Mallory was making great strides in mind control. Carly drifted back and forth between Mallory's testing and mine, and gave me updates on the ride home. "She's scary good," Carly said, gripping the steering wheel. She glanced over to see if I was paying attention. "Don't let her touch you, Russ. I mean it. I wouldn't let that girl get within five inches of me."

"It's not like she's going to do it to me without me

knowing it," I said. "She's my friend. Besides, I can do a bit of mind control too, you know."

"You haven't seen her lately," Carly said. "Your mind control is nothing like hers. Now she can implant memories and make people hallucinate. I overheard some of the guys from the Praetorian Guard say they've never seen anything like the three of you *ever*. And your powers seem to be increasing all the time. I'm afraid, Russ. I'm really afraid. After this, they're not going to let you go." She lifted a hand and I saw her wipe her eyes. "If you survive this mission, they will want more and more and more. You will never be able to have a normal life."

We were both quiet for a moment and then I said, "I'm not so sure I want a normal life."

She shook her head sadly. "Oh Russ, you have no idea."

About three weeks into our training, Nadia was finally able to get away from her mom long enough to astral project to me. That night, I was already in bed, eyes closed and nearly asleep. I felt her presence and knew she was there. "Nadia?" I whispered. I didn't need to talk out loud because she could hear my thoughts perfectly, but sometimes I forgot and fell into old habits.

She looked like a beautiful ghost drifting through the window. I watched her float to the foot of my bed, her image the same size as her body in real life but as ethereal as smoke. I knew that when she wanted to, she could enter a room invisibly, but she was also able to show herself at will. And with me, she always did.

Russ? she said cautiously. I sensed a careful happiness coming from her, the kind you have when you don't want to get your hopes up. I didn't want to answer out loud so I switched to thoughts. My parents were downstairs and probably couldn't hear my voice, but it was better to be careful.

I sat up and asked, *What's wrong?*

Nothing's wrong. I'm just…

What?

Glad to see you. I wish I could really talk to you though.

We're talking now.

I mean in person.

I know. But this is almost better, right?

I felt the equivalent of a sigh from her. She said, *It doesn't matter if it's better or worse. It's all I can do right now. Believe me, my mother is tireless in her efforts to make me miserable.*

I'm sorry, I said.

I know. She sighed again. *I don't mean to be so negative. I'm happy to finally see you but this is all so virtual. I just wish I could touch you.*

I felt her essence sweep through me like a warm breeze. As close to touching as we could manage at the moment.

Really touch you, she added

That made two of us. Before Nadia and I connected in Peru, I had no idea how addictive another person could be. I craved being close to her, smelling her, feeling her hands wander over my skin and through my hair. Day and night, thoughts of her haunted me. I replayed our times together and tried to relive the feeling of our kisses and the press of her body against mine. I said, *She can't keep you trapped in that house forever. We'll be together again.*

Yeah, but when? By the time that happens you'll have forgotten about me and be with someone else.

That's not going to happen, I said, sort of insulted. How could she say that? Didn't she know everything about her was etched onto my soul?

I've been told it happens with teenage romances, she said, her tone bitter. *My mother has made that very clear to me. More than once.*

Well, she doesn't know us.

I guess you're right.

I decided to change the subject. *So what else is new?*

She was quiet for a moment. *Nothing, really.*

You didn't notice anything different about your face?

Oh! Yes. I mean, thank you! I didn't notice at first, and then when I did I couldn't tell you. I can't believe I didn't thank you first thing.

I grinned. *Were you surprised?*

Confused, and then surprised, and then happy. When did you do it?

On the plane, when you were sleeping.

That's what I thought! she said.

What did your parents say?

My dad thought it was because I was using this ointment he gave me. My mom, as usual, was highly suspicious. She asked if I'd been worshipping Satan.

She did not. But even as I said it, I knew it was true.

Yes she did. But don't worry about it. That's just life at my house. One more thing to add to the list. I'm overjoyed that you fixed my face, and really, really grateful. I can even open my eye all the way now. And I'm letting my bangs grow out. It's amazing really. The skin looks better all the time. Like it's regenerating. I never used to look in the mirror, but now I can't stop and when I do, I think of you and what you've done for me. You've changed my life in so many ways, I can't even begin to thank you...

You don't need to thank me.

Of course I do. What you did for me is everything.

That's just what you do for someone you love. The words were out without a thought, but when I felt her surge of joy fill the room, I was glad I'd broken through my tendency to hold back and just put it out there.

I love you, Russ.

I love you too. The words felt so right, but being apart when we said them was so wrong. We should be in the same room. The novelty of astral projecting had completely worn off. I wanted Nadia, the real Nadia, right next to me. Body and soul. I wanted it all.

My biggest fear, she said, *is that you're going to die on this mission. If that happened, I'd be lost. I wouldn't want to live without you.*

I'm not going to die.

You could. We almost did in Peru.

I promise you, Nadia, no matter what happens, I'll find my way back to you.

If I could go on the trip we'd be together no matter what happens.

That reminded me: *The Praetorian Guard guys who are training us said they've been trying to get someone into your house to try mind control on your mom. Are they making any progress?*

Ha! They've been trying but my mother is formidable. They've offered her free carpet cleaning, told her she's won prizes, and said they're from social services and that they are there to check on me.

Really? I asked, fascinated. *What happened?*

My father let them in. My mother wouldn't even shake their hand. She wouldn't even go within five feet of them. They pretended to inspect the house, which is spotless, by the way, asked me a bunch of questions and left. My mother told them she'd be contacting her attorney and reporting them for harassment.

Did she?

I don't know. Maybe. She seems to have an awful lot of free time.

I really wanted you to go with us to Washington D.C.

Yeah, me too, but unless I jump out the window, it doesn't look like I'm going anywhere.

The Praetorian Guard will come up with something, I said. *David Hofstetter said your astral projecting would be invaluable. And Mallory's mind control is getting to be really powerful. Maybe your mom would let her in the house?*

Maybe, Nadia said, sounding doubtful.

But the weeks went on and the Guard didn't come any closer to arranging for Nadia to come on the mission. Her mother had eased up a little so she was able to astral project to me at night, and I kept her filled in on what we were learning. Her days were filled with homework and studying and bad television, so she listened to my descriptions with rapt attention, laughing at my observations of Jameson and speculating, with me, what it all meant.

Why would someone want to kill the president? she asked.

I don't know, I said. President Bernstein was the first female president in the history of the country, and fairly well-liked by most. There was a very vocal group of dissenters that wanted her gone but it was only two years until her term was up. It seemed like it would be easier to wait than commit murder. Not to mention that the vice president would just take office and he was on the same side, so really, what would that accomplish?

Nadia said, *What do they think might happen at the Bash?*

I don't know. They said they'd tell us more when it gets closer. I guess we'd just have to wait to find out.

CHAPTER TEN

RUSS

B y the end of the summer, all three of us had amped our powers to levels far beyond anything we'd ever envisioned. It was hard not to use it in everyday life. So many times I desperately wanted to put on a light show for my nephew, heal my mother's headaches, or use a little mind control on Dad to convince him I could put off mowing the lawn for another day, but admirably I held back. Carly would have been really angry with me for one thing, not to mention that showing my powers in public might jeopardize the mission, and the Praetorian Guard in general. I didn't want to be the stupid teenager who lacked impulse control and couldn't be trusted.

One Thursday night we arrived at the burial vault factory and knew something was up. It was a few days before we were scheduled to leave and we still didn't have a clue as to our role on this trip, other than that we were going to attend the Presidential Black Tie Bash. At some point we'd stopped wondering and asking, and just focused on the training.

That night, Carly and I were met at the door by Tiffany, one of the administrative assistants. Instead of directing us to the warehouse, she ushered us into a conference room where we were told to wait. Mallory, Jameson, and Rosie were already there; Mallory said hello as we entered and Rosie smiled, but Jameson was too busy leaning back in his chair with both feet propped up on the polished table to acknowledge our entrance. "What's this all about?" Carly asked.

"I don't honestly know," Tiffany said apologetically. "Some kind of announcement, I believe." She closed the door behind her and then the five of us were sealed in the windowless space. The conference table was large enough for twenty. The surface was polished light wood, all one color except for a glistening spiral pattern in the center. It reminded me of Dorothy's yellow brick road or our very own lux spiral. One wall was covered with a white veneered surface, like it served as a screen for video clips or PowerPoint presentations. The two long walls were covered with photos of the founder of the company and his sons and grandsons. Generation after generation, all of whom opted to go into the burial vault business. The plaques were industry awards and commendations for employee safety. In the corner, a triangular bookcase held a decanter and glasses, along with a bowling trophy and a few random books. It looked like a standard business conference room, but I sensed electricity where there should be none. Besides the outlets and light fixtures, there was electricity pulsing out of the picture frames and the bowling trophies. Hidden cameras was my guess.

"Take a seat," Rosie said, gesturing to the chair next to her with a smile. I'd heard her say the same phrase many times when we'd visited her in the diner. The familiar words were comforting. I sat next to her, but Carly, in a small bit of rebellion walked around to the head of the table and took a high-backed swivel chair clearly intended for whoever would be leading the discussion.

"That's the chair I wanted," Jameson shifted his feet to the floor and sat up straight. "But Mallory wouldn't let me sit there."

Carly shrugged. "You have to learn to think for yourself, young man. If you keep waiting for approval you're going to miss out on a lot."

"I can think for myself," Jameson said, clearly offended. "I was being polite."

"Being polite doesn't get you very far, believe me." Carly was definitely in a mood. It was like there was something in the air only she could sense and she wasn't liking the smell of it.

"Not knowing what's going on can be a little stressful," Rosie said soothingly. "But I'm sure it's all going to work out fine."

"Where's Dr. Anton?" Mallory said. "He's usually here by now." There was a hint of worry in her voice.

Rosie said, "I talked to him this morning and he said he's going to be here, so don't you worry about him. Probably just delayed by traffic. As long as we're waiting though, I might as well take the time to tell you how thrilled we are at how well you all are doing. You've worked hard and honed your powers, but that's just part of it. Dr. Anton and I are also impressed with your maturity and focus. All three of you make us proud. We know we're putting a lot on your young shoulders, but we trust you'll get the job done."

From anyone else that speech would have sounded a little condescending, but Rosie delivered this speech with conviction. I think she really was proud of us and thrilled at our progress and everything else she said. Jameson and Mallory must have felt the same way, because they both said, "Thank you," at the same time I did.

Mallory grinned. She'd gotten really tan this summer and it made her teeth look extra white. I noticed she'd been wearing a lot of white lately too, probably to show off her darker color. "We're glad we've earned your trust," she said. "And we'll do everything we can to get the job done."

At the end of the table I saw Carly roll her eyes as she mouthed the words 'suck up' to me. Luckily, no one else spotted it. It took all I had not to laugh.

A few seconds later, the door opened again and Dr. Anton walked in followed by Mitch and Will, along with a man and woman we'd never seen before. Both of the strangers wore business attire. The woman seemed to be in charge. The four men fell in place along the edge of the room while she strode forward, greeting each of us with an official handshake. She was tall, slender, and edgy-looking with spiky red hair and funky glasses, but her attitude was all business. "I'm Dr. Wentworth," she said and listened as we each said our name. I sensed she already knew who we were and I also sensed that she and the other man were wired for sound. The devices, hidden underneath their clothing, pulsed in a way that was impossible for me to miss. Now that I could detect electricity I had to remind myself that other people didn't have that ability. It was the one superpower that I hadn't brought up during our training sessions. At times like this I appreciated my new awareness and the knowledge that someone somewhere was watching us and listening to our every word. I was careful not to say too much when I knew I could be overheard.

When we were finished with the pleasantries, Dr. Wentworth gestured to her colleague, "My associate, Dr. Habush." Dr. Habush, a short man with a large briefcase under one arm, nodded mutely. Compared to Dr. Wentworth, he looked twitchy and out of place. Already I noticed he had a nervous habit of running his fingers through his stiff brown hair. The five of them pulled up chairs and sat, with Dr. Wentworth taking the seat at the end of the table opposite Carly. "I want to thank you for meeting with me on such short notice. This is an emergency meeting, as I'm sure you know."

Carly opened her mouth but before she could speak, Jameson jumped in and said, "We don't know anything. This was our regularly scheduled practice time and we were told to wait in here. That's all we know."

"My apologies," Dr. Wentworth said, twiddling a pen between her fingers. "I thought you knew you were called here to be prepped." She gave Dr. Habush an irritated look. "I won't make any assumptions from now on." She cleared her throat. "Let's get started. Habush, can you give the preliminary statement?"

Dr. Habush scurried to his feet, his chair squeaking as he rose. "Everything said during this meeting is confidential. There will be no note taking. No recording devices allowed. Please take a moment to turn off your phones." He waited while everyone shut down their phones, then continued. "Anyone who violates the security code and reveals what we discuss here can be prosecuted for crimes against the United

States. We will follow up. The safety of every citizen relies upon your discretion."

Like a dark cloud covering the sun, the mood in the room turned somber. I glanced over at Jameson, expecting him to have a smirk on his face, but even he took this seriously.

"Thank you, Dr. Habush." Dr. Wentworth stood, a cue that she was taking over. "We'd planned on briefing you on the flight to D.C., but something has happened and we feel the need to fill you in ahead of time. The first thing I need to tell you is that the trip has been moved up. You will be leaving a day early."

"I'm not sure my mom will be okay with that," Mallory said. "She sort of had it all planned out day by day." She extended her fingers and frowned.

Dr. Wentworth assured her that parental permission would be their department. "Believe me," she said dryly, "what your mom has to say on this subject is the least of my worries. You're going, regardless."

"Why are we going so soon?" Jameson asked.

Dr. Wentworth said, "As you're aware, the original mission entailed the three of you attending the annual Presidential Bash in Washington D.C. to provide added protection for the President and her daughter in the event the Associates try to harm either one of them. The Bash is one of the biggest social events of the year. To cancel it is out of the question."

"Canceling isn't even an option!" Dr. Habush said. Dr. Wentworth gave him a sharp glance and he took a step back.

She continued. "Once again, the Bash will also be a celebration of the president's daughter's birthday. As you may know, Layla will turn nineteen this year."

Mallory said to no one in particular, "I can't believe we're going to meet Layla!"

"Yes, you will meet Layla," Dr. Wentworth said. "In fact, Russ will be her date and you and Jameson will be going as a couple, posing as good friends of the first daughter. Your presence adds another measure of security for the first family, the kind of security the Secret Service can't provide."

Dr. Habush said, "Because so far none of them has been able to zap a lightning bolt from forty feet away." He chuckled.

Dr. Wentworth ignored him and continued. "The Bash was our original reason for sending you on this trip, but recently, there's been another complication." She pointed across the table. "Habush, start the presentation."

Habush got up to switch off the light. For a split second we were in complete darkness. Before my eyes could adjust, an eerie glow rose up over the center of the table. A second later, a three dimensional image took shape, a movie of President Bernstein working in the Oval Office. There was no sound, but we saw her clearly as she hung up the phone, then spoke to a young man who came into the room to hand her some papers.

"You should know that this was two days ago," Dr. Wentworth said. "The last day our president was at work."

"She's on vacation?" Mallory said the words tentatively.

"No. She's in a coma. It hasn't been announced publicly because it would put the country in a panic. Only a few people know. Most of her staff has been told she's unavailable—too busy for any meetings or calls. The medical staff taking care of her is small and is working in seclusion to ensure the information is contained."

"What happened?" I asked.

"We're not entirely sure, but we believe she's been exposed to something that essentially caused the equivalent of a brain aneurism. We've been keeping her on life support."

Mallory looked at me across the table with shining eyes. "Russ can heal her."

I had a sick feeling about this. Every time I healed someone it felt like a fluke, something I could never do again. Mallory sounded so positive, but what if I failed? I was willing to try, but I wasn't sure it would work.

"Maybe," Dr. Wentworth said. "We've been impressed with what we've seen, but his healing powers are nowhere near definitive. And of course, if there's brain damage, it may not be reversible."

"Russ can do it," Mallory said, giving me a smile. "I'm sure he can."

"Moving on," Dr. Wentworth said and the image switched to Vice President Montalbo as he walked through a crowd of school children shaking hands, and patting the smaller ones on the head.

"Is the vice president going to be taking over?" Rosie asked.

"Not if we can help it," Dr. Wentworth said. "Our president is firmly on the side of the Praetorian Guard. Vice President Montalbo, on the other hand, was recently discovered to be affiliated with the Associates. As far as we know he is not aware that the president is incapacitated. The vice president is out of town right now but he'll be back right before the Bash. Under no circumstances can we allow him to take office."

"The first order of business involves Russ trying to heal the president," Dr. Habush said. He was starting to remind me of a hyper kid who couldn't wait for his turn.

"So Russ heals the president and gets to be the Layla's date and all Mallory and I do is hang out at the Bash?" Jameson asked.

"Hardly," Dr. Wentworth said, with a sour expression. "Both of you will be entrusted with protecting the president and her daughter. Your powers of telekinesis might make the difference between life and death. And Mallory's mind control will be used to influence the vice president and others. Believe me, you won't be just hanging out at the Bash." She put finger quotes around the last five words.

"Okay, okay." Jameson leaned back in his chair and put up his hands. "I get it."

"We're also counting on all three of you to watch the crowd to determine if there are any Associates present. Anyone who attempts to approach Layla Bernstein without advance clearance should be perceived as a threat. You have our permission to use your powers as you see fit."

"The same with the president?" Mallory asked. "They can use their powers to protect her?"

Dr. Wentworth nodded. "Assuming the president is there."

"Oh she'll be there." Mallory shot me a knowing look.

"And we can do this in front of four hundred people?" Jameson asked.

She nodded. "Do whatever you need to do to safeguard the presidential family. Don't worry about witnesses. We'll do damage control later." She gave Dr. Habush a sign to move on.

The image in front of us changed to a crowded ballroom. "This is footage from last year's Black Tie Bash," Dr. Habush said. The 3D visual showed it as if we were moving through the crowd. "You can see that the dance floor gets packed on occasion. This could be a trouble spot for Layla who can be a bit unpredictable. If she wants to dance, all three of you need to be right there, as close as possible. Human shields."

"Hear that, Russ. As close as possible," Jameson said.

"I've got it," I said. Jameson thought he was such a riot.

Dr. Habush took us through the schedule of the evening. Guests would move through a receiving line which would consist of the vice president and his wife, and the first family. "Assuming President Bernstein is well by then," he said. Afterward, there would be dancing and drinks.

"No alcohol for any of you," Dr. Wentworth piped in. "You're on duty."

"At the end of the evening, a cake will be wheeled out for Layla's birthday. Everyone will sing and slices of cake will be made available for guests to take home," Dr. Habush said. "If everyone is safe and sound at that point, the Praetorian Guard will consider it to be a rousing success."

"Any questions?" Dr. Wentworth said.

Mallory raised her hand. "So are we supposed to bring fancy clothes...?"

"No, they will be provided. You will have an appropriate gown and the guys will wear tuxes. A stylist will be assigned to do your hair and makeup."

Mallory smiled so wide I swore I could see all her teeth.

The fact that formal clothing would be provided was a clear selling point for her. For me, not so much.

I held up my hand. "I'm assuming the Bash will be covered by the media. Won't they wonder how Layla knows us?"

"Good question," Dr. Wentworth said with a smile. "She knows you because she met you at the academic decathlon in Miami earlier in the summer."

"She met us at the academic decathlon?" Jameson said, his brow wrinkled. "But we weren't actually there."

"Layla Bernstein was there, though, handing out the awards," Dr. Wentworth said. "And Mallory is going to convince her that she met the three of you there and all of you hit it off. Think you can do that, Mallory?"

"Yes, I can do that."

"Very good." Dr. Wentworth went over to the wall outlet and switched on the lights. "You will get more information when you arrive in D.C. Tonight's briefing was just to give you a general idea of what will be happening. Now if there aren't any other questions, I believe we are finished."

CHAPTER ELEVEN

— • ○ ● ○ • —

RUSS

I had to see Nadia one more time before we left and it had to be in person because I had a gift I wanted to give her. The night before our flight to Washington D. C., I snuck out of my parents' house after they'd gone to bed, and headed out to Nadia's house. Being out at night was like old times back in the days leading up to witnessing the lux spiral.

On the walk over I wished once more that Nadia was coming on the trip with us, not only because I wanted her there, but because I knew she would be an asset to the group. Her presence might make the difference between life and death.

The subject of my life and death was definitely on my mind after finding out my name was on the Associates' hit list, something I learned after the briefing at the burial vault factory. Dr. Wentworth stopped Carly and me as we headed toward the door, saying she wanted a word with us in private. The rest of the group trooped out, with only Dr. Anton glancing back to notice that we were being held back. He didn't look the least bit surprised.

"Please," Dr. Wentworth said, indicating the chairs we'd just been sitting in. "Have a seat."

My sister and I sat down side by side. "Are we in trouble?" Carly said, with a smirk.

"Possibly," Dr. Wentworth said, taking a seat at the head of the table. "We've known for a while that the Associates now have a new commander and there are a number of changes going on in the organization."

"Who is this new commander?" Carly asked.

"We don't know the identity of the commander, but your brother is definitely on his radar." Dr. Wentworth rested her palms on the table and tented her fingers. "There's no easy way to say this: I am sorry to tell you that Russ might be a target at the Black Tie Bash."

"A target?" Carly asked, confused. She didn't get it, but I did. For a split second I felt a hitch in my chest, like my heart was about to stall. I pushed the fear down, and kept my face steady, the mask of someone completely unconcerned. On the outside I looked cool. Inside I had a ball of anxiety trying to surface. "Really," I said.

"Yes, apparently they are aware that Russ will be there and they see him as a threat."

"Are you sure?"

Dr. Wentworth peered at me over her glasses while answering Carly's question. "Yes, we're sure. We have a reliable source who's reported that the new commander was very clear on this."

"So what does that mean—he's a target? Like they're going to take him or kill him?" Carly said.

"They'll try."

"They'll try. That's all you have to say when a sixteen-year-old boy's life is on the line?" Her voice was frantic.

I said, "Excuse me. Did you notice that I'm sitting right here?" I knocked on the table. "Right here. It would be nice to be included in the conversation, especially since it's about me."

"Not quite," Dr. Wentworth said, still speaking only to Carly. "We have several options for him."

"Like what?" she asked. "Whatever it is better keep him safe, or I'm not going for it."

"He can go on the trip and work with us to heal the president, but skip the Bash, or another option is for him to—"

"He'll skip the Bash," Carly said. "No way is he going."

"Still sitting right here," I said loudly, my hand raised.

"I'm not going to have my brother's life jeopardized—"

I pushed back from the table, and stood up. I put one palm out and sent a flash of electricity in the airspace over their heads. The electricity sizzled and crackled, making them duck. Startled by my electrical outburst, the room got quiet. The sparks scattered and died before they hit the table. "If there are any decisions to be made, I'll be making them," I said. "I'm the one whose life is at stake, and believe me, I can protect myself."

When Dr. Wentworth finally spoke, she directed her words right to me. "You have two choices, Russ. You can go on the trip and try to heal the president, but not attend the Bash. That should almost completely eliminate the threat to your life for now. Or, you can go to the Bash to protect Layla and help us smoke out the Associates in the crowd. Our source says the commander is going to be at the Bash.

This is the first time in over a hundred years that the PG has been aware that the leader of the Associates will be appearing in public. This new commander is either very bold or very foolish. This is a rare opportunity for us to figure out his identity."

"I will be attending the Bash," I said. "Nothing could keep me away."

"Very good." Dr. Wentworth nodded her approval.

Carly said, "I don't like this."

I said, "You don't have to like it."

Her face fell. "Are you sure about this, Russ? Really sure?"

"I'm sure." I kept my attention on Dr. Wentworth, like it was just the two of us. "Is there some reason you've told me about the commander being at the Bash and me being on his hit list but you haven't told Mallory and Jameson?"

She said, "Yes, there is a reason. We trust you."

"Oh." I waited for her to elaborate on this, but she didn't say another word and the room grew uncomfortably silent. Finally I said, "You know if you're trying to find out the commander's identity, you really need to have Nadia there. She can read people like you wouldn't believe. She picks up on emotions and can tell if people are lying. Give her a little time and I'm sure she could pick him out of the crowd."

Dr. Wentworth tipped her head slightly, considering what I said. "Why do you assume it's a him?"

"What?"

"The commander. You said she could pick *him* out of the crowd. Has it occurred to you that their leader could be a woman?"

I felt myself flush red. I had a bossy sister and a

strong-minded mother and I'd always treated girls well. No one could accuse me of being sexist. "Of course I know it could be a woman. I believe you referred to the commander as a male yourself." I shifted uncomfortably. "So Nadia? You see what I'm saying? She'd be perfect for this."

She exchanged a glance with Dr. Habush before answering. "I understand exactly what you're saying, Russ, and believe me when I say we've weighed all the pros and cons in this matter. The team leader in charge of Operation Nadia has determined that the only way to get Nadia on this trip would be to come up with an excuse to forcibly remove her from the house. And that would require something like a faked abduction or accusing her parents of abuse. Either case would potentially create media coverage, something that would attract attention." She shook her head. "We're trying to minimize our risks here. Even having you three in attendance is risky, but your talents are so valuable we've opted to include you in spite of it."

*

That night, when Nadia astral projected to me, I'd told her what Dr. Wentworth had said. *They really called it Operation Nadia?* she asked, pleased. *Wow!*

As usual, I was in bed underneath my cotton sheets during this discussion, as relaxed as a person could be. Nadia was with me, both in my mind and as a presence, hovering, spirit-like alongside me. Sometimes I forgot that she was actually in her own bed on the other side of town. I answered, *That's what she called it—Operation Nadia.* I pictured a team sitting around a table, plotting ways to get into Nadia's house.

I could believe they'd never encountered anyone like Nadia's mother. She was a force.

Nadia must have read my mind, because she said, *I think my mom is on to them, because she's noticed that we've suddenly had a rash of people offering different stuff besides the scholarships and academic achievement trips.*

Like what?

All kinds of things. One guy offered to demonstrate carpet cleaning, another company wanted to meet with my parents for a free session of financial advising. Then there was something about earning money from home doing something online, and they'd be happy to come over to show you how it's done. It's been nonstop. People come to the door, they leave brochures in our mailbox, they call. They're unbelievably persistent. My mom has been really paranoid. She says that people are trying to get into our house to take over.

But is it really being paranoid, if she's right? I asked.

I guess not. There was a moment of silence between us and then Nadia said, *I don't really want to talk about her anymore. I want to hear about you and what you've been doing.*

So even though they swore us to secrecy, I told her everything about the meeting, that we'd be attending the Presidential Bash, that the president was in a coma, that the leader of the Associates would supposedly be at the Bash, and that the vice president was one of the evil Associates. The only thing I left out was the part about me being a target.

The part about the vice president disappointed her. *Oh no. I always thought he seemed so nice,* she said.

Me too. I remember when they'd won the election. The people of the Philippines were so proud that one of their own had come to power in the United States. Never mind that he was a third generation American, they still claimed him. He was a slight man, with wavy dark hair, and a thoughtful concerned look that made him seem gentle and kind. At least that's how he came off in the media coverage of his public appearances. It just showed that you never knew about a person.

What else?

Um, I guess at the Bash I'm going to be escorting Layla and Jameson and Mallory are going to be going as a couple.

So you're going to be her date? she said. *I don't think I like that.*

It's not as if I like her or anything. I don't even know her. It will probably be totally awkward. Plus, I'm just supposed to be making sure she's safe.

Nadia sighed. *She's so beautiful.*

I don't think she's all that beautiful. She's like gigantically tall.

Some guys like that.

Not me.

Well, don't fall in love with her.

Not a chance. To deflect her worry I said, *I really miss you, Nadia.*

I miss you too. It's killing me that I can't go with you on the trip. I guess I was lucky to go to Peru, considering how my mom is.

There will be more trips in the future. We'll travel the world together someday.

I would love that, she said, *but someday seems like it will never come.*

I know.

I'll try to astral project to you at night.

I said, *Then I'll have something to look forward to every day.*

She sighed, a sigh that spoke volumes. It said that we shouldn't be apart, that astral projecting wasn't enough, that she was afraid this trip would cause us to grow apart. *I won't be able to think about anything but you but you'll be too busy to even think about me.*

I told her that wasn't true, but nothing I said helped her get past her insecurities. And then, thinking I was just making conversation, I made the mistake of mentioning how tan Mallory had gotten this summer. I guess I'd forgotten how girls are when you talk about other girls, or maybe I just thought that Nadia was beyond that. I'd been pretty clear that I wasn't interested in Mallory, but as she explained, she felt trapped at home, and the thought of Mallory and me bonding over this trip made her insane. And then I'd said something like maybe we wouldn't even survive the trip, which was not the smartest thing to say. Now she had something new to worry about.

To cheer her up, I told her I was coming to see her the night before we left. She said she'd be at her window at the appointed time.

As I headed to her house that night I thought about my stupid comment about Mallory and hoped my present would help with damage control. It was a serious gift, the kind you wouldn't give a girl unless you were really crazy about her. I'd chosen it partly because I wanted her to have something to remember me by if I died, although I wasn't planning on telling her that.

Once I got to her house we'd only be able to talk through her window. With me on the ground and her up above, it wasn't as good as really being with her, but it was the best we could do for now. It didn't escape me that we were like a fairy tale couple; she the princess locked in the tower, me the suitor on the ground. Her mother, of course, was the wicked ogre keeping her imprisoned.

As I walked, a breeze picked up. I was going into the wind, so my T-shirt and shorts clung to my front and billowed out in back. The forecast had been for rain and thundershowers. The air was heavy with moisture and I sensed conditions were right for electrical activity. When lightning appeared a few seconds later, it was impressive, a giant zig-zig that cut the sky in two. For an instant it was light as day. I hurried, not because I was worried about the storm, but because I wanted to beat the rain. Seeing Nadia with my clothing soaked and water streaking down my face wasn't the look I was going for.

When I turned onto her street, I glanced at my phone, glad to see I would make it right on time. The boxed gift was a lump in the pocket of my shorts. I couldn't wait to see her reaction when she opened it.

Her neighborhood was quiet at this late hour and the tall trees and full bushes provided perfect coverage for me. Hopefully her parents, like mine, were fast asleep. I approached the house from the side, and looked up at the window we'd used the last time. As expected, Nadia's room was dark. I took a few steps back, pulled a laser pointer out of my pocket, and aimed it upwards. If I calculated correctly, it would land on her ceiling. I swiveled the pointer around and around, creating my own lux spiral show for her benefit.

Within seconds she came and threw open the window, then stuck her head out. In preparation for my coming, she'd taken the screen out so there'd be nothing between us. "Hey

Russ," she said, and my heart literally swelled with happiness. I was still getting used to seeing her without her hooded sweatshirt. Her dark hair fell freely over each shoulder, but she didn't have it over her face anymore, so I got a full view of her warm eyes and huge smile.

"Nadia." As satisfying as it was communing via astral projection, this had a different feeling. Less dreamlike, more real. Even though the wind whipped at my clothing and the air felt like rain, I was glad to be here, glad to see her in person. She pushed her upper body out the window and leaned over as far as she could, then reached down. Even standing on tip-toe with my hand outstretched we didn't connect, but we tried. Both of us felt it. The gap between us was charged with longing.

She whispered loudly. "I'm so glad you came!"

"Me too." I pulled the rubber-banded box out of my pocket. "I have a gift for you." Off in the distance, a flash of lightning filled the sky.

"You do?" She clasped her hands together, clearly delighted. "You didn't have to do that."

"Well, I did." I swung my arm back, prepared to toss it in air. "Ready to catch it?"

"Yes."

I swung back and up it went, falling just out of reach of her outstretched hands.

She swiped the air but didn't make contact. "Sorry," Nadia said, giggling.

"That's okay, it was a practice throw."

We tried again, but this time my aim was off and it hit the side of the house before floating back down. The problem, I decided, was that it was too light. Plus, my throwing sucked because I was a little nervous. "Maybe if we tied it with a string you could swing it up to me?" she suggested.

"Good thought. Do you have some string?"

"No."

Both of us were grinning now. This was the most ridiculous thing ever. The thunder rumbling in the distance seemed to mock my failure. But it also gave me an idea. "Can you take the screen off your other window?" I said pointing around the corner to the bedroom window facing the street. The porch roof jutted out just below the window. If I could get on top of it, we'd be close enough to touch. I'd also be visible from the street, but hopefully no one would notice this late at night. There was only a light mist in the air now. If I waited too long it would start raining and I wasn't looking forward to losing my footing and falling off a wet roof.

"Sure I could take the screen off." She glanced over her shoulder. "Why?"

"I think I can get up there. Just take it off, okay?"

Nadia looked puzzled, but she trusted me and went to work on the other window. I saw her fumbling with the screen and I got ready, putting the box back in my pocket and waiting for the next round of lightning. I'd never told Nadia about my ability to achieve lift-off by shooting electricity at the ground, so she didn't have a clue as to what I was about to do. Mitch and Will didn't think this particular ability had any practical applications. Ha! If I could eject myself onto the porch roof and get close to Nadia it would be the most practical, best application ever.

I watched in anticipation as Nadia lifted the screen out of the window and lowered it into her room, then stuck her head out facing me. She lifted her finger to her lips to remind me to be quiet. I saw a flash of lightning close by, and waited for what I really wanted. Thunder. Luck was with me. The next time it thundered it boomed loudly, shaking the earth and providing the perfect cover for the sound of a teenage guy landing on a roof. I released a short burst of electricity out of my palms and rose in the air, overshooting the roof by about three feet, then coming down with a thud. I landed in a crouched position, and struggled to keep from sliding toward the edge. Fortunately the thunder still raged, covering the noise. Below, on the ground, the grass smoked where I'd lifted off. In the morning the scorch marks would make it look like lightning had hit the lawn.

"Whoa!" Nadia's eyes widened in astonishment. She extended a hand and guided me toward her. My heart pounded at her touch. Our time, I knew, was limited. I wanted to fit in everything I wanted to say and do. Just in case I never saw her again.

I knelt in front of her and put my hands on either side of her face. Our noses met and I took in her smell and her touch. "You're really here," she said, and then blushed. "That sounded stupid. What I meant—"

"I know what you meant." I leaned in and our lips met, Nadia kissing me with such passion, it took my breath away. It was completely right. I was on a roof in the middle of a thunderstorm and there was nowhere else I'd rather be.

Nadia pulled away, but we were still close, I saw tears in her eyes. "This, right here, right now. This is the best moment of my life," she said.

I swallowed. This was the best moment of my life too, but there was a lump in my throat that kept me from saying so.

"Do you believe in fate?" she whispered.

"I'm not sure."

"Well, I do," Nadia said. "I believe in it enough for both of us. I think we were fated to see the lux spiral, and get superpowers, and meet. What were the chances that the one person I'd fall crazy madly in love with would be the only person in the world who could heal my face? I mean, really— what were the chances?" She leaned in again and planted a forceful kiss on my mouth, like she was trying to leave an impression. "I'm telling you, it was fate. We're destined to be together."

I nodded, and images surged through my brain: every moment I'd spent with Nadia since we'd first met behind a dumpster at the industrial park. My first impression wasn't good, frankly. Lurking underneath her hood, she seemed like a character in a comic book. I never got a handle on what she was really like until the day I was outside of the frozen custard shop and I saw her at a table next to the window being berated by her mother. When her mom got up from the table, she saw me and put her hand on the glass. Instinctively, I'd placed mine on the other side, over hers. We'd connected that day. After that it was a journey of discovering who she really was, and I liked everything I'd discovered. She was grateful that I'd fixed her face, but she'd done more for me than she'd ever know.

"Destined to be together," I repeated.

"Like the heavens aligned just for us." She reached up and touched my cheek, then smiled playfully. "I believe you said something about a gift?"

"Oh yes!" I shifted my balance and reached into my

pocket. When I handed her the small white box, I said, "It's not much but I hope you like it."

She pulled off the rubber band holding the lid to the bottom and casually dropped it onto the roof. While she lifted the lid, I kept my eyes on her face. I'd bought the ring at a jewelry store in a strip mall at the end of town. When I'd gone into the store I didn't have a set idea on what to get her. She didn't seem to wear much jewelry. I knew it couldn't be flashy or tacky. And I wanted it to be significant to the two of us. Oh, and I had to be able to afford it. A tall order. I stood at the counter for the longest time looking at the charm bracelets, and diamond earrings, and engagement rings. None of it seemed right and I almost left, but just then the saleswoman, a portly lady with a bouffant hairstyle, suggested I might want to look at some of their antique jewelry. "We buy it from estates," she said. "Perhaps you'll find just the perfect thing for your lady friend. We have lots of unique pieces."

I thought about Nadia. "She is unique," I said.

The saleslady brought out a wooden tray lined with velvet and covered with various rings and bracelets. I spotted it right away and picked it up to examine it. A silver ring made up of interlocking spirals. At the top a clear stone was set in the middle of one of the spirals. "That's a nice piece," she said approvingly. "Custom made by a gentleman for his wife when they were first dating more than sixty years ago. The woman who brought it in was their daughter. She said the ring was designed to symbolize their interlocking lives and never-ending love." The saleswoman tapped on the ring. "See how the spirals are linked together?"

"What about the stone? Is it a diamond?"

"No, Austrian crystal. Not as valuable, but pretty nonetheless."

The saleslady told me the price and I said I'd take it. I pulled a roll of twenty dollar bills out of my pocket, and peeled off the right amount while she boxed the ring and rang it up. It didn't occur to me until later that it might not be the right size, but in fact, it wound up fitting Nadia perfectly.

She gasped when she lifted the lid, but I had a feeling she'd have been happy with anything I gave her. "It's an antique," I said. "Not an engagement ring or anything," I added hastily. "I just thought you'd like it."

"I love it," Nadia said, slipping it on her finger. "It's perfect." She held out her hand to admire it.

"It has the spirals, which I thought was cool."

"Like the lux spiral."

"Yes." I tried to remember what the saleslady said. "And because they symbolize our interlocking lives and our never-ending love."

It was apparently the right thing to say because Nadia surged forward and gave me a big hug. She was halfway through the window now and I realized it wouldn't take much more to free her completely. We could both leave right now, right this minute. We could be gone before anyone noticed; it wouldn't matter to me where we went. Except. Tomorrow I was going to Washington D.C. to cure the president and save the nation. My lips caressed her ear. "Oh, I would love to take you away with me."

"Then do it," she said.

Leaving her behind was the hardest thing I've ever done.

CHAPTER TWELVE

RUSS

My dad drove Carly and me to the airport the next afternoon. Before we could leave, my mom stopped us at the front door to obsessively shower us with hugs and kisses, as if she thought she'd never see us again. I'd overheard her the night before telling Dad she was worried about the two of us flying together because if the plane went down she'd lose both of her kids. She was good at coming up with pretend reasons to be afraid. If she knew the real truth about the trip she'd have been catatonic with fear. One thing was good though—both my parents totally accepted our change of schedule. They seemed to think that the excuse the Praetorian Guard gave, which was that leaving earlier would allow us additional opportunities, was completely acceptable.

As we gathered up our luggage in the front entryway, my mother was overcome with emotion. "I'm so proud of both of you," she said, cradling Carly's face in her hands. My sister allowed it for a moment before gracefully pulling away.

Because I was taller, I was spared the same treatment. When she came in for a hug, I patted her head and said, "Mom, let's not make this into a big deal. We'll be back before you know it. Besides, you'll have Frank to keep you company."

My nephew Frank had been hopped up all morning. He'd rifled through my things while I packed, tearing apart my shaving kit and other personal items. His nonstop talking made my head hurt. When I heard my mom heading up the stairs with more clean laundry for me, I yelled, "Mom, Frank Shrapnel is annoying me." Using his middle name always amused me.

"Frank, stop bothering Russ," she'd called back. Like that would help.

I grinned at the kid. "You heard the woman. Stop bothering me." It was hard to stay mad at Frank though. He idolized me, copying everything I said and did. Believe me, I didn't get that kind of admiration very often. Like never. And now that I knew he was David Hofstetter's son, I found myself studying his face on a regular basis. Once I saw the resemblance, I couldn't unsee it. It was as obvious as the nose on his face. And it wasn't just his physical appearance, it was in mannerisms too: the way he walked, how he gestured with his hands when making a point. The narrowing of his eyes when he was deep in thought. He was more David than Carly. How my parents never noticed it, I don't know. Maybe they weren't looking for it.

At the airport, Dad pulled up to the baggage claim area, helped us get our bags out of the trunk, and said good-bye. He gave Carly a warm embrace and me a man-hug, then reminded us to call as soon as we arrived. "If you don't, your mother will really worry," he said. "And I will too."

Once the car pulled away Carly took the lead, navigating her rolling luggage around scatterings of people moving too slowly for her taste. Every now and then she'd glance back to see if I was keeping up. With Nadia gone and Carly here, this trip had a different feeling than our trip to Peru. I was more nervous, more stressed. The previous night I'd tossed and turned, dreaming the president was in a coma in a locked room and I couldn't reach her. I woke up with a feeling of failure, and even now, in broad daylight, I was still trying to shake it.

After we'd checked our bags, we met up with the others in the sitting area right outside of security. The other four had arrived before us and were waiting. I was glad to see Dr. Anton in his suit and bow tie, stroking his goatee and talking to Rosie, while Jameson and Mallory lingered nearby. I was grateful that the parents had been instructed that there were to be no prolonged good-byes at the airport, because the students, meaning us, needed to embark without the emotional attachment of our home life pulling us back. Or something like that. Anyway, I didn't miss having my mom make a big fuss in front of the others. As it was, I was the only one bringing a family member, which was weird enough. Hopefully Carly wouldn't make a scene or do anything embarrassing. She could be unpredictable.

"Hail, hail, the gang's all here," Dr. Anton said, jovially as we approached. "And with plenty of time to spare too." We'd been told to come two hours early, so we would have extra time in case there were long lines, but at this time of day, the airport wasn't too busy.

"Next we go through security?" Jameson suggested. He had his arm resting over Mallory's shoulder. His hand dangled, like this was a casual gesture. I knew better.

"Not just yet," Rosie said. She had a large purse clutched

under one arm. Several magazines peeked out of the outside pocket. "We have to wait for the others. Oh, here they are now!" She waved enthusiastically, her arm making a wide arc over her head. I looked to see Mrs. Whitehouse and Kevin Adams hurrying toward us.

"Are they going with us?" I asked.

"No," Rosie said. "Just coming to say good-bye."

Kevin Adams, carrying a large plastic bag, reached us first. Mrs. Whitehouse, right behind him, struggled to keep up. When she got to us, Mrs. Whitehouse insisted on giving everyone a farewell hug. Being pressed against her front was like sinking into an enormous flabby pillow. She kept me in the embrace a few seconds longer than I was comfortable with. As I tried to ease out of it, I saw Carly slip away from the group on the pretense of having to go to the restroom.

After they'd both wished us well, Kevin pulled stacks of comic books out of his bag. "A little going away gift," he said, parceling out a stack to me, Mallory, and Jameson. "Something to read on the plane."

We thanked him and stuffed the comic books into our respective carry-on bags. Mine, like the others, was held together with a strip of paper with my name on it. I wondered if he'd hand selected comics for each of us, or chosen them randomly. I'd have plenty of time to find out later.

Not to be outdone, Mrs. Whitehouse said. "I too have presents for the kids." She rifled in her purse and handed each of us a polished stone, the type you see in shops selling crystals and miniature pyramids. Each stone had a word engraved on it. We compared. Mine said *Peace*, Jameson's said *Hope*, and Mallory's said *Love*. We all said thank you with as much enthusiasm as we could muster.

"Those stones were all blessed with a protective prayer. You must all promise to carry your stone with you every day. Just put it in your bag or pocket, or what have you. It will keep you safe." Mrs. Whitehouse's wide face was made wider by a big grin. "Make sure you take them with you to the Bash, okay?"

"Okay," Mallory said, turning the stone over in her palm. I stuck mine in my pocket for the time being. I appreciated the thought, although I wasn't buying the whole protection thing.

"I also," Mrs. Whitehouse said with flourish, "have something extra for Mallory." She pulled a jeweler's box out of her purse and held it out. "Sorry boys, this is a girl thing."

"What is it?" Mallory asked, taking it from her. Even though none of us were crazy about Mrs. Whitehouse, Mallory couldn't resist the allure of a present.

"Open it and see," she said gleefully.

"Oh pretty," Mallory said. She lifted a chain out of the box, and held it up for all of us to see. Dangling off the chain was a white rose with petals edged in gold. "It looks old."

"It belonged to my grandmother," Mrs. Whitehouse said. "Carved ivory. I was hoping that you'd do me the honor of wearing it to the Bash."

Mallory's mouth dropped open. She hurriedly put the necklace back in the box. "I couldn't possibly take something that belonged to your grandmother."

"No, no, no." Mrs. Whitehouse took a step back and held out a hand. "I insist. Please. I would be honored if you would keep it and wear it." She smiled in a sweet way. "I don't have any daughters to pass it on to and it would make me happy to know someone I care about can wear it and enjoy it."

"Well." Mallory seemed undecided, but only for a moment. "All right then. Thank you."

"That's my girl!" Mrs. Whitehouse put her arm around Mallory and whispered something to her before moving on to me. Before I realized what was going on, Mrs. Whitehouse pulled me off to the side for a little conversation. I tried to pretend I was listening to Dr. Anton and Kevin make small talk about the flight schedule but she saw right through me.

"It just doesn't seem right that poor little Nadia isn't here," she said quietly to me. "I bet you really miss her, Russ."

"Yes, I do."

"Remember how on the last trip you went and got her at the last minute?" She smiled sweetly.

I nodded.

"I bet you'd love to do that again. Go charging out of here and save her. See if you can pull it off again like you did last time."

I stared right into her eyes, wondering what she was getting at. We'd been told that the lux spiral was only witnessed by teenagers with exceptional intellectual capabilities. In other words, geniuses. Mrs. Whitehouse had once been an Edgewood teen who'd witnessed the lux, and she'd developed superpowers afterward. In theory, in order to qualify, she would have been highly intelligent at the time. I wasn't seeing it now though. How could she possibly think I could get Nadia when so much was on the line? And knowing how much I wanted Nadia there, it was mean to goad me like that. Last time I'd been able to successfully get Nadia's dad to allow her to come. But things were different now. Nadia's mother was on high alert, and more was at stake on this mission. I wasn't about to jeopardize national security.

She continued. "I bet you'd like to hop into a taxi just like last time and go right to Nadia's house."

"Yeah, well, unfortunately, that's not an option," I said. "I'd miss my flight."

"Oh, I don't know about that. I bet you could get back on time."

She put her hand on my shoulder and gave it a squeeze. I'm not normally rude but she was seriously creeping me out. I said, "Please don't do that." I took a step back and walked around to where Mallory and Jameson stood. Her eyes followed me, but luckily she stayed planted.

After Carly came back from the bathroom, Dr. Anton took it as a cue we should be on the move. He had an authoritative but friendly way of wrapping things up with Kevin and Mrs. Whitehouse. "I wouldn't dream of keeping you any longer," he said, grabbing onto the handle of his rolling carry-on. "I'm sure you both have a million things you should be doing." He said it as if he were being considerate of their time, instead of just blowing them off. I'd have to remember that trick for future reference.

Mrs. Whitehouse got a stricken look on her face. "Kids, don't forget to carry the stones with you everywhere. They've been blessed!" We all nodded before grabbing our bags and following behind Dr. Anton. As we headed away, I could still hear Mrs. Whitehouse complaining to Kevin that she didn't have enough time to talk to us.

"Man, she's annoying," Carly said loudly, and no one in our group contradicted her.

We passed a large metal waste can on the way to the security area. Carly spit out a wad of gum as she went by, and Jameson, walking right behind her, tossed in the stone Mrs. Whitehouse had just given him.

"Jameson!" Mallory said, coming to complete halt. "I can't believe you threw that out."

"Why, did you want it?"

"Well, no, I have my own." Mallory pulled hers out of her pocket and ran a thumb over the letters. "Love. What did yours say again?"

"Hope." He sighed. "So pointless. I don't waste my time *hoping* things work out. I'm a man of action. I either do what I set out to do or I don't. And I plan on doing it. Besides," he added, "I don't believe in new age garbage and stones that have been blessed. Blessed by whom, I ask? And what kind of blessing? No, I'm a little too savvy to just accept what I've been told. Especially by an unreliable source like Mrs. Whitehouse."

Mallory turned to me. "He makes a good point." She lobbed her stone into the trash and then turned to me. "What do you think, Russ? Want to make it three for three?"

With a shrug I pulled the stone out of my pocket and deposited it in the waste can. Normally I'd feel bad about throwing out a gift, but I wasn't a fan of Mrs. Whitehouse and it wasn't a very thoughtful gift. Who needed a stone that said *Peace* when we were leaving for a trip to guard the president's daughter? I needed to be on guard and ready in case of attack. Peace was nice in theory, but it wouldn't help me with what I needed to do.

"I'm not getting rid of the necklace though," Mallory said. "That's worth keeping."

116

CHAPTER THIRTEEN

RUSS

We were picked up at the airport in D.C. by a black stretch limo. Normally a limo stocked with chips and nuts and a full bar would be a reason to indulge, but the seriousness of our trip held everyone back. Mallory helped herself to a diet soda but no one else had anything. The windows were tinted but we could still see out. I watched the city stretch out before us and admired the clean streets and impressive buildings. I'd never been to D.C. before but it had a familiar look, probably from watching the news.

The driver had told us we'd be there in about forty-five minutes. I didn't ask, but I assumed "there" would be a hotel or government office, so it was a surprise when we entered a parking structure, drove around and around all the way to the fourth floor, and then stopped in the middle of a row of parked cars. When the driver shut off the engine, got out, and opened the trunk, we realized we'd arrived.

"I guess it's time to get a move on," Rosie said, gesturing us to the door. Dr. Anton got out first, thanked the driver and made sure everyone had their stuff. Then he said, "I need to collect everyone's electronics." We all stared, not connecting the dots. "I mean it," he said. "I need your cell phones, iPods, Kindles. Anything you have that's electronic in nature."

The women rifled through their purses, while the guys pulled their phones out of their pockets. The limo driver held out a cloth bag and one by one, we reached in and added to the pile. We'd been told we couldn't make any calls while we were gone (and our parents knew not to expect them), but I didn't know they'd be taking our phones.

"Are we getting them back?" Mallory asked.

"Eventually," Dr. Anton said all too cheerfully.

After the driver finished gathering up our things, and got back in the limo, Dr. Anton gestured us to follow him across the parking structure.

"Where are we going?" Carly asked Rosie, who only shrugged.

"Just follow the doctor," she said. "He's the one in charge on this trip."

The wheels on my rolling luggage squeaked until we came to a stop in front of a large steel door. Dr. Anton got out some keys, expertly unlocked it, and ushered us through. The next thing I knew we were headed down a short hallway to an elevator.

"Where exactly are we?" Mallory asked as the elevator descended. We dropped lower and lower, exchanging worried glances all the way. We seemed to be in an elevator heading toward the center of the earth.

"You shall see," Dr. Anton said, a twinkle in his eye.

When the elevator lurched to a halt, I expected to come out somewhere damp and dark. Maybe a concrete bunker or cave or the lower level of the same parking structure. As it turned out, I couldn't have been more wrong. When we stepped out we were in a space that reminded me of the Mall of America crossed with Grand Central Station. The ceilings were high and arched, the space was light and spacious, and the architecture was modern American with the addition of Roman columns flanking each side.

"Come on," Dr. Anton said. "If we hurry we can catch the next subway."

"Holy crap there's a subway down here?" Carly said.

Mallory stood stock still, just staring. With her chin raised and eyes wide, she had the amazed look of a toddler seeing snow for the first time. People in business attire criss-crossed all around us. A security guard stood watch, his back against a column, while customers waited in line at a coffee stand that also sold baked goods. Two young men manning an information kiosk looked bored. We could have been in almost any public place except for two things that really stood out: no one was talking on a phone and there were no kids around. We were, in fact, the youngest people I'd seen so far.

"What is this place?" I asked, catching up to Dr. Anton. He was walking quickly, making the rest of us scramble to keep up.

"PGDC," he said. "There's a whole city beneath the city. And this is it. Everyone you see here is with the Praetorian Guard."

"No one else knows about this?" I looked around.

"No."

How could something this big be secret? "But like the FBI must know about this, or the CIA?"

119

"Only if they're members of the Guard."

I saw the subway terminal ahead. A large monitor off to one side listed times and destinations. "But doesn't anyone question people coming and going and all the electricity being used and everything else?" I asked.

"No," Dr. Anton said, "no one questions it." I must have had a worried look on my face because he added, "Don't worry about it, Russ. There are systems put into place to ensure nothing is disclosed to the public. If anyone gets wind of it and tries to go public with the information, they are discredited or they wind up changing their mind. Entrances to PGDC are periodically changed and they're always monitored." Dr. Anton paused to look up at the subway schedule display. "Looks like our timing is going to be perfect."

Rosie came up behind us and said, "That's good because I am ready to take a load off. Traveling always wears me out."

"Have you been to this place before?" Carly asked.

Rosie shook her head. "I've been hearing about it for years, but this is my first time."

When we got to the subway platform, Dr. Anton finally filled us in. "We'll go to the hotel first and drop off your things. Then dinner and then the briefing room."

"You don't want Russ to do his thing right away?" Mallory asked patting my arm.

Dr. Anton said, "We follow the schedule we're given." He cast a wary glance at two men who came up alongside us. They were talking to each other and had no interest in us as far as I could tell, but he was still being careful. I remembered Dr. Wentworth saying that only a few people knew that the president was in a coma. Even among other Praetorian Guard members there were still secrets.

The subway ride was comfortable and fast, and before we knew it we'd arrived at the hotel. Since everything was indoors, the space from the subway to the hotel felt like we were walking in a mall or airport. Once inside the lobby, Dr. Anton checked us in and got key cards for our rooms. Just like in Peru, I was rooming with Jameson, but with Nadia gone, Mallory was now doubling up with Carly. As the leaders of our group, Dr. Anton and Rosie had their own rooms.

I was hoping the rooms would be special in some way, full of Praetorian Guard spy gadgetry or photos of PG history throughout the last century, or at least luxurious beyond belief, but our room had the standard hotel layout. Our headboards were bolted to the walls as was the hair dryer in the bathroom. We each had our own dresser. Between the two dressers hung a flat screen TV, and over by the window overlooking a courtyard, sat a desk and chair. I threw my suitcase on the bed closest to the window and said, "I call this one."

Jameson grinned. "This is mine." He pointed to his suitcase and used telekinesis to lift it off the floor and onto the bed. "Are you sure that's where you want your suitcase to be?" He raised one eyebrow and turned his attention to my bed. A second later my suitcase hovered over the bed and started levitating around the room. "Oh look, I'm Russ's suitcase and I'm confused about where to go. Doh. Doh. Doh. Maybe I should go see if I can heal someone in the bathroom." I watched as my suitcase turned into the open doorway to the bathroom. "I think your suitcase wants to take a shower, Russ. Better go check on it before it gets all wet."

I hated Jameson when he got like this. I didn't think he could turn the water on from the next room, but I wasn't taking any chances. "You're an idiot," I said before going to retrieve my suitcase. When I came out he was still grinning, hands on his hips, like he'd done something clever. I said, "Don't push me, Jameson. I could send a blast of electricity and fry that smile right off your face."

"Yes, but you won't," he said. "Because then you won't be the golden boy of this whole trip. The savior of the nation."

"That's right," I said. "And don't forget it." My words were more confident than my feelings. Golden boy? Savior of the nation? Who nominated me for that kind of responsibility? Until recently I had trouble remembering to put the lid down on the toilet. Who in their right mind expected a sixteen-year-old guy to fix the problems of a whole country? And how could it be that I was so valuable someone wanted me dead? The whole thing was messed up.

By the time the others knocked on the door and collected us for dinner, I was done with Jameson. The guy had a lot of good qualities, but every time I'd decided he was okay, he made some jerk-move and undid every bit of good will. I couldn't decide if he was immature, insecure, or just had a flawed personality. Nadia, a much better person than me, said Jameson had a terrible home life and I should cut him a break. Easy for her to say. He wasn't threatening to give her suitcase a shower.

Dinner was fine dining and included some of the best food I've ever had. We never actually ordered; they just brought food. And more food. Soup and salads and rolls. Trays of crab cakes, medallion-sized slices of beef tenderloin, shrimp on skewers. Fish stew in a kettle. Pasta primavera.

I kept eating thinking each course was the entrée only to find out that there was still more to come. By the time they brought the dessert tray we were all stuffed. I had a harrowing thought during all of this, remembering that condemned prisoners always got one last outstanding meal. And that led to me thinking about another last meal, the Last Supper from the Bible, the one Jesus shared with his apostles before his crucifixion. And another example: the tradition of fattening up animals before they went to slaughter. I looked around the table at our group of six, all of them satiated and raving about how great the meal had been and all I could think was: this is the beginning of the end and we are totally screwed.

I hoped I was wrong.

CHAPTER FOURTEEN

RUSS

After dinner we were off to a briefing, which was, we were told, was one short subway ride away. I was glad Dr. Anton knew the way, because the rest of us were clueless. I was struck by how perfect everything was. This underground city, PGDC, was like the idealized version of the real world. There was no graffiti here or smog or rude employees. It was the Disney World of the Praetorian Guard. I wondered if this was where the top PG members would hole up if the Associates succeeded in their plan and everything topside went to hell. The rest of us would be fending for ourselves while they waited safely underground.

Finally after we'd walked a few blocks, we arrived at our destination. The briefing room was bigger than your average room, to say the least, closer in size to an auditorium and shaped like a boomerang. Like half of an IMAX theater. The long curved wall ahead of us was a screen with nature images that changed periodically. "A giant screen saver," Carly observed, taking a seat next to me. "I almost feel like I'm in the Grand Canyon right now."

"I'd rather be at a fake Grand Canyon than be back at

home right now," Mallory said. She and Jameson had taken seats on the other side of the aisle. "Hey Russ, how do you feel about missing the beginning of junior year?"

The next day was the first day of the school year. I always hated the first day—the getting used to a new schedule, memorizing a new locker combination, getting up early after three months of sleeping in—but still I regretted not being there. If I could have been two of me, I would have played it both ways, living as Russ the average teenage guy and also seeing how it went for Russ, the guy with superpowers. But I didn't have that option and if something had to go I would choose to let go of the conventional life. I shrugged and said, "I'm okay with it. I'm sure we'll get caught up when we get back."

We'd arrived at the briefing area right on time, but still they made us wait. Dr. Anton went to confer with some unseen person in charge, leaving the rest of us behind. Carly assumed they were unorganized, but I knew the real reason for the delay because I sensed the electricity all around us. Cameras and microphones were planted everywhere in the room. I wasn't sure why, but they were deliberately leaving us unattended and paying attention to everything we said and did. Carly snapped her gum, while Jameson made Mallory's ponytail rise off her shoulders. In response, Mallory shrieked and grabbed at her hair. Whoever was watching saw all of this. "Stop it, Jameson," Mallory said, slapping him in a flirtatious way. Knowing we were being watched, I made a point to come off as the mature one in the group. When Rosie, sitting to my left, leaned over and asked if I was nervous, I said, "No, not nervous. Ready."

"That's good," she said giving me a motherly smile. "I have a feeling you're going to do fine, Russ."

"Thank you, Rosie," I said. "I appreciate it."

By the time Dr. Anton returned, followed by ten other people, Jameson had teased Mallory into a giggling fit so severe she was practically convulsing. During all of this he periodically gave me a superior look that was supposed to make me jealous that they were having fun together while I was stuck in between Rosie and Carly. Little did he know that I felt like they were at the kids' table while I'd been promoted to sit with the grownups.

"Attention everybody," Dr. Anton said, "We're about to begin."

Mallory coughed back a laugh, while Jameson, feigning innocence, looked straight ahead.

They began with the introductions. We'd already met the red-haired Dr. Wentworth and her mousy assistant, Dr. Habush, as well as Mitch and Will, our mentors from back in Edgewood. The other six, two men and four women, quickly became a blur of names and faces. They ranged in age from late twenties to early fifties, and all of them looked serious and professional. Each of us in the Edgewood group stood one at a time and gave our name, even though I'm sure they already knew everything about each of us. Most likely all of them had viewed the footage from our practice sessions and studied the data that came from those tests.

Again Dr. Wentworth led the presentation. "We're happy that all three of you have agreed to join this mission. We value your time and talents." After that she talked about the history of the Praetorian Guard, how they'd been around since the days of the Roman Empire. On the screen behind her flashed images of Roman soldiers. "Although as the guards of the Roman generals, they played a different role back then. Still, our name is synonymous with the word 'protector.' We are the protectors of the average citizen, almost like guardian angels in that we watch over them without their knowledge. No credit, no glory, just doing our duty to make the world a better place."

On the screen flashed a photo of a lux spiral, the fragments shimmering in formation on the ground. I sat straight up to really take a look at it. Since I'd witnessed the Edgewood lux spiral last spring, I hadn't seen any photos or video footages of it. When I thought about it, it almost seemed like a dream, but here it was exactly as I remembered it. "This is not an actual photo, but a recreation of a lux spiral as it would appear after just having landed on the ground," Dr. Wentworth said. "We were able to create it via CGI using the descriptions of witnesses. No one has ever actually photographed it. It seems to not occur to people to photograph it." She shook her head. "We don't know why. We've established that it's a natural event, and that the fragments are supercharged with energy that is then passed on to those exposed to it in various ways. All of the witnesses have been sixteen years old, give or take six months."

Jameson raised his hand. "I have a question."

She pointed. "Yes?"

"Are there others like us on this mission? And if so, will we be working with them?"

"Simply put, there are no others like you. You three have been chosen out of hundreds considered," Dr. Wentworth said, "You'll be getting your orders and will work on your specifically assigned tasks. Don't worry about anyone else. Just stay focused on your assignment." The image on the screen changed. "Moving on," she said in a way that conveyed she wasn't going to take kindly to anymore interruptions.

The next twenty minutes were a recap of what we'd learned in Edgewood: that the president was in a coma, that Vice President Montalbo was with the Associates, and that the Associates had a plan that put Layla and President Bernstein at risk. Dr. Wentworth said, "Having President Bernstein back in office is imperative. If Vice President Montalbo takes power, it won't be long before the Associates seize control of the government. When a government no longer has the interest of the citizens at heart, all of society suffers. We've seen this happen historically many times over, the most memorable being the Nazis in Germany."

I think she repeated all this to make an impression on us, but I'd gotten the picture clearly the first time around and it was always in the back of my mind. Life as we now knew it? Enjoy it, because it might all be flushed away overnight.

After the formal presentation, we were allowed to ask questions. Jameson said, "But even with Montalbo as president, things couldn't happen that quickly, could they? We have three branches of the federal government, and the Constitution is set up as a system of checks and balances to help ensure that no one branch becomes too powerful, right?"

Dr. Wentworth said, "The Associates have found a way to circumvent the system of checks and balances. You should have gotten a handout during your practice sessions in Edgewood explaining how they plan to do just that if given the opportunity."

"Ah, yes," Jameson said. I could tell by the look on his

face that he was remembering the sheet he'd crumpled up and thrown away thinking it was the same old, same old. Meanwhile, I'd taken mine home and read it, so I knew exactly what she was talking about. It doesn't help to be a genius if you don't follow directions.

Carly raised her hand and said, "I've been monitored by the Associates for the last sixteen years, and I assume they're watching Russ as well. How do you know they aren't on to us? I mean, if they're following along at all, they'll know we're here and they'll be able to figure things out..." Her voice trailed off and she gulped. Carly always came off as tough, but now her more vulnerable side was showing. She was afraid for both of us. "I mean, they actually told Russ they'd be in touch with him at the end of summer, which is right about now."

Dr. Wentworth got up and stepped into the aisle to get closer. Her voice was low, like she was speaking just to Carly. "You and your brother are as safe here as you would be at home. Maybe more so. We are taking every precaution."

"But every precaution might not be enough," Carly said.

"And yet it's the best we can do," Dr. Wentworth answered, her voice once again businesslike. "I think that should wrap things up. Make sure you get your rest tonight because tomorrow is a big day. Russ will meet the president. With his help we have high hopes for her recovery. And later, the three of you will meet Layla Bernstein. Mallory will convince her that she's already met you in Miami. We want all of you to spend time together so that you're close friends by the evening of the Bash."

CHAPTER FIFTEEN

RUSS

That night I had trouble relaxing. In the bed next to me I listened to the sound of Jameson's breathing until it got slower and heavier. When it did, I knew he'd dropped off to sleep. How he managed it, I don't know. We'd been slammed with so much information my head was spinning. After the briefing, Carly and I lingered behind the others because she couldn't let go of her question. "I don't understand why you aren't concerned about my being watched by the Associates." She had one hand on her hip, a challenging pose.

Dr. Wentworth said, "I didn't want to get into this in front of the group, but I think you should know that we've investigated and there's no evidence that the Associates have been monitoring your activity at all."

"Well that's where you're wrong," Carly said, "because I find bugs and cameras in my apartment and tracking devices on my car on a regular basis. Also, I've had messages on my cell phone played back, and not by me, I might add. This has been happening to me for years."

Dr. Wentworth sighed. "I can't tell you why that is.

Someone with a grudge? All I know is that it's not the Associates."

"It's not someone with a grudge!" Now Carly was getting mad. "Whoever is doing this is very sophisticated. I'm telling you, it has to be the Associates."

"But they'd have no reason to monitor you. You don't have any superpowers or anything else they want," Dr. Wentworth pointed out. "You're of no value to them."

"But I know things," Carly said. "I mean, even the fact that I know they exist—wouldn't that make me a person of interest?"

"Not really," she said.

"But I could go to the media and tell them everything I know about the Associates if I wanted to!"

"With what proof? And who would believe you?"

"But…" Carly's argument was growing thin, but she didn't want to let it go. "But what about the teenagers that disappear or die every sixteen years? Isn't that suspicious?"

Dr. Wentworth looked bored. "Teenagers die. They run away." She shrugged. "It happens." She took a deep breath and said, "For the record, I understand where you're coming from. It must be very upsetting to know that you're being spied on. I don't doubt what you're saying. But I can tell you that it's not the Associates. You might want to contact your local police and see if they can help. It might be a former love interest or someone who has something out for you. That's the most likely scenario."

I read the anguished expression on Carly's face and felt a surge of guilt because I knew that David Hofstetter had been the one monitoring her apartment. He told me so in Peru.

He said it was his way of making sure she was safe and the only way he had of keeping tabs on Frank, his son. A little creepy and stalkerish if you ask me, but the guy had been locked away in a research lab for sixteen years and was apparently a little out of touch with the definition of appropriate social boundaries.

After that Dr. Wentworth said, "As long as you're here, Russ, I have a few questions I've been meaning to ask you about Mallory."

"What about Mallory?"

"I'd like to ask you about the time Mallory spent with Mr. Specter in Peru when she was under the influence of the device he called a Deleo."

"Jameson and I answered questions like this back at home," I said.

"Humor me," she said. "Just one more time." She'd taken a tablet out of her briefcase and was typing as we talked. "I believe you said that Mallory left the group and went with Samuel Specter for some testing."

"Yes, Mallory went first, and then me."

"But when it was your turn, you were able to mentally fight off the effects of the Deleo?"

I nodded. I could still recall the way the Deleo, a goggle-type device, suctioned itself to my head once Mr. Specter activated it. He'd said it would measure how strong my superpowers were, but I quickly realized it was a brainwashing device and I fought it with everything I had by blocking his suggestions with something more powerful—my feelings for Nadia. I came out of it dazed, but it didn't take long for me to recover. I was absolutely certain that none of the ideas he'd tried to implant had taken hold.

"And Mallory?" she asked.

The doctor's steely gaze made me uncomfortable. I said, "I don't know. She was in a daze when she came out of the room, but later on she seemed fine. Whatever happened, it wore off, I think."

"You think?"

I met her stare head on. "As far as I know. I can't get inside Mallory's brain. Maybe you need to ask her."

For a second I thought she was going to do another round of questions, but instead Dr. Wentworth just pursed her lips and said, "Fair enough."

That night, I was lying in my hotel bed, staring at the ceiling and thinking about all this, when I saw the first glimmer of energy enter the room. Nadia! At least I hoped it was Nadia. I sat up, but didn't speak aloud. *Nadia?* Next to me, Jameson snorted and rolled over, turning to face the wall.

Yes, it's me!

Her astral projecting entrances always reminded me of Glinda arriving in her bubble in The Wizard of Oz. It didn't look the same, but I got the same feeling as I did when I was a kid watching the movie. Magic. Pure magic. *See?* I teased Nadia. *And you were so worried about not being able to find me.* I pointed to Jameson's sleeping form. *You can see that it's very exciting around here.*

Why are we underground? she asked.

There's a whole city underneath the city. Praetorian Guard headquarters. PGDC. It's massive and deep.

It was creepy as hell to get here. I sensed I was going into the ground and then I kept going down, down, down. At first I thought someone had buried you alive.

I filled her in on everything that had happened since the last time we talked. When I asked what was new with her, she responded by telling me her mom had gotten worse.

She's always been controlling and critical, Nadia said. *But lately it's been over the top. She watches me like a hawk and questions everything I do. Today she got mad because she said my face doesn't look right.*

What does that mean?

I don't know. You can't have a regular conversation with her, so I don't even try. My dad thinks she stopped taking her medication.

Nadia's energy was invisible but having her next to me was as soothing as a rush of warm air on a cold winter's day. Still, I wished she were really here so I could comfort her in person. I said, *Maybe when this is all over, I could come over and talk to her? Or maybe to your dad? I had good luck with him before. Maybe he'd let us see each other as long as it's at your house.*

Maybe, she said, but she didn't sound convinced.

I do love you, Nadia.

I love you, too, she said. *I'm not sure if I'll be able to do this again. If I don't come back after this, just know that it's not that I don't want to—*

And then she was gone.

CHAPTER SIXTEEN

NADIA

I was yanked back into my body with a shocking force. When I got my bearings, I realized I was in bed, with my mother on top of me, the force of her knees digging into my hip bones. The overhead light was on, making a halo effect around her head but she looked anything but angelic. She held my arms in a tight grip. From the stinging on my left cheek it was clear she'd just slapped me. "Let go," I cried, struggling to get free.

The whites of her eyes ringed enlarged pupils. She said, "What have you done? What have you done?" It was a wail, an accusation, a tormented cry. "Tell me now before it's too late!"

"I don't know what you mean," I said. "Mom, stop it. You're scaring me."

"I will shake the devil out of you," she said. "I will not rest until you're free of his grasp." Her voice was a deep growl I didn't recognize.

"Dad!" I yelled, hoping he was within earshot. "Help!" I had never seen Mom this way. Her intense stare gave me the chills. I felt her fingernails gouging into the fleshy part of my upper arms. "Dad!"

"Don't bother," she said. "He's not home."

"Yes, he is," I said, gesturing with my head. "He's right in the doorway. Dad!"

She hesitated and let go just for a moment to look, and that's all it took. I took advantage of the element of surprise and pushed her off of me. She lost her balance and fell off the bed. I shook off the covers, ran past her and flew down the stairs.

"Liar!" she yelled from behind me. "Lying to your own mother. You're not my daughter. Nadia would never treat me this way."

I paused at the front door, but when I saw she'd locked the deadbolt with a key, I gave up without even trying. The odds were good that she'd secured the whole house like that. The only chance I had was to reach my father. I had no idea where he'd be at this time of night, but he wouldn't have gone far. I ran to the kitchen to use the landline. It was an old-fashioned phone attached to the wall above the counter. A curly cord kept it tethered to the base. The phone was there when we'd moved into the house and my mother saw no reason to update it as long as it still worked. I punched in the number for my dad's cell phone and listened as it rang. *Come on, come on. Pick up the phone, Dad.* I pictured him in line at the grocery store or in the car. If that was the case, it was going right to voice mail. He was old school concerning phone etiquette. He'd never answer the phone when he was driving or if he were talking to a cashier. One was unsafe, the other was rude. I heard my mother clumping down the stairs, her breathing heavy. Right now she didn't even sound like Mom.

The call went to voice mail. *Oh no.* I clutched the phone and waited for the beep. I spoke frantically. "Dad, it's me Nadia. I'm at home and..." Stupid. Of course I was home. I was never *not* home. "Something's wrong with Mom. She's acting crazy and I need you here right now. Please..."

She rounded the corner and came at me with both hands, pushing me against the wall. I lost my hold on the phone and it dropped, dangling from the cord. "Leave my daughter now!" she shouted.

"Mom, it's me, Nadia." I tried to talk sense to her but there was no reasoning with someone who had no reason.

"You're not fooling me," she said with a sneer. "I knew as soon as I came into the room that you went into my daughter's body. I saw the change with my own eyes. Believe me, I will cast you out!" She put her hands around my neck and squeezed. I reached up and tried to pull her hands away, but she was incredibly strong. I slapped at her head and kicked with one leg, but it only made her madder and she increased the pressure on my windpipe. Her eyes narrowed. She yelled, "Out I say!"

The sound of the garage door opening didn't distract her, but I got a rush of hope. *Hurry Dad, hurry.* I croaked the word "help" but it was barely audible. When the door opened and I saw Dad walk in carrying a paper grocery bag, I was on the verge of passing out. I slammed my fist against the wall to get his attention and it worked.

"What's going on here?" He set the bag down on the counter and rushed over.

"Out I say!" she said, as if he wasn't even there.

Dad grabbed her arms and pulled her away from me. I staggered back and gasped, pulling in deep gulps of air. She faced him. "Leave me alone!" Again, her voice was deep and angry. And she thought *I* was possessed. "I need to do this. I need to get Nadia back."

"Nadia, are you okay?" he asked. I nodded and he looked relieved. "I'm sorry. I shouldn't have left." Suddenly he looked old and tired to me. "I thought a quick trip to Pick 'n Save would be okay." Dad held Mom's arm while she struggled to get to me. "Honey," he said to her. "I can help you. Let me get your medication. You've had a rough time of it lately."

"No," she roared. "I will not be silenced." She broke free of his grasp and ran to the other side of the island counter, opened the drawer and pulled out a butcher knife. "You're with them," she said, pointing the tip of the blade in his direction. "I should have known."

"Put the knife back," he said in a careful, measured manner. "I will help you, I promise. Just put down the knife. You know I love you."

This is how it happens, I thought, breathing heavily. Every time you read about a violent domestic death in the news it starts like this: family members living in the same house, going along with their lives day to day, never knowing that one day one of them will become unhinged and take things a little too far. I saw how easily my family could become one of those families. When she'd had her fingers around my neck, her thumbs digging into my windpipe, I'd felt my airway close and my life slipping away. And now she held the knife like she meant business. If she succeeded, we would be one more family on the police blotter, one more article in the news. And everyone who read it would wonder how in the world could this happen? Why would a mother murder her daughter or her husband? But honestly? It's not as complex as you'd think. A knife, some rage, a moment of insanity, and it's all over.

I picked up the phone and pressed the button to hang up, then dialed 911. At the same time, my dad moved cautiously toward her. "It'll be okay," he said. "You know I love you. You know Nadia loves you. We only want to help."

Her eyes darted back and forth from him to me and back again. I could sense the distrust from several feet away. She was certain we were both against her.

"911, what's your emergency?" The operator sounded so calm.

"My mother is completely out of control," I said, my voice coming out raspy. "She tried to choke me and now she's got a butcher knife."

"Nadia," my father said, giving me a sideways glance. "We don't need to get the police involved. Tell them it's okay and hang up the phone."

"Who else is there with you?" From the way the operator spoke you'd have thought we had all the time in the world.

"My father is here," I said.

"No!" my mother yelled, tearing around the counter and past my father who tried unsuccessfully to hold her back. She held the knife up over her head like we were at the Bates Motel and came right at me.

"Dad!" I cried out as I watched the whole scene in slow motion: my mother surging toward me, my father making a grab for the back of her shirt, and me, standing frozen with the phone against my ear. I saw the knife coming at my neck, dropped the phone and swung my leg out, kicking her in the thigh. The knife nicked the base of my neck right before she doubled over in pain.

"Demon child!" she yelled. My father went to restrain her but somehow she got a second wind. She turned on him then and they grappled for control of the knife.

I picked up the phone and yelled into the receiver. "Please send help. Please!"

The 911 operator rattled off our house number and street name. "Is that correct?"

"Yes."

"We have a car in the neighborhood. The police will be there in a few minutes. Just stay on the phone with me. Can you do that?"

"Yes," I croaked. My father wrested the knife out of Mom's hand. Relieved, I slid down the wall until my butt hit the floor. "I can do that."

CHAPTER SEVENTEEN

RUSS

I barely got any sleep because I was so worried about what had happened to Nadia. I didn't want to think about how I would live in a world without her. No, I decided, she was fine. Something had happened to pull her back into her body and after that she just couldn't come back. Maybe her mother's cat Barry had barged in and jumped on her bed. It had happened before so Nadia usually kept her door closed, but it was possible that she forgot this one time.

At least that's what I told myself. In my heart, I knew she wouldn't forget.

When morning came, the artificial light from outside of the building mimicked the rising of the sun. Jameson was still just a lump under the covers, but I was wide awake so I raised the blinds and watched the courtyard below come to life. A young couple sat on a bench holding hands while an employee, a man in a beige jumpsuit, swept the walkway behind them. Another employee, a young woman, fussed with flowers in the planters. The flowers couldn't be real, I thought, not without bees and true sunlight, but they sure looked authentic. It was a typical hotel courtyard scene, the only difference being that this hotel was located deep below the surface of planet Earth. Anything could be happening topside right now and we'd never know it. Everyone I loved could be gone while I stood here watching a man sweep, a woman arrange flowers, and a couple holding hands. I missed Nadia desperately right then. She always knew the right thing to say to make me feel better. All we wanted was to be together. It didn't seem to be asking too much.

I wondered if she was safe. I wondered if she thought of me as much as I was thinking about her. And I wondered if I should have fought against my good sense and pulled her through the window that night. The two of us could have taken off and gone somewhere, anywhere. Between the two of us we would have figured it all out.

At eight o'clock we all gathered for breakfast in the hotel restaurant and afterward we met in the lobby where we were broken into smaller groups and told our schedule for the day. Jameson and Dr. Anton left to scope out the hall where the Bash would be held, while Rosie and Mallory went off with one of the guard officials to be schooled in how to approach the vice president. As Rosie said, "You can't practice mind control on someone if you can't get close to him."

Mallory was excited about the upcoming Black Tie Bash. Typical girl concerns—what she would wear and how she was going to do her hair. She'd changed her look on this trip, losing the ponytail and letting her hair just fall naturally on her shoulders. I noticed she tucked it behind her ears a lot. When we'd talked about the Bash earlier, she'd asked, "Up or down?" scooping her hair up and piling it on top of her head to give us the full effect.

"Either way is fine," I said. I used to find Mallory so

fascinating, but now her endless talking put me on edge. I was glad when everyone left and Carly and I could sit in peace. I kept thinking about Nadia and what was going on at her house. Once again I hoped the interruption had been something as simple as the cat jumping on her bed. I wanted that to be it.

My thoughts of Nadia were interrupted when Dr. Wentworth came to pick up Carly and me in the hotel lobby after breakfast. "Ready for your big day?" Dr. Wentworth asked. She had a forced smile, the kind that says *let's get on with this.*

I nodded. I was keyed up and nervous about meeting the president, even though she would be unconscious. Dr. Wentworth was all business this morning. The three of us walked silently to the station. We'd been told the hospital was a short subway ride from the hotel, giving me just enough time to mentally prepare. On the subway I found myself interlocking my fingers and flexing my hands over and over again, my way of getting ready for a morning of healing. Or maybe I should say, a morning of *trying* to heal. I said a silent prayer that I'd be able to do it.

Carly sat next to me with the doctor in the row behind us. The seats were red leather edged by a row of brass rivets along the top. The PGDC appeared to be a mix of old style and new architecture. Nothing in this city down below was scuffed or worn or faded. Everything looked new. I ran a finger over the top of the seat in front of us, trying to keep my mind off the enormity of what they were asking me to do. Carly must have sensed my nervousness because she leaned over and said, "Look at us. Two outcasts from Edgewood, Wisconsin off to see the president. Who'd have thought?"

"Outcast? Speak for yourself," I said.

She leaned back and gave me a hard look. "I stand by my statement. You and I, we're both outcasts."

"Yeah, I don't think so." I knew kids at school who had trouble making friends and didn't seem to fit anywhere and even they weren't outcasts. Just too outside of the mainstream. "I have plenty of friends."

"You can have plenty of friends, but still know on some level that you're not the same as them. Inside we all have secret lives. Trust me, you're an outcast. If your so-called friends at school knew about your superpowers, they'd never treat you the same."

"Maybe so, but that doesn't make me an outcast."

"Okay, have it your way."

Carly didn't do it that often, but I hated it when she assumed the wiser older sister role. I had parents to give me advice I didn't want to hear. I didn't need it from her too. "Thanks, I will."

She squeezed my arm. "Don't get me wrong. I'm proud of you, Russ. You're doing the right thing even though you know it might not end well." She had a thoughtful look that made me wonder if this was about more than just me. "Believe me, I've seen it not end well."

"Are you thinking about David Hofstetter?" I asked.

Carly looked down at her shoes, and didn't say anything. At first I thought she hadn't heard me, but then she nodded and I saw her eyes were filled with tears.

"Even after all this time, the thought of him still makes you cry?" I said.

"I'm always thinking about him," she said. "It never

stops. Just when I think I've got him out of my system I hear a song that reminds me of him, or something he said pops into my brain and it starts all over again. Sixteen years this has been going on. You'd think it would have faded by now. It makes me crazy. Why is it still so painful?" When she locked eyes with me her gaze was steady. "Believe me, I don't want to feel like this, Russ. I *hate* feeling like this, but I can't seem to get past it. I miss him and I'm so angry that he's gone. There's no changing the past, but if you can help bring down those lying murderers, the Associates, it might bring me some peace. That's one of the reasons I wanted to come with you on this trip. I want to be there when it happens."

"But what if it doesn't happen?" I was already feeling the pressure; now it was escalating, like a ball of stress climbing from my chest to my throat.

"You're going to do fine," Carly said firmly. She leaned in and whispered. "There's something I need to tell you. Once when you were a baby, Mom and Dad were out of town and I was babysitting you, and I took you with me to meet up with David at the old train station late at night. We fell asleep and David woke up when the lux spiral hit. He had you in his arms when he went outside to see what it was. I think that's why your powers are so great. You've been exposed to it twice."

Carly didn't know that I'd heard this story from David already. I tried to look surprised, but I guess I didn't have the right reaction because she felt the need to repeat herself.

"Twice, Russ," she said, making a peace sign. "The first time as a little baby. Who knows how long the power has been inside you, growing, growing, growing?" She was still whispering but her voice was excited. "It's probably been in every cell of your body, building this whole time, but lying dormant, just waiting. And then, when you saw the lux spiral this past spring, it activated every bit of it, like someone had flipped a switch. Boom!"

I nodded.

She said, "You're probably the first person in the history of the world to get exposed to it as an infant and then again as a teenager. I've never told this to anyone."

In the rows ahead of us, people were gathering up their things, preparing to get off at the next stop. "Thanks for telling me that," I said. "That's pretty incredible."

"You must have been three months old that first time, but David said you had a look of awe on your face. Like you'd been touched by something great."

Something shook loose in my memory and pushed its way forward. Before I could stop myself, I blurted out, "Maybe because I had a piece of it clutched in my fist?" No sooner were the words out of my mouth than I realized my mistake. Carly hadn't told me that my infant self had gotten hold of a piece as it dropped from the sky. David had been the one who'd given me that piece of information. Confused, Carly did a double take. I watched her face and it didn't take long for her to realize that I shouldn't have known that fact.

"Time to go." I felt a tap on my shoulder and glanced up to see Dr. Wentworth in the aisle looming over me. "Quickly now."

I was saved, for now. But I knew my sister, and there was no way this was going to fade from her memory. The subway slowed to a stop and we got up to follow the doctor out the door. Not one person pressed forward or grumbled. Instead, every single passenger filed out courteously. I was learning that everyone in PGDC was orderly and polite. This was the world as it should be.

Security at the hospital was crazy intense. We walked hallway after hallway, going through multiple doors and up an elevator. Signs everywhere said: *Authorized Personnel Only.* Dr. Wentworth had a laminated card that hung from her neck which allowed us access through the first set of doors. After that, she entered numbers into a punch pad in the elevator in addition to using the card. When we exited the elevator we faced another locked door. This time, she lined her eyes up in front of a recognition scanner. A woman's voice said, "Maxine Wentworth, welcome. Please state today's password."

Dr. Wentworth spoke each syllable in a clipped, clear way. "Russ Becker."

My name was today's password? Carly caught it too—she grinned and jabbed me in the ribs with her elbow just as the door slid open. Dr. Wentworth strode forward, her heels clicking on the linoleum, and we followed down a long hallway, past a nurses' station to the president's room. We walked in without even knocking.

The room was nicer than your average hospital room, much bigger, with the kind of decor you'd see in a luxury hotel, but the bed in the middle was set up exactly the way I'd seen it in countless movies and TV shows. The air had a faint antiseptic smell reminding me of Lysol. In the middle of the room was a large hospital bed, and in the bed, under a thin sheet, lay President Bernstein looking worse than I'd expected, completely pale and tiny in the midst of all the medical equipment. Up close, I saw that her curly, black hair was threaded with silver strands. Unconscious, she didn't look like our leader, the one who inspired confidence with her rousing speeches and assured manner. Wires and tubes snaked from her body to the various monitors measuring her vital functions.

"How is the president doing?" Dr. Wentworth asked the doctor who stood alongside the bed. He hadn't looked up when we walked in, seemingly engrossed in reading something on a clipboard. He had horn-rimmed glasses and wavy hair slicked back with an abundance of product. I could even see the comb lines over the top of his head. He was shorter than me and wore a blindingly white jacket with a stethoscope slung around his neck, like a kid at Halloween wearing a doctor costume.

"About the same," he said, sighing, but then he looked up, saw us and smiled a greeting. "But it looks like help has arrived." He extended his hand. "Russ Becker?"

For a second I thought he was saying that *his* name was Russ Becker, which would have been a really amazing coincidence, but before I could make a comment about it, which would have made me look really stupid, I realized that wasn't the case. "Yes, I'm Russ," I said, reaching out my hand.

"I'm Dr. Karke," he said. "We've been looking forward to your arrival. I've heard good things about all you can do. I can't wait to see you in action."

"Thank you," I said.

Dr. Wentworth introduced Carly to him and they exchanged small talk about our plane ride and how we were enjoying our stay. Dr. Wentworth was telling him that we'd spent our first night at the hotel but that we'd be transferring to a luxury suite tonight, which was news to me, but I wasn't interested in being part of that conversation. Instead, I was drawn to President Bernstein. I found myself walking around the bed, trying to determine where to start. Every cell in my body buzzed with electrical anticipation. I sensed all the electricity in the room keeping her alive, and I instinctively knew it hadn't been enough to keep her here the whole time. Somehow I knew President Bernstein had crossed over the line from life to death and back again.

"She died already?" I said, interrupting the conversation in the room.

"What did you say?" Dr. Wentworth's head whipped back in my direction.

"The president. She died and you brought her back with the paddles?"

Dr. Karke hesitated, then said, "That's right."

"I wasn't told that," Dr. Wentworth said sharply.

Dr. Karke shrugged. "It happened. We acted quickly, did what we had to do, and stabilized the president. The details are in the patient notes."

I walked to the head of the bed. "More than once?" I looked at Dr. Karke, whose face flushed red. "You had to revive her twice?"

Embarrassed, he didn't meet my eyes. "Yes, it happened twice."

Dr. Wentworth looked at me in amazement. "How did you know that?"

I didn't answer. Not that I didn't want to, just that I was afraid to break my concentration. Once I locked in to heal someone, that was it. It required everything I had and more. I went to the head of the bed, and stroked the president's hair, something that wasn't necessary to heal her, but something I felt compelled to do. Touching her established a connection between us. It said, *I am here. I will help you.* From that brief touch I could tell that President Bernstein's essence was in there, lingering inside her damaged body. I guessed from the concerned look on the two doctors' faces that they wondered if she was too far gone to save. Dying and being resuscitated twice was a lot for a body to go through.

"Can you help her, Russ?" This from Carly who stood right at my elbow.

I gave a quick nod, before extending my arms over the president's body. I heard the squeaky wheels of a cart being pushed through the doorway—one of the medical staff making a delivery, I assumed. Both doctors spoke at once.

"Not now!"

"Get out!"

Whoever it was pulled the cart back through the doorway and out into the hall. My palms pulsed with energy as I tried to detect the area that needed healing. I held my hands about six inches above the president's body, and slowly went from head to toe and back again. The trouble spot, the worst of it, was her head, but that wasn't where the problem ended. Her entire body had been affected. To me, her organs felt stressed. Every muscle was weak. Her empty stomach churned and her heart strained to pump blood to her extremities. Without these machines and the medicine she'd been given she would already be dead. Part of her spirit yearned to go; but the other part, the warrior part, struggled to stay. I knew all of this, but I wasn't sure *how* I knew all this. I just did.

After making an assessment, I concentrated on her head, holding my hands on either side above her ears. I felt a pressure on her left side and intense pain, like a terrible, horrible headache. The pain medication had dulled it, but it was still there underneath. I focused all my energy and emotion on fixing the president. I knew from past experience that I couldn't let my thoughts muddle the process. Words and ideas didn't matter to energy. I ignored the fidgeting sounds of the other people in the room. Dr. Karke cleared his throat and shuffled his feet at one point. I heard it, but I didn't let it break my concentration. My palms moved from her head to her heart and when I felt my energy depleting like a balloon running out of air, I did one last swoop over her arms and legs, before quitting. "I'm done," I said. I shook my fingers loose and stretched my arms.

"Already?" Dr. Wentworth said, not hiding the disappointment in her voice.

"Yes."

"But it's only been fifteen minutes."

"That's all I can do for now," I said, flexing my fingers. "I feel like I'm going to have to do this in stages. The damage is too great to fix all at once."

The two doctors stared down at the president's still form. Dr. Wentworth glanced up at the monitors hoping to see some indication that my work had helped, but everything looked the same.

"Could you please try again?" Dr. Karke asked. "We need to have the president fully recovered by the night of the Presidential Bash."

"I understand that," I said. "Believe me, I want to see President Bernstein healed as much as anyone." Maybe more, since everyone was counting on me. "I'm not refusing to do more. I *can't* do anymore. I'm depleted. You know how a bucket can only hold so much water and after it's all poured out, you're not going to get another drop out of it no matter what you do? That's how it works for me. I can only do it until I'm done."

"But would it hurt to try a little longer?" Dr. Karke asked, looking to Dr. Wentworth for back-up. "I told the first gentleman that I'd have good news for him today." A note of desperation tinged his words. He wrung his hands.

I felt for him, I really did. I just couldn't help him.

"You heard what my brother said," Carly said, speaking a little louder than necessary. "His bucket is *empty*. When he can do more, he will." She turned to me. "When do you want to come back again, Russ?"

"I don't know. Maybe tonight?" I said. "By this evening I think she'll be ready for more." As I said this, I felt a frequency of awareness in the air and sensed that the president could hear everything being said. I leaned over and said, "President Bernstein? My name is Russ Becker. I'm the one who alleviated the pressure in your head. You get some rest. I'll be back tonight to do another session. Hang in there, you're doing really well." She didn't respond in any way, but I knew she understood.

"Could you two excuse us?" Dr. Karke said to me and Carly pointing to the door. "We need a few minutes to confer."

Once we were out in the hallway, I heard him say to Dr. Wentworth, "What the hell was that? I thought you said he could heal her!" Dr. Wentworth shushed him and said something in my defense. I couldn't quite make it all out, but I caught something about test results and data and allowing more time.

Carly put her hands on her hips and frowned. She said, "I don't care if he is a doctor, that little man is a complete dick."

"Cut him a break. He's not so bad," I said. "Just disappointed." I knew the feeling. I was disappointed in myself.

"You are way too nice," she said.

"Not really."

Shaking her head, she turned her attention to her purse, unzipping the top and rummaging through the contents. When she located her pack of gum, she popped a piece into her mouth. "I was ready to tell him we were done and going home. Ingrate."

"Don't even talk like that, Carly," I said. "We're not going home." A pretty nurse smiled at me as she came past pushing a cart. She hesitated in the president's doorway, and when Dr. Wentworth called to her, she went in.

"It just makes me mad that they're second guessing you." She snapped her gum, a habit that drove my mother nuts.

"That's his job. He's just doing what he thinks is best." I leaned my back against the wall and rested the sole of one foot flamingo-style. "I actually feel sorry for him. Now he has to tell Mr. Bernstein that his wife isn't miraculously recovered like he promised. That really bites for him."

"He shouldn't have promised it."

"Yeah, he shouldn't have promised it. But he did."

Carly leaned in and quietly asked, "Do you think you can fix her? In time for the Bash?"

"Yeah, I think I can." I thought about how her brain woke up after my energy infusion. President Bernstein wanted to get better, but every part of her body was fatigued and strained. "I'm going to try my best anyway."

CHAPTER EIGHTEEN

RUSS

That afternoon I found myself in Layla Bernstein's bedroom. Most guys my age would think this was a dream come true, but for me, it was just part of the job. After we found out we were going to the White House, the three of us dressed appropriately: Mallory in a flowery dress with a ruffle around the v-neckline and Jameson and I in button-down shirts and khaki pants. When we first arrived, a Secret Service agent directed us into a small sitting room with the kind of furniture preferred by elderly women. The agent assured us Layla would be with us shortly, and then departed, leaving us to wait alone. Mallory and I sat in stiff upholstered chairs, while Jameson took the loveseat across from us. On the cream-colored wall behind him hung an oil painting of a bonneted woman who looked down on him in disapproval.

"Imagine all of the history that took place in this room," Mallory said, looking around. "First ladies having tea here, and diplomats sipping brandy and hammering out agreements by the light of the fire." She gestured to the fireplace. "I can picture it."

"Of course you can picture it. I don't think they've

redecorated since Lincoln was in office," Jameson said, stifling a yawn. "Didn't you think the rooms would be bigger here?" He leaned back and extended his long legs. "What's the deal with that? Even the furniture is tiny."

"I did think it would be bigger," Mallory said. "Didn't you, Russ?"

I sized up the room and shrugged. "I didn't have any preconceived ideas one way or another."

She and Jameson went on about the size of the furniture, and wondered if the Secret Service would notice if Jameson rearranged the room. "It's probably all wired with explosives." Mallory joked. "If you move something, we'll get blown to bits."

"None of the furniture is wired," I said. "But I wouldn't try to take that picture off the wall, or an alarm will sound."

Mallory looked startled. "Why do you say that?"

I raised one eyebrow. "If you don't believe me, give it a try."

She jumped up quickly, to go test my theory I thought, but I was wrong. A second later I knew the real reason she got up off her chair when I spotted Layla Bernstein leaning against the door frame peering in on us, an amused expression on her face. Who knew how long she'd been watching us and listening to everything we'd said? I was glad I hadn't done anything embarrassing.

"Hello," Mallory said politely, gesturing to us to rise. "It's nice to see you again."

Layla walked in and immediately I saw that she had it—the thing that all the magazines talked about. She had a presence. She strode in as if she was in a perpetual spotlight.

Layla was beautiful and slender, with glossy black hair and chiseled cheekbones, but her beauty appeared to be effortless. I doubt this girl ever had a moment in life when she lacked confidence. Next to her Mallory looked ordinary.

Layla sat down on the loveseat next to Jameson, but her eyes were on Mallory. "I was told we met in Miami, but I don't remember being introduced."

"It was so hectic at the decathlon," Jameson said, sitting back down and resting his hands on his knees. "You probably met so many people..."

Layla put her finger to her lips. "Shh. I'm thinking." She gestured to Mallory. "You have a sort of standard high school girl look. And you," she turned to Jameson. "Smartest guy at your school? Top nerd. Am I right?"

"Actually I'm homeschooled," he said. "Doing university-level work. They're the ones who go to the public school."

"I saw a million nerd boys in Miami," Layla continued. "You could have been one of them, for all I know. But you, sweetheart, what's your name?" She snapped her fingers at me and pointed.

"I'm Russ Becker."

"Russ Becker." Coming out of her mouth my name was as smooth and sweet as honey. Her intense scrutiny made me uneasy. "You I'd remember. We've never met. I know I've never seen you before."

A woman came in carrying a tray of tall glasses filled with a light brown liquid, a wedge of lemon floating in each glass. "Would anyone care for a cold drink and some cookies?"

Layla stood up. "Send them to my room. We're going upstairs." She beckoned to me with one crooked finger. "Cute boy, come with me." Mallory and Jameson looked unsure as to what to do so they just tagged along behind. Layla took my hand and pulled me through the doorway past two Secret Service agents, both in dark suits with earpieces. They said hello to her but she didn't answer. She said to me, "We have to go through the Diplomatic Room to get to the private residence. Hopefully there won't be anyone there. I hate it when I get stuck talking to people."

I didn't say anything, because I didn't know what to say. Her hand clasping mine was warm and soft, and I couldn't stop looking at her. She practically glowed with perfection and she smelled like a wonderful mixture of something like roses and cinnamon. It felt all wrong to be noticing these things when I was in love with Nadia, but it's not like I had a choice.

Layla glanced over her shoulder and frowned as she saw Mallory and Jameson behind us. "We're not going to lose them, are we?"

"Afraid not," I said. "The three of us are supposed to stick together."

"That's a shame," she said. "Because I'd love to get some alone time with you."

I felt my face flush red but Layla didn't seem to notice. Nearly as tall as me, her strides were long and she was making good time. We passed another Secret Service agent talking to a woman wearing business attire. I tried to see if the woman was someone famous, but Layla yanked me along before I could tell.

When we got to the Diplomatic Room she exhaled in relief and looked up at the ceiling. "Thank you." She turned to me. "Once we're through here we're home free. Literally.

After this I can finally be myself." We walked through the room and around a set of brown, room-dividing screens, the kind they use in restaurants to give diners a sense of privacy. We ducked behind the screens to get to the stairs. She was right, going from the public portion of the house to the private part did have a different feeling. Home free, as she said.

We walked up a staircase and down a hallway. "Welcome to my museum bedroom," Layla said, as we approached a closed door. She opened it and went in first, beckoning for us to follow. Once inside, she kicked off her shoes, sending them skittering across the floor. The room did look like it could be in a museum. Ornate crown molding lined the edges where the walls met the very high ceiling. Opposite her bed was a sitting area set up in front of a fireplace like the one downstairs. An oval gold-framed mirror was mounted over the mantel. Heavy velvet drapes were held back from the windows with a gold cord which ended in tassels.

But there were some personal touches too. The mantel and dresser were topped with dozens of framed photos of Layla with friends, just like you'd see in any other teenaged girl's room. The fact that most of these friends were famous rock stars and actors was beside the point. And the rug next to the bed was a fake full-sized grizzly bear, which was, I'm guessing, not original to the room.

"So cool," Mallory said, her voice bubbling with excitement. She examined the celebrity photos above the fireplace. "I can't believe we're here, in Layla Bernstein's bedroom. This is amazing."

"You're here all right," Layla said. "By the way, you don't need to worry about snipers. The glass in my windows is bulletproof."

"Has there been a problem with snipers?" I asked.

"Well, no," she said, "because the glass is bulletproof." She padded over to the nightstand and picked up the phone, turning to me before dialing. "Did you not hear me tell that girl to bring the drinks up? Where the hell could she be?" She drummed her fingers on the wooden surface. "Yes, this is Layla. Tell the girl to bring the tray with the drinks and cookies up to my room. Really? Okay then." She hung up and made a face. "She's on her way."

"This was so nice of you to invite us up here," Mallory said.

"Please," Layla said, indicating the chairs by the fireplace. "Have a seat." After they'd occupied both places, she grabbed the front of my shirt. "You. You're coming with me." Half laughing, she pulled me over to the bed, then climbed up and sat with her legs tucked beneath her. She patted the space next to her and I went along with it, sitting down on the edge with my legs hanging to the floor. She said, "So Ross Becker, what do you think?"

"Russ."

"What?"

"My name is Russ. Not Ross."

She laughed. "Okay, if you want to play it that way."

"It's not that I want to play it that way. It's my name."

"Okay, then. *Russ*." Like I was being difficult and she was humoring me. "Let's start the conversation over and get it right this time. What do you think of my room?"

"It's nice."

"Just nice?"

I had the feeling I was being tested and I didn't know the right answer. I ventured a guess. "*Very* nice?"

"Do you like my rug?" She indicated the fake grizzly bear rug underneath my feet. It actually looked pretty real, but the plastic beady eyes reminded me of the stuffed animals Carly used to give me when I was little. I never really played with them and eventually my mom donated them to Goodwill.

I shrugged. "It's cool."

She leaned in and in a confidential tone said, "Sometimes I like to roll around on it naked."

"Excuse me?" I heard her, but I wasn't quite sure I heard her.

"I like to take off all my clothes and roll around on it," she said with a laugh. "I love the way it feels against my skin. Do you know what I mean?"

Jameson called over from his side of the room. "Are you comfortable there, Russ? Because you look decidedly *un*comfortable." He laughed his Jameson cackle. I could never decide if it was an actual laugh or if he was faking it. Either way, it had an unmistakable mocking tone.

"I'm fine, thanks," I said to both him and Layla.

I was happy when there was a knock on the door and it turned out to be the woman we'd seen earlier carrying the exact same tray of refreshments. Two minutes later we were served iced tea along with cookies that looked like dog biscuits. None of us opted for a cookie, but the tea was pretty good. Before the woman left, she reminded Layla not to drink near her bed, because tea stains were hard to remove. As soon as the door shut behind her, Layla called Jameson and Mallory over to sit with us on the bed. "They won't give me diet Coke anymore," Layla said, sighing and taking a sip of her tea. The ice clinked in her glass as she raised it to her lips. "Not since my mom started advocating for a healthy lifestyle. As the first family we have to set a good example."

"I read about that," Jameson said. Out of the four of us he seemed the most awkward sitting on the bed. He tried about three different positions before settling on cross-legged, but I don't think he found it natural. He had the look of a spring about to be unsprung. Any second I expected his limbs to come undone and send him sprawling. "That's why they won't serve fish sticks in public schools anymore."

"In fourth grade I was addicted to fish sticks," Mallory said. "With French fries and lots of ketchup. Yum. I didn't even think about calories back then."

"Imagine how much grease you were consuming," Jameson said. "And your gall bladder had to deal with all that fat."

"My gall bladder was cool with it," Mallory said. "It didn't mind."

Layla watched them discuss fish sticks and gall bladders with amusement. She set her glass down on the nightstand, moved closer, and gave my knee a squeeze. "So if you're thinking you'll meet my mom, you're out of luck. She's working on some big project and even I haven't seen her for days. You might be introduced to her at the Bash, if you're lucky, but don't count on talking to her. She's going to be super busy."

"Okay," I said. I always had trouble talking to someone when there was another discussion happening nearby. Jameson and Mallory had moved on to the topic of tator tot casserole and, like a true Wisconsinite, Mallory was rhapsodizing about melted cheese. Stretchy melted cheese, which was, in her opinion, the very best kind. I had to really pay attention to catch what Layla was saying.

"Okay what?" Layla said.

"Okay, whatever. I don't really care, Layla. I wasn't planning on talking to your mother. I'm here to go to the Black Tie Bash with you."

She tilted her head to one side, giving me a look of careful consideration. "So what's the story, Russ? Would you care to fill me in?"

"Fill you in on what?"

She gave my knee another squeeze and then started to stroke the inside of my thigh. "Why exactly are we pretending that I met you before?"

"Um." I gulped and took a quick sip of my drink. "What?"

Mallory's head whipped around. Amazing the way girls can carry on one conversation but still catch what other people are saying. "Layla, I heard that you have problems with back pain, is that true?"

And just like that, Layla dropped the subject and turned her attention to Mallory's question. Apparently she was one of those people who jumped at the chance to talk about herself. "I wouldn't call it pain," she said, putting a hand to her back. "More like torture. Absolute torture. And when it's bad, nothing touches the pain. I mean, I can't get any relief. I'm in total agony. My dad gets it too. I must have inherited my spine problems from him."

"I'm a certified massage therapist," Mallory said, flexing her fingers. "I bet I can help."

"It's not too bad today—"

But before Layla could really object, Mallory handed her

glass to Jameson and scooted over behind Layla. She placed her hands on Layla's shoulders and began kneading the base of her neck. "Man, you are tense. You must be under a lot of pressure."

"Tell me about it." Layla's head dropped forward and her eyes closed. "That's really good, but the trouble spot is lower."

"I'll get there," Mallory said, continuing to massage Layla's shoulders and then sliding her fingers down her back.

I was one hundred percent certain that Mallory was not a certified massage therapist and that it was all a ploy to allow her to get close enough to exert mind control. Mallory had to have heard about the back pain from one of our PG contacts. It wasn't public knowledge. At least I had never heard about it.

"This is really nice," Layla said, practically purring like a kitten. Her head drooped and bobbed as Mallory worked on her back.

"I knew I could help," Mallory said.

While all this was going on I took a good look at Jameson. The massage was getting to him, I could tell. Each of his hands had a tight grip on the iced tea glasses, and it had to be cold, but he didn't seem to notice. "Jameson!" I said, breaking the spell.

"What?" It was like he came up for air.

"Why don't you put the glasses down?" I gestured to the coffee table over by the fireplace.

Layla's eyes were closed now and her chin was against her chest. Her glossy black hair hung down leaving only a sliver of her face in view. She made a small moan of pleasure as Mallory continued working on her back. Instead of answering me, Jameson grinned and let go of the glasses, which hovered in front of him. He swiveled his thumb toward the coffee table and the glasses obediently traveled across the room, coming to rest on the tray in the middle of the table. I held my breath as this happened, but neither of the girls seemed to notice. Without the drinks to hold onto, Jameson was able to stretch his legs.

"Okay then," Mallory said after a few minutes. She tapped Layla on the shoulder. "I think that should do it."

Layla opened her eyes and rotated her head. "Wow, that's amazing. I've been to physical therapists, chiropractors, the works. This is the best I've felt in a long time. Thank you." Her gratitude seemed genuine. I could only think that Mallory had implanted the idea that the pain was gone. Whatever she did, it was a good thing.

"You're welcome." Mallory smiled.

"It was a lucky day when I met you guys in Miami. I hope we can stay in touch," Layla said, overcome with emotion.

"Well of course we'll stay in touch," Mallory said, her voice indignant. "Why wouldn't we? We're friends, aren't we?"

"Yes, we're friends," Layla said. She didn't have the dopey look that I associated with mind control. Carly was right; Mallory had really fine tuned this talent. She was scary good. "Of course we're friends. I think you guys understand me better than anyone."

"We're here for you," Jameson said.

"It's hard being me. The media mobs me. I can't even go to a concert with friends like normal people. I have to sit backstage and watch."

"You poor thing," Mallory said. "It must be rough."

"It is."

Jameson said, "So what do you do for fun around here? I think I heard something about a White House bowling alley? We could give that a go." His self-assured grin made me think that he was planning to get a perfect score. Who needed a ball to knock down pins when you could do it with your mind?

"Oh no," Layla said, blowing out a puff of air. "Bowling's not my thing. How about a movie?" She explained that the White House had a movie theater on site, and that they received films before their release date. "I'll call down and get them to set it up and get the popcorn ready."

She picked up the phone and said, "I'd like to watch a movie with my friends, please." I hadn't heard her say please before. I wondered if that was something Mallory had implanted. "Really? Why not? Oh, that's disappointing. Well, maybe another time. Thank you." She hung up the phone and gave us the bad news. "There's an event I have to attend—a sick kid in a hospital, and I have to leave in an hour to go visit her. It was on my schedule, but somehow it slipped my mind."

"We can come back another day," Mallory said, like she was soothing a small child. "We'll be here for a few more days."

"Another day," Layla agreed. "Maybe tomorrow?" She looked around the room like she was seeing it for the first time. "I suppose I should get ready. There are always photographers at these things." She exhaled loudly. "They expect me to look a certain way. I definitely need to do something with this hair." She pulled a lock away from her face and looked at it, then let it drop. I thought her hair looked nearly perfect, but from the disgusted look on her face, it needed a lot of work.

"We have to go anyway," Mallory said, taking the glass from my hand and crossing the room to set it on the tray. I slid off the bed, followed by Jameson, and finally Layla. "I don't know why they get so weird," Layla said, smoothing the bed spread. "We didn't spill a drop."

Jameson ambled toward the door and Mallory and I followed his lead. "I guess this is good-bye for now," Mallory said, pausing.

"Wait a minute!" Layla said, striding toward us and for a split second I thought she was on to us, that she'd figured out the mind control and that she knew she'd never met us before today. But what she said next erased my worries. "You don't think I'd let you leave without a hug, do you?"

She embraced Mallory and then Jameson, thanking each of them for coming to see her and saying how happy she was that we came out for the Bash. When she got to me, the hug lingered and I felt the unmistakable sensation of her knee working its way up between my legs. She whispered in my ear. "We are going to have some fun, Russ Becker. Just you wait and see." Then she planted a forceful kiss on my startled lips. I didn't see it coming and I was too shocked to react.

When she pulled back three seconds later, I knew my face had reddened because I felt the warm, embarrassed flush go from my cheeks all the way up to my hairline. I hoped it wasn't obvious, but of course it was. "Look, Russ is blushing," Jameson said. He nudged Mallory. "How cute is that?"

"Very cute," she said.

I couldn't get out of that room fast enough. We were

halfway down the stairs when Mallory said. "You don't have to thank me Russ, but you can if you want."

"For what?" I said.

She laughed. "For the little something extra I implanted in Layla. Not only does she remember meeting you in Miami, she now wants you in the worst possible way. More than she ever wanted anything in her entire life."

CHAPTER NINETEEN

—••●•—

RUSS

To say I was pissed off at Mallory would be an understatement. She knew how I felt about Nadia and she went and did this? What kind of friend does something like that? I stopped midway down the stairs and said, "What did you do that for?"

Her eyes grew wide in surprise. "I thought you'd like it," she said. "Layla obviously has a thing for you anyway. I just gave her an extra nudge in that direction."

Jameson said, "It's a gift, Russ. If you don't want it, I'll take it. She's totally hot."

I gave him a steely-eyed look. Was he serious? "You'd want some girl to want you just because she's been brainwashed to want you?"

"Well, yeah," he said. "A sure thing. What's wrong with that?"

If he didn't see anything wrong with that, there was nothing I could say to convince him otherwise. I said, "You heard him, Mallory. Switch Layla over to him."

"Oh, I don't know if I can do that. You're her date

and having her get all crazy over Jameson would be really awkward."

"Guess you're stuck with her," Jameson said, slapping me on the back. "Tough to have to take one for the team."

"Seriously Mallory," I said. "You have to undo this. We're supposed to be protecting her at the Bash. How can I do that if she's hanging all over me?"

Mallory tucked a strand of hair behind her ear. "I don't know if I can get close enough to her to do it again. Besides, if she's hanging all over you, we don't have to worry about her wandering off. If anything, I did you a favor. She'll be easier to keep track of if she's attached to you."

"So you won't change her back?"

"I'll think about it." I knew that 'I'll think about it' was Mallory's code for 'not in a million lifetimes.' I was screwed. Unless I wanted to tell on her to the Praetorian Guard officials I was stuck with a presidential daughter determined to seduce me. A year ago I would have thought this was a good problem to have, but not anymore.

I was too mad to even talk to either of them so I kept going down the stairs and didn't say a word. When we met with our PG escorts and they said we could have some down-time before dinner, I opted to go back to our room alone, grateful that Jameson and Mallory were leaving to explore PGDC. "You really aren't going to go with us?" Mallory said puzzled, as if she hadn't just done this heinous thing. It occurred to me that she actually thought she was doing me a favor and I would enjoy having Layla obsessed with me.

"No, you guys go ahead. I just want to decompress."

"Suit yourself," Jameson said, leading Mallory away. With

old Russ out of the way, he thought he had a clear path to Mallory's heart. Good luck with that. He was welcome to it.

Back in the room, I finally had time to hear myself think. As far as the mission went, everything was on track. Mallory had convinced Layla that we'd met before, I had started my healing work on the president, and Jameson hadn't screwed anything up with his show-off moves. Still to come: Mallory working on the vice president and me going back to the hospital to try again with the president. So much to think about.

I settled back on the bed and watched a little TV, first viewing *Underworld*, a movie I'd seen a million times before, and then the beginning of an old *CSI: Las Vegas*, before I finally got bored with it and clicked it off. I grabbed my carry-on and rifled through the pockets until I found the packet of comic books Kevin Adams had given me at the airport. I might be sixteen, but I loved comic books as much as I did when I was eight. The great graphics, the action-packed plots, the way I didn't have to strain my brain to follow the story. They were so visual it was easy to see why so many of them were made into movies. Sometimes a guy just needed some fun reading.

I rifled through the stack, looking to see which ones I'd already read and which ones were new to me, when one caught my eye in a big way. It had a large yellow sticky note on it that said, *Russ, this is a comic book that Sam and I made when we were a little older than you. He did the story & I did the pictures. I thought you might like it.* I put the sticky note on the pillow next to me and I flipped through the pages. It was clearly handmade, but well done. The same size as a typical comic book and about as many pages. The drawings were pretty good too, considering Kevin wasn't a professional artist. I thought of the two of them working together on this project, a young Sam Specter and Kevin Adams, totally getting into this nerd enterprise. They must have had copies made somewhere and then stapled the pages together themselves. Things didn't line up perfectly, so it was a little off. Not too bad though, considering.

The title on the cover said: *Superheroes of the Twenty-First Century!* Interesting. Especially because it was written during the twentieth century. The twenty-first century must have seemed way off in the distant future to young Sam and Kevin.

I started reading and by the second page, I thought I was going to have a heart attack. Seriously, I was hyperventilating and my heart began pounding when it hit me that the comic book story was about us. Four teenagers from a small town gifted with superpowers. Their names were Persuasa, Spark Boy, Secret Weapon Girl, and Mover! (with an exclamation point—it was part of the name, apparently). Kevin's drawings had been done more than twenty-five years ago, way before the four of us had even been born, and yet there we were in the pages of his homemade comic book. Persuasa had the power of mind control, just like Mallory. Spark Boy could shoot electricity out of his palms. Clearly that was me. Secret Weapon Girl walked around with her face obscured by a hood. Her superpower was forcing people to tell the truth. Not quite like Nadia, but close. And Mover! was Jameson, without a doubt. He was tall and lanky, with white-blond hair. In the story, Mover! had a sort of know-it-all attitude that had Jameson stamped all over him. Mover!'s power was telekinesis, of course.

The similarities were too much to be a coincidence. Puzzled, I flipped through the pages and then read Kevin's note again. *Russ, this is a comic book that Sam and I made when we were a little older than you. He did the story & I did the pictures. I thought you might like it.* And then it hit me. Sam did the story. Sam Specter, who had the power of seeing the future, wrote the story. He knew about us before we even existed and knew what was going to happen. But why make a comic book out of it? Maybe to keep it fresh in his mind? His powers had since faded, in the same way that Kevin and Rosie and Dr. Anton's powers had also faded. Could it be that he knew that would happen and didn't want to forget? It would have been more than a quarter of a century ago—a long time and details could easily fade from a person's memory.

I read through the comic book, paying attention to each word and every illustration. I got chills reading the story. In *Superheroes of the Twenty-First Century*, the teenage superheroes got called to Washington D.C. by a secret organization that needed their help avoiding a national incident at a charity ball the president will be attending. The biggest problem is that the lady president is in a coma. Spark Boy is called to use his healing electricity to make her well again.

Layla had a role in this story too. Just like in real life, she was the president's daughter, but in this version her name was Lola. Pretty close. In this version of events, Lola was vain and a real man-eater. In the comic book she wore a low cut gown and had one of those long cigarette holders, like you see in old movies. Very dramatic and elegant. Unlikely to happen in real life, but a nice comic book touch.

Although all four superheroes are invited to the charity ball, Secret Weapon Girl (Nadia) has to stay behind to fight crime in their small hometown. A crazy woman is on the loose in the town of Edgemont, jumping out of hiding after dark, and attacking people with a large butcher knife before retreating and getting away. No one knows her identity, but Secret Weapon Girl is sure she can figure out who she is and bring her to justice. "I will join you as soon as I can!" she cries to her friends, who board their Superhero jet and wave good-bye.

The bad guys, aptly named the Associates, just like in real life, planned to kill the president and Lola at the charity ball. The head of the Associates, Commander Whitlock, arranged to be at the ball, to oversee the actions of all his underlings. The three superheroes are there to protect Lola and watch out for anything underhanded. Spark Boy tells Lola: *Do not worry, gorgeous, you are safe with me! I will be at your side all night.* And then Lola gratefully grabs him and plants a kiss right on his mouth. *Swak!* It must have been one great kiss because in the next panel, she swoons. Literally swoons. The room spins for her and stars swirl above her head.

For the second time today I felt a flush of embarrassment realizing that Mr. Specter knew all about this, the whole time. Did he know it would be me? All of sophomore year in his science class did he know that someday I'd be Spark Boy? And if so, why didn't he destroy the comic book? He was on the Associates' side, but this comic book was a manual on what they were planning to do and could tell me how to defeat them.

I read on. At the ball, Persuasa uses mind control on the vice president to convince him to switch sides, so he's no longer aligned with the Associates.

Now the story flipped to the other side. The Associates, who'd caused the coma in the first place, were shocked to see the president arrive at the ball in perfect health. *She was supposed to be dead!* the commander screams. In a fit of rage, he instructs his minions to create a distraction. He wants the president and the daughter killed at the same time. An explosion is set off and the room fills with smoke. People panic, scream, and run. The commander pulls out a missile the size of a canoe and sends it toward the president. Mover! uses his power to turn the missile around so it bursts through the ceiling and explodes up in the sky like fireworks. Looking closely at the page, I recognized Mover!'s self-confident expression. It was all Jameson, every bit of it.

Persuasa ushers Lola and her parents out a side entrance and they are able to escape. In the confusion, a member of the Associates who has the same power as Spark Boy, goes to electrocute the president. Spark Boy sees him and counteracts his power with a mighty blast. Lightning bolts intersect from each side of the room, but Spark Boy is more powerful and he wins.

Commander Whitlock and the rest of the Associates beat a hasty retreat. In the getaway car, Commander Whitlock pulls off what looks like a latex mask covering his entire head, and reveals that he's actually a woman. On the last page, she says to her sidekick, a man with a pointed nose, *This isn't over. We'll be back.*

The three superheroes return home, but before they get there, tragedy befalls Secret Weapon Girl. As she's outside tracking the Edgemont killer, Secret Weapon Girl is confronted by the same Associate who was overpowered by Spark Boy. "Your little boyfriend messed with the wrong guy," he jeered, before electrocuting her. Spark Boy finds her lifeless body in the town square and rushes to her side, but it's too late. In the pavement next to her body, are the words,

REVENGE IS SWEET. In the panel, Spark Boy is shown cradling her in his arms, wailing. He weeps over her lifeless body and kisses her forehead. *I realize it now. You were my one true love. And now you're lost forever.* I stared at this panel for a long time. A wave of emotion came over me, and my eyes filled with tears. I could imagine Spark Boy's unending sorrow because I knew how I would feel if Nadia died. Thank God her mother never let her leave the house and she was safe at home. Maybe her mom wasn't so crazy after all.

I shook off my grief reminding myself this wasn't real. I kept reading. Next, Spark Boy vows revenge on the Associates. *They won't get away with this!* he says, his fist raised. *I will avenge her death!*

And below that: THE END. I turned the page and on the back, printed in large letters, it read: Watch for *Superheroes of the Twenty-First Century Part II, Coming Soon!*

CHAPTER TWENTY

NADIA

I sat in the waiting room at the hospital for what seemed like a really long time. The visitor center of the psychiatric ward had a different feeling than the rest of the hospital. More security, for one thing. We had to sign in and get buzzed through to get past the entry point. And the other visitors' faces were grim and no one carried flowers or balloons. I sat on the fake leather couch and paged through magazines. I looked at the wall clock at least a hundred times waiting for my father to come back from talking to the doctors.

My dad referred to what happened as "the incident." Much nicer than saying "when your mom went crazy and tried to kill you." When the police arrived in response to my 911 call, the incident became too big for us to take back. My dad couldn't make it go away by saying it was a minor family dispute, although he tried doing just that. The cops might have been able to ignore my mother's wild-eyed look, our disheveled kitchen, and the yowling of the cat, but the sight of me holding a dishtowel to my bloody neck was a game changer.

One of the cops called for two ambulances. He actually

said, "We're going to need two buses," just the way they do on the police shows on TV. After that, they separated the three of us for questioning. My dad gave me a begging look as they led me away and I knew he wanted me to come up with a story that would get Mom off the hook. He was always holding things together. I didn't want to be the one to get my mom in trouble and break up the family, but it was too late. I'd already told the 911 operator about my mom wielding the knife and the blood gushing out of the side of my neck sort of backed up that version of events. In the end, I couldn't lie. I told them everything that had happened from the time I'd woken up to find my mother on top of me, determined to get the devil out of me, until they arrived.

At the same time as I was telling them my version, I heard her in the next room frantically trying to convince them that I was possessed by a demon. "That is not my daughter, Nadia! I saw it take over her body. If you were there you'd know I'm telling the truth. Whatever is in there is trying to fool us, but I saw right past it. I was trying to save my daughter, my baby girl!" I hadn't heard her call me her baby girl in a long time and it made my heart hurt to hear it now. I heard the lady cop talking quietly and trying to get Mom to calm down but that only made her more agitated. "How do you explain her face healing like that?" Mom yelled. "I say it's the devil's work!" Another officer was asking my dad to get the vial of my mom's pills to bring to the hospital to give the doctors.

Listening to my mom, I felt bad. Some of what she was saying was true. She had seen my spirit leave my body and then watched it reenter when I'd returned. And she was right in saying I had been different lately. My father missed a lot of details around the house, but she didn't miss a thing. The most obvious change, my face, was noticed by both of them, but my dad thought it was due to the ointment he'd given me. Mom saw beyond that. Now that I didn't look hideous, living in my body became a whole lot easier. I found myself stopping in front of the very mirrors I used to avoid. I no longer felt repugnant and that influenced how I moved and the clothes I wore. I'd retired the hoodie and started wearing the tank tops and tees that before had just been layering pieces. And the biggest change? I was in love with Russ, and that changed everything.

When the paramedics arrived, they set to work evaluating me, putting pressure on my wound, and monitoring my vitals. They checked my blood pressure and took my temperature, both of which were fine. The cut had nearly stopped bleeding by then, but still they had me lie down on the stretcher and wheeled me to the back of the ambulance where they put an oxygen thing in my nose. Once I felt the vehicle start to move, it all went by in a blur.

My dad had decided to drive our car and meet us at the hospital, but not before assuring my mom that he'd bring her purse. I guess she didn't realize that when you were committed to a mental health ward you couldn't keep your personal belongings with you.

The whole thing was surreal, like it was happening to someone else's family. My mother had always been extreme, but never so bad that we couldn't handle it ourselves. My dad thought of her as moody and quirky. He'd tell me when to leave her alone because she had some things to "work out." He never told me what her medication was for and I never saw the vial of pills. They kept it hidden somewhere in their bedroom—off-limits for me. My dad always kept her on an even keel. He steered the ship, I followed his lead, and generally everything was okay. But now, my astral projecting had steered us off course and put her over the edge. Her increased insanity and my father's sorrow all sourced right back to me. My family was a mess and it was my fault.

At the hospital that night I got eight stitches. The doctor who did it frowned as he worked. "I'm afraid this will leave a slight scar. Your folks might want to consult with a plastic surgeon. I can give you a referral if you'd like."

Just to be polite, I nodded. I took the piece of paper with the referral even knowing I would never visit a plastic surgeon. I didn't need plastic surgery; I had Russ. If he could heal my burn scars, which were several years old, this incision should be easy for him to fix. I imagined his hands hovering over my neck before finding their way to either side of my face. I loved his touch and the intensity of our eyes meeting right before he leaned in to kiss me. He looked at me like I was a miracle: the sun rising after the end of the world, rain after a long, harsh drought. Looking through his eyes I saw myself the same way.

They sent me home with my father while Mom stayed behind to be evaluated. Once we were in the car in the parking lot, he gripped the wheel and looked up at the lit hospital windows. "I hope they treat her well," he said with a tired sigh before starting the engine.

That night I fell into a deep sleep. Before I drifted off, I tried to astral project to Russ, but I couldn't make it work. I couldn't get my head in the right place and my body wouldn't relax enough to make it happen. Astral projecting had caused the problem and now I couldn't even do it. Totally ironic.

The staff in the ER filed paperwork saying my mother was

a threat to herself and others, the others being me, I guess. Dad said they were going to keep her for seventy-two hours for observation, but he was going to try to get them to release her sooner. "She doesn't belong there," he said, as we drove back the next day. "Last night I heard one of the patients screaming at the top of his lungs that he was going to kill everyone. Hearing that gave me chills. I can only imagine being stuck there and having to listen to it all night. I'm sick that they wouldn't let her go, but there was nothing I could do about it." He ran his fingers through his hair. "This is such a disaster."

I didn't say anything, just kept my eyes on the road ahead. I felt my eyes well up with tears and my nose start to run and I sniffed to hold it all back. Fumbling, I reached into the glove compartment to grab the tissues we usually kept there, but there was nothing but a wad of paper napkins from a fast food place. The napkins were scratchy but I used them anyway.

"Don't worry, Nadia. We'll get it sorted out," he said kindly.

"It's all my fault," I said, my voice choked with emotion. I blew my nose and swallowed.

"It's no one's fault, honey. Things just happen sometimes. Just when you think you've got everything figured out, life throws something else at you. I've seen it happen time and time again."

We went back every day after that, today the doctor wanted to talk to Dad alone, so I was directed to the waiting room, a square area lined on three sides with faux-leather furniture and end tables that were actually shelves attached to the walls. One of the fluorescent lights flickered and I finally got up and turned off one of the light switches so only half the room was lit.

When Dad finally returned to the waiting room, he sat down next to me and didn't say a word.

"Did you get to see Mom?" I asked.

He nodded, "Briefly, but she can't come home just yet. She's taking her medication and no longer says you're possessed, but they still want to keep her because they're concerned about your safety. She can come home on Friday. They asked if there was a relative or friend you could stay with for a week or two, but I told them no, we really don't have anywhere you can go." He put his arm around my shoulder to console me, not knowing that what he said had given me an idea. I was suddenly filled with hope. He said, "It's okay, Nadia. I told them I'd assume responsibility for your safety. We'll be fine. We'll get through this."

"I could go away for a while though, if it would help Mom," I said slowly, being careful not to let my enthusiasm show. "Remember how I was chosen to go to Washington D.C. with the National High School Student Initiative?"

His nose wrinkled as he thought back. "The two men that came over that day?"

"Yes. It wouldn't cost anything. The whole trip is covered by them and it would look great on my college application. Plus, they give scholarships. Mallory went and she's there right now. You know Mallory, right? I'm sure I could still join the group. I still have the card they gave me." Despite wanting to play it cool, all the words came out in a rush. When I was through, I waited for him to say that it would be too complicated to arrange things at the last minute, or that he wanted me home to help with Mom, but he didn't say either of those things. He just looked at me with a thoughtful expression on his face.

"But isn't it half over already?"

"That's okay," I said, trying not to sound too eager. "They said a shortened visit is fine. And I'd make it in time to go to the Black Tie Bash."

"Wouldn't that be something? My baby girl at the Presidential Black Tie Bash," Dad put his arm around my shoulder. He sighed. "Seems like someone in this family should be having fun."

"So I can go?"

"That might be best for now," he said finally. "If you can arrange it, I'll sign the paperwork and do whatever else needs doing. Maybe by the time you get back, things will be better with your mom."

CHAPTER TWENTY-ONE

RUSS

I shuffled through the rest of the comic books looking for *Superheroes of the Twenty-First Century Part II,* but it wasn't there. Presumably Mr. Specter and Kevin never got around to making a sequel or it would have been included in the bunch.

When I heard a key card unlock the hotel door and Mallory and Jameson laughingly entering the room, I glanced up to see them sort of tumbling in, almost tripping over each other and their multiple shopping bags. At that moment, I'd been reading the comic book again for the third time. I was sure Kevin had deliberately given it to me so that I could prevent the outcome of the story and I wanted to have all the details committed to memory.

"Hey Russ," Mallory said enthusiastically. "Guess what?" She had a large plastic cup in one hand and she took a loud, slurpy sip from the straw.

"He'll never guess." Jameson dumped his purchases out onto the bed and they fell in a scattered heap. Clothing, packaged food, books, and an assortment of other items fell onto the bed. "Never in a million years."

"Let me tell him," Mallory said, turning to tell me the big news. "Get this—everything in PGDC is free."

"Free," I said.

"Absolutely free, as in no money. Nada. The food vendors, the clothing stores, the grocery, none of them even have cash registers. If you want something, it's completely free. They do have signs asking that you not take advantage of the system, but no one enforces it or anything."

"Huh. Interesting." I closed the comic book.

Jameson said, "I got all this stuff and I never even got my wallet out of my pocket. This place is freakin' awesome. And you missed out, old buddy. Sitting here like a lump while we were out claiming our territory."

Sitting like a lump? "While you two were out acting like you're on vacation, I was reading this." I held the comic book up. Since neither of them looked in my direction, I knew that I hadn't quite emphasized its importance. "It's a comic book from Kevin Adams. He and Mr. Specter made it when they were teenagers and it's about us."

"What do you mean it's about us?" Mallory said, putting down her drink and taking the comic book from my hands. She sat on the edge of Jameson's bed and examined the cover.

"I mean, we're in it. The characters are us and they're in Washington D.C. just like we are now."

"Mr. Specter and Kevin made this?" She flipped through the pages.

"Thirty years ago. Mr. Specter came up with the story. Kevin did the illustrations."

Jameson sat next to Mallory so they were elbow to elbow. They silently read it together. Mallory took charge turning the pages, waiting until Jameson nudged her before flipping to the next one. I watched their faces and knew exactly when Jameson had spotted Mover!'s entrance on the page because he got a big grin on his face. He'd made the connection that it was supposed to be him.

I was dying inside for them to finish it. I wanted someone else to experience it with so we could discuss it, note the similarities, and strategize. We could talk about what Sam Specter had in mind when he wrote the text, and what Kevin Adams expected us to do with the knowledge. As impatient as I was, it felt like it took them forever to finish, giving me only their facial expressions to go on. When they reached the end, they looked pleased, but neither one said a word.

"What do you think?" I asked.

Jameson gave me an amused grin. "I think that Mover! is one cool dude. The best one in the bunch, clearly."

"Okay, if you can't be serious for one minute—"

Jameson held up his hand. "Chill, Russ. I can be serious and still think Mover! is the best character in the story." He rubbed his forehead. "Pretty trippy that Specter came up with this so long ago. I wonder if he saw the future exactly like this, or if he just got glimpses and filled in the rest of the story with guesswork?"

"Does this worry either of you at all?" I stood up and took the book back. "It doesn't end well for Nadia."

"I'm wondering why Kevin gave it just to you and not to me and Jameson." Mallory sounded slightly irritated at being left out.

"Neither of you got a copy of this?" I asked.

She shrugged. "I know I didn't."

"I haven't even looked at mine yet," Jameson said, getting up to pull his carry-on out of the closet. He knelt down to unzip the side pouch. Once he'd pulled out the stack of comic books, he didn't waste any time leafing through them. "Nope, I didn't get it either. You'd think that if it was a warning, he'd have specifically mentioned it and given us each a copy."

"Okay," Mallory said, "Let's talk this through." And suddenly I was reminded of the old Mallory, the one I'd first noticed in Science class sophomore year. Pretty and smart. The one with her hand raised because she thought she knew the answer and wasn't afraid to be wrong. "Mr. Specter wrote the book. Kevin did the illustrations. Is it possible Kevin hasn't looked at it recently and didn't realize the similarities between us and the characters?"

"No." Jameson shook his head. "He has to know. What would you do if a friend died and you came across something like this, a project you worked on together? You'd read it, right? You'd pour yourself a drink and read it in memory of your friend."

"Unless it's too painful to read," Mallory suggested.

"No," Jameson shot back. "Too painful, that's a chick thing to say. A guy would read it, right Russ?"

I had to give it to him. When Jameson was right, he was really right. I said, "Kevin would have read it before he gave it to me. Without a doubt."

"So he read it," Mallory said. "Without a doubt." She

gave me an amused smile. "Did he give it to you as a warning or just for fun?"

I pulled the sticky note off the pillow. "I thought you might like it," I read.

"Fairly generic sentiment," Jameson said. "So that doesn't help. But let's assume he did want to issue a warning and to Russ only. Is that because he thinks we're inconsequential? Weak links? Or, does he think we can't be trusted?"

"I don't think Kevin is that deep of a thinker," Mallory said. "He probably just figured Russ would share it with us."

Jameson nodded, but I wasn't entirely convinced. I said, "But how did he know I would even read it? I could have gone the whole time and never even looked at it."

"He knew you would," Mallory said. "Because you're that kind of guy."

Sadly, she was right. I was the kind of guy who would read the comic book. If I'd thought about it, I would have read it on the flight over. "In the story, the commander turns out to be a woman dressed as a man," I said. "And the Nadia character dies. Mover! levitates the missile out of the way." Jameson smiled at the reference. "And there are explosions and bedlam and the villain escapes. It ends badly."

"I'd say it ends well," Jameson said. "At the end, the president and the president's daughter are safe and they figure out the identity of the leader of the Associates. All of our objectives are covered."

"I'm sure the part where they give Persuasa and Mover! awards for heroism is covered in the next book in the series," Mallory said. She and Jameson high-fived each other.

"I think you're missing the point," I said. "Ideally we

don't want to have to save anyone. Ideally there shouldn't even be an explosion. We have an opportunity to prevent all this from happening."

"You're assuming things will happen the way they do in the story," Jameson pointed out. "But they couldn't possibly. For one, Nadia never leaves her house. Secondly, the PG and the Secret Service are anticipating problems, so there's no way a missile could be smuggled into the Bash."

"And believe me, I'd never wear a green dress like that," Mallory said, shuddering at the thought of actually wearing her comic book character's gown. "It's the color of cat vomit."

"I bet you could make it work," Jameson said to her. "You'd look good in anything."

"Thanks."

"So what do we do with this?" I held the comic book up in the air, like I was a 1920s newsboy. "I'm thinking we should give it to one of the Praetorian Guard officials." I liked the idea of getting the higher ups involved. Let them tighten the rein on security. We had enough to do.

Mallory left Jameson's side and came to sit next to me. She put her hand on my neck and gave it a squeeze, then worked her fingers over the muscles. I felt my shoulders drop in relief. "This has really got you worried, I can tell."

"It should have all of us worried," I said. "If this comic book is right, we're going to a formal event that's going to turn deadly. We can't ignore something like that."

"I agree," Mallory said. "I'm meeting with one of the top PG guys tonight. He's prepping me to meet the vice president. If you want, I can give it to him and let him take it from there."

I knew she wasn't an official massage therapist, but she really had a knack for loosening up muscles. The tension melted away. "Yeah, that would be good," I said. "Make sure you say that Samuel Specter had the power to see the future and that the events in the story really might happen. Tell them they need to beef up security and be extra careful who they let in the door."

"I will."

"And tell them to call Nadia and warn her."

"Yes. Got it."

"You have to really emphasize it or they'll think it's just a kid's comic book."

"I will. I Promise."

For the tiniest, briefest moment, I doubted her, but it went by in a flash. Mallory had promised and her word was good enough for me.

CHAPTER TWENTY-TWO

RUSS

After dinner, Mallory and her chaperone Rosie left to go to a briefing about Vice President Montalbo. Presumably, the more she knew about him, the easier it would be to get her hands on him and apply her mind control magic. Mallory had changed clothes and was now wearing a sundress she'd gotten when she and Jameson went shopping that afternoon. She also had a pair of large sunglasses perched atop her head, even though we were hundreds of feet underground without a real sunbeam in sight. As they got up to go, I reminded Mallory about the comic book and she patted the side of her bag. "Don't worry about it, Russ. I've got it right here."

Jameson's chore for the evening was to take another dance lesson. Frankly, I gave him credit for trying but I thought it was pretty much hopeless. His long legs were way too spastic to ever keep in time to the music, but another lesson couldn't hurt. Maybe this new dance teacher wouldn't hit him with a fan and he'd be able to relax a little. With any luck he'd improve enough not to step on Mallory's feet the night of the Bash.

As for me and Carly, we were summoned back to the

hospital for another healing session with President Bernstein. Dr. Wentworth came to escort us and we followed along just like before. On the subway, she filled us in.

"This evening while you're out, your things are being moved from the hotel to luxury suites. You're not going to be sharing rooms anymore. It's a security measure. Each of you will have your own space from now on. We're supplying you with formal clothes for the Black Tie Bash. You'll be fitted and coached on what will be expected of you."

"Me too?" Carly asked.

"Yes, you'll be getting your own suite too." Dr. Wentworth said.

"No, I mean what about my formal wear?" Carly asked. "I didn't bring anything appropriate." She didn't own anything appropriate, is what she meant. How many people have something in their closet they could wear to a Presidential Bash? Prom clothes maybe, but Carly was way too old for prom and she never was the prom type in the first place.

"That won't be necessary for you."

"What do you mean it's not necessary? Didn't you hear me? I said I didn't bring anything I could wear to a formal event."

"Which is fine because you won't be attending the Bash."

"Wait a minute." Carly said, her voice rising. The other passengers in the subway glanced over to see who was causing a ruckus. "What do you mean I won't be attending the Bash? The deal was that I go wherever Russ goes."

"No, the deal was that you're lucky to even be here at all. You're a chaperone. Chaperoning the trip. That doesn't give you carte blanche to go anywhere you want and you're certainly not going to be attending the Bash."

Carly lowered her voice. "I was under the impression I would be going."

"Your impression was incorrect." Dr. Wentworth said. The loudspeaker announced the next stop. "That would be us." She stood up and walked briskly to the door, motioning to me and Carly to join her.

Carly wasn't going to leave it at that. "I don't think you understand. I need to be at the Bash. I can't let Russ go alone."

The doors slid open and Dr. Wentworth stepped out full speed ahead. "Come along," she said without turning around.

"Did you hear me?" Carly said, tapping her on the shoulder. "If I don't go, Russ doesn't go."

This got Dr. Wentworth's attention. She stopped, and we practically ran into her. "Now you listen to me," she said curtly. "This isn't a negotiation and it isn't personal. Not everyone is going to the Bash. I'm not going, none of the other chaperones are going. This is a Praetorian Guard mission." She leaned her head in and lowered her voice. "We're already taking a risk by involving teenagers with superpowers. We don't need overly emotional family members there to screw things up. And don't tell me you're not overly emotional." She jabbed a finger in Carly's direction. "Because clearly you are." The three of us were standing in the middle of a pedestrian path and oncoming walkers had to go around us. We were the clog in the pipe.

Carly folded her arms. "If I don't go, Russ doesn't go. And that's final."

Dr. Wentworth sighed. "Well let's put that to the test,

shall we?" She turned her attention to me. "Russ, if your sister is not allowed to go to the Bash, do you still want to go?"

"Absolutely. I'm going no matter what."

Carly glared at me, but Dr. Wentworth looked vindicated. There was no way I could have made both of them happy, so I had to choose for myself.

"Okay, then," Dr. Wentworth said. "The subject is officially closed."

Now that the subject was officially closed, Carly didn't seem to have any more to say but in one small sign of rebellion she snapped her gum every ten yards or so.

At the hospital we followed the same route as earlier in the day, walking hallway after hallway, going through multiple doors and up an elevator. The *Authorized Personnel Only* signs were everywhere and we ignored all of them since we were apparently authorized. The guard at the first set of doors nodded when they saw Dr. Wentworth's laminated card. From there she entered numbers into a punch pad in the elevator. When we exited the elevator we faced what I knew would be the last locked door. Once again, she lined her eyes up in front of a recognition scanner. When a woman's voice said, "Maxine Wentworth, welcome. Please state today's password," I knew what the password would be.

"Russ Becker," Dr. Wentworth said making each syllable clear and distinct. And then we were through.

Having been there once, everything was now familiar. I knew the corridor and could have found the president's room myself, but I let Dr. Wentworth take the lead. When we arrived at the room Dr. Karke stood alongside President Bernstein's bed but he wasn't the only one in attendance. Sitting in a chair on the other side, holding his wife's hand, was Mr. Bernstein, the first gentleman of the United States. Dr. Karke said, "Oh here they are now," as if they'd known we were on our way.

Mr. Bernstein stood up to greet us. I'd seen photos of him many times, but never looking like this. His eyes were puffy from lack of sleep and he had an overall rumpled appearance like he'd slept in his clothing. His hair too, looked like it could use a combing. And his eyes and nose were red as if he had a bad cold or had been crying. When he caught sight of me, his expression turned to one of hope. "You're the one who's going to heal my wife?" he asked, clasping my arm.

"I'm going to do my best, sir."

Dr. Karke regarded me warily. "This is Russ Becker, his sister Carly, and one of my colleagues, Dr. Wentworth. As I told you before, there are no guarantees—"

"No, no, no." Mr. Bernstein wagged a finger in his direction. "I don't want to hear it. I *refuse* to hear it. We must stay positive."

Mr. Bernstein spoke directly to me, "You, young man, what have you done?" Seeing my puzzled expression he clarified. "When you healed other people. What problems did they have?"

"What he's done before is really not relevant to this case," Dr. Karke said. "Medically this is a difficult situation and I don't want you to get your hopes up."

"Why not?" Mr. Bernstein said sharply. "All I've got right now is hope. Why would you take that away from me?"

Dr. Karke exhaled and looked down at the president's immobile body, slowly shaking his head. "I'm not taking anything away from you, sir. Just advising you to keep your expectations realistic."

"Could you please do me a favor?" Mr. Bernstein said. "Could you please take your realistic expectations and leave the room while the boy works on my wife? I don't want your negative energy anywhere near her."

The room filled with awkward silence until Dr. Wentworth said, "I'll be here to cover for you." Dr. Karke took his clipboard and left, his hard-soled shoes clicking against the linoleum as he went out the door.

"Now I will ask you again, son, what other healing have you done?"

You know how sometimes you meet someone and you like them right away? I mean like within two or three minutes? That is exactly how I felt about Mr. Bernstein. I wasn't expecting to like him because his daughter was kind of a snob, but I'm guessing that was no reflection on him. He seemed like a good guy, a man who loved his wife, and someone who knew his own mind. I said, "I've healed bullet wounds, teething pain, electrocution, skin cuts, an intestinal problem on an infant, and I once revived an elderly woman from near death after a heart attack." There might have been more, but those were the ones that came to mind.

"Really?" Mr. Bernstein said with enthusiasm. "Very good. A regular miracle worker you are." He gripped my shoulder. "And now you are going to heal my wife."

"I'm going to try my best, sir."

Dr. Wentworth said, "Russ was here earlier and said it might take a few times before we see results." I could tell she was trying to do the same thing Dr. Karke had done—let him down gently. She had a better way about it though.

Mr. Bernstein nodded. "Of course. I understand. But before you begin, may I ask a favor of all of you?" He waited until we'd all responded affirmatively and then held out both arms. "Would you join me in prayer?"

On the other side of the bed Carly reached over and took his hand, and indicated with a nod of her head that I should take the other. Dr. Wentworth looked a little uncomfortable, but must have decided to go with it. When we were all joined there were two of us on each side of the bed, our arms linked over the president's body.

Mr. Bernstein prayed for his wife's recovery, he prayed for the safety of the nation and for world peace. "And last, but certainly not least," he said, "If it's your will, please help Russ Becker to do your good work."

Mr. Bernstein's eyes were closed and it was quiet for a minute until Carly said, "Amen," more out of reflex than anything else, I think, because she hadn't been inside a church in years. Dr. Wentworth repeated, "Amen," and then we let go of each other's hands and the praying was done.

Mr. Bernstein said, "Go ahead, Russ. Do what you need to do."

CHAPTER TWENTY-THREE

NADIA

When we got home from the hospital I dug out the business card PG officials had left behind the day they'd tried to get my mother to listen to their presentation. My mom had thrown the card out, but I'd retrieved it from the trash and hidden it in my sock drawer. No one ever looks underneath the socks, at least not in my house.

The card looked official, embossed and glossy. At the top it said: National High School Student Initiative – Rewarding High School Students for Distinguished Academic Achievement. Underneath was the guy's name, "Preston Moore," along with his number and email address. The NHSSI website address was at the very bottom. I flipped over the card and read where someone had written, "We'd love to provide Nadia with the opportunities she deserves—completely funded by the NHSSI of course."

I don't think my mom had even glanced at it before she tossed it out, but I'd read it over dozens of time. Read it and wished I could go on the trip and be with Russ. And now I could.

When I ran downstairs to give the card to my dad I found him sitting quietly on the couch, the television remote in one hand like he was considering using it. I handed the card to him and he set the remote down to look. "Very good, Nadia. I'll call in the morning."

I plunked myself down on the other end of the couch. "Thanks, Dad." My mom's cat, Barry, walked into the room, let out one lonely yowl and then went into the kitchen and did the same thing, then moved on to the next room. Yowl, move, repeat. Calling for my mom.

Dad looked in the direction of the yowling, sighed heavily, rested his head in his hands and closed his eyes. "What a nightmare this has been."

"I know." I knew where he was coming from, but I wanted to say that I thought it was good my mom was getting help, that things had been going downhill for a long time and it was too much for him to keep on top of, but I sensed he wouldn't agree with me. He liked saving her, being the one to keep things steady. And he loved her too, crazy as that sounded, even to me. She wasn't always so mean and unbalanced. Sometimes she could be sweet and thoughtful. The problem was that you never knew which side of her was going to pop up until after it came out. And it could switch just as quickly.

He opened his eyes and held the card between two fingers. "You don't mind going away? I don't want you to feel like you're being banished. None of this is your fault, you know."

"No, I don't mind," I said. "You know Mallory? She'll be there."

He nodded. "Nice girl, that Mallory."

"And I have a good shot at getting a scholarship through this organization. That would be good."

"You deserve a scholarship. You work hard, always studying and learning. I am so very proud of you, Nadia. I know I don't say it often enough."

I didn't remember him ever saying it, but this didn't seem like the right time to bring that up. As I watched he rested his head in his hands again and began trembling ever so slightly. And then the trembling became shaking. I realized with horror that my father was crying. I had never seen him cry and it was unsettling because he was supposed to be the steady, strong one. If he fell apart, what would happen to me and my mom?

I slid next to him and put my arm over his back. "It'll be okay, Dad, you'll see."

He coughed. "You think so?"

"We've been on a downward slide for awhile now. Once Mom is on the right medication and she sees I can leave the house and not have anything catastrophic happen, she can relax and maybe let go a little bit. Who knows, maybe I can even go out with friends or have them over here. We could be like a normal family. Wouldn't that be something?"

Dad looked at me amazed. "Would you even want to have friends come over?"

"Well sure. Of course."

"Really?"

"Well yes, you know that."

"But your mother always told me…never mind, it doesn't matter."

"No, keep going. What did she say?"

"I was under the impression that socializing was extremely stressful for you. That you felt safer at home with all the alarms and everything. So nothing could get to you."

"Oh Dad." I rested my head on his shoulder. "Have you ever known a girl my age that wanted to hang out with her parents and the cat night after night?"

"I guess not." His voice was sad. "It's just after you were attacked on the bus, you seemed to prefer to stay home. Right?"

"That was four years ago, Dad. And since then I've been to—" I stopped to think, almost saying 'Peru' but catching myself, "Miami and coped just fine."

"Yes, you did." He set the business card on the coffee table. "First thing tomorrow we'll see if the offer still stands. If it does, you will go on this trip. That will give me time to figure out what your mother needs. You're absolutely sure you don't mind going?"

"I'm sure."

CHAPTER TWENTY-FOUR

RUSS

I leaned over the president and held my palms over her head, trying to get a reading on what was happening underneath the dark hair, pale skin, and the hard shell of her skull bone. I sensed that beneath the layers, she was more aware than the doctors gave her credit for. She'd heard her husband's prayer and drawn comfort from it, and even added a prayer of her own. Mentally she'd been able to tabulate who was in the room and where each person was located. There was nothing wrong with her brain, it just wasn't able to send signals to the rest of her body just yet.

I was hyper aware of my surroundings as well. When I heard Mr. Bernstein say to Carly, "Is there something we should be doing to help?" I sensed the slight shake of her head, as if the movement created a stir of air which then radiated out to me.

I closed my eyes and willed my energy to enter the president. I pulled the love I felt from her husband and directed it toward her, so that the damaged areas were bombarded with positive rays. Mr. Bernstein hadn't been too far off making

Dr. Karke leave the room. There was no time for negativity here.

Normally if you hold your arms out zombie-like, they eventually get tired, but when I was doing the healing work it was another thing altogether. Hard to put into words. I almost felt like I was channeling energy from somewhere else and it was just coming through me. Maybe the lux spiral was the originator and I was the connection. My arms didn't get tired because they were being held up by energy from outside of my body. The energy radiated off my hands and jumped the gap between me and the president. All of her muscles, tissue, blood vessels, and bones, were waiting to be nourished, and the places that needed it the most absorbed the energy and went to work repairing the damage. I felt a sigh coming from the president. At first I thought it was just a thought in her head, but when Mr. Bernstein gasped, I knew it had been audible.

"It's working," he said excitedly. "She's coming to."

Dr. Wentworth tried to shush him, but he wouldn't be quieted. "Hang in there, dear," Mr. Bernstein said, "we're coming for you."

It was funny he phrased it that way because that's exactly how it seemed to me too—that her essence had fallen into an abyss and needed a hand up. *We're coming for you.* Metaphorically she grabbed his words and my energy and it became the rope she needed to claw her way to the surface. It took everything she had, but with great effort, she was able to open her eyes. For a moment, I saw the room as she did. Everything bleary like she was looking through a windshield smeared with Vaseline. When she located her husband, her heart surged with joy.

Mr. Bernstein kept talking to her, holding her hand and weeping with happiness, but I didn't stop. I moved slowly over the rest of her body, pausing when I sensed there was a need, covering every single damaged inch, until finally my bucket was empty. When I was done I stood up straight and shook out my hands.

"Finished?" Dr. Wentworth asked and when she saw my answer was yes, she pressed a button above the bed. "I need the entire team in here stat."

Dr. Karke, who must have been right outside the door the entire time, came running in first. Instinctively, Carly and I moved back to make room for the doctors and nurses who rushed in. They exclaimed over the fact that President Bernstein was awake and responsive and began talking medical speak.

"BP one ten over seventy."

"Pulse is steady and normal!"

"Temperature ninety-nine degrees."

The staff surrounded her, checking her reflexes, calling out vitals, and generally just examining her like she was an unusual specimen. Her husband had been pushed back, his spot claimed by a white-jacketed woman who was placing a stethoscope on the president's chest. "Steady heartbeat!" she proclaimed, as if she was adding something of value to the dialogue.

Dr. Karke got out a small flashlight and checked the patient's pupils, then raised his pointer finger. "Madame President, can you follow the movement of my finger?" He went from side to side. "Very good."

I knew what a gargantuan effort it took just to open her

eyes. I'd felt how she'd heroically struggled to the surface when it would have been so much easier for her to stay submerged. And I instinctively knew that at this moment all this commotion was way too much for her. "Enough!" I said. "She needs to rest."

Dr. Karke turned his head and frowned at me. "Thank you for your help, Mr. Becker. We'll take it from here." Just like that, the guy totally blew me off. I stood there, with my mouth open thinking: *you've got to be kidding me.* They'd had the president for three days and there had been no change in her condition. I had two short sessions with her and she was on the road back to recovery. And he was telling me they'd take it from here?

My back had been against the wall but now I stepped forward and forced my way into the inner circle. "Stop! All of you need to stop right now!" I held my hands over the patient and got a small faint feeling of gratitude, confirming my hunch. "This is too much for her. If you keep going, you're going to slow down her progress. Her body needs quiet time and rest to repair itself."

"With all due respect, Russ," Dr. Karke said, his eyes narrowing. "I don't think—"

"Do what the boy says." Mr. Bernstein's voice thundered from behind me. A second later he'd forced his way forward and was standing next to me, his hand on my shoulder in solidarity. "My wife needs quiet. I want this circus out of here."

"Mr. Bernstein, it's important that we assess your wife—" Dr. Karke spoke hurriedly but he still didn't get to finish.

"Now," Mr. Bernstein said. "All of you. Out. I will call if you are needed."

Everyone froze looking from Dr. Karke to Mr. Bernstein

and back again, waiting to see if the doctor would counter. When he threw up his hands in defeat, they filed out of the room one by one, leaving Carly, Mr. Bernstein and myself behind.

Like most of the country, I'd always thought of Mr. Bernstein as the man behind the woman. Having a wife who was so educated, strong-minded, and accomplished, I'd sort of assumed he was a mild-mannered guy, a pushover. But I could see now how wrong that kind of thinking was. His kind of strength didn't need to be front and center, but it was definitely there, ready to be pulled out at a moment's notice.

"Much better now," he said, to no one in particular, rubbing his forehead in relief. "I can hear myself think." His gaze was on his wife who now looked like she was sleeping; he stroked her cheek with one finger. "Will she open her eyes again?"

"Yes," I said. "It took a lot of effort for her to do it the first time. She just needs time."

"You'll be back?" he asked.

"First thing tomorrow," I promised.

CHAPTER TWENTY-FIVE

RUSS

As Carly and I were leaving the room, Dr. Karke asked if he might have a word with me. "I was hoping to speak with you alone," he said, looking nervously at Carly. "If you can spare a few minutes. Please?" After being yelled at by Mr. Bernstein, he'd suddenly become super polite.

"Is there a reason I can't be part of this?" Carly said, her eyebrows raised. It cracked me up that she sounded like our mother. My opinion of Carly was changing for the better all the time. She used to seem flaky and unpredictable, changing jobs, apartments, and cell phones, but now I knew that many of her actions were precipitated by a fear of the Associates. I had been guilty of judging her based on that and the way she dressed. The jeans with the bedazzled back pockets and the long hair, both of which made her look like a teenager from behind. Even though she was Frank's mom, I never saw her as a grown-up until recently. It's like she grew up before my eyes. "Is there something you're not telling me?" she probed. "Something you want Russ to do that I wouldn't like?"

"Nothing like that," Dr. Karke assured her. "Just a few questions about the president's recovery. It's technically classified since it regards national interest. I was instructed to speak only to Russ about this matter."

She gave me a hard look, and must have decided his explanation was plausible. "Well, okay, but don't keep him too long."

Dr. Karke said, "Ten minutes or so. If you go down the hallway and to the left, you'll find a waiting area. We'll come and get you when we're done."

Carly hoisted her purse over her shoulder and headed that way, giving me one last forlorn look as she went. We weren't allowed cell phones in PGDC and didn't need money, so I had no idea why she carried that purse everywhere she went.

"Right this way, Russ," Dr. Karke said, heading in the opposite direction. "This won't take long."

We walked toward the elevator, but turned down a side hallway I hadn't noticed on the way in. The walls were lined with fake windows showing outdoor scenes. The sunshine slanted in, just like you'd see above ground. "Are these images computer generated," I said pointing, "or are they from cameras somewhere?"

He didn't pause. "CG," he said. "The sunlight coming through the windows moves in real time in order to regulate our circadian rhythm. Even though we're underground, steps have been taken to mimic a natural environment. If you spend too much time in our outdoor area, you can actually get the equivalent of a sunburn. Sometimes they'll have it set for a breezy day or it will mist or drizzle. After awhile most people forget they're underground."

"No kidding." I kept up with him step by step. "That's amazing."

He shot me a sideways glance. "No one told you this?"

"No, we just got into an elevator and went down and they were like, 'now you're in PGDC'."

"Okay, here we are," he said, opening a windowed door labeled with Dr. Wentworth's name. Inside the room, a man stood with his back to us, looking at the framed photos on the opposite wall. I sized up the room and saw standard office furniture: mahogany desk, bookcase, and filing cabinet. In one corner, a pedestal held a large luminous globe. Next to the doorway was a tan-colored leather couch, with a bedroom pillow on one end, making me think Dr. Wentworth occasionally slept here.

The man turned around when we walked in and I had an immediate flash of recognition. The last time I'd met this guy he'd been wearing a white lab jacket embroidered with his name, "Dr. David Hofstetter." He'd lost the lab jacket somewhere along the way, and now wore a dress shirt and suit coat, but otherwise he looked the same—dark hair, thin nose, and deep-set eyes. I imagined my nephew Frank would look a lot like him when he grew up.

"David?" I said in disbelief.

His smile was wide. "Russ!" He came over and pulled me into a bear hug. "Good to see you again. I hear you've been doing your magic on the president."

"Trying my best."

"Atta boy! I told them you could do it. Didn't I, Karke?"

Dr. Karke, who'd been standing quietly next to the door said, "Yes, you assuredly did."

David said, "Thanks for bringing Russ here. I won't keep

him for very long. If you want to come back in ten minutes or so, that should work out fine."

It was amazing to me how people around here said things without coming right out and saying them. *You can get lost now* is what David really meant, but he managed to tangle it up in all kinds of nice words so it came off well.

"Very well," Dr. Karke said, slipping out into the hallway. David reached over and shut the door. I could see through the glass that Karke was walking away from the room, but he was taking his sweet time about it.

"No one told me you would be here," I said. The last time I'd seen him we were in South America. "You told me there was a big mission coming up, but I didn't think I'd be meeting the president."

"Of course we didn't know about the coma until it happened," he said leaning against the desk. "But the rest of it is still the same. The Associates are moving in and getting closer. If they manage to overthrow this president and install their man, it will be end times for all of us, Russ. A dictatorship. And those who don't go along with what they want will be wiped out. Have they explained that to you?"

"I know all that."

He pinched the bridge of his nose and blinked. "Sorry. Of course you were briefed. I didn't mean to be patronizing."

"It's okay. Don't worry about it."

He said, "I wanted to see you before the Bash, so you won't be surprised to see me there."

"You're going to be at the Bash?"

"Yes, in a professional capacity," he said. "One more person to help keep the first family safe. My powers aren't what they used to be, but I can still do a pretty good blast if I have to. You want to see?" I nodded and he pointed to the globe in the corner. At first nothing happened but eventually I saw a thin stream of electricity shoot from the end of his finger to the globe. The impact made the globe spin around, first in slow circles, then faster and faster. A high-pitched thrum filled the room until the moment he stopped.

"Pretty good," I said approvingly.

"I know it's nothing compared to what you can do. Hell, it's nothing compared to what I used to be able to do." He shrugged. "You lose power as you get older, you know."

"I know. I heard."

"Still, if I was standing close enough, that amount of electricity could down a man, or at least bring him to his knees. And that's what you'd need in an emergency. Anyway."

I sat down on the couch so I was looking up at him. He'd stopped, but it seemed like one of those momentary pauses that didn't require a reply, so I waited.

"The real reason I wanted to see you is that I wanted to know about Carly and Frank." The statement just hung there. He'd suddenly become nervous, resting his backside against the desk, which caused Dr. Wentworth's pencil cup to knock over. Pens and pencils spilled out, several of them rolling off the desk and onto the carpet. Embarrassed, he leaned over and scooped them up.

"Carly and Frank are okay," I said. I wasn't going to give him too much. Don't get me wrong. I liked David Hofstetter a lot. The guy had saved my life in Peru, and he seemed to be honest and have good intentions and all that. But I wasn't okay with how he'd broken my sister's heart by faking his own death, reappearing a few years later under the guise of being his own cousin, impregnating Carly and then not being around for Frank's childhood. Add that to the fact that he'd been spying on them for years because he wanted to see them (which seriously freaked Carly out every time she came across a bug or camera planted in her car or apartment), and there was no way we were going to be really friendly.

"Just okay?" He turned back to face me.

"Okay and doing fine."

"You didn't tell Carly you met me?"

"What do you think? You're the one monitoring her apartment. Did you notice anything different?" Yeah, I knew I sounded like an ass, but it was because I was offended. I'd told him I wouldn't tell and I didn't tell. I didn't say a word to my sister, even though I wasn't sure it was the right thing to do and it killed me to keep the truth from her. And now he doubted me?

"I stopped having her apartment bugged after you told me how much it upset her. Listening to them used to be the high point of my day. It feels empty not to have that anymore. It's been killing me not to be part of their life."

He sounded sincere, so how could he be so clueless? Unbelievable. I swallowed to keep my anger in check. I needed to stay level to make my point. "David, I hate to tell you this, but you never *were* part of their life. Watching and listening to them is not even close. You're like the guy who watches TV and feels like he's friends with the characters on the show. You feel like you know them, but it's all one way. They don't know you. You're nothing to them." I'd been picking up speed as I went. I knew I'd gone too far with that last sentence when he flinched like I hit him.

"Ouch." He squinted and looked away from me, having acquired a sudden interest in arranging the pencils in a jar.

I don't have any trouble saying I'm sorry when I really am, but I wasn't going to say it this time. What I'd said was cruel, maybe, but it was true. Sitting at a monitor watching your son grow up is no substitute for being there. I'd been the one Frank had asked, "Why doesn't my dad love me?" Try explaining that one to a ten-year-old kid. I knew his pain, and I knew Carly's pain too. No way was David Hofstetter getting off the hook.

"Okay," he said finally. "So I screwed up. I can't go back in time, Russ. There is no rewind. What would you suggest I do?"

"Man up right now," I said pointing. "Carly is just down the hall. Go talk to her, tell her everything."

David looked down at his feet. "She will hate me."

"Yeah, you're right. I guess it's better that she thinks you're dead."

"You're young, Russ. You think things can be fixed, that I can go have a heart-to-heart talk with Carly and that she'll be mad at first, but then later she'll forgive me. Then I'll move back to Edgewood and get a job and slide into Frank's life and become the dad he deserves to have. He'll buy me a gift for Father's Day and Carly and I will get married. We'll come up with an excuse for my absence to tell other people. We'll say I survived the car accident but I had amnesia or something. People will think it sounds fishy at first, but over time they'll accept it. And then maybe Carly and I will have another child, maybe a girl this time. Carly can quit her job and stay home, or go back to school and follow her bliss.

And everyone will be happy and everything will be fine." His mouth turned upward, but his eyes weren't smiling.

"Yeah, that could happen," I said. "Why not?"

"Because life doesn't happen that way, Russ. Sometimes it's just too late. Too many years and the wounds are just too deep."

"Still. You could try."

"And I will. But not today."

"If not today, then when?" I asked.

"I need to get through this week first. After the Bash I promise I'll talk to Carly."

"Are you sure you won't chicken out?"

"No, I'll do it."

"If you don't, I will." I couldn't keep lying to my sister. My conscience was killing me, and besides, as Carly had pointed out, I was a terrible liar.

CHAPTER TWENTY-SIX

RUSS

When Carly and I were finished at the hospital, we were escorted to a different building and shown our new luxury suites. Some mysterious person, or maybe a crew of people, had transported all our stuff from the hotel to our new suites, and it was already set up like we'd been staying there for ages. My toothbrush stood at attention in a cup in the bathroom, and my clothes, which now looked pressed, hung in the closet and were arranged a lot more neatly than if I had done it. Each suite was like an apartment with homey touches like fresh flowers on every flat surface, and food and assorted beverages in the fridge. It felt a little creepy, actually, like I'd crashed someone's house and they might come back any minute.

My luxury suite was conveniently located down the hall from Jameson and Mallory's, while Carly and the other chaperones were on the other end of the building. When Carly asked about it, Dr. Wentworth said, "We need to establish some space between now and the Bash. These young people will be involved in a potentially dangerous situation and

I don't want their heads cluttered up with worrying about other people's expectations."

Carly had a lot to say on that subject, but she knew enough not to argue. I did hear her muttering to Rosie and Dr. Anton about it as they headed down the hall to check out what Rosie called, "their new digs."

I'd just started looking around when I heard a loud thumping on my door, accompanied by the sound of a girl's voice. I opened it to find Jameson and Mallory out in the hallway. Jameson pushed past me and came right in with Mallory on his heels.

Right away I asked the question that had been nagging me. "Did you give the comic book to the Praetorian Guard guy?"

"Of course," Mallory said. "I told you I'd take care of it, didn't I? Have I ever let you down before?"

"Did you emphasize how important it was and tell him about how Mr. Specter could see the future?"

"All that and more, so you don't have to give it another thought."

"And they said they'd amp up security so none of that would happen?"

"Yes, they'll amp up security so none of that will happen." Mallory patted my arm and walked past me, stopping in the center of the room. "Can you believe this place?" She raised her arms above her head and gracefully did an impromptu pirouette. When we'd had our dance lessons with Prima Donna she'd mentioned she'd had ballet lessons as a little girl. I could see her in a tutu at age ten, front and center at a recital. "We're like celebrities."

"I won't lie," Jameson said, giving me a jab. "I'm not going to miss sharing a room with you, Russ. Your snoring made me crazy."

I knew I didn't snore because if I did, my nephew would have mentioned it ages ago. Frank had been sleeping over since he was a little kid and I can't tell you how many times he'd come into my room to wake me up during thunderstorms or after a bad dream. And believe me, Frank Shrapnel Becker was not a kid to hold back from saying something just to be nice. No. I didn't snore, or I definitely would have heard about it. Before I got a chance to say as much though, Mallory crossed the room and opened the doors of a large wardrobe. "Did you check out your formal clothes for the Bash? I have four different dresses to pick from, while all your suits look about the same," Mallory said, stepping back to reveal several tuxedos and white shirts hanging within. "You guys are going to look like James Bond."

Jameson said, "I'll be Jameson Bond, his good-looking nephew. Russ can be my manservant." He snapped his fingers and switched to a British accent. "Russell, I need you to lay out my clothing. And then, mix me a martini, shaken not stirred."

I peered into the wardrobe and rifled through the hanging suits. "Wow. I didn't even know that stuff was in there," I said. "We just got back from the hospital."

"How's that going?" Mallory asked, as if just remembering. "Is President Bernstein healed now?"

Even Jameson seemed interested in hearing how the president was doing, so I gave them the lowdown, telling them first about the annoying doctor and my meeting with David Hofstetter afterward.

"David's going to be at the Bash?" Jameson said. "Doing what?" His tone implied that we had things covered at the Bash and wouldn't need any extra help.

"He'll be doing the same thing we are—protecting the president and Layla."

"Assuming the president is well enough to go," Jameson said.

"She'll be there," I said, with far more confidence than I felt. "Believe me, she's almost there now." For someone who wasn't that great at lying, I managed to really bring it when goaded by Jameson. I sincerely hoped the president would make it to the Bash, for a lot of reasons, but especially because if she wasn't recovered by then, I'd never hear the end of it from Jameson.

Mallory plunked herself back on my couch, slipped off her sandals, and put her feet up on the coffee table. "So you're not going to tell your sister that David is here?"

"He said he'd come clean after the Bash. I said if he didn't tell her then, I would." I sat down next to her and put my feet up as well. It didn't seem like the kind of table you were supposed to put your feet on, but then again, we were in a secret city below our nation's capital. The rules on what was allowed were getting a little fuzzy.

"So how's he going to protect the president?" Jameson said.

"His superpower is that he can shoot electricity," I said.

"Like you?" Mallory asked.

"Almost. His powers have faded a lot, but he can still give someone a good jolt if he has to."

Jameson said, "But can he do this?" He tilted his head

in our direction and a second later, the coffee table, the very one our feet rested on, began to rise, forcing our legs up to an uncomfortable angle.

"Stop it, Jameson," Mallory said in a flirty girl way. "Put it down!" Her laughter contradicted her words and fueled him to keep going. In some ways he was such a kid.

"Put it down," I said, jumping up off the couch. I pressed down on the coffee table with both hands but I couldn't move it, no matter how hard I pushed. "Now."

"Not going to do it. Can't make me."

"I'm not in the mood, Jameson. Just put it down."

"Yeah, I don't take orders from you." He made the coffee table shimmy back and forth, which really made Mallory laugh.

He had pushed my patience to its limits, apparently not caring that this was my room. A guy should be able to pull rank in his own space. "That's enough," I said. "We get it. Just put it down."

"Make. Me." He became an orchestra conductor, his hands directing the coffee table to tilt and spin.

"Last chance, Jameson. Knock. It. Off." I raised my voice, making the message clear.

"Uh unh," he said with a shake of his head. The coffee table was halfway to the ceiling now.

I blasted a lightning bolt over his head, and it hit the far wall with a sizzle. The electricity briefly made contact with the top of Jameson's head and the smell of burnt hair filled the room. The coffee table dropped to the floor with a clatter.

"Becker, you moron!" Jameson shouted. He put a hand up to his head. "You could have killed me!"

"I didn't even come close to killing you." It was true that for a split second I'd wanted to kill him, but admirably, I'd held back. "I warned you to stop."

"Do you know how hot that was?" he said. "And my hair is scorched, thanks to you. How are we going to explain that?"

Mallory got up to look at the top of his head and he bent over obligingly to make it easier for her to look. "Your hair is burnt off all right," she said, running her fingers through it. "Yuck. Smells terrible."

"Is my scalp burned?" he asked. "I feel like it's burned. I bet it's red and blistering."

"Your scalp looks just a little pink," she said. "But you're definitely going to need a haircut before the Bash. A nice military cut would get rid of all the burned ends."

"Great. Just great." Jameson's mood turned sullen. "Now I'm going to look like a freak at the Bash."

"No one cares how you look. They don't care how any of us look," I pointed out. "They only care about what we can do." To make my point I held out my hands and began juggling with a ball of sparks. I tossed it from hand to hand so quickly that it blurred like the lights on an amusement park ride at night.

"Nice, Russ," Mallory said, marveling at the light show. "You could headline in Vegas."

I let the ball fizzle out and bowed dramatically toward Mallory, who applauded loudly. I said, "Thank you. Thank you very much." My best Elvis impression. I even curled my lip.

Jameson let out an exasperated sigh. "Good boy, Russ. I

can see you're very proud of yourself, so good for you. But guess what? I have a few surprises up my sleeve too." He gestured with a flick of his finger. "Mallory, go sit on the couch."

"Let's not do this again," I protested, but my words were ignored.

Mallory went to sit on the couch, her legs tucked underneath. "This okay?" she asked, smoothing her hair.

"Come on, Jameson. That's enough." I shouldn't have blasted him, I saw that now. Instead of stopping him, he'd turned it into a competition.

"Don't worry about it, Russ. It's nothing bad. You're going to like this." Jameson turned his attention back to Mallory. "Ready?"

Mallory leaned back like a magician's assistant, ready for the next trick. "I'm ready."

"Watch this," Jameson said, holding his palms up and wiggling his fingers. "Couchicus, Upicus!" I couldn't look at both of them at once, so my eyes had been on Jameson, the one most likely to do something crazy. When I glanced back to the couch, it was already hovering a few inches off the floor. Mallory's mouth dropped open in delight. The couch with Mallory on it had to weigh a few hundred pounds. I'd never seen Jameson move anything anywhere near that size.

"How are you doing this?" I asked.

Jameson's eyes narrowed as he concentrated on the couch. It inched upward until Mallory's head was almost to the ceiling. She pressed her hand against its surface and Jameson dropped the couch in response. It became a game. He'd raise her up, she'd push against the ceiling and it would go down, and the whole thing would repeat. Mallory said, "Don't drop me, Jameson!"

"I would never drop you, Miss Mallory," he said, bringing the couch gently to the floor. "Your safety is my only concern." Somehow he'd acquired a Southern accent.

"Thank you kindly, sir," Mallory said, playing along. She leaped off the couch like a kid jumping off a swing. "I'm much obliged."

He bowed low. "My pleasure, truly."

I said, "No, seriously, how long have you been able to do this?"

Mallory threw her arms around Jameson's neck. "Isn't he good? He's been practicing on the sly. He moved a refrigerator back home."

Jameson's mouth spread into a toothy, satisfied smile. He said to Mallory, "I think I finally impressed our friend Russ. And you know that's not easy to do."

CHAPTER TWENTY-SEVEN

—••●•—

NADIA

I went to my room, shut the door, and lowered the blinds before settling back onto my bed. My mind buzzed with everything that had happened lately: my mom in the hospital and my dad giving me permission to go to Washington D.C. to join the others. I didn't want to be happy about my mother's breakdown, but I was a little. She would get the medical attention she needed and I would be released from being confined to my house. My prison door would be swinging wide open very soon. Now all I needed was permission from the Praetorian Guard to meet up with the rest of the group. I didn't even want to think about the possibility that they'd say no. That would really suck to be able to go but have it be too late. I put it out of my mind, settled back on my pillow to get comfortable, but not to sleep. I was way too hyped up to do that and I needed to talk to Russ.

I let myself sink into the bed and willed myself to enter the zone. The world faded away and I let out a sigh of relief when I felt it working. Not being able to do it before had made me doubt I would ever be able to do it again, but now that I was feeling more relaxed it had to work. It just had to. I thought the words: *Take me to Russ Becker.*

I soared through the air, across land and time. Minutes and miles meant nothing. The way I traveled couldn't be measured in increments. I wasn't grounded anymore. I was an angel, a ghost, a thought, a wisp of air. And the sensation? Indescribable freedom.

When I started my descent deep into the earth, I wasn't worried like I'd been the first time it happened. Underneath was where Russ was, so it's where I wanted to be. Once I got to the city beneath the city, my spirit flew like Peter Pan and the Lost Boys, but this wasn't Never Never Land and I wasn't lost.

Russ's room was dark but I could make out his form under the covers. He wasn't in the same place he was the night before. This space looked bigger and he was alone. Better, I thought, not to have anyone else around. No Jameson in sight. I moved closer and his face came into view. His beautiful face. I could look at him all night and for the rest of my life. Unaware of my staring eyes he slept, quietly and deeply. I watched intently as he exhaled in and out. Peaceful breathing, I thought. At one point he smiled and rubbed his hand over his nose like he had an itch.

My ethereal form nestled up against him, waiting for him to sense my presence, but minutes went by and that didn't happen. Instead he slept the sleep of the truly exhausted. Working on the president must have worn him out.

Russ. My thought waves nudged at him. *Russ, can you hear me?*

He sighed audibly and sounded pleased. I had to think that on some level, he knew I was there. I let my mind meld with his. *Russ, it's me—Nadia. I'm here with you now. Can you hear me?* I couldn't break into his thoughts, but I tapped into his emotional essence and grabbed hold of three things floating around his consciousness. He felt good about what was happening here in PGDC. He knew he was capable of performing what needed to be done on this mission. And he missed me.

I pulled back and looked at the outline of his face in the dim light of the room. If I'd actually been there I would have traced his profile with my finger, starting at the top of his forehead and ending at his strong jaw-line. In Peru, a woman named Elena had said he looked like a young John F. Kennedy. I hadn't really seen it then, but I saw it now. Not a dead-on resemblance, but a little bit the same. Like JFK, Russ had the air of someone who would someday be very important. The potential for greatness was obvious. *Russ,* I said. *My mother is in the hospital and my dad is letting me come join you.* Russ didn't show any signs of having heard me. Man, he was out of it.

In the end I decided to let him sleep. Soon enough he'd know I was coming, or maybe when he woke up my words would linger, like something he'd heard in a dream.

I wasn't quite ready to go home just yet. I wandered from room to room looking at the ornate framed pictures and the vases of flowers everywhere. Fancy. More like something a woman would like than a guy. The furniture was fussy and stiff. Nothing you'd flop down on after a hard day's work, that's for sure. The oversized bathroom had a shower and a separate, deep tub. A lot of room for just one person. This place was more like a suite or an apartment than a hotel room. Eventually I got bored of checking it out and I went back to Russ's bedside. *Good-bye Russ.* I said. *I love you. I'm leaving now but I'll be back later.*

I saw his lips move. I didn't hear a sound, but I felt the words as they came out. *I love you, Nadia.*

When I left his side I intended to go home, but at the last minute, I had a sudden thought. *Mallory.* Back home Mallory had said my astral projecting to her had creeped her out, but since she now was in a strange place on a stressful mission, it would be different, I thought. Who wouldn't want to hear from a friend in a difficult time? Just to stay on the safe side, I decided not to reveal myself until I was sure she was up to having a visitor. If she wasn't alone or was showering or whatever, I could just slip away and she'd never know the difference.

Take me to Mallory, I thought. Like smoke drifting through an open window, I slipped into Mallory's suite. The place was dark except for a light shining through a slightly open door. Doors, slightly open or otherwise, never held me back. I slipped into the room and saw Mallory sitting on the floor of the bathroom in front of the toilet. The room was dimly illuminated by the light above the shower. I saw she was only wearing a camisole top and matching underwear, both lacy and dark pink in color. It was a very personal scene and I almost drew back, the equivalent of saying, 'oops, sorry!' but I stopped when I noticed what she was doing. Mallory had some kind of pamphlet or notebook in her hand and she was burning the pages one by one. She'd tear off a page, hold it over the toilet, light it with a match, and then let it drop into the water when it was nearly consumed by the flame.

She hummed as she did this little ritual. The song was nothing I knew and I didn't recognize the look in her eyes either. Mallory was most definitely not herself. She didn't look tired or scared or angry. Her gaze was vacant, but focused. She'd tear off a page slowly and carefully, set it on fire, then drop it into the water with a flourish. I moved forward and saw that the pages were from a comic book, but it wasn't one I knew. Once I was closer I could see it wasn't a traditional comic book. It looked homemade, the kind small presses put out by indie artists. Alternative comics, I thought they were called. Mallory hummed and ripped and set pages on fire and dropped them into the toilet and flushed. She did this over and over again, sitting on the tile floor of a bathroom wearing only her pink underwear. I had no idea what to make of this.

When she was done, she brushed the soot off her front and gave the toilet one final flush, watching in fascination as it swirled downward. Before leaving the room, she washed her hands and stopped to check her face in the mirror. When she brushed her hair and smiled in a satisfied way, she looked like her old self again, my friend, the one who had befriended me at the homeschooler's social during the time I had no friends at all. I sighed with relief. Mallory wasn't possessed after all. There had to be a plausible explanation.

I thought I'd wait until she got dressed or into pajamas or whatever and come into view then. Maybe she'd explain about the burning pages, or maybe not. I'd let her bring it up. I went into the bedroom area and waited for her to come.

Before long, she came strolling out of the bathroom, right through me and into the arms of a man who stood in the shadows. I felt a jolt of shock, my own personal horror show moment.

"I did it," she announced, resting her palms on his chest.

"Good girl." His voice was a purr of approval. I tried to see his face, but it was hidden in the dark. It wasn't Jameson, I knew that much. This voice was older and deeper. Familiar too, but I couldn't place it.

Mallory said, "Every page destroyed."

"You've passed the test of perfect obedience," he said. "And you know what you need to do next? At the Bash?"

"I know what I must do," she said.

"And you'll do it?" His hands slid over her shoulders and from the light coming from the bathroom I saw hairy knuckles and a gold watch.

"Yes, I'll do it."

"Don't let us down, Mallory, we're depending on you."

"You can depend on me, Commander."

I did a double take. Commander? I realized, with a start, that I only knew of one commander, and that was the head of the Associates. But that couldn't be right. Why would she be half naked and hanging out with the enemy?

"Good," the commander said. "Now go get the necklace you were given at the airport."

Mallory walked out of the room in slow, measured steps and headed toward the bedroom. Again I strained to see the man's face, but he hadn't moved an inch and was still hidden in the dark. I followed Mallory into the bedroom and watched as she turned on the bedside lamp before going to unzip a compartment in her suitcase. By the time she looked up, a necklace dangling off her fingertips, I'd decided to confront her.

Hello Mallory. I was right in front of her, but I purposely didn't become visible. She could hear me, but she couldn't see me.

I thought she'd jump out of her skin, but she didn't. Her eyes were dull, her voice nonchalant. "I can't talk right now Nadia," she muttered, very quietly. She gestured to the other room with a nod of her head. "I'm doing important work right now. Come back later."

Mallory, what is going on? She ignored me and kept going. Her deliberate, slow pace reminded me of the way sleep walkers moved in movies. And that's when it hit me. Mallory had been brainwashed. Someone in the Associates had used mind control on a girl who had incredible mind control powers herself. And as a trusted member of the Praetorian Guard, she could work against the rest of us, giving the other side secrets and using her powers for their side while pretending to be on ours.

Still hiding my presence, I followed her back into the other room. I saw now that it was a sitting area almost exactly like the one in Russ's suite. "Here it is," Mallory said, handing over the necklace, a white rose dangling on a chain.

The commander did something to the rose and I heard a click. "When you press on this side and hold it," he said, "a tiny needle pops out. Like this, see." Mallory leaned over and watched as he repeated the motion. He asked, "Do you understand?"

"Yes," she said robotically.

"And you know what you need to do with it?"

"Yes."

"Just one quick prick, that's all it takes." He turned the necklace around. "When you press on the opposite side a different needle comes out. That is the antidote. You won't need that. It's for emergency purposes only. Understand?"

"Yes."

"After you use the first needle the way we talked about, you'll need to distance yourself from the necklace. Put it in another lady's bag or leave it under a napkin or whatever. Just get rid of it."

"But Mrs. Whitehouse gave it to me." Mallory's confusion came to the surface. "She said I could keep it always."

"I know, I know," he said, like soothing a small child. "But we'll get you another one. A much better necklace than this one. I'll even let you pick it out. Any necklace you want. Would you like that?"

She smiled. "Yes, I'd like that."

"Now let's go over the plan one more time. You know how to use the needle in the necklace?"

"Yes."

Don't listen to him, Mallory! I sent a message right to her, but she showed no sign of hearing me.

"Wait until you see the Specteron," he said proudly. "I'm unveiling it that night. Some say it was impossible, but I've managed to improve on Tesla's design. The particle beam is most impressive. If you want to live, you'll manage to get behind it. Those in front of it will be getting a not-so-nice surprise. Do you understand?"

"I'll need to get behind it if I want to live."

Oh Mallory, how can you be part of this?

"Have you gotten control of Jameson?"

"Yes, I think so."

No! Jameson is your friend. Do not involve him.

"Good girl!" the man said. "And what about Russ?"

Oh, not Russ. Leave Russ alone, Mallory...

"I keep trying but my mind control doesn't work on him. It's like he's got a shield over his brain," Mallory said.

"Keep trying. Use your feminine wiles, do a lap dance, just do whatever you need to do to get him up next to you."

"I'll try. But..."

"But what?" he asked, his voice stern.

"I don't think it will work. He won't let me get too close because he loves Nadia."

I held my breath thinking that next she'd tell him that she'd just seen me a minute ago, astral projecting to her in the other room. But either she forgot or else her loyalty to me as a friend had survived the brain washing, because she didn't say anything else.

"Teenage boys are notoriously fickle. Nadia's not here. You are. Make it work. Do you understand?"

"Yes, I understand," she said. "I will make it work."

"I'm going to leave now. You need to go to bed and when you wake up you'll forget I was here. You will, however, remember all your instructions and you will carry them out to the letter. Do you understand?"

"Yes, Commander."

"And Mallory?"

"Yes."

"Don't answer the door in your underwear ever again. If it had been anyone but me you could have encountered big trouble." He leaned out of the shadow then and I got a full view of his face: the high forehead, receding hairline, and glasses. Behind the dark rimmed glasses and beard and mustache, his facial features had a familiar look. I puzzled over this for a split second until he took another step and his button-down shirt and sweater-vest came into view.

The commander was Mr. Specter.

"One last thing, Mallory," he said, pushing his glasses up his nose.

"Yes?"

"I need to know Russ Becker's room number."

"Two-oh-eight," she mumbled.

"That was last night, at the hotel." Mr. Specter sighed and rubbed his forehead like he had a headache. "You've moved remember?" And then quietly, almost to himself. "Probably to shake our trail."

"We moved from the hotel to the luxury suites," Mallory said, her voice lifeless and flat. "I put the ribbon on my doorknob like I was supposed to."

"Yes, that's right. But I need to know where Russ's room is because I have to speak to him." He reached down and patted his pants pocket where I saw, to my horror, the bulge of what looked like a gun.

Mallory's mouth twitched. "I don't remember the number, but he's two doors down from here."

"On the same side of the hallway?"

"Yes."

"Not the next room, but the one after that?"

"Yes."

"In which direction, dear?"

When Mallory hesitated he said, "Remember that wonderful session we had in Peru trying out my Deleo?"

"I remember," Mallory said, nodding.

"It was such a pleasant feeling having the Deleo rays wiggling into your head sending soothing messages to your brain. Remember the beautiful feeling?"

"Oh yes, I remember." Mallory's chin lifted heavenward. She closed her eyes and the expression on her face said she was recalling something wonderful.

"What is the number one thing you were told to do?" he pressed.

"Always do whatever Mr. Specter tells me to do," she said.

"Now I'll ask you one more time. What direction is Russ's room?"

Mallory's arm rose in one swift movement pointing to the left. I almost showed myself then and confronted Mr. Specter, but stopped when I realized I'd be as threatening as a dust mote. There was nothing I could do to stop him, but I wasn't going to wait for him to hurt Russ either. "That's my girl!" he said patronizingly, but I was out of the room before he said another word.

Take me to Russ Becker. I was like the wind only better, because the wind couldn't go through walls. In a second I was next to Russ's bed, and once again I tried to wake him up. *Russ! Russ! Russ! Please, open your eyes. Mr. Specter is on his way to your room with a gun.* I pleaded. He didn't move, not even a muscle. Again, what I wouldn't have given to have a real body in the room with him at that moment. So frustrating not to be able to reach him.

Panic swelled inside of me. Astral projecting, I could travel hundreds of miles in seconds and move invisibly through walls. I was as big as the world and as small as a microbe. I heard conversations without being detected and could get past locked doors. But I couldn't stop a man with a gun.

I wished myself into the hallway. Once there, I needed a half a second to get accustomed to the sudden brightness. When I'd adjusted, I realized I'd landed about ten feet behind Mr. Specter who now stood in front of Russ's door. From behind I watched as he patted the pocket that held the gun.

I struggled to make myself visible to the world. It was easy to do when I was with Russ, but I found it harder to achieve when alone and terror-stricken. I pushed to burst out of my shell of anonymity until I finally felt my shape develop like a Polaroid picture. As I forced myself into view, I noticed Mr. Specter swiping a plastic card key in the slot above Russ's door knob. Instinctively I screamed out *No!!* and surged toward him. At that moment I heard a ding and saw a man in a waiter's uniform pushing a cart through open elevator doors and down the hall. Room service for someone. The linen covered cart held domed plate covers, a bottle of wine chilling in an ice bucket, and one red rose in a silver bud vase.

The man pushing the cart didn't notice me or Mr. Specter at first. His head was down as if he were determined to get to his destination. But something made him glance up. Maybe he'd heard my "No," ringing in his head, or maybe he caught a glimpse of Mr. Specter standing in the hallway. It really doesn't matter. What matters is that he looked up and saw as I rushed at Mr. Specter. I knew he'd spotted me when his face went from confusion to horror. "Dear God, what is that?" the waiter screamed, picking up one of the covers off the cart and throwing it at me.

It didn't hit me, of course. I was still at home in my bed with my eyes closed, fingers laced together on top of the covers. Mr. Specter, however, was very much there and the cover came right at him. "Get out of here," the waiter yelled, clearly terrified.

The metal cover bounced off Mr. Specter's front but before it even landed on the floor, he turned and ran down the hall. The speed with which he took off made me think he didn't want to be identified.

Mr. Specter had taken a physical hit, but I was shaken to my metaphysical core. The waiter looked at me like I was something vile, monstrous. It was worse than my mother thinking I was possessed by the devil—this man thought I *was* the devil. I tried to hold on, I even thought: *Take me to Russ*, but it was no use. I felt myself fading from sight and being pulled back, back, back to Wisconsin, then Edgewood, and finally under the covers of my very own bed.

CHAPTER TWENTY-EIGHT

RUSS

I woke to a sharp rapping noise. Minutes before, in a dream, it had been the sound of a woodpecker, but as I woke up I realized it was someone knocking on the door to my suite. I struggled out of bed and flung the door open, so sure it was Jameson that the words 'get lost' had already taken shape in my mouth, so I was a little taken aback to see Dr. Wentworth there. "Dr. Wentworth." I rubbed my eyes. "I wasn't expecting you."

"Obviously," she said, giving me the once over.

Self-consciously I ran my fingers through my hair. "What time is it?" I looked down at my bare feet, glad to see I had pulled on a T-shirt and pajama pants before going to bed.

"Five-thirty. You need to get dressed and come with me right away. The president has asked to see you!" Her eyes shone and her mouth stretched into a wide smile. I'd never seen her look so enthused.

"Really?"

"Yes. She's made enormous improvements during the night. The medical team is very pleased with her progress."

"Let me jump in the shower..."

"We don't have time for that. Get dressed. We need to go immediately."

I can't tell you how much it goes against my way of doing things not to shower right away in the morning. At home there'd have to be a fire to get me to skip it, but since Dr. Wentworth followed me into the suite and plunked herself down in the sitting area, I didn't have much choice. I ran my hand under the faucet and managed to wet down my hair (which always stuck up funny in the morning), brush my teeth, and throw on some clothes. We were out the door in five minutes.

When I got out to the hallway, I almost walked into a man standing guard by my door. He wasn't wearing a uniform, but something about him said military to me. It might have been the close-cropped hair, flak jacket, and the semi-automatic weapon held at his side. "Hi," I said. He just nodded.

As we made our way down the hall, I asked Dr. Wentworth, "What's up with that?"

"We had a slight security breach the other night," she said. "Nothing to worry about, but we're covering our bases."

"A slight security breach?" That didn't sound good.

"You didn't hear anything in the hallway last night?" she asked.

"No." I drew in a sharp breath. Something happened while I was sleeping?

"A minor disruption. We're not entirely sure what happened. Probably just someone goofing around," she said, sounding bored. "Come along. We don't want to keep the president waiting."

I was starting to know the route, so this time around I kept pace with Dr. Wentworth rather than letting her take the lead. If I'd had her laminated pass and her retinas (for the scanner), I could have made my way to the hospital room by myself.

When we got to the hospital room President Bernstein was sitting up in bed, a tray positioned in front of her. Her husband stood at her side, holding a cup with a straw to her mouth. "That's enough," I heard her say, and he pulled it away. Her voice made me smile; it was strong and familiar, exactly the voice of the Commander-in-Chief I'd heard giving presidential speeches. When Mr. Bernstein caught sight of us, he waved us over. "This is the young man I was telling you about," he said to his wife. "Russ Becker, the miracle maker from Wisconsin."

I strode over to the bed to shake President Bernstein's outstretched hand. She clasped it gently while I said, "I'm very pleased to meet you." Next to me, Dr. Wentworth beamed up at me like a proud mother.

"The honor is all mine," she said. "I am very grateful you agreed to travel here for my benefit."

"Of course," I said.

"And for the benefit of the country," Dr. Wentworth added.

On the other side of the room Dr. Karke was talking quietly to one of the nurses. He'd given me a nod when we walked in, but it was a safe bet I wasn't getting any thanks from him. The president called out, "Doctor? Would you mind if I had a few moments in private with Russ?"

Dr. Karke raised his eyebrows, but he said, "Of course that would be fine." The nurse took the cue and left first, followed by Dr. Karke. When the president raised her eyebrows at Dr. Wentworth she took off too, although she walked slowly as if hoping it was a mistake and she'd be called back. No one did call her back though. As she went through the doorway her head turned and I caught one last lingering look.

"Now that we got rid of them," President Bernstein said, holding my hand in hers, "I can say what's really on my mind." She squeezed my fingers as if afraid I might bolt out of the room. "I don't know what it's like for you to heal someone, but I can tell you how it feels being on the receiving end." Her eyes twinkled. "I couldn't move and I couldn't talk, but I could feel the warmth coming off of your hands and it felt like just what I needed. Even more than that, I could feel the energy and love radiating out of you and pouring into me. It was remarkable."

I didn't want to get too full of myself, but I'd be lying if I didn't say I felt a surge of pride just then. I mean, how many people get to pull the president of the United States back from the brink of death? "I'm glad to be able to help," I said. "It was my honor."

Mr. Bernstein spoke up. "You should know that you will be the first recipient of the Civilian Medal of Honor for acts of valor above and beyond the call of duty."

The Medal of Honor? When he said the words, I felt my ribcage seize hold of my heart. The Medal of Honor was a big, big deal—too big for me. I thought about the men and women who gave their lives during battle or performed heroic acts at great cost and suddenly I felt insignificant. I'd done something important, but not because I was brave or willing to sacrifice my life but just because it was the right thing to do. Under the same circumstances anyone would have done it. "That's not really necessary," I said sheepishly. "I'm not in the same category as the other Medal of Honor recipients. It wouldn't be right."

"Now I don't want to hear any of that," Mr. Bernstein said. "You are worthy, believe me. Interestingly enough, the hallmark of a true hero is denying that they've done anything heroic. You're clearly in that category."

"But the Medal of Honor? I don't know about that…"

"It's the Civilian Medal of Honor," Mr. Bernstein said, holding up one finger. "An important distinction."

The president briskly said, "It's not up for discussion, Russ. The decision has been made."

"Well, if you insist. Thank you."

"We insist," Mr. Bernstein said.

"Of course, we can't literally award you a medal," she said. "And for security reasons, there won't be a ceremony. This is more or less an understanding between us."

"So I can't take it home with me?" The mental image I'd had of posting it on Facebook instantly vanished.

"Well no. Because you won't actually be getting a medal. And you can't tell anyone about it. Officially, it will be like it never happened."

Seeing my disappointed look, Mr. Bernstein said, "But you'll know what you did, and so will we. That's another hallmark of a true hero. They don't do it for the glory."

President Bernstein said, "If I could change the topic?"

"Of course." Her husband and I said the words at the same time. Even sitting in bed wearing a hospital gown, she had an air of authority.

"I understand, Russ, that you will be escorting our daughter to the Presidential Black Tie Bash?"

"Yes ma'am."

"I have been briefed about the threat, and as a mother, I'm very worried, but as the leader of the country, I know the importance of not letting the enemy see our vulnerability. We will not let the Associates see us cower in fear. The Presidential Bash will go on as scheduled. I know I can rely on you and your friends to protect Layla."

"Absolutely," I said. "You can count on us."

Mr. Bernstein said, "My daughter can be a firecracker, Russ. She's been given special treatment for far too long and it's gone to her head. Don't let her intimidate you."

"I won't, sir."

He rubbed his chin thoughtfully. "I have to warn you that she can be rather bossy. Pushy, at times. It's not really her fault. It's a family trait." He grinned at his wife who smiled back.

"Yes sir." Clearly the night of the Bash would be full of challenges. I thought about my last encounter with Layla and found myself blushing. To get my mind off the thought of her knee working its way up to my crotch I said, "As long as I'm here, I'd like to do another healing session, if I could."

"Of course," President Bernstein said.

"It would help me if you would lie flat," I said, instructing the president. "And then close your eyes and stay completely still." As it turned out, Layla Bernstein wasn't the only one capable of being bossy.

This time around when I had finished, I sensed that the healing energy had completely saturated every inch of her being. I rubbed my hands together and wiggled my fingers. I said, "I'm finished." President Bernstein opened her eyes and I knew she had completely recovered. Her color was good, her eyes sparkled, and energy pulsated off of her body. Such a difference from a few days ago. "Aren't you getting kind of tired of lying in that bed?" I asked.

"Funny you should mention it," she said, sitting up. "I was just thinking that I've been away from the office for far too long." The president swung her legs over the side of the bed, holding her hand out for her husband's assistance. "If you'll excuse me, Russ, I think I need to get dressed and get back to work."

"Of course." I nodded.

"Thank you, again," Mr. Bernstein said. "I am very grateful." Tears came to his eyes.

"No problem," I said. "Glad to help."

"We'll see you at the Bash," the president said.

"Okay, see you then." We said our good-byes and I left pretty quickly after that. Seeing me come out the door, Dr. Karke, who lurked in the hallway, rushed back in. As I made my way to the elevator, I heard him say, "President Bernstein, you shouldn't be out of bed—"

And the president's voice thundered, "Karke, get out!"

When I heard Karke's footsteps scrabbling out the door, I had to smile. The president was back.

CHAPTER TWENTY-NINE

NADIA

I listened in the next room as Dad called the PG official and explained that I could go on the Washington D.C. trip after all. He didn't go into details about his change of mind, for which I was thankful. My mother's attack was on record with both the police department and the hospital, so it wasn't a secret, but I didn't think announcing it to the world was the way to go. When I heard Dad say, "Okay, wait a second while I grab a pen," I knew for sure things were going my way.

After he hung up, I stuck my head in the doorway. "Well?"

"They still want you." He grinned. "They gave me a number to call in about half an hour to find out the flight arrangements. You'll leave this afternoon."

Hearing those words, my heart nearly burst with happiness. I know that sounds dramatic, but it was true. Over and over all I could think was that I'd get to see Russ. I wasn't going to be left out. I was going to be part of this mission. Meeting the president and going to the Bash? That was frosting on the cupcake as far as I was concerned. I didn't care what the mission was, I just wanted to be there because it meant being part of something big with Russ at my side. It could have been a mission reviewing dinner at Denny's for all I cared. The important thing was that I'd be there when it happened.

My suitcase and carry-on were packed by the time Dad made the second call. He was relieved to find out they'd be sending a car for me because his mind was really with Mom at the hospital and taking me to the airport was one less thing to worry about.

When a black limo pulled up in front of our house right after lunchtime, I turned to Dad and said, "I guess this is it." One of our neighbors, the very nosy Mr. Johnson who had nothing better to do since he retired, came out on his porch to stare. Limousines weren't a common sight in our neighborhood. Mr. Johnson held his hand over his forehead to get a shaded view.

Dad helped me carry my bags out. "I'm going to miss you, Nadia." He patted my shoulder and sighed. "But this is for the best, I think. When you get home things will be better."

"I think so too."

The limo driver got out and shook Dad's hand, then wordlessly loaded my things into the back. "Take good care of my daughter," Dad said.

"Yes sir," came the muffled reply from the back of the vehicle.

"Thanks for letting me go on the trip, Dad," I said.

He held me by the shoulders before giving me a fierce hug. "They said I won't be able to call you once you're in D.C. so you'll be on your own kiddo, but know that I'll be thinking about you. Your mom and I are really proud of you and we love you," he said, his voice overcome with emotion. "I will miss you."

"I know. I'll miss you too. Tell Mom I love her." It was easy to be generous with words of love when I was getting what I wanted, but there was more to it than that. Since my mom had been hospitalized I realized that I really did love her. All this time I'd resented her and saw her as the enemy, when it suddenly clicked that the part of her I hated wasn't really her at all. The harsh words, the mean decisions—all of that came from the disease of her mind. Her paranoia and fear were holding me prisoner. Underneath it all was still the mother I remembered from when I was a little girl, the one who read me picture books, sang me to sleep, and took me to the park. Our relationship for the last several years was so horrendous I'd almost forgotten that things had once been different. Maybe in the future it could be different too.

After I waved good-bye to my father and we'd pulled away from the curb, I left the problems of home behind me. Being in a limo would normally have been exciting, but the experience didn't fully resonate because my thoughts were already in Washington D.C. with Russ. At home I didn't wear the spiral ring he'd given me, because my parents would question it, but now I felt comfortable taking it out of my bag and slipping it onto my finger. I tilted my hand underneath the sunlight coming through the limo window, and smiled at the way the gem stone glistened. Russ's words about the spirals echoed in my memory: *symbolizing our interlocking lives and our never-ending love.* Our interlocking lives and never-ending love. I couldn't wait to see him again.

The plan was that I would be flying from Milwaukee to

a second airport, and from there taking a connecting flight. Once I'd landed in D.C., I'd be escorted by a PG official, but in the meantime, I was on my own. My Dad had said that they'd apologized for the flight arrangements. Ideally they'd have given me a nonstop flight, but since it was so last minute this was the best they could do. I didn't care. As long as I made it in time for the Bash, that was the important thing.

The first flight was uneventful. It wasn't until I got to the second airport that things fell apart. Once I disembarked, I pulled out my boarding pass to see the time difference between flights. Two hours. Plenty of time to find my gate, and once I was there I could grab something to eat. The next flight would be shorter. And then I'd be on my way to Russ.

That was the plan anyway.

When I got off the plane, I found an open seat where I could watch the monitor above the desk to be sure my D.C. flight was still listed as being on time. And it was on time, right until it wasn't.

"Attention passengers of Flight 1709," a woman's voice said over the loudspeaker. I looked up to see a perky young woman talking into a microphone behind the counter. "Due to extreme weather conditions, all flights have been cancelled. Your luggage can be picked up on carousel four."

All around me other passengers grumbled and muttered profanities. I think I had my mouth open for about three minutes because I was totally in shock. Weather conditions? How could that be? All of us collectively wondered what in the world she was talking about. The view through the floor-to-ceiling windows told us it was gorgeous outside. Sunny with a light breeze. At home the weather had been the same and I'd heard birds chirping while I got a whiff of my neighbor's freshly mown grass. It was the kind of day where flowers smiled while woodland animals helped a Disney princess dress for the ball. It was definitely not the kind of day where a flight would be cancelled because of extreme weather conditions. Please. Around me people gathered up their things and began to line up at the counter to find out their options. All of us had somewhere we wanted to be and it wasn't here.

As the line inched forward people relayed information to the others in line saying that the reason for the cancellation had nothing to do with the weather where we were, and everything to do with the weather in the flight path. Dangerous wind currents or some crap like that. If it made us feel any better, we were told that all of the flights in the airport, not just ours, had been cancelled. It didn't make me feel any better.

When I got within earshot of the desk, I heard each person making a case for getting on the next possible flight. One man was going to his brother's wedding, another guy would be seeing his girlfriend for the first time in months, and an elderly woman was taking her little granddaughter to see a doctor, a specialist. The little girl, cute as a button, but obviously thin and sick, with a scarf over her head, had a rare form of cancer. "The doctor fit us in," the grandmother wailed, wiping away tears with a tissue. "He usually has a three month wait for an appointment, but he worked us into his schedule because her case is so serious. We can't miss our appointment." The airline representatives (now there were two behind the desk) tapped on their keyboards, looking for options. For the grandmother I think they made a special exception because I saw the employee lean over the counter and whisper something the rest of us couldn't hear.

I had a bad feeling that my excuse—a student trip to D.C.—wasn't going to cut it. Bit by bit the line moved forward. Each person dragged their bags or moved them ahead with a shove of their foot. I had my backpack slung over my shoulder. I held it there until my muscles ached and I was forced to put it on the floor.

When it was my turn at the counter, the woman didn't even look up. Her head was tipped down so far her chin seemed to be pinning down the jaunty red scarf looped around her neck. "Flight 1709?"

"Yes," I said, putting my boarding pass on the ledge. "I need to get on the next available flight. It's really important."

She still didn't meet my gaze, but her eyes crinkled in amusement. I had the feeling that this wasn't the first time she'd heard that. She tapped at the keyboard, "The next available flight is on Sunday at two o'clock."

"Sunday at two o'clock?" I couldn't keep the shock out of my voice. "No way."

She looked up. "That's two o'clock in the afternoon. You're arrival time will be 3:57."

"No, you don't understand," I said putting both hands flat on the counter and leaning forward. "I can't fly on Sunday. I have to be in Washington D.C. as soon as possible."

"Believe me, I do understand," she said gently. "All of these people have to be there as soon as possible." She gestured to the line behind me, which snaked back as far as I could see. "But you have to understand that we only have so many flights. We're working to get everyone to their destinations as soon as possible. If you want, I can refund your money and you can make other arrangements." Her frustration and weariness rolled off her in waves. I knew she was having a bad day, but I didn't care. I wasn't having such a great time myself.

"I don't want a refund. I want a flight out of here." Why did other people get what they wanted while I had to struggle for everything? I wanted to cry but I wasn't going to. For years I'd been Nadia the one who never protested, the girl who just went along with what other people wanted, but today I was pulling out a reserve of strength I didn't even know I had. Love could do that to a person. "I understand that you have to accommodate everyone but you seem to be able to make exceptions. How come you found a way for that little girl and her grandmother to get to Washington D.C. today?"

She looked up now and I saw that the red scarf around her neck was knotted in the front. She leaned forward and whispered. "Yes, we made an exception for that woman, but it was a matter of life and death." Her eyebrows narrowed in irritation. "A child's life."

"Well I'm legally a child, and my getting to Washington D.C. is a matter of life and death too," I said. "So I need for you to make an exception for me too."

CHAPTER THIRTY

RUSS

The Praetorian Guard decided that I needed to get together one on one with Layla Bernstein one more time and since she had a gap in her schedule this morning and I was already up, Dr. Wentworth said I could go right from the hospital to the White House. "Carly's going to wonder what happened to me," I said.

"Don't worry about Carly." Dr. Wentworth guided me down the hallway with her hand against my back. "I'll fill her in later this morning."

She said it so nonchalantly it was clear she was clueless about how angry Carly would be when she discovered they'd taken me somewhere without her. I wouldn't want to be Dr. Wentworth during that conversation. At my house, Carly's wrath was legend.

"I'm not sure why I have to get together with Layla again," I said. "I mean, we've already talked and she thinks we met in Miami."

"The Guard feels it's important to cement your relationship."

"There's really no relationship," I told Dr. Wentworth, as we approached the elevators that would take me topside. "I'm just her date for the evening of the Bash. We did dance lessons back home, so that's covered, and I know how to make small talk. I really don't get why we're doing this."

"So you're saying you don't want to do it?"

"Well, of course I'll do it," I said. "I just don't think it's completely necessary."

"I know, Russ, and I agree," she said. "But it's really not up to me. If it makes you feel any better, we all have to do things we don't want to do for the benefit of the greater good."

"It's not that I don't want to get together with Layla," I said. "I just don't think it's the best use of my time." I was tired too, something I hated to admit. I'd just come from doing a healing session at the hospital and it had worn me out. Not that it wasn't worth it to save the president, but it did come at a personal cost.

"I think you can spare a few hours," she said dryly, pressing the button for the elevator. "You know, a lot of guys your age wouldn't find spending time with Layla to be such a hardship."

"It's not a hardship. It's just…"

"What?" The elevator doors opened; she held it with one hand.

"The last time we got together she was really pushy."

"What do you mean? How so?"

I was starting to regret even mentioning this. "I mean physically pushy."

"She pushed you? Like an attack?"

"No, the opposite." How to put this? "She was encroaching on my private space."

"Like making moves on you?" Dr. Wentworth's eyebrows raised in amusement.

I nodded. "I think I'm going to have to tell her I have a girlfriend."

Dr. Wentworth barked out a laugh and patted my arm. "Oh Russ, you've totally made my day."

She was still chuckling as the elevator doors closed and I dreaded the thought that she'd be sharing this story with the rest of the staff. I wished I'd had the chance to explain that it wasn't that I couldn't handle Layla's advances. I could. It's just that I didn't need her stuck barnacle-like to my front while I was trying to scope out a banquet hall looking for Associates. Not only that, but I wasn't attracted to her that way, although I had a feeling that under certain circumstances my body might respond as if I were attracted to her that way, which could be really embarrassing.

I tried thinking about things that were not sex all the way to the White House and even while waiting in the same sitting room that Mallory, Jameson, and I had been in the last time I'd been there. I sat opposite the oil painting of the gray-haired woman in a bonnet, the one who'd stared down disapprovingly at Jameson. She didn't look like someone who'd ever had sex or took much pleasure in anything, for that matter. Yes, as long as I had the image of that old woman in my mind I'd be in complete control.

When Layla walked in, I was ready to fight off her advances, but I shouldn't have worried, because from the look on her face, she wasn't interested in romance. Barely through the door, she skipped a traditional greeting and said, "We need to talk."

I stood up. "Okay, what about?"

"Not here." She beckoned with one finger and turned around.

I obediently followed. "Are you planning on telling me where we're going?" I asked. She was a tall girl who took long strides, and I was right on her heels. She moved at such a fast clip that the purse hanging off her shoulder swung as she walked.

"Breakfast." She shot this word over her shoulder and kept going.

We went into an empty dining room with yellow walls, a blue and yellow rug, and a large chandelier. Layla said, "This is the Family Dining Room," and kept going. She pushed through a swinging door and I followed her into a long narrow work area comprised of white walls, cabinets, fluorescent lights, and chrome counters. I felt the electricity in the walls powering industrial sized refrigerators and other appliances. There was a lot of power in this room, and not the presidential kind. Two women dressed in white shirts stopped talking as we walked in. One was folding napkins, the other putting away a rack of glasses. "Good morning, Miss Layla," they said in unison.

"Good morning," she said. "My friend and I are going to be eating here for the next hour or so and we'd like some privacy please." She pointed to a chrome counter fronted by three red vinyl covered stools. The same style as those in Rosie's Diner back in Edgewood.

"We'll be out of here in a second," the woman said, and

true to her word, they finished up what they were doing and left almost immediately.

As if on cue, an elevator door opened on the other side and a man in a bow tie, white shirt, black jacket and trousers, came out and placed a tray of food on the counter in front of us. "Good morning." He nodded to each of us, then raised the covers of the plates revealing omelets and fresh fruit. Besides the food, he'd also brought each of us a cup of coffee with cream and sugar, and a glass of orange juice. The coffee smell was strong, like walking into Starbucks in the morning. "Can I get you anything else, Miss?" he asked cheerily.

"No, this will do fine," she said, depositing her purse on the counter next to her plate. "Thanks."

When we were completely alone, Layla said, "You're probably wondering why we aren't eating in the dining room." She spooned some sugar into her coffee and stirred before looking up to meet my eyes.

"Well no, this is rather…" I looked at the open garbage can next to me. On the top of the heap were coffee grounds and orange peels. A nearby counter held an open notebook with a list like someone had been taking inventory of the contents of the refrigerator. "…cozy?"

She laughed. "Nice try. This is the Butler's Pantry. I wanted to go someplace where we wouldn't be overheard. This is as good as it gets. We probably have about an hour before they'll need this space."

"Okay." I took a sip of my orange juice. "You were saying we needed to talk."

"Yes we do, Russ Becker. You've got some explaining to do."

I tried to read her face. Clearly she wasn't happy with me which was a huge change. The last time I'd seen her she'd looked at me like she'd been waiting her whole life for a caramel sundae and I was a perfect caramel sundae. "Okay. What do you want to know?" Despite my curiosity I was suddenly really hungry. I dug into the omelet, watching as she pulled a book out of her purse.

"Do you know what this is?" she said, showing me a leather bound volume secured by a lock.

"A diary?" I guessed.

"Fourth graders keep diaries," she said. "This, young man, is a journal. *My* journal." She set it on the counter and put a possessive hand over the cover. "I carry it with me at all times and it's always locked. It's hack proof, virus proof, and can never be accidentally deleted or forwarded. Old school security. I've been keeping it for ages. My grandmother gave it to me. She thought it would be a good idea to document my years in the White House."

"Nice," I said.

"When she first gave it to me, I thought I'd never use it," Layla said. "I was like 'thanks, Gram,' and then I stuck it in a drawer. It was there for months. I almost tossed it out, but one day it occurred to me that maybe old Gram was on to something. I mean, maybe someday I'd want to write a memoir or something and it would be good to have a written record to jog my memory. But of course, once you write something down, there's always the thought that someone else might get hold of it and read it, and God forbid, maybe publish it, so that's when I decided I'd always carry it with me. I also came up with abbreviations and codes that only I know, so now all of my entries are written in secret code."

Layla spun the dial on the lock back and forth until it clicked open. Removing the lock, she opened the journal and showed me a page. "To most people this looks like the ramblings of a crazy meth addict."

I took a look and nodded. First of all, her handwriting was terrible, worse than my sister's even. And once you got past the messy writing, there was more trouble because the text appeared to be a mixture of letters and numbers sprinkled in between actual words. I couldn't make sense of it. I doubted it was as secure as she thought, but it wasn't something that could be solved quickly either.

"Good idea, using code," I said, spearing a melon ball. This breakfast was really hitting the spot.

"One interesting little bonus is that sometimes I catch people in lies." She closed the journal. "Or worse." Her tone turned icy. "Sometimes they try to turn *me* into a lie. And that's something I won't stand for."

I stopped mid-chew. The food in my mouth sat like paste on my tongue as I realized where this was going. She searched my face for a reaction. Trying not to give anything away, I quickly looked down at my plate, but it was too late. She knew I knew something. I swallowed the food and the lump in my throat at the same time. "Really," I said.

"Yes, really." Her expression softened just a bit. "Okay, Russ, I'm giving you a chance here to be straight with me. Would you like to explain why I suddenly remember three people I've never met before and why I'm haunted by thoughts I'm in love with you when we barely know each other?"

"You're haunted by thoughts that you're in love with me?" Despite my best efforts, the corners of my mouth tugged upward.

"Yeah, that's what I said." She tucked a piece of hair behind her ear and gave me a thin lipped smile. "But I know it's not real love. It feels like when I was eleven and I used to obsess about some actor in a movie. An immature crush based on nothing."

"Oh." Suddenly the omelet lost its appeal. I set my fork down. "You don't remember meeting us in Miami?"

"No, I actually have very distinct memories of meeting you in Miami, and yet, I know that it never happened. I know that because—" She opened the journal and flipped through the pages until she found the right spot and began to read. "I wrote this: Delphine has scheduled me to meet with three high school kids she says I met in Miami. Not true. I don't think I've ever seen them before and I know I've never met Russ Becker." She looked up at me.

"Who's Delphine?" I asked, buying time.

"She handles the schedule." She narrowed her eyes. "Nice try changing the subject." When I didn't say anything she continued. "I checked all three of you out on Facebook ahead of time. Mallory and Jameson had a vaguely familiar look. I meet a lot of people and sometimes they all blur together in my mind." She waved her hand for emphasis. "But you? You have a look I wouldn't have forgotten. I knew instantly that I'd never laid eyes on you before."

I scrambled for an explanation. "I don't update my Facebook page all that much. My profile picture is old."

"Nice try." She continued, "I also know I'm not in love with you because I'm involved in a relationship with someone else, a secret, scorching hot love affair, which is why having you constantly in my thoughts is really annoying. I think something happened to me once we were all up in my bedroom. Something that affected my brain and inserted memories I didn't have before."

"What do you think happened?" I asked cautiously. The door from the dining room swung open, but I didn't turn to look. Someone started coming in, spotted us, and backed out again.

"I believe I was brainwashed, but I'm a little unclear on how it was done," Layla said, taking another sip of her coffee. "I know I wasn't drugged because we all had the iced tea. The same thing with the air. Anything I could have breathed in would have affected everybody in the room. I think it's more likely there was some kind of hypnosis, but I think I would have remembered something like that." She leaned toward me and spoke quietly but firmly. "I feel like I'm going insane. I need you to tell me the truth here, Russ. Can you do that? Are you man enough to come clean?"

I wished she'd stop staring at me—it was making me feel guilty. "I can't tell you everything," I said reluctantly. "But I can tell you that you're not going insane."

"That's a start. Keep going."

I shook my head. "I can't say anymore than that. It's a national security issue."

"National security requires that I lust after you?"

I felt the familiar flush of my face turning bright red. "Well, no."

"So then it's not a national security issue." She folded her arms. "You can't have it both ways, Russ. It's either a matter of national security or it's not."

I leaned in. "Can you keep a secret?"

"Please." She exhaled audibly. "All I do is keep secrets."

"Mallory, Jameson and I are attending the Bash as added protection for you and your mother. They thought it would seem more natural for us to be there if you'd met us before. Like inviting friends to come."

"Who is this *they*?" She put the words in finger quotes.

"I can't say."

"Why would my mother and I need added protection when we have the Secret Service?"

I shook my head. "That I can't tell you."

"Well then, why would they choose high school kids from Wisconsin to protect us? Seems kind of lame. No offense."

"None taken." I thought for a second. "Let's just say we have some specific talents that not too many people have."

"Specific talents?" She raised one eyebrow.

"Yes."

"Like martial arts training?"

"No. I mean, yeah, something like that, only different." Every time I opened my mouth I dug myself in deeper.

Layla tapped her fingers on the counter for a minute, deep in thought. When realization dawned, her mouth stretched into a wide smile. "Aha! Now it all makes sense," she said, snapping her fingers and jabbing a finger toward my chin. "You're one of them."

Now I was the one with a question. "One of what?"

"One of those kids, those meteorite kids." Her eyes gleamed. "I've been hearing about you for years. When my mother was with the NSA I used to listen at doors. Sometimes I'd pretend to fall asleep on her couch in the office. You wouldn't believe what I heard." She tilted her head to one side and smiled. "Or come to think of it, maybe you would."

"I have no idea what you're talking about," I said. "I think we should just forget this whole conversation. We'll have a nice time at the Bash and that will be the end of it. Hopefully your boyfriend won't find out and beat the snot out of me."

"I don't have a boyfriend," she said.

"You mentioned a secret relationship?" I tried to think of the phrase she used. "Scorching hot?" I prompted.

"All true. But it's not a *boy*friend."

"Oh."

She laughed. "Don't look so surprised, Wisconsin."

"I'm not." I rearranged my expression to convey a look of nonchalance. "I mean, it's cool."

Layla put her hand up to my cheek and leaned in. "Our next order of business," she said, and paused. To me the pause seemed deliberate.

"Yes?" I said.

"Will be to undo the brainwashing before I go insane." She sat back and started to tick off on her fingers. "I need to get you and your incredible body out of my head. I also need—,"

I felt my cheeks flush crimson. "My incredible body?"

She leaned toward me and whispered. "That's one of the thoughts I keep having. Over and over again I find myself thinking, 'I bet he has an incredible body. I'd love to see him with his clothes off. I want to run my hands over his incredible body.' Trust me, between that and knowing we hadn't met before, I knew something wasn't right."

I looked away, embarrassed. "I can't believe Mallory did that. I'm sorry."

"So it *was* Mallory who did it," Layla said with a satisfied expression. "I thought as much. One of the other thoughts I keep having is that I trust her implicitly. Without question. 'Blind obedience to Mallory' is the phrase that keeps popping into my head. I need to get that erased too."

"Blind obedience to Mallory?" I said. "Are you serious?"

"Absolutely."

I shook my head, confused. "Why would she do that?" If Mallory thought that was funny, it wasn't.

"I don't know." She held her palms up. "Why do people do what they do? I just need you to fix it. Can you do that for me?"

I wanted to help, but I sure wasn't positive I could make it work. "I can try."

"Or do you need Mallory to reverse the curse?"

I pushed my stool back and stood up next to Layla. "Let's see what I can do."

It was true I couldn't touch what Mallory could do in the mind control department, but still, I thought I could help Layla. I got up and stood behind her, placing a hand on each of her shoulders. She relaxed at my touch, and I concentrated on transmitting energy.

Unlike Mallory, I needed to speak aloud. I leaned in, purposely keeping my voice low so only Layla would hear me. "Layla Bernstein, you are not in love with me, Russ Becker. You no longer feel any attraction to me. You will not have obsessive thoughts about me." I hesitated, letting it sink in. "You feel no blind obedience to Mallory. You have free will and will use your own judgment. These troubling obsessive thoughts are gone now. You no longer have the memories of meeting us in Miami. You know that you just met us for the first time the other day." Layla's head dropped forward. I wasn't sure if she'd relaxed fully on purpose or if this proved my words had sunk in. Just to be safe, I slowly repeated everything again. When I felt like I was depleted, I shook out my hands, and said, "Okay, that's the best I can do."

Layla lifted her head, turned to me, and blinked. "You're done?"

"Yes, that's all I've got. How do you feel? Did it work?"

"I no longer have the urge to grab your crotch, so that's an improvement."

What does a person say to that? "Well that's good."

Her forehead scrunched as she thought. "The feelings I had for you are gone, I think. I remember having memories of meeting you in Miami, but now they don't feel real. It seems more like a movie I saw a long time ago or something I heard about once. I'm pretty sure that what you did worked."

"Pretty sure?"

"Let's test it, shall we?" She stood up and pushed her stool aside, and then grabbed my face with both hands. Before I could even process what she was doing, her mouth was pressed hard against mine. Layla Bernstein was gorgeous and her lips were warm and soft, but all I could think of was how much better it was to kiss Nadia. When she pulled back, her mouth made a sort of smacking noise.

"So?" I said. "What do you think?

Layla wiped her mouth with the back of her hand. "Nope," she said. "I've got nothing. My feelings for you are officially gone."

We shared a smile. "Good," I said. "If you wouldn't mention this to Mallory, I'd appreciate it." The fact that Mallory had implanted the words 'blind obedience to Mallory' confused me. That hadn't been part of the training.

Layla shrugged. "I wasn't planning on talking much to Mallory. After what happened, I don't want her anywhere near me."

I didn't stay too much longer after that. Right after we finished our meal, the staff needed the space to prepare lunch and so we slipped out to talk in a sitting area for a bit. After about half an hour, Layla's personal assistant came to remind her that she had to leave shortly to speak at a fundraiser for a children's charity. "Russ, this is Chloe. Chloe, Russ," she said, introducing me to her assistant. Chloe was slim and tall like Layla, with cocoa brown skin and hair pulled back into a French braid. If she hadn't been wearing office attire— navy pants and a white button-down shirt with a clunky gold necklace—she could have passed for a college freshman. "Russ is my date for the Bash tomorrow night." The two of them exchanged an amused glance and burst out laughing.

"Something funny?" I asked.

"Not at all," Layla said, grinning.

But I got a hint of something I couldn't put my finger on. Later on, when I was back at the hotel resting before our final briefing, I figured it out. The something I couldn't put my finger on was a silent vibration between Chloe and Layla, something, I guessed, that was scorching hot. I wondered if I was right, but I wasn't going to ask.

CHAPTER THIRTY-ONE

NADIA

The woman behind the airline counter said, "Legally a child? How old are you?"

"Sixteen."

"And you're by yourself?"

I nodded.

"Okay, that changes things," she said, tapping into her keyboard. She must not have liked what she saw because she picked up the phone and the next thing I heard was her saying, "I've got an unaccompanied minor here. She needs to be on the next flight to IAD." She listened and frowned. "Okay," she said. "Yes, will do." She gave me a small smile. "Today's your lucky day. We're working to get you situated. My supervisor is checking with other airlines. Please take a seat and I'll call your name when I hear what's been arranged."

Interesting that when I said it was a matter of life and death no one even blinked, but the fact that I was a minor got some attention. "Thank you," I said, gathering up my boarding pass.

"Can you call your parents and whoever is picking you up at Dulles?" she asked. "Or do we have to do that?"

"No, I've got it, thanks."

"Great! We're kind of shorthanded." She smiled apologetically.

To get to the seating area I had to walk along the queue of passengers. All of these people were tired and worried and not able to go where they wanted to go. I was getting better at shutting out the emotions of people around me, but right now it was overwhelming. Feelings of frustration, sadness, and worry poured off of them. They were all screwed and they knew it.

I settled back in my seat and watched for a good long while. As unhappy as people looked while they were in line, they were even more unhappy when they were done talking to the airline officials. Each one trudged away from the counter, pulled out their cell phones and gave someone on the other end the bad news. No one was getting what they wanted. I watched for an hour or so, and despite the bright lights and the nonstop sounds of people talking, I found it hard to keep my eyes open. Finally I gave in to it, closing my eyes, letting myself drift and thinking: *Take me to Russ.*

Just like that I felt my spirit leave the bustle of the airport terminal and I traveled through time and space, all of it going by like I'd fast forwarded over the boring parts. Before I knew it, I was standing behind Russ, but he wasn't alone so I didn't show myself. I seemed to be in a very bright narrow space filled with metal counters and serving dishes—a restaurant kitchen maybe? Russ stood in front of Layla Bernstein, who was sitting at a counter with two half-eaten plates of food in front of her.

I wished he were alone so I could tell him I was on my way, that Mallory had gone over to the dark side, and that Mr. Specter was still alive and had a sinister plan for the Bash. Instead, all I could do was wait and hope that Layla would have to go to the bathroom or have some other reason to leave the room. I listened, trying to figure out what was going on.

"Pretty sure?" Russ said to Layla in a flirtatious way.

"Let's test it, shall we?" She stood up and pushed her stool aside, and then grabbed his face with both hands and kissed him, wrapping her arms around his neck to hold him close. Layla was the same height as Russ, and (I feel sick saying this) absolutely beautiful. Her black hair gleamed like in a shampoo commercial, her skin lacked visible pores, and worst of all her mouth was on top of my boyfriend's and he wasn't pulling away. My heart stopped and then it broke into a thousand pieces. Heartbroken. A real word and a real thing. How could Russ do this to me? He'd given me a ring and said he loved me and I'd thought his word was his promise. I thought he felt the same way about me as I felt about him, but I never would have betrayed him like this. Watching them kiss was excruciatingly painful, but I couldn't make myself look away.

When they finally pulled apart, she took a second to look into his eyes, connecting with him the way I always did. "So?" he said. "What do you think?"

I strained to hear her answer, when with a violent shake, I was yanked out of the scene and back into my own body. A nanosecond later I was in my seat at the airport, my head spinning from the suddenness of it.

"Nadia?" I opened my eyes to see the woman from the

airline counter standing above me, her hand squeezing my shoulder. "Nadia? Honey, are you okay?"

"Yes?" I rubbed my eyes. Even under normal circumstances being jolted out of an astral projection felt a little like waking up in the back seat of the car after sleeping through a road trip. Add that to the shock of seeing the love of my life kissing another girl and I wasn't in a good place emotionally. I tried to pull it together. I mean, maybe there was a good reason for that kiss? Honestly though, I couldn't even imagine what that would be. "I mean, yeah, I'm fine."

She chuckled, a bit indulgently. "You had me worried for a minute. I've never seen anyone who was so out of it sitting upright like that."

"No, I'm okay." My eyes began to fill with tears and I wiped them away. "Just dozed off for a second."

"Well I have some news for you," she said. "It's not the best news, but it's not the worst either. We got you on a flight for tomorrow afternoon." She held up a hand and spoke hurriedly, like she was expecting me to protest. "It was the absolute best we could do, and believe me, they tried everything."

"Is there a train or a bus? Some other way I can get to D.C.?" I looked around and saw that the crowd had thinned, but there were still a fair number of people in line, while others hunched over laptops and tablets, trying to make other arrangements to get to their final destination.

"I'm sorry, but no." She shook her head and I saw that her once jaunty scarf looked a little droopy. "I have a voucher for you to stay at the airport hotel and then all you need to do is come back tomorrow. This is not normal procedure for an unaccompanied minor, but we're short staffed and—"

"I'll be fine," I said. "You don't have to worry about me."

"That's what I told my supervisor," she said. "I told her that you seem very capable. Now remember, your bags will be on carousel four. And the hotel is right here inside the airport, on the far end. Follow the signs."

"Carousel four. Airport hotel. I've got it." I took the voucher and new boarding pass from her hand. "Thanks."

"There's a number on there," she said, pointing to the folder holding the pass. "Any problems, day or night, just call."

"Okay."

"And you did call your parents? And the person who's picking you up?" She asked, craning her neck to see the desk.

"I've taken care of everything," I said. "Don't worry about that."

"Good girl!" she said, flouncing away. "Good luck to you and safe travels!"

CHAPTER THIRTY-TWO

RUSS

After Layla gave me a good-bye hug, I wandered out through the Family Dining Room. Before I could even wonder what to do next, I was approached by a Secret Service agent. He could have come direct from a movie set—clean cut, dark suit, one of those ear things. "Russ Becker?" he said, without even a trace of a smile. For a second I wondered if I was in some kind of trouble.

"Yes?"

"Your car is waiting."

The driver knew where to go and I returned to PGDC in time to hear that there was big news. "Two major announcements," Mitch said in a gathering in a conference room. "The first thing is that it looks like your friend Nadia has gotten permission from her father to join us."

My lips involuntarily stretched into a wide smile and I felt my heart float upward like a bobber in a stream. Nadia. It seemed like forever since we last saw each other at her window and I'd given her the spiral ring. Having her with me made everything better. But I couldn't stop thinking about the comic book and the image of her dead on the ground. But that had been at home. Maybe she'd be safer here with me?

All eyes were on me. Mallory clapped, Jameson whooped, and even Carly looked pleased for me. "You know what this means, don't you?" Jameson said, running a hand over his newly shorn head. He looked better with short hair. I think I did him a favor scorching the top of his head. "I'll have two dates for the Bash and one of them will be your girlfriend."

I ignored him. "When? When will she get here?"

Mitch said, "Her flight comes in later this afternoon, so she will be at the luxury suites by the time you get back from what is big news number two—your visit with Vice President Montalbo!" The Praetorian Guard officials buzzed with excitement and anticipation. Dr. Wentworth clasped her hands together. "This is huge," she said, her eyes widening. "We were afraid you wouldn't see Vice President Montalbo until the night of the Bash and that might have been too late."

The news of Nadia was overshadowed by the preparation for our upcoming White House visit. We spent an hour in the conference room being told how to dress and practicing the protocol for a meeting with the vice president. Mitch and Dr. Wentworth were running the show, but our lovely Edgewood chaperones, Dr. Anton, Rosie, and Carly were there as well, all of them with advice for us. Dr. Anton asked Jameson and me to push the conference table aside to give us space for some role playing. Of course I wound up doing it the old school way while he did it with his arms folded using the power of telekinesis. "Show off," I grumbled.

"Nah, just lazy," he said, for once not trying to prove anything. "Plus I can use the practice."

"Firm handshake, good eye contact!" Will exclaimed with enthusiasm during our rehearsal. "Try not to talk too much, but feel free to ask a few polite questions about neutral topics. Ask him about Tipper. He loves to talk about his dog."

Mitch said, "Jameson, make sure you keep your hands out of your pockets! Remember, good posture is important, but keep it natural." Not clear on the concept, Jameson slouched less with his hands hanging awkwardly on either side.

Mallory seemed worried. "So I'll do it during the picture taking?" she asked. We'd been over this half a dozen times but she seemed to need constant confirmation.

"That will probably be your best opportunity to touch him for any length of time," Mitch said, nodding. "A handshake will be too quick."

"What if I don't have enough time?" she said, her voice tinged with worry.

"Improvise," Will said with all the vigor of a drama teacher. "I know you'll figure something out."

Mallory fiddled with the ends of her hair. "Okay,"

"Just get the job done," Will said. "You need to stop him from teaming up with the Associates. Implant the phrases we suggested and we have a good shot."

Vice President Montalbo, we'd been told, had an enormous ego and Mallory was instructed to use that to our advantage. The idea she'd be implanting was that the Associates were going to use him and then discard him, whereas with the help of the Praetorian Guard, he had a good chance of becoming the presidential candidate and ultimately getting voted into office during the next election. That would be a real achievement, and he would ultimately have the power, prestige and admiration he craved. Of course, the Praetorian Guard had no plans to actually have him become a presidential candidate, but he wouldn't know that.

Hopefully Mallory wouldn't go off script like she did with Layla. I still didn't think it was funny.

"Remember to just use word associations if you're pressed for time," Dr. Anton said. "Praetorian Guard equates to honor, prestige, and power. The Associates equals corruption, and disrespect. He's got a huge thing about being disrespected. That word is heavy for him."

Mallory nodded, the enormity of the task seeming to weigh on her. Rosie put an arm around her shoulder. "Don't think about it too much Mallory, or you'll make yourself crazy. You're a smart, capable girl. Believe me, you can do this." Rosie and her particular brand of motherly love had a calming effect on Mallory, who exhaled in relief. Rosie continued, "It all starts with a handshake and 'it's a pleasure to meet you, Mr. Vice President.' Just start there and do it the way we practiced and you'll do fine."

All the way to the vice president's office at the Eisenhower Executive Office Building, and even while sitting in the waiting area, I noticed Mallory practicing as she periodically mouthed the words, 'it's a pleasure to meet you, Mr. Vice President' over and over again. "You're going to do great," I said, squeezing her hand in the waiting room, but she didn't look reassured.

Mallory leaned in close and quietly said, "Russ, can I ask you a question?"

I resisted the urge to say, 'you already have,' (something

my dad always said and thought was absolutely hilarious), and just answered, "Sure." Next to us Jameson was amusing himself by juggling wrapped peppermints he'd taken from a dish next to him. He'd started with three and had worked his way up to six. His juggling was less impressive when you knew that he wasn't actually juggling at all.

Mallory dropped her voice to a whisper, "Russ, when we were in Peru and Mr. Specter had that Deleo strapped to your head, how did you manage to fight it off?"

I was sure we'd had this discussion before, but I didn't mind telling her again. "I figured that if he was trying to change my feelings and thoughts, I'd block them with my own feelings and thoughts." With some quick thinking at the time, I'd called to mind the strongest weapon I had in my arsenal of emotions, the way I felt about Nadia.

"So you just thought things?" She said, raising her eyebrows significantly.

I nodded. "I built a wall out of what I knew to be true and I blocked what he was trying to add. It's like ignoring people who are talking too loudly on the bus. It takes a lot of effort, but you can do it."

Relief washed over her face. "You built a wall out of what you knew to be true and blocked what he was trying to add. And that worked."

"Yes, it worked," I said. "I filled the space with truth and love and then there was no room left for lies and deception." Man, was I poetic! I had half a mind to write that down.

"No room left for lies and deception." Mallory said, almost to herself, letting out a slow breath.

When the vice president's assistant told us he was ready

to see us, Jameson dropped the candy back into the dish and we trooped into his office.

"Come in, come in," Vice President Montalbo greeted us from his desk with a wide smile. His dark hair was smoothed back, not a strand out of place. He got up and met us halfway, his arm extended. He was shorter than me, which surprised me. He always looked so tall standing next to President Bernstein. "I've been looking forward to meeting all of you."

He had a slick handshake, one I'd never experienced before. While he was grasping your hand, he pulled you toward him. For the guys, he then placed his other hand briefly over yours. For Mallory, he pulled her in giving her sort of a half hug. It's not as creepy as it sounds because it was quick and accompanied by smooth compliments. Mallory got, "Now who's this lovely young lady?" and Jameson was "statesmanlike with a strong handshake," while I was told I had "the presence of a leader." The thing with phony compliments is that even when you know you're getting them, it's still okay. Vice President Montalbo was shoveling it hip deep and we were all standing in it, straight and proud.

I noticed Mallory said the words, "It's a pleasure to meet you, Mr. Vice President," just as Rosie had coached her. I looked at Mallory's face as Montalbo held her in a half-hug and it was scrunched in concentration, so I could only think she was using the brief moment of contact for her mind control.

After the greeting, Vice President Montalbo said, "I'm pleased I was able to meet you today, but unfortunately I only have a few minutes before my next meeting. Did you have any questions or concerns before our photo session?" He leaned back against his desk with his arms crossed.

We exchanged uneasy glances, all of us momentarily caught off guard and speechless.

Jameson stepped forward, his arm extended. "Would you like a peppermint?" In his palm was one of the candies he'd filched from the waiting area.

"How kind of you," the vice president said, taking it from his outstretched palm. "Thank you." He tucked it into his pocket.

Jameson's offer of stolen candy jarred us out of our shyness. Mallory sidled up to Montalbo asking, "Do you have any pictures of Tipper? I just love dogs!" She slipped her hand into the crook of his arm, which looked kind of weird, but he didn't seem to mind. Turned out that he had an 8x10 of his dog, Tipper, right on his desk. He picked it up and Mallory fussed over the image. Not to be left out, Jameson went around to his other side and admired Tipper too. I'd seen my share of dogs in my lifetime, but I pretended to care while the vice president answered Mallory's questions about Tipper's age and health. We all listened to cute stories about the dog and nodded and smiled as he spoke.

Nothing about the vice president struck me as being out of the ordinary. How could this nice man who told boring stories about his dog be secretly aligned with an organization determined to overthrow the government? Hard to imagine. If only there was some way to get him to reveal the man within.

The vice president set the photo on the desk behind him and said, "I'm afraid I've been talking too much," he said.

"Oh no," Mallory assured him, her arms still linked in his. "We love your stories."

"If you have any questions about national policy or about

the White House, I'd be glad to answer them," he said, smiling down at her.

"I have a question." I stepped forward, my hand half raised. "Is it hard to always be second string?"

He frowned. "Second string?"

"Second in command. Understudy to President Bernstein. Whatever. You know what I mean." I smiled.

"I would hardly say I'm the understudy to President Bernstein," he said. "The vice presidential office serves a much bigger role than most people realize. I travel quite a bit serving as the country's representative, I speak on behalf of the president when she's otherwise occupied, I'm Presiding Officer of the Senate, and the Chairman of the Board for the National Aeronautics and Space Administration." His chest puffed out with pride.

"I see," I said, "but still, you don't have much power, do you?"

An expression crossed his face like a storm cloud covering the sun. I'd clearly struck a nerve. The room got quiet and Mallory shot me a look that said I had gone too far. I wished Nadia was here. She'd have been able to sense what was going on below the surface. Was he just irritated that I was being a smart-ass kid or did he have a real problem with his lack of power? If I had to guess, it was the latter. I was starting to believe he was one of the Associates.

"I don't think Russ means it the way it sounds," Mallory said, glaring in my direction. "He's not usually so rude."

Vice President Montalbo said, "No, he's right. I don't have much power." He pulled his arm away from Mallory, took off his glasses and rubbed the bridge of his nose. "Not much power at all. At least not right now."

He picked up the phone and asked his assistant, Kimberly, to come in to take a group photo. We lined up as instructed and she took several photos. Afterward, she told us they'd be mailed to the address she'd been given.

As we walked out of the room, Mallory spoke out of the side of her mouth. "Nice job insulting the vice president, Russ."

I shrugged. "I just wanted to know how he felt about being number two."

CHAPTER THIRTY-THREE

NADIA

At the hotel, I dropped my bags at my feet, put my voucher on the counter and said, "The airline made a reservation for me. I'm checking in."

The two young women behind the counter (they didn't look any older than me) stopped talking and gave me a look that said they didn't appreciate the interruption. "Excuse me?" one of them said, adjusting a headband attached to a hair piece. The hair above the headband was straight and brown, a stark contrast to the reddish brown curls cascading below.

"I'm checking in," I said. "My flight was cancelled."

"Everyone's flight was cancelled," she said, acknowledging me. As her head was bent over my paperwork, she popped in a breath mint. I held back from asking for one even though I desperately wanted to. My mouth felt so gross. "I don't know about this. I thought we were completely booked."

I had a bad feeling, not just from what I was picking up from these two women, both of whom radiated apathy and laziness, but also from what she was saying. The flights had been cancelled hours ago. It did seem likely that the hotel was full. "The woman at the airline said they'd reserved a room for me."

"They say a lot of things," she said with a snort. "Just let me look." She typed on the keyboard, the other girl looking over her shoulder.

"Maybe they…" The onlooker whispered something I couldn't hear.

"No, because that guest still occupies the room," the other one answered. "Hmmm." She tapped her fingers on the counter, deep in thought. They both stared at the screen until finally the one who seemed to be in charge said, "The airline did call about a room, and it does look like someone at the 800 number booked it, but the reservation is for a room that's already occupied."

My stomach sunk. "How can that be if it's my room?"

"The guest who was expected to check out extended their stay."

"Can they do that?" I asked, aghast.

She shrugged. "They did."

"Can't you honor my reservation? Ask the person to leave?"

"No, we can't really do that. Sorry." Both of them looked like they wished I would go away. Well I had news for them. I had nowhere to go.

I was so tired. All I wanted was to wash the airport dust off my body and sink into a soft bed, where I would astral project to Russ and confront him about that kiss with Layla Bernstein and then get some sleep, in that order. I needed a room and I wanted it now. "Can I speak to a manager?"

The one with the fake hair said, "I am the manager."

My stomach sunk. "You need to find me a room. Please. Don't you have anything?"

She shook her head. "All booked up. After all the flights were cancelled, we got swamped. It's been crazy."

"I'm an unaccompanied minor." I didn't want to pull this one out, but it had worked with the airline, so I figured it was worth a shot.

Her eyebrows arched upwards, echoing the line of the headband. "Is that true? Because if it is, the airline should have made arrangements for someone to accompany you. Would you like me to call someone in authority?"

Someone in authority? Meaning the airport authorities or the police? I wondered, but I wasn't going to ask. I sensed she didn't really want to pursue it. Lazy. "No it's not true," I said. "Just forget it."

"Okay then." She gave me a knowing smile. We both knew I'd just lied, but she didn't care enough to make good on her threat. Or maybe she was cutting me a break. Either way, I was in the clear.

I picked up my bags. They'd gained about fifty pounds since I set them down. Every muscle in my body ached. I would have given up five years of my life for a comfortable bed and a firm pillow, that's how tired I was.

Her expression softened. "If you want, you can sit in the lobby," she said, pointing. "Normally we only allow it for guests, but I'll make an exception for you." I must have looked unsure because she added, "Unless you have somewhere else to go?"

I nodded wearily. "No, I'll just stay here for now. Thanks."

The lobby furniture looked more comfortable than the chairs in the airport. It would have to do. I pulled my suitcase over to a chair and sat down, defeated. I found myself touching the cut on my neck and running a finger over the stitches. It bothered me. I couldn't wait until the stitches were out and the cut healed.

Another airport refugee, a middle-aged man, sat in a chair opposite me. He was slouched in his seat, head back, mouth open. Breathing through his nose in loud, raspy bursts. Great. Just great. We'd be lobby roommates for the night. I opened my phone to call my PG contact. I'd already decided not to call my dad. He had enough to worry about. The Praetorian Guard was a different matter. I needed them to pick me up at the airport if I was ever going to get to Russ. I waited while it rang three times and when it went to voice mail I said, "Hello, this is Nadia. My flight has been cancelled and I won't be there until tomorrow." I explained about the weather and that they'd rebooked my flight, gave my new flight number and the time I'd be arriving. I hoped they'd still have someone there to pick me up. It just occurred to me that I had no idea where to go once I got to Washington D.C.

My night in the hotel lobby stretched on endlessly. I couldn't get comfortable, for one thing, but it wasn't like I would have been able to sleep anyway. All kinds of totally bizarre fears filled my head. I worried that if I dozed off someone would take my stuff, or molest me in my sleep, or that I might drool or snore. I sat and watched as the seconds turned into minutes, taking so long that time seemed to be moving in slow motion. Finally, after hours had gone by, I decided to risk astral projecting to Russ again. I closed my eyes, ignored the noises around me, and let myself sink into a trance. When I felt ready, I thought the now familiar words: *Take me to Russ.*

Immediately I was in his darkened hotel suite, next to the bed. He'd left the bathroom light on and the door was slightly open, wide enough so that I could see his head and one arm above the covers. Underneath, the rest of his body created a hilly terrain of blanket.

Russ! I said. *Wake up!* It took all my energy, and it still wasn't enough. Except for the rise and fall of his chest with every breath he didn't move at all. *Russ! This is an emergency. Wake up now.* I wanted to shake him and wake him, but physically I was less than a puff of air. If I couldn't tap into his thoughts, I had nothing. *Russ!* He shifted and pulled the covers tighter. I took this as progress. *Russ, can you hear me?*

And then, victory. He mumbled, "Nadia?"

Yes! Yes! It's me, Nadia. Wake up, Russ.

His eyes were still closed. The words he spoke next came out haltingly. "Is this a dream?"

No, it's not a dream. I'm really here. Open your eyes!

One eye opened just a little bit. "I can't see you at all."

Good grief. I'd forgotten to show myself. I made an effort to make myself clearly visible, but in the half minute it took, he'd closed his eye again. No! *Don't fall back asleep, Russ! Listen to me, you can't trust Mallory or Jameson. Watch out for them, okay? They're in league with the Associates.* Technically I wasn't sure if Jameson was in league with the Associates, but if he was under Mallory's spell it was pretty much the same thing. I continued. *Mr. Specter is not dead! You hear me? I've seen him with Mallory. They've got something planned for the*

Bash. There's a needle in Mallory's necklace. I don't know what it does, but I can tell you it's not good. Try to get the necklace away from her. There's going to be trouble. Be careful.

He didn't show any sign of having heard me.

Russ? Did you hear what I said? For a split second I was tempted to channel my mother and ask him to repeat things back to me so I knew without a doubt that he'd heard me. I always resented the way mom did that when I was a kid—so patronizing, but I could see the value now.

Russ scrunched his forehead and said, "Trouble. Be careful." He'd gotten the gist of what I'd said, but I wasn't completely sure how much was just being repeated and how much had actually penetrated his skull. I tried again. *Russ! This is very important. Do not trust Mallory or Jameson. Keep Mallory from going near the president with that necklace. Mr. Specter is the commander and she's following his orders. Do you understand?*

I watched for signs he'd heard me but was getting nothing. His breathing was slow and regular now, like he'd lapsed back into sleep. A restful, happy sleep judging from the slight smile on his face. You had to be kidding me. *Russ!* This time I screamed his name in my head, but it didn't matter. Still no movement. I kept trying, though, repeating my message again and again, each time pounding on every word. His lack of response was infuriating.

I stayed for a few minutes, frustrated and emotionally spent from trying to get through. I was on the verge of anger, and then felt guilty for being mad about something he couldn't help. If only he would wake up. I had to know he understood and I wanted to know why he kissed Layla

Bernstein. I was sure there was an explanation that made sense and I wanted to hear it and believe it.

I tried, and then I tried again, and kept talking over and over again, but nothing worked. After deciding I'd done as much as I could, I gave up and said, *Good-bye Russ. I love you. See you at the Bash.*

I paused then, wondering if there was someone else I could go to for help. It had to be someone connected to the Praetorian Guard, so that eliminated most of the world. Mentally I checked off the possibilities. Mallory and Jameson: no. Mr. Specter, definitely not. I considered Rosie and Dr. Anton, but besides my visits to Rosie's Diner, I didn't feel like I knew them all that well. It was so hard to know who to trust. Mrs. Whitehouse? Absolutely, positively no. She was so awkward and patronizing I didn't even want to talk to her in real life, must less go to her for help.

My last choice, Kevin Adams, struck me as the best possibility. We'd spent time with him in Peru, so I felt like I knew him. He also seemed truly devastated by Mr. Specter's death. Certainly he had no idea that it was faked and that Mr. Specter was a double agent working for the Associates. Kevin was a good-natured, unassuming guy. Down to earth. Likeable. Happy hanging out in his comic book store. Simple in his view of the world. Someone like that would want to help, even if the enemy was his old friend, Sam Specter. Maybe *especially* since it was Sam Specter. Kevin was probably going to feel angry and betrayed when he found out. Yes, Kevin was the one to go to. He could reach out to his Praetorian Guard contacts and warn them for me.

I hovered over Russ one last second and then took the plunge. *Take me to Kevin Adams.*

I'd been worried that I'd catch Kevin sleeping, so it was nice to see him sitting up and wide awake, sipping from a tall glass of what looked like dark beer. As I watched, he smacked his lips appreciatively. I almost made myself visible, but caught myself when I noticed he wasn't at home. And he wasn't alone either.

He was sitting at a round table, across from Mrs. Whitehouse, who didn't look quite like herself. And judging from the slight thrumming sound, the curvature of the beige walls, and the squarish shaded windows, they were on a plane. No, a jet. A private jet, judging by the spacious design and lack of rows of seats. So very curious. I moved closer, careful not to let them know I was there.

Mrs. Whitehouse nervously drummed her fingers on the tabletop while Kevin Adam took a long pull on his glass of beer. "This is good. A really good tasty brewski," he said, setting the glass down on a cardboard coaster. "I should see if I can get this brand at home."

"Hmm." Even without words, she managed to show disapproval.

"I'm going to get a refill on this," he said, reaching over to press a button above the table. Mrs. Whitehouse slapped his hand to get him to stop, but it was too late. "I'd like another beer, please," he said.

Mrs. Whitehouse lowered her head to talk directly into the speaker. "Cancel that. There will be no more beer."

"Yes ma'am," came a man's voice through the speaker.

"Who died and made you boss?" Kevin asked. He ran a hand over his Elvis-styled hair, and gazed forlornly into the bottom of the glass.

Mrs. Whitehouse barked out a laugh. "Funny you should mention it. Commander Specter died and made me boss, that's who. Second in command, that's what I'm going to be."

"Yeah, well it hasn't happened yet."

"Oh, it will," she said, with complete confidence. "You wait and see. Sam promised. He saw it in one of his visions."

If I'd actually been there, my mouth would have hung open in disbelief. Kevin Adams and Mrs. Whitehouse were in league with Mr. Specter? Easygoing, lovable Kevin and nerdy, annoying Mrs. Whitehouse were aligned with the Associates? No! Couldn't be. I heard it but found it hard to believe.

"Yeah, yeah," he said, not convinced. "That and a buck fifty will get you a cup of java." He ran a finger around the rim of the glass. "But what I'd really like is another glass of beer."

"Show some discipline, would you?" Mrs. Whitehouse said. "That's the key. How do you think I lost so much weight? And ten years I've kept it off." She put a hand on one hip and I realized then that this was why she looked so different. She was thin, for her. I'd seen her in Peru earlier in the summer and she must have been fifty pounds heavier then. How had she lost so much weight so quickly? Her face too, looked different. It was like she'd wiped off stage make-up with wrinkles and age spots, and revealed a softer, younger version of herself.

"Taking off the fat suit helped too."

She nodded. "That thing was hot. Wearing it behind the cafeteria line was torture. I was broiling inside that thing. Glad I'm not doing that anymore."

"What was the point of that? You were a lunch room lady, not an international spy."

"Even lunch room ladies have identities. And I knew that eventually I'd be changing mine. Having a different look to begin with will make the transition much easier. Sam suggested it, you know."

"I know."

"I've been waiting for this for a long, long time. Back when my last name was Whitman—"

"Oh, here we go," Kevin muttered.

She continued on. "Whitman was just such a boring name. The only time anyone ever asked about it was when they wanted to know if my family was related to Walt Whitman. You know Walt Whitman, the poet?"

"Not personally, no." He lifted the window shade and looked out into the darkness.

"We weren't related to Walt Whitman, but I always said we were. Even as a child I knew I was born for better things. And then when we were teenagers and Sam said he saw me in a vision of the future and saw both of us in power in Washington D.C., it came to me." She snapped her fingers. "My name would be Mrs. Whitehouse. A sort of inside joke. Sam loved it when I told him my idea. I remember getting it legally changed and the man at the courthouse asking if I was sure this was what I wanted. I was about twenty then, and skinny as a twig. They probably thought it was a whim, but believe me, it wasn't."

"Why not Miss Whitehouse?" Kevin asked, suddenly interested. "Why Missus?"

"Mrs. Whitehouse sounds better and it's easier to say,"

she said. "Try saying it both ways and you'll see." She flapped her hands at him. "Go ahead. Try it."

"I'll take your word for it."

"I knew that someday Sam would be in power and I'd be right by his side, like the first lady, only better. I've been preparing to be Mrs. Whitehouse for almost thirty years." She tucked her hair behind her ear. When I'd seen her last, her hair had been dowdy and shapeless. Since then she'd gotten a sleek new cut and color. It almost looked chic.

"You seem very confident that this is going to work," Kevin said.

"Of course it will work," she exclaimed. "Everything we've worked for all these years has led to this. Do you think I wanted to be a lunchroom lady for the last twenty-five years? Criminy. Those high school kids are idiots and I walked around and made friends with them every single lunch hour. Every single lunch day. I chatted them up and earned their trust. Did the whole dimwitted lunch lady act so no one would be suspicious. And I did this for years. *Years!* Just waiting and watching to see when the Edgewood four would show up. The ones with all the power. The ones Sam predicted would come. And then we found them, one by one." She ticked off on her fingers. "Mallory, Russ, Jameson, and Nadia." She stared at a spot beyond Kevin, like envisioning all of us standing behind him. "Slippery little devils, what with two of them being homeschooled. That's what threw me off. I was looking for four of them in the cafeteria. Rosie had her suspicions when they started coming into the diner, but Sam was the one who confirmed they were the ones. He had it all figured out."

"Sam, Sam, Sam," Kevin muttered. "You think the sun

rises and sets by that guy, don't you? Well, I've got news for you. He's a regular human being just like the rest of us."

"That's where you're wrong, Mr. Adams," she said, jabbing a finger in his direction. "Sam Specter isn't like the rest of us. He was born for greatness. He's going to change the world."

"I kind of like the world the way it is."

"That's because you lack vision," she said, sniffing. "I've been lucky enough to hear Sam's plans, and believe me, they are inspiring."

"I've heard them too," Kevin said, clearly not impressed.

"Sam says the reason most governments can't get anything done is that there are too many people muddying the waters. Ruling by committee never works. The laws that finally do get passed are diluted, the rules get bent, and there are too many changes implemented to make any kind of difference. Ultimately no one benefits from all the wishy-washiness. Having one all-powerful leader would be ideal, except that citizens resent not having a say in things. But what if," she said, and here her eyes gleamed with excitement, "you could have a government with the appearance of a democracy, but which has just a few people making all the decisions behind the scenes? Wouldn't that be better for everyone concerned?"

"I've heard all this," Kevin said abruptly. "I know the plan and in theory it sounds great. I even used to agree with Sam. Seriously, I used to sit in his basement drinking beer and listening to all the crap you're spouting now and I totally thought he was on to something. Yeah, I'll admit it made sense to me. Why not seize control? Why not take power? The government's pretty messed up and Sam's a damn genius with a gazillion ideas for making things better. So a few people have to die." He blew a raspberry. "Tough blow, but ultimately the entire world will come out ahead. Sam called those deaths collateral damage. People die. Too bad, so sad. Move on and prosper, just like he said."

"So what's your problem, then?" She leaned back, crossing her arms.

Kevin poked a finger on the table top. "My problem is that Sam never said the plan included joining up with the Associates. We both know those people are ruthless, power mongers lacking in human decency."

"And the Praetorian Guard are all angels? Please, Kevin." Mrs. Whitehouse exhaled loudly. "The good guys and bad guys concept is completely outdated. Everyone is corrupt. At least the Associates get things done."

"Yeah, by murdering people."

She let out a cynical chuckle. "People die. That's a fact of life. Most of the time there's not even a good reason. At least this time there's a benefit that comes out of it."

"But see here, that's the problem," Kevin said, shifting uncomfortably in his seat. "I know these kids and I don't see a benefit to them getting murdered. Russ, Mallory, and Jameson—they aren't just nothing. They have names and families and futures. I like them. I don't want to see them die."

She sighed. "You always were a soft touch. Why you even wanted to come on this trip, I don't know."

"I don't know either. I guess I just couldn't stay at home and let things happen without me."

"You know the kids have to die, don't you? Sam saw the

vision clearly. They're the only thing standing in our way. Once they're gone, the path is clear, that's the way he saw it."

Kevin shook his head slowly, and then reached over and pushed the button. "I'm gonna be needing another beer." His voice was defiant.

The same man's voice came over the loudspeaker. "You have approval for a beer?"

Mrs. Whitehouse said, "It's okay. You can bring him his beer." She tilted her head and gave him a withering look. "You're not holding up very well, are you, Kevin?" He said nothing so she continued. "If it makes you feel any better, you won't see them die." She lifted up the shade to look at her reflection in the window, then tucked her hair behind her ears. "I'll be there. Luckily I'm not as squeamish as you are."

"You can really watch three kids die?" Kevin said. "And what about Rosie and Anton? They don't have a clue what's going on and they could wind up getting killed too. You don't feel bad about that? That's pretty cold, even for you."

"Rosie and Anton? Those two always felt they were better than me."

"No they didn't."

She slapped her hand on the table. "Believe me they did, and they still do. Pompous fools, that's what they are."

"So you're okay with having someone you've known since high school getting killed? You don't feel even a little bit guilty about that?"

"Oh, I'm sure I'll feel guilty about it afterward, but I've made my decision and I can live with it. And I can't reverse it even if I wanted to. The die has been cast. Before those kids even got on the plane they were goners."

"What are you talking about?"

"The inspirational stones I gave them at the airport?" She grinned. "Not so inspirational, as it turns out. Peace, love, and hope? Kaboom!"

Kevin's face turned ashen. "Oh, no."

"Oh yes," Mrs. Whitehouse said gleefully. "They're actually powerful explosives timed to detonate during the Bash. Since the stones will be in their pockets, they'll be killed instantly. That means no pain, if it makes you feel any better," she said, with a wave of her hand. "Yep, Sam has it all planned. About a third of the Secret Service at the Bash are Associate plants, so they're on our side. The smoke that's created will supply the diversion needed to allow us to kill the president. Getting rid of the daughter is just a little extra Sam dreamed up since she's so well liked. The country will be so preoccupied by these events that the vice president will easily slide into power and make half a dozen major changes before they even know what hit them." She slapped the table. "It's gonna be a revolution."

Kevin said, "But why do the kids have to die? No one said anything about that to me."

"We kept you in the dark on purpose." She gave him a mean smile. "Because Sam saw that you'd turn traitor. You haven't been part of the equation for a very long time."

CHAPTER THIRTY-FOUR

RUSS

When they told me Nadia wouldn't arrive in time for the Bash, I felt sick. There was some story about a weather delay and her flight being cancelled, which supposedly left her stranded. The whole thing sounded ridiculous to me. Couldn't someone go and get her?

But no. Mitch said that the voice mail she left only gave her new flight information. They didn't know where she would be spending the night, and when they called back, she didn't pick up.

"Can't you track her phone and find her location?" I asked.

"Someone's been watching too many crime shows," Will quipped with a grin. "It's not that easy, Russ. Believe me, we've thought of everything." He told me that Nadia would be arriving sometime after the Bash started. A PG contact would pick her up from the airport and rush her to the event where someone would be waiting with her evening dress and accessories. "It will be close. Hopefully her plane won't be delayed or she'll miss the whole thing."

And then in a condescending tone (which I totally hate), Mitch said, "Don't worry about a thing, Russ. You'll be able to see Nadia as soon as she gets here."

From their flippant attitudes, I don't think they understood how valuable Nadia could be to the mission. Her sense of who was telling the truth was the ultimate bad guy filter. Just because she couldn't shoot electricity out of her palms or make someone think they were in love with me didn't make her talents any less important. A superpower doesn't have to be flashy to make a difference.

Will turned serious. "Don't let the fact that Nadia's not here be a distraction," he said. "You'll need to focus completely and you won't be able to do that if you're watching the door waiting for her to show up."

"I know," I said, a little insulted. We'd covered this many times. I wasn't a hyperactive kid that was going to let my attention wander. I knew this was important and I was going to give it my all.

After a short briefing where they reminded us yet again how important this mission was, we were sent to our rooms to get ready for the evening. Each of us had an assistant who would be helping us get dressed in our formal attire. We already knew the sequence of events: a meet and greet with the president, followed by dancing and drinks in the ballroom and ending with Layla's birthday cake being wheeled out and the guests singing "Happy Birthday." If the evening ended with no security issues and the presidential family safe and sound, it would be considered a success.

I tried to get rid of my sister, but she wasn't having any of it. "I think I can manage on my own," I said as she followed me back to my room.

"If I can't come to the Bash, I can at least help you get ready," Carly said, not getting the hint. She hoisted herself up on my bed, like it was her room instead of mine. Once she'd adjusted the pillows as a backrest, she settled back, hugging her purse to her front. "Did I tell you that I get to watch the Bash on a monitor right outside the ballroom? Dr. Anton, Rosie, and I get to hang out in the control room with the security guys and see the whole thing. They promised me that if there's any trouble they'll get you out of there right away."

I got the tuxes out of my closet and started to lay them side by side on the end of the bed. They all looked remarkably similar. Different sizes, maybe? Hopefully when the assistant guy got here he'd know what I was supposed to wear. "You sound like you're not so worried anymore," I said.

"Oh I'm still worried," she said. "I just know it won't help to talk about it. We're both too far into this to go back now."

She was right. We'd reached the point of no return and that was a scary thought. If I was being completely honest, the possibility that I might die tonight was on my mind. I didn't want to die. Not now, not ever. No one does, at least not usually, but it would be especially bad for me at this point since I hadn't even started to live yet. If I died now I would die without ever having had sex, without ever having my own car or house or having traveled to all the places I wanted to see. I'd never know what my kids would have looked like and what kind of man I would have turned out to be. I wouldn't know what I could have accomplished given more time. My story would end abruptly. It's like reading a book that's just starting to get interesting, turning the page and bam, there's no more there. An abrupt, unsatisfying ending.

Like anyone else, I had big dreams. Dying as a junior in high school wasn't one of them. But if I did die, there was one thing I didn't want left unsaid. "Carly?"

She'd been rifling through her purse, looking for gum no doubt, but the urgency of my voice made her look up. "Yeah Russ?"

"I haven't been completely honest with you. There's something I wanted to tell you before, but I just couldn't. It's about David."

Carly's eyes narrowed and her gaze cut right into me. "Tell me now."

There was no way to say it but to just say it. "We found him in Peru."

"Alive?" Her voice quavered. I'd known Carly as long as I'd known myself and rarely had I seen through the cracks of her tough girl façade, but here it was—Carly about to burst into tears from the joy of finding out the love of her life was still alive.

"Yeah, he's alive. He's been working for the Praetorian Guard doing scientific research. They're making some amazing world-changing discoveries, he said."

"You've got to be kidding."

"No, it's true."

"You actually saw him and talked to him?"

"Yes."

"That asshole!" She spit the words out. "All this time he let me think he was dead and he's just fine?"

"He wanted to tell you, he really did—"

"Don't you defend him, Russ." Her eyes narrowed. "There's no excuse for this. For years I've been grieving for him while he's been off tra-la-la doing research? That's so lame. Really lame. My life has been on hold while David Hofstetter gets to go on and do whatever the hell he wants to do? How nice for him. I suppose he's got a wife and six kids too."

"No wife," I said. "Only one kid."

Carly swung her legs over the side of the bed and hopped off. Without saying another word, she disappeared into my bathroom where I heard her blowing her nose. When she came out, she had a wad of tissues in her hand and makeup smudged around her eyes. "I don't even know what to say," she said, sitting down in the chair next to the bed. Her head drooped and she rested her chin on her hands. She'd gone from euphoric to angry to defeated in about three minutes.

I rested my hand on her back. "I'm sorry I didn't tell you sooner. He made me promise. He said I'd put you in danger if you knew."

"Oh Russ, don't you know you can tell me anything?" Carly lifted her chin and sorrowfully shook her head. She exhaled loudly, exasperation coming through. "So you've known for two months then."

I nodded. "Yeah, I came close to telling you a few times."

"I knew you were lying about something." She lowered her nose into the lump of tissue and blew hard.

"I did lie to you. I'm sorry."

"Well, I wish you had told me right away, but after sixteen

years of not knowing I guess that little bit of time wouldn't have made that much of a difference."

Whew. At least she wasn't mad at me. "I wanted to tell you."

"So you said." She wadded the tissue into a ball. "So how does he look? Did he ask about me?"

I tried to think. "He doesn't look too much different. Just older, I guess. And he did ask about you. You were pretty much the whole topic of conversation."

"Like what did he say?"

I was starting to regret telling her. This whole thing felt familiar. My mom had this habit of wanting a play-by-play description of things. If I came back from dinner at someone's house, my mom wanted to know what they had and who cooked it and how many siblings were home and what the parents did for a living. Was their house nice? Bigger than ours? I had to tell the whole thing in order and she wanted details. My dad called it "the interrogation." I noticed that Carly did the same thing to Frank. The women in my family wanted to hear every bit of our experiences away from them like they were going to recreate it with puppets for YouTube or something. "I know you want the details," I said. "But can I give them to you after the Bash? I'm supposed to be getting ready."

Carly started to say something, but her words were interrupted by a knock on my door. I went over and opened it to find a young woman, carrying what looked like a plastic tool box. She was dressed like my sister in T-shirt and jeans, but over the tee she wore a jacket with a scarf looped loosely around her neck. Her sleek black hair was held back by a plaid headband. "I'm Tasha, your assistant," she said, pushing past me and coming into the room.

"*You're* my assistant?" I said, taken aback.

She smiled. "In a word—yes."

Carly got up and gave a little wave. "I'm Carly. The sister." Tasha gave her a nod before setting her case on the bed and flipping it open. Just like a tackle box it had multiple tiered compartments, but instead of fishing lures it held what looked like cosmetics.

"I thought I'd get a guy helper," I said. "Since I'm going to be getting dressed and everything."

Tasha blew a loud puff of air through vibrating lips. "No need to be shy, sir. I've seen it all. Now strip down to your skivvies, so we can get started."

"Not with her here," I said, pointing to Carly.

"You give me news like you just did and then want me to leave?" Carly said.

"Please?" I asked gesturing for her to go. "I promise we'll talk after I'm dressed."

"I'll go in the other room," Carly said. "But that's all. I still want to hear more about that thing we were talking about." She pulled her purse over her shoulder and loped out out, clearly not in any hurry at all.

I was wrong about the tuxes. They were all the same size—my size. The difference, Tasha said, was in the cut and the designer. She stood back and sized me up, her fist resting against her mouth. "You have the perfect body for a tux," she said finally. "Tall, trim build, broad shoulders, narrow waist. Perfect." She went back to the bed and pulled at a hanger. "I'm thinking we'll go with the Armani. It's a classic.

Timeless. Try it on, with—" she grabbed a white shirt, "this shirt. We'll worry about everything else after we see the fit."

Despite her assurance that it would be fine for me to strip down in front of her, I decided to change in the bathroom. When I came out, Tasha clapped her hands in delight. "Just as I thought," she said. "So handsome. Come see." She took hold of my sleeve and pulled me over to the mirror.

Whoa. Seeing my reflection, I saw myself as others would, and I had to admit, I liked how I looked in a tux. "Do I get to keep this?" I asked, turning to see myself from all sides.

"Do you get to keep a thousand dollar tux?" She laughed. "Short answer: no."

"Can I look?" Carly yelled from the next room. Without waiting for a response, suddenly she was there, reminding me of Frank, who had the knack of showing up at inopportune times. "You clean up nice, Russ," she said, nodding approvingly.

After that, Tasha and Carly tag teamed me, supervising the putting on of socks and shoes, artfully inserting the cuff links, slicking my hair down with some kind of product, and painfully tweezing half a dozen of the eyebrow hairs they called strays. When they were done fussing over me, both women stood back to assess their work. "Magnificent," Tasha said.

"Not too shabby," Carly agreed.

Tasha put her supplies back in her case and snapped the lid shut. "Just hang the rest of the formal wear in the closet," she said. "Someone will come by to pick them up."

"Will I see you again?" I asked.

"In a word," she said. "No." Hesitating halfway through

the doorway, she glanced at her watch. "We made good time. You have five minutes until you're supposed to meet everyone down in the lobby. Have fun at the Bash." And then the door clicked shut and she was gone.

Carly couldn't wait even one more minute. "Tell me everything David said."

CHAPTER THIRTY-FIVE

NADIA

It wasn't until the plane was up in the air and the pilot had greeted us over the loudspeaker that I let myself believe I would actually get to Washington D.C. The lack of sleep hadn't hit me yet—I was running on adrenaline, crazy with worry that my friends and the love of my life were going to get murdered before the day was done. I spent all day in the airport pacing and eating. For breakfast I bought a blueberry muffin and iced coffee from a kiosk, and lunch was a burger. Neither meal was satisfying. When I realized my phone was dead I wandered around looking for an open electrical outlet, but didn't have any success. Hopefully the PG contact I called had gotten my message and someone would be at the airport to pick me up.

My seat on the airplane was near the window, so I could watch the runway recede from sight as the jet lifted off. I loved flying, loved the split second moment when the plane lost contact with the pavement and began to rise. Besides our trip to Peru, I hadn't flown since I was a little girl. If my mother's goal was to keep me home for the rest of my life, my goal was the exact opposite. I wanted to travel the world, go everywhere and see everything. I wanted to hike the Grand Canyon, and see the Hoover Dam. Stand in Times Square on New Year's Eve when the ball dropped, tour vineyards in Napa Valley, touch the Great Wall of China, see the pyramids in Egypt, and feast my eyes on the great paintings of Italy.

I wanted to stand in Anne Frank's Secret Annex, and ride a trolley car in San Francisco. Scale Mount Everest and visit the Skydeck of the Sears Tower in Chicago, just like Ferris Bueller did. I wanted to do all those things and a thousand more. And I wanted to do it with Russ. But first we had to get through tonight.

I looked at the ring Russ had given me, twisting my hand so it caught the light from the window. Every time I thought about what he'd said about the spirals symbolizing our inter-locking lives and never-ending love, I was so overwhelmed with happiness I wanted to cry.

The ring was so perfect. The spirals circling it were deli-cate but distinct, and the gem stone on top looked enough like a diamond that at a glance it could have been an engage-ment ring. How could he have given me a ring like this and still kissed Layla Bernstein? There had to be an explanation.

A round-faced older woman sitting next to me said, "What a gorgeous ring. Was it a gift?"

I flushed red, but managed to nod.

"Your boyfriend?" She leaned toward me, uncomfortably close.

"Yes. I'm going to be seeing him tonight."

"Well, he has excellent taste in jewelry, I must say."

For a split second I wondered if I'd said more than I should. What if she was one of the Associates, planted to spy on me? But after the next ten minutes of listening to her talk about her children and grandchildren (complete with photos on her phone), I was pretty sure that wasn't the case. Finally I said, "If you don't mind, I think I'm going to close my eyes for a few minutes and rest." She looked a little hurt, so I added, "I was up all night. I didn't sleep at all."

Her expression softened. "Oh, of course dear." She sat back and began leafing through a magazine she'd taken from the seat pocket.

With my eyes closed, I was able to shut out the world. After a night spent guarding my luggage, it felt good to finally be able to relax. I calculated the time of my arrival against the start of the Bash and knew I would be touching down right before the Bash began. I could tell the driver what I knew about the inspirational stones and they could call ahead and take them before Russ, Mallory, and James even walked into the event. I wasn't exactly sure what the plan was involving the needle in the necklace, but if the explosions didn't happen, maybe that would throw off the plan and save them from harm.

At least I hoped so. But what if no one met me at the airport? And what if I couldn't find an outlet to charge my phone? Even if I did find an outlet, what if I got voice mail again? The thought of all of this hinging on me made me sick with fear.

I decided to try one more time. *Take me to Russ.* And whoosh, I was rushed to his room, where I witnessed him standing statue-like in a tux and shiny shoes, while his sister Carly and another woman fussed over him, pulling on his sleeves, and brushing off his shoulders. "I think something should be done with his eyebrows," Carly said.

"My thoughts exactly," said the other woman.

Russ grimaced. "Oh please, tell me you're kidding."

There was no way I was going to be able to get his full attention for very long. Reluctantly I left his side and returned back to my seat in the plane. How frustrating to be so close but not be able to communicate with him.

If only there was someone else I could go to who could give the Praetorian Guard advance warning. Someone I could confide in who would give my message to the right people. Again I went through the list. Rosie and Dr. Anton were possibilities. Both of them seemed solid but I didn't know either one very well. Could I rely on them when lives were at stake? Trying to figure out who to trust was making my head hurt.

Finally, inspiration hit and I knew exactly who I could trust. I took a deep breath and thought: *Take me to Layla Bernstein.*

CHAPTER THIRTY-SIX

RUSS

Carly pestered me about David all the way down the hallway. "You can't just leave me hanging, Russ. You have to tell me what you know."

I'd made a big mistake in telling her when I did. With only an hour to go before the big event, I needed some downtime to recharge and concentrate—I didn't want to get sidetracked with Carly drama. I could tell she wasn't going to give up though, so when we got into the elevator, I said, "Carly, I've got like no time here. I'll give you until we get to the lobby. What do you want to know?"

"Everything."

I shook my head. Her idea of everything included detailed descriptions of the room and the expressions on David's face. I didn't have time for everything. "I'll tell you what I remember." I reached over and pressed the button for the lobby. The doors slid shut. "Basically, the Praetorian Guard helped him to fake his death in a car accident to save him from the Associates. He's some kind of scientist now, doing research for them in a lab. The research facility where we found him was pretty cool. It was underground." I decided to skip over the part where the facility was blown up while we were there, forcing us to escape through underground passages, just narrowly avoiding getting killed.

"I don't care about any of that," she said. "Tell me what he said about me."

"He still loves you, if that's what you want to know."

Her look of impatience softened. Clearly I'd said the right thing. She said, "He actually said that?"

"Pretty much. He's been keeping up with you and your life, and I sensed he had a lot of regret about leaving you behind."

Her smile dropped. "Keeping up, how?"

"He used to come back to Edgewood in disguise to visit his grandfather, and he heard about you that way."

Carly gripped the railing and looked down at the floor. "Gordy sometimes said he saw David, but I thought it was the dementia. He was so confused about so many things. I can't believe he would visit his grandfather and not me. I could have kept a secret, you know."

"I know."

"Maybe…" She lifted her head and I could see the tears glistening in her eyes. "Maybe he didn't come to see me because it would have been too hard to leave me again."

"I think that's probably it," I said. The elevator doors opened and I motioned for her to walk ahead of me. I hoped she would be satisfied until tomorrow. If David kept his word, he would see her then. Let him explain everything to her. I didn't want to be in the middle.

Carly and I walked to the lobby where the rest of our

group waited. I couldn't wait to meet up with them so my conversation with my sister could officially be over.

"Just a minute!" Carly whirled around and blocked my path. Even though she was shorter than me, she could still be intimidating. "You said he had a kid."

"Yeah?"

"Boy or girl?" She put a hand on one hip. Her stance said, *I'm not going anywhere until I get answers.*

"A boy."

"Is David still in a relationship with the mother?"

"Not really."

Her lips came together, and a thinking look came over her face. Just when I thought she might be done, she said, "How did it come up that he had a son? Did you see the kid?"

"He had a photo in his lab and I asked about it."

"What does the boy look like? What's his name?"

She was edging into the danger zone. There was no good way to put her off and I sure didn't want to answer. "Can we talk about this after the Bash?" I craned my neck to look at the group. Jameson gave me a quizzical look, wondering what was holding us up.

"No, we can't talk about this after the Bash," she said, drawing out the words to show me she was in no hurry at all. "We're talking about it now."

"What was the question again?" I could see Jameson gesturing for us to hurry. Standing in his tux he looked less like a praying mantis and more like a super skinny penguin.

"What's his son's name?" Carly asked.

I took a deep breath before answering and looked her right in the eyes. "His name is Frank."

"Oh." I saw a wave of confusion cross her face. "The same as my Frank?"

"Carly, his son *is* your Frank."

CHAPTER THIRTY-SEVEN

NADIA

Leaving my body in seat 26D, I astral projected through time and space, finding myself in a bathroom not too much bigger than mine at home, but definitely nicer. My view of Layla Bernstein was from behind. She was fully dressed in a gorgeous silver ball gown. Her hair was swept up with little tendrils framing her face. Teardrop earrings and a matching necklace completed the ensemble. I saw all of this in the mirror, the same view she had as she leaned over the counter, putting on her makeup. If I had looked half as good as she did, I would be overjoyed, but Layla had a scowl on her face. She expertly lined her eyes with liquid eyeliner, then stood back and assessed her handiwork, not looking pleased at all. She sort of shrugged as if to say, this is as good as it gets, then moved on to applying mascara.

I'd only astral projected to a few people, but I knew there were times when it wasn't a good idea to show myself. When someone was holding something close to their eyeball was one of them. I waited until she was done, mentally rehearsing what I was going to say in the meantime. I imagined that she'd scream and maybe run out of the room. If not that, she might become paralyzed with fear, which would be hor-rible but at least she'd be in one spot which would give me a chance to explain. I hoped she wouldn't faint or become hysterical. I didn't want to scare her, I just needed to talk to her. If I could have texted I would have, but astral projecting was all I had.

When she was done with the mascara and eye shadow she looked a little happier. Apparently the eyes had shaped up fairly well. She'd achieved the smoky nighttime eye that every girl practices at some point in time. She was my boyfriend's date for the evening and she looked like a goddess.

As she paused to double check the whole look, I took the opportunity to come into view. I was behind her, and off to one side. I saw my reflection in the mirror as I made my energy visible. First I was just a shimmer, a mirage, and then the form of my body took shape. When I was finished, I was transparent but it was clearly me, a girl-shaped form complete with the impression of facial features, and hair. The clothes were less defined but still there. A memory of the clothes I wore on the plane.

I came into view and watched Layla as she noticed the flickering image in the mirror. She turned to see and I expected a horror movie screen, but she surprised me. Puzzled at first, her expression turned to delight. I tried to make contact.

Layla Bernstein?

"Are you talking to me?" She pointed to herself with a long-handled makeup brush, the kind women used to apply blush or bronzer. I'd thought she looked perfect but appar-ently she had more to do.

Yes, I need to talk to you.

"Are you a ghost?" The grin on her face told me she wasn't afraid of ghosts.

No, I'm a real person. My name is Nadia.

From outside the bathroom door, a female voice, said, "Layla, did you call me?"

Layla didn't even turn her head. "No, I wasn't talking to you, Chloe. I'm speaking to a spirit."

Chloe giggled. "Oh okay, as long as you're all right."

I'm not a spirit. I'm alive. I said. *I'm astral projecting to you from somewhere else. I'm a friend of Russ Becker's.* That didn't sound quite right so I amended it. *I'm his girlfriend, Nadia.*

"Fascinating!" She reached forward and put her hand closer until it was through me. It didn't feel like a physical touch, but I picked up on her essence. She was trustworthy. "So you're one of those meteorite kids too?"

I wasn't sure how much she knew, but there wasn't time to get into it. *I can astral project,* I said. *I need to send a message to Russ.*

"I'm going to be seeing him tonight," Layla said, as if this was a major coincidence. "I'd be glad to give him your message."

A rap on the bathroom door, and then Chloe said, "Layla, are you on the phone?"

"No, I'm talking to this girl who astral projected to me." She turned to me and said, "Is it okay if I let her see? Chloe would be cool with it, trust me."

No, no, no! I said. *You can't tell anyone besides Russ that you saw me. Seriously, you have to promise.*

Layla said, "No dice. I tell Chloe everything. I'd trust her with my life. She is my life." She set down the makeup brush and folded her arms, a definite sign that this wasn't negotiable.

Okay, so I couldn't call the shots here. I let it go and continued on. *Okay, well do you know anything about the Praetorian Guard?* When she shook her head, I knew I had to give her the condensed version. *Just tell Russ that the inspirational stones Mrs. Whitehouse gave them at the airport are actually explosives set to go off during the Bash. Tell him not to trust Mallory or Jameson. Mallory's necklace is dangerous. Russ needs to get it from her.* I told her there was a plan to kill her and her mother, which I thought might freak her out, but she didn't seem all that concerned. *Mr. Specter invented something called a Specteron. It shoots some kind of dangerous particle beam.* When I started relaying the conversation between Mrs. Whitehouse and Kevin Adams, she seemed to lose interest.

"That's a lot for me to remember," Layla said. "You do know all the guests will be screened like they do at the airport? And the Secret Service will be there too. It's totally safe."

It's not safe. These people are ruthless, I said. *Be very careful and tell Russ to be careful too.*

"I will," she said. "Don't worry I'll take good care of your boyfriend."

Yeah, about that...

She laughed and said, "Don't worry, I have no interest in Russ. He's not my type."

We talked a little while longer. Layla asked me what powers Russ had and I found myself telling her everything. I'm not sure why. Usually I can keep a secret, but she seemed trustworthy enough and I even sensed she might prove to be helpful. "Really?" Her eyes widened. "He can shoot electricity and heal people?"

Yes, but you have to keep this to yourself. Even as I said it, I saw her eyes dart to the door and I knew she was going to be telling Chloe. Well, too late now.

Layla said, "I knew he could undo brainwashing, but I never would have guessed everything else. Fascinating."

I told her not to go anywhere alone with Mallory, and she said, "Believe me, I wasn't planning on it." Then she said, "You're lucky you caught me alone. Usually I have people for these events, but the last time the makeup artist made my eyes look so weird I decided to do it myself this time around."

Her world was so unlike mine, that even if we met in real life we probably wouldn't be friends. Still, I liked her well enough. When Chloe knocked again, saying it was almost time to go, I said, *I better get back. My physical body is on an airplane and my flight should be landing soon. I will be at the Bash, but I won't get there until after it starts.*

"Will I know you when I see you?" Layla asked. "Do you look the same in person?"

I don't know. How do I look to you?

She cocked her head to one side. "Petite. Pretty. Dark hair."

That's me, I said. I could have cried from happiness. For years I'd thought of myself as monstrous, but I guess that wasn't me anymore.

"Well, I guess I'll see you at the Bash then," she said, a cheerful note in her voice.

When I got back to the plane, I opened my eyes to see the matronly woman next to me regarding me with wide eyes.

Her face was so close to mine I could smell her coffee breath. "Well, look who's back," she said with a smile. "I was getting worried. You looked like you were dead to the world."

I feigned a yawn. "Just a power nap. Did I miss anything?" I moved my head from side to side to loosen up my neck muscles.

The woman said, "The pilot just announced we'll be landing in fifteen minutes. Right on schedule."

CHAPTER THIRTY-EIGHT

RUSS

The news that Frank was David's son rendered Carly speechless, and for a split second I regretted laying such a load on her. But only for a split second. After all, she'd been there for the conception, so in theory this shouldn't have been news at all.

"We have to join the others," I said, taking her arm and steering her forward.

"But…" she said, confused. "Frank is David's son? How can that be?"

I shrugged. "The way I understand it, you didn't know it was David that night because you were drunk and he told you he was his own cousin. Then you went with him to his hotel. Nine months later Frank was born."

We were only ten feet from the group when she stopped walking, a stricken look on her face. "How could I not have known?" she whispered.

I'd been impatient with her because I was anxious about the upcoming night, but when I heard how upset she sounded, everything else melted away and my heart took over.

"It's okay," I said, giving her a hug. "You didn't do anything wrong. You were lied to. Plus you'd had too much to drink."

We stood there for a second, until Dr. Anton said, "Everything okay there, Russ?" His forehead furrowed in concern.

Carly pulled away and wiped her eyes. "I'm fine," she called out over her shoulder. "Just wishing Russ luck." And then she leaned in and whispered in my ear. "Be really careful tonight. I couldn't bear it if anything happened to you."

"Okay then," Dr. Anton said, rubbing his hands together. "Shall we get this show on the road?"

The five of us followed him like ducklings. Tonight Mallory looked even better than usual in a long shimmery blue dress with her hair mostly pulled up except for a few pieces that curled around her face. Besides the fact that her eyes had all this dark stuff on the lids, she looked pretty spectacular. Jameson, on the other hand, was a different story. He didn't wear the tux well, in my opinion. He tugged on the sleeves like they bugged him, reminding me of a kid who couldn't wait to change back to his normal clothes. I think I pulled off the whole look much better. Carly, Rosie, and Dr. Anton were wearing their usual clothes, of course, so standing alongside them we looked like kids going to the prom. I almost expected someone to ask us to line up so they could take pictures.

Leaving PGDC and entering the world topside was an adjustment. Even the air felt different—not as fresh and clean and with a gustier breeze. Getting into the limo in the parking structure I got a whiff of exhaust fumes and realized this was something you'd never smell in the world below.

Was PGDC a microcosm of goodness, or an artificial elitist society? I honestly didn't know, but the air smelled better anyway.

When we arrived at the building where the Black Tie Bash would be held we were escorted to a back room to wait for our final briefing. A table off to one side held a pitcher of water and bottles of soft drinks, along with an ice bucket and some glasses, but nobody wanted anything. We milled around for a little bit before taking a seat on one of the leather couches. We'd all been pretty quiet up until then, but now our nerves came out. Mallory kept fiddling with her necklace, a carved white rose on a chain, and began talking about who might be at the Bash. "Last year all the actors who won Academy Awards were invited. Wouldn't that be fabulous if it happened again?"

"Really fabulous," Jameson said, cracking his knuckles one at a time. Even though he answered, he wasn't looking at her. I wasn't an empath like Nadia but it was apparent he was nervous. He reached over the arm of the couch and raised his palm upwards, lifting the lamp on the end table with his telekinesis. Just to prove he could do it. He was like a nervous ballplayer tossing a few balls to warm up.

"You'll see a lot of famous people," Dr. Anton said, "but don't let that be a distraction. I wish you could just relax and enjoy the evening, but unfortunately that's not why you're here." He rubbed his goatee thoughtfully, a gesture I'd seen many times before when I was his patient.

"What do you think is going to happen tonight?" I asked him.

He raised his eyebrows. "Well Russ, there's no way to know for sure…"

"I realize that. But I value your opinion. How do you think this is going to go?"

Dr. Anton cleared his throat. "In all honesty? I think this is going to go badly. If it were up to me they'd cancel the Bash."

Jameson released his hold on the levitating lamp, which clattered down onto the table. Carly looked like the breath had been knocked out of her. "Why do you say that?" she asked. "Do you know something?"

"I don't know anything for sure," he said, holding up a hand to indicate time out. "And I'm not trying to alarm anyone. I just know what the Associates are capable of."

Again, I didn't have Nadia's gift for reading people, but I suspected he knew so much more than he was telling.

"Well maybe they should cancel the Bash," Carly said. "Or not send them in. They're high school students for crying out loud." Her voice was ragged with emotion.

Rosie reached over and patted her arm. "Carly, it's all gonna be fine, trust me. Yes, they're high school students, but they also have incredible capabilities and the security at the Bash is rock solid. There's nothing to worry about." If you could bottle Rosie's reassurances they could sell it to every worried person in America. Her words had a calming effect, at least on Carly, who seemed to have backed away from hysteria and now only looked worried.

"Besides, it's too late now," Jameson said. "I'm wearing the tux." He stood up and put his arms out, welcoming the world to the Jameson show.

"I'd say the tux is wearing you," I said.

A second later, Mitch and Will came walking into

318

the room, all smiles. "Good evening, Russ, Mallory, and Jameson," Mitch said, giving us a slight bow. "And of course, a good evening to your esteemed chaperones."

Will said, "We just want to go over a few things before you join the procession. First of all, kudos go to both Russ and Mallory for fulfilling your objectives. Because of Russ's incredible healing sessions, the president is back to work and feeling one hundred percent better." He paused as if there might be applause. When there wasn't he kept going. "And Mallory's visit with the vice president went well, I hear, so excellent work there, Mallory."

Mitch said. "As you know, our main objective for you this evening is to protect the president and her daughter Layla. Two things to remember—watch for anything or anybody who is acting suspiciously and report them to the Secret Service. An agent will be near you at all times. Secondly, stick together. If Layla has to go to the bathroom, someone needs to go with her, most likely you, Mallory, and one of the boys. She should never be alone for a minute, got it?"

"Got it," Mallory said, beaming, while Jameson and I nodded to show we understood. We'd been through this so many times before that it was practically tattooed on my brain. I could only guess that they thought we were teenage screw-ups who were going to forget all our training once we walked through the door.

"Eyes and ears open, the whole time," Will said. "Practice your observational skills and scan the room continuously. Don't let your guard down. Anything is possible."

"We're on it," Jameson said. He unbuttoned his jacket, then seemed to reconsider and buttoned it again.

"Glad to hear it," Mitch said. "Are we ready to head out then?" He looked to Will, who nodded in approval.

Mallory slipped her hand into the crook of Jameson's elbow. "Let's do this thing."

CHAPTER THIRTY-NINE

NADIA

At the baggage claim area, a young man held a sign with my name on it. I let out a huge sigh of relief. "I'm so glad to see you!" I said rushing up to him. "I was afraid no one would be here."

He smiled, his teeth so straight and white they almost looked fake. "Not to worry. I wouldn't have left you stranded. You've been on the schedule since last night."

When my suitcase came around on the conveyer, he grabbed it out of my hands, insisting that he'd take care of everything. I followed him out of the airport and to the car parked outside, not surprised when I saw a waiting limo. I slid into the back seat, and was greeted by the driver, an older man with a fringe of white hair. He didn't turn his head all the way around, so I only got a partial view of his face. It occurred to me that I was being awfully trusting, but it also occurred to me that I had to be. My Praetorian Guard contact, Preston Moore, was the only one who knew when I was arriving. But were these guys with the PG, or were they a hired car service?

The young man, after putting my suitcase in the trunk, got in the passenger seat up front. "Do you have your seat belt on?" he called back to me. When I said yes, he said something to the driver and we took off, tires screeching. Once we exited the airport, our pace increased and my stomach lurched. The driver put a flashing red light on the dashboard and we sliced through traffic, forcing lines of cars to move aside for us and going over medians when intersections were too crowded. I guess I didn't have to tell them I was in a hurry to get to the Bash.

When the driver pulled off the street, we passed a crowd, all of them excitedly waving at the limo as if they thought I might be someone important. A guard stopped the car and the driver rolled down the window, showed him some paperwork, and we proceeded into a u-shaped driveway and stopped under an overhang. I realized then we'd arrived at a fine hotel. The younger man hopped out and opened the door for me.

"Are we here?" I asked, but he'd already gone back to get my suitcase out of the trunk.

I climbed out, feeling unsteady like I'd just gotten off a roller coaster. The entryway of the building was brightly lit with red carpeting and velvet ropes leading up to the main door. An hour or so earlier celebrities had walked the red carpet and the place had swarmed with paparazzi. Now the place had been cleared out and there was only one bored valet standing at a wooden podium.

"Have a good evening, miss." The younger man dropped my suitcase next to me and jumped back into the limo before I could even respond. The limo pulled away and I was left standing alone in front of the building.

"Nadia?" A young woman with curly dark hair and cocoa-colored skin approached me.

"Yes?"

"Come along, we don't have much time."

"Is this where the Bash is?"

"Yes." She grabbed the handle of my suitcase and led the way. I trailed after, trying to figure out what was going on. I wanted to ask questions, but keeping up with her took everything I had. We passed security at several points and she showed them her badge. When we reached a door further into the building, we were stopped by a guard sitting in front of a full body scanner like at the airport. She turned to me and said, "Is there anything in your bags that you might need in the next three hours? Medication, an inhaler, anything like that?"

"No." I shook my head.

"We're going to leave them here for now," she said. Now that we were closer, I spotted an earpiece with an attached spiral cord that dangled behind her ear and threaded into her clothing. The whole thing was nearly camouflaged by her thick curly hair. Her badge, now two feet in front of my nose, listed her name as Nedra Babish.

"I need to get a message to the security people," I said. "It's really important."

Nedra titled her head to the security guard, as if to tell me not to say anymore in front of him. She guided me toward the scanner. "Let's wait until we get through, shall we?"

I went inside the booth and held my arms up like I was surrendering. When the guard gave me the okay, it was Nedra's turn. Once through, she hurried down the hallway, until we reached a bank of elevators. I followed her inside, and she pushed a button for the third floor. When the doors closed and the elevator shimmied upwards, she said. "You were saying?"

We were close enough for me to pick up her vibe, and I sensed she was on our side. I opened my mouth and it all spilled out, every detail. I told her that Jameson, Mallory, and Russ would be carrying stones that were going to explode and that Mrs. Whitehouse was going to be attending the Bash in disguise. "Russ's old science teacher, Mr. Specter, invented something called a Specteron and it shoots some kind of dangerous particle beam and it sounds like it's going to be at the Bash. And Mallory is still under the mind control of Mr. Specter from when he had her brainwashed by this device he invented—the Deleo." Even to me, the things I was saying sounded like crazy ramblings, but Nedra listened carefully. When we arrived on our floor, we left the elevator but I kept talking. When I was done, she spoke into a piece on her wrist, repeating everything I'd said. Once she was done, she looked to me. "Anything else?"

I racked my brain, thinking. "I think that's it," I said finally.

She signed off with whoever was at the other end, and said to me, "They all went through security and emptied their pockets, and none of them had the stones you talked about, so no worries there, okay?"

"Okay," I said, relieved.

"Now let's get you in hair and makeup and into your gown so you can join the event."

CHAPTER FORTY

—••●••—

RUSS

After we went through security, Dr. Anton hurried us into the banquet hall. I was glad for his sense of urgency because it enabled me to give a quick goodbye to Carly. Given enough time there would be awkward hugs and anguished goodbyes; unnecessary signs of Carly grieving the loss of me before I'd even shown signs of dying.

The first part of the Bash involved an official procession where all the guests lined up to meet the president, her husband, Layla, the Vice President, and Mrs. Montalbo. All of them looked glamorous, the men in tuxes, the women in long dresses. Evening gowns, I guess they're called. Layla looked incredible, taller than usual and elegant in a dress that left one shoulder bare. Her mom's dress was navy blue and basic-looking, but she had some pretty sparkly earrings that caught the light when she moved her head.

We were instructed to file past like we were in a receiving line at a wedding. An aide would announce our names and we were to exchange greetings for no more than ten seconds and then move on. Ten seconds, seriously, that's what we were told. With close to four hundred guests, this part of the evening could take nearly an hour. The three of us were scheduled to go first, so that we could step to the side afterward both to guard the presidential family and also to observe the other guests as they went through the line.

Jameson, pulling Mallory by the hand, pushed past me so he could be the first to go through. I let him, because why not? I had nothing to prove. They were announced to the president and vice president, and then to Layla, who told her parents, "I've already met Mallory and Jameson. They're friends of Russ, my date." I hoped Jameson caught that.

Mallory said, "Happy birthday, Layla!"

"It's really tomorrow, but thanks."

I went next, and the president said she was very glad to meet me as if I hadn't held my hands over her at the hospital and infused her body with healing energy.

I said, "You're looking well tonight, President Bernstein."

"Thank you, Mr. Becker," she said with a wink. "I've never felt better."

Mr. Bernstein grasped my hand and said, "Take good care of our little girl, Russ. Make sure she behaves."

I said, "Of course, sir." Out of the corner of my eye I saw Vice President Montalbo take Mallory's hand and lean in to whisper in her ear. Meanwhile, Jameson was saying something funny to Mrs. Montalbo, causing her to laugh. When I got to Layla, she shook my hand and leaned over to kiss my cheek. "Here's the man of the hour," she said. And then more quietly, "I got a visit from your girlfriend asking me to give you a message."

"Nadia?" Stunned doesn't begin to touch my reaction.

Shocked is more like it. I lowered my voice. "She astral projected to you?"

"Yes." And then so quietly I barely heard the words. "She had some concerns about this evening. I already told the Secret Service. I'll fill you in after I'm done here."

"Can you tell me now?" The hall was getting noisy as guests entered and mingled. It looked like not everybody was choosing to get in line, or maybe they were just waiting.

She tilted her head to indicate the encroaching line. In another five seconds, I'd be in the direct path of the man next to me. I vaguely recognized him as the lead singer of a rock band Carly had loved in high school. "Later," Layla whispered.

It killed me to walk away without hearing more, but rock and roll guy was extending his hand to Layla saying, "It's awesome to meet you."

Vice President and Mrs. Montalbo greeted me and said it was nice to meet me. There was no sign that he remembered me as the young man who'd insulted him in his office just recently. So that was good.

I took my place along the wall next to Mallory and Jameson. Across the room, servers offered guests glasses of champagne, while others walked around with trays of hors d'oeuvres. The line leading up to the president snaked around the side of the room, and Secret Service agents were everywhere, not even trying to blend in. Mallory nudged me and said, "Can you believe we're here? Isn't this wild?"

"Yeah, pretty crazy." I kept my eyes ahead, looking for suspicious behavior, but also looking for a woman disguised as a man. I'd had trouble sleeping the night before so I'd mentally gone over the plot of the comic book Mr. Specter and Kevin

Adams had written. *Superheroes of the Twenty-First Century!* Most of the action in the story had taken place in a banquet hall, much like this one. And from there, the similarities kept coming. Just like Spark Boy, I had healed a lady president who'd been in a coma and like Persuasa, Mallory had used mind control on a vice president who'd previously crossed over to the Associate side. Those two things alone made me think I needed to pay attention to the story. Interesting that back when the story was written the idea of a lady president was pretty farfetched and here we were more than twenty years later, with a woman president and it was no big deal.

The rest of the story hadn't played out yet. We were at a ball, although it wasn't a charity ball, but that was a minor point. If the evening followed the comic book, the commander of the Associates, a woman, would be here disguised as a man. An explosion would go off, causing the room to fill with smoke. And then, pandemonium as the crowd panics trying to escape. What happened after that? I thought about the next panel in the comic book. One of the Associates aims a shot of electricity at the president which is intercepted by Spark Boy who stops it with a bolt of lightning of his own. Jameson had his own heroic role in this when his character, Mover!, propels the missile away from the president and shoots it out of the ceiling.

The rest of the story was the most troubling to me because it involved Nadia's death, something that made me sick to my stomach just thinking about it. But of course that would never happen. Nadia was on her way here, not Edgewood. The scenario didn't fit, so it couldn't possibly happen.

So the comic book wasn't completely accurate, but it still held clues, I thought. But what if, even as a teenager,

Mr. Specter anticipated crossing over to the other side, and through the comic book he purposely tried to steer us wrong? That would take a lot of anticipation and planning. It seemed unlikely, but then again, everything that had happened since the night I saw the lux spiral seemed unlikely.

Mallory and Jameson had been talking quietly to each other this whole time, pointing out celebrities and debating if anyone would stop them from having a glass of champagne. They caught me listening to their conversation and I shook my head in disapproval. Jameson said, "Russ is a killjoy."

"Not a killjoy," I said, turning my attention back to the line. "Just a superhero of the twenty-first century."

"Whatever," he said.

I watched the line approach the first family, and when the aide announced, "Dr. David Hofstetter," I did a double take because I'd forgotten he was going to be here. I thought of Carly watching this event on a monitor in an adjoining room and wondered if she'd recognize him. Who knew? Maybe she had audio and even heard them say his name. I tried to catch his eye. Not to talk to him or anything, just to let him know we were there, but he didn't look in our direction. David was too busy talking to the president and Mr. Bernstein. From their familiar greeting it seemed that they'd met before. As he went through the line I noticed that his exchange with Vice President and Mrs. Montalbo was clipped and brief. I didn't think they had met before.

When a server came by with a tray of soft drinks, I shook my head, but Jameson and Mallory each took a glass. My stomach growled but I turned down hors d'oeuvres too, even though they looked delicious. Next to me, my friends ate and drank and talked like we were at a party where nothing terrible could happen, but I couldn't shake the feeling that in the upcoming hours this lovely social event could turn into tragedy. I remembered Dr. Anton's answer when I asked him how he thought things would go: *I think this is going to go badly. If it were up to me they'd cancel the Bash.* I didn't think he'd try to scare us unnecessarily. That's just how he felt.

I flexed my hands by my side, ready to shoot out the electricity coursing through my body on a moment's notice. I was on edge, but I had to be.

CHAPTER FORTY-ONE

NADIA

Nedra took me to a room that held three barber chairs and two small makeup stations complete with vanity mirrors and more trays of cosmetics than you'd find at Macy's display counter. An older woman who'd been sitting in one of the chairs, jumped up when we walked in. Her eyes narrowed while she looked me up and down and she didn't look happy with what she saw. When Nedra introduced us (Maisy this is Nadia, Nadia this is Maisy), and we shook hands, I sensed that somehow without even knowing her, I'd become a disappointment. Maisy shook her head sternly, "I have no idea if I have a dress that will fit her."

Nedra said, "Surely you must have something."

"I have a lot of somethings, but this Bash is for grownups. I have nothing that will fit an eighth grader." She gestured to a rolling rack filled with dresses and scowled.

"She's tiny but certainly you have dresses in a size two?" Nedra turned to me. "Is that your size, Nadia?"

"Maybe," I said, not really certain. The clothes my mother ordered for me were women's small. My jeans were purchased by waist size and length. I wasn't used to getting clothes by size, but I was pretty sure size two was for models.

Maisy said, "The size isn't the problem. It's the length that's going to kill us. Not only that but her shoulders are way too narrow."

Nedra strode decisively over to the rack and started pulling dresses. "Strip down, Nadia," she said. "I'm going to need you to try these on."

"Can't I go to the Bash like this?" Even as I asked I knew the answer was no. Showing up at the Black Tie Bash in jeans and T-shirt under any circumstances was never a possibility.

Nedra dumped an armful onto the chair. "Start with these."

Maisy said, "Even if we find a dress, there's the problem of her hair."

"What's wrong with my hair?" I kicked off my shoes, and unzipped my jeans and stepped out of them.

"It looks like a three-year-old cut your bangs."

"I'm letting them grow out," I said, pulling off my T-shirt. To minimize the amount of time spent in my underwear in front of two strangers, I took a yellow dress off the pile, pulled it over my head, and let it shimmy over my hips. The excess fabric at the bottom pooled around my feet like I was standing in a spotlight.

"Maybe with high heels?" Nedra said doubtfully.

"Not even with stilts." Maisy stood with her arms folded. I had the feeling she'd be on a break right now if not for me. "By the way, Nadia, you need to lose the bra. All the gowns have built in cups."

I tried on dress after dress, all of them too long. When

I pulled the last one over my head, I was so flustered that at first I tried to put my head through the opening for my arm. Lost inside a sea of red chiffon, it was Nedra's voice that saved me. "Let me help you." I felt her hands guide my arms toward the sleeves and pull the fabric around my head until everything came out of the right opening. Part of the cloth was still over my head even as the rest of the dress fell to the floor. "It has a hood?" I asked.

Nedra flipped it back. "No, it has a low back which drapes at the bottom." She looked at Maisy. "I think this is perfect for her."

Maisy begrudgingly agreed. "But only because the dress is supposed to fall mid-calf. On her it's all the way to the floor."

"It doesn't matter," Nedra said. "It's perfect." She led me to a full-length mirror, where I saw the image of someone who could have been me, if I were beautiful. For an instant the crisis faded and time paused while I gaped at myself in the dress. I pinched the chiffon fabric and pulled it up, then watched as it floated down.

"Oh, it's so beautiful," I said, turning to see the view from the back.

"You look absolutely gorgeous," she said. "The only problem is that the dress will be too short with high heels. I'll find you some flats. Size five?"

"Six please." She took off into an adjoining room, leaving me to stare at the dark-haired girl in the mirror who looked almost perfect to me.

Maisy came up behind me and said, "While Nedra's hunting for shoes, let's do your hair and makeup." She steered me into a chair and stepped back to appraise my face. "Your skin is nearly perfect, so there's not much to do there."

"Oh no, my skin is awful," I said, lifting a hand to the side that had been burned. "The worst."

"From where I'm standing it looks great." She shrugged. "If you normally have breakouts, you don't have them today. Since you're in a hurry, we can skip the foundation and make do with some lipstick and a touch of bronzer and, I have to tell you, I do a really great dramatic eye. I usually do Layla Bernstein's makeup so you're in good hands." She took a long handled brush and dipped it into some powder and began sweeping it over my cheeks. She stepped back to survey her work.

Oh man, this was going on for way too long. I needed to get out of here pronto. "You know I don't usually wear much make-up and I'm going to miss the whole Bash if we don't hurry. I want to skip the rest."

"Skip it!" she exclaimed, clearly dismayed. "You can't skip it."

Nedra came rushing in, holding a pair of black and red flats. "Not a great match, but good enough."

I stood up and slid my feet into the shoes. "The dress covers them anyway," I said.

"It won't cover them when you're dancing," Maisy said, her voice grumpy. She grabbed a comb off one of the vanity tables and ran it roughly over my head, then pulled my hair up in the back and pinned it quickly in place.

Nedra took my hand. "That's enough, Maisy. I have to get Nadia to the Bash."

"Geez, what's with you two? You're like Cinderella rushing to go to the ball."

Cinderella actually rushed to get *away* from the ball, but I wasn't going to correct her. We said our good-byes and Nedra led me out the door. We were halfway down the hall, when we heard the clatter of Maisy's feet coming up behind us. "Wait!" she yelled. I turned to see her brandishing something curved and shiny. A red gem-studded headband. She skidded to a stop right behind us, and taking a comb from her pocket, quickly brushed my bangs to one side, the placed the headband on my head. "There," she said. "You needed that."

A wave of professional pride rolled off her. It bothered her that I'd left her with uneven bangs. "Thanks," I said.

As we continued down the hallway Nedra said, "I must say it does add just the right touch." Off in the distance I heard music playing from the Bash hall. I'd missed the meet and greet, but it wasn't as late as I'd thought. And at least I wasn't hearing explosions.

Nedra took me right to a set of double doors blocked by a heavy-set guard. She flashed her security badge and he stepped aside. "This is where I leave you," she said bowing slightly. "It has been a pleasure, Miss Nadia."

"Did anyone tell Russ I'm here?"

She pushed the door open and ushered me through. "You can tell him yourself."

CHAPTER FORTY-TWO

RUSS

After the last of the crowd came through the receiving line, a man strode up to a podium in the front of the room, and spoke into a microphone. "Good evening ladies and gentlemen. I give you the president of the United States!"

A hush fell over the crowd and President Bernstein stepped forward. She adjusted the microphone and with a smile said, "Welcome everyone, to the third annual Presidential Black Tie Bash!" She waited for the applause, which came thundering. When it died down, she said, "I am proud to see assembled here some of our brightest and best citizens. Whether you're an entertainer, a scientist, a diplomat, a politician or what have you, please know that you play an important role in making America a great country. This evening is a thank you for your talents and support. As a nation we still have our challenges, but just for tonight, please set those concerns aside and enjoy our hospitality. Very soon the band will begin and dancing will commence. In the meantime, we'll keep the champagne flowing. If anyone imbibes too much and needs a ride home at the end of the evening, please let us know." A few people in the crowd laughed and a smattering of applause came from somewhere in back.

I felt a hand on my arm and glanced over to see Layla standing next to me. "Hey there," she whispered. "Now I can relax. The worst is over." I hoped she was right, but the night was young. A lot could happen.

The president wrapped things up by saying, "And now, let the fun begin." She had a joyful look on her face, such a contrast to the hospital scene of a few days ago. When she'd said the part about the evening being a thank-you for your talents, I felt like she was talking right to me. But maybe everyone in the room felt that way.

The president stepped away from the podium, and the noise level in the room rose as people resumed talking and drinking. I heard the clinking of glasses and more laughter, a sign the champagne had begun to kick in. People milled around and several guests approached the president and her husband to talk. I watched worriedly, but didn't notice anything that looked threatening. On the other side of the room, a young woman I recognized as an actor from the Syfy channel had Vice President Montalbo's attention. She chattered away gesturing wildly with her hands, while he listened, amused. Next to me, Mallory and Jameson were watching too.

The staff began setting up table and chairs around the perimeter of the dance floor. Each circular table was covered with a linen table cloth and topped with a candle. On the raised platform on the far end of the room, the band was setting up their equipment. Someone, somewhere, lowered the lights to give the evening some ambiance, and my heart fell as I realized this would make it even harder to check out the guests. I clenched my fists again, ready to strike if I had to.

"Lighten up, Russ," Layla said, giving my arm a squeeze. "You look like you want to kill someone."

"Believe me, I don't want to kill anyone," I said. "But I'm ready to do what I have to." Now that I had her next to me, I was able to say it. "Tell me about Nadia."

Her eyes widened. "Oh my, that was amazing! One second I'm alone in the bathroom, the next she's right there like she beamed up from the Enterprise. She's really super cute, by the way. At first I thought she was a ghost—"

"But what did she say?"

Layla laughed. "Someone's impatient! If you'll give me a minute I'll get there."

There was no stopping her; she was determined to tell the story her own way. I listened politely while she told me the whole thing, complete with her reactions and how Chloe kept knocking on the door because she couldn't figure out who Layla was talking to. Nadia had told her there was a plan to kill her and her mother, which didn't seem to alarm Layla in the least. "It's a big country," she said, waving her hand dismissively. "There's always some crazy who wants the president and her family dead. We get threats all the time." She had trouble remembering it all. "And something about a Specteron. You know what that is?"

"No."

"Well she seemed all worried about the safety here. I assured her the Secret Service has it all locked up tight. That's sort of what they do." She waved her hand. "I told her I had no interest in you, which I think made her feel better."

When she finished, I felt the need to recap. "So she said the inspirational stones Mrs. Whitehouse gave us contained explosives?" Layla nodded. Good thing we threw the stones away at the airport. Somewhere a landfill full of garbage would be exploding. I continued, "And she said I shouldn't trust Mallory or Jameson?" I glanced in their direction but nothing in their faces said they had traitorous intentions.

"Yes, young man, that's pretty much what she said. I told her not to worry. The security at this thing is crazy, but she was all concerned about you. It was pretty adorable."

"Did she say anything else?"

Her pursed lips moved from side to side as she thought. "There was something else, but I'm having trouble remembering." She snapped her fingers. "Oh!" she said. "I know what it was. She was on a flight here at the time, and it sounds like she's going to make it to the Bash. She'll be late though."

"What time? Did she say?"

Layla shook her head. "I don't have a clue. But remember that you're my date so I'm not giving you up once she gets here. She can have you for the rest of your life, but tonight you're mine." She linked her fingers through mine and said, "Time to dance!" The band had started with a slow song and some guy at the mike was doing his best Frank Sinatra impersonation.

The next thing I knew, I was being dragged to the middle of the empty dance floor. Mallory and Jameson, following the instructions that we all stick together, were right behind us. We were the only ones out there. When we got to the center of the floor, Layla very theatrically curtseyed to me. This hadn't come up in our dance training, but I played along and bowed. On the sidelines, the crowd's attention shifted to us, and when Layla and I finally came together and began dancing, applause broke out. It was mortifying to know that every pair of eyes in the room looked our way. Luckily for me, my worst dancing beat Jameson's best dance moves any day of the week, so by comparison I was doing pretty well.

Layla's pressed her body tightly against mine and breathed into my ear. "You're probably wondering why I wanted to be the first on the dance floor."

"Yeah, I did wonder. Isn't the president supposed to dance first?"

"Technically yes, but trust me, my mom doesn't care," Layla said, shifting her head in the direction of her mother, who watched us with a pleased expression. "She's just happy to see me touching a man."

"So I qualify as a man?" I felt my lips tug upward into a grin.

"More or less. But to get back to my point..."

"Yes?"

"If we're looking for infiltrators, this provides us with an excellent opportunity to scope out the crowd. They're stationary but we're moving. Look at the faces," she urged. "Are there any in particular that are looking at me in a strange way? Calculating, maybe? Or impatient, like they're waiting for their moment?"

As we swayed and twirled I kept my gaze on the rest of the guests. Dressed in tuxes and ball gowns, they all looked vaguely alike. We might as well have been at a costume party. "I'm not seeing anything odd."

"Keep looking," she said, "because I noticed a few suspicious looking people and I want your opinion."

Next to us, Jameson valiantly tried to keep in rhythm. With each step I saw his lips move. I swear he was counting to himself. When we first got on the dance floor Mallory had laughed at his jerky moves, but if he stepped on her toes one more time, she'd be losing her patience real fast.

Layla took over, pulling me around to give me the right view. "That guy right there," she said with a tilt of her head. "See him? The one with the dark hair? Kind of good looking? He's been staring at us in a really creepy way. I swear I can feel his eyeballs boring into me right now."

I grinned. The creepy guy whose eyeballs were boring right into Layla was David Hofstetter. "Trust me, he's okay."

"Are you sure?"

"Absolutely. I know him. He's a friend of my sister's, that's why he's staring."

She exhaled audibly. "Okay, if you're vouching for him, that's good enough for me. Okay, now I want you to check out two other men."

"Where?"

"Don't look around like that. It's too obvious," she said through gritted teeth. "It's those two near the bar. When they went through the line they were announced as being father and son, but they don't look at all alike. The father is small and puny, and the son is massive like he's a wrestler or body builder. They don't fit."

I craned my neck to see. Sure enough, a gray-haired older gentleman with a mustache and goatee and glasses stood a head shorter than the guy who was supposed to be the son. The son, who didn't look much older than me, had broad shoulders and a military haircut. It wasn't that unusual for a father and son to look different. But the younger guy had a familiar look. Where had I seen him before? "Who are they?" I asked.

She shrugged. "The line moved so quickly I didn't catch their names."

"I've seen the son before, I think. I don't know the father."

"Maybe they've been in the news? Most of the people here are well known in their field. I just thought there was something not quite right about them."

"No, not from the news…" I strained my mind trying to figure out where I'd seen this young guy. Another place, another time, a different context. And I had the feeling that something about him was different. Like watching a movie and trying to figure out where you've seen an actor before. The idea that I'd met him nagged at me, but I couldn't pull up the specifics. I shook my head. "I can't place him."

When we got off the dance floor, Layla went to point the two out to one of the Secret Service agents, who nodded and said they'd keep watch. I stood back to give them space to talk. Jameson and Mallory, who'd followed us, watched curiously as Layla gave the agents the update. "What's up?" Jameson asked.

"Layla's just checking in with them."

"Anything we should know about?" Jameson said.

He sounded so sincere that I almost told them, but no, Nadia had said not to trust them. I shrugged and said, "Nothing so far."

Jameson took a step in that direction, trying to hear what Layla was saying. Mallory took this opportunity to sidle up to me. "Can you do me a favor, Russ?" Without waiting for me to answer, she grabbed my hand, pressed something into my palm and closed my fingers over it. She stood on her tip-toes and whispered into my ears. "Keep this for me and don't give it back to me even if I ask for it. Can you do that for me?" I opened my hand to see an ivory rose on a chain—the necklace she'd gotten from Mrs. Whitehouse.

"Sure I can do that, but why—"

Mallory put a finger over my lips and shook her head. "No matter what I say, don't give it to me. Promise?"

"Well, sure but—" I said, stopping when I saw the terrified look on her face.

"You have to promise me, Russ." She stared up at me with big eyes.

"I promise." I slipped the necklace into the inside pocket of my suit coat.

A second later, Layla returned, with Jameson right behind her, and said, "Okay, that's set." The four of us came together in a four leaf clover configuration. Anyone watching would think we were planning something.

"What was that all about?" Jameson asked, tipping his head in the direction of the agents.

"Just talking about my birthday," she said nonchalantly. "People have been bringing gifts. I never keep them and now I have to write thank you notes."

The air in the room seemed different to me now—more charged with electricity, more menacing. I saw the president and Mr. Bernstein making small talk with guests, every one of them a potential Associate. How quickly the room changed before my eyes. Was I getting paranoid, and if so, was that a bad thing? I opened and closed my hands, assuring myself that I had energy on hand and that at a moment's notice I could shoot a bolt of electricity across the room, an idea that reassured me and terrified me at the same time.

As we walked away I felt a hand grip my shoulder. Startled, I wheeled around to get loose and reflexively I let out a zap of electricity. Just a small one, a flash of silver between my hand and the guy's chest, but even that little bit was too much, because a nanosecond later I realized it was David Hofstetter and I'd nailed him a good one. The impact caused him to stagger and drop to his knees. "Dammit, Russ," he said, clutching his chest.

CHAPTER FORTY-THREE

NADIA

I walked through the double doors into the Bash and was transported into another world. Somehow I'd thought the event would be like a wedding reception or a prom (both of which I'd only seen in movies and on TV), but this room, these people, surpassed anything I could have imagined. Ornate pillars, like Roman columns lined the long sides of the hall. Overhead, semi-sheer fabric draped in between crystal chandeliers supplying soft lighting, making the place look dreamy. Floor-to-ceiling curtains were held back by gold cords which were looped around the fabric multiple times ending in tassels as big as my fist. The men in tuxes and the women in their elegant gowns floated across the dance floor. I'd been sent back to one of Gatsby's parties. It would be so easy to get lost in this piece of heaven and forget why I was here.

My first objective though was to find Russ. I'd thought it would be easy, that all I'd have to do was look across the room and I'd spot him, but I was short and couldn't see past those standing in front of me. I looked for an empty chair, thinking I could get up on one, but every single one in sight was occupied. I weaved my way through the crowd, searching as I went. A waiter stopped to ask if I wanted a glass of champagne. I started to say no, then reconsidered and took a glass. "Thanks." I hadn't realized how thirsty I was until I took that first sip. The golden liquid went down smoothly. As I walked around, glass in hand, I recognized almost everybody. Actors, politicians, scientists, they all had a familiar look, which added to the feeling that I'd dreamed this whole thing. When I was done with the champagne, I set the empty glass on the edge of a deserted table and kept walking.

"Hey sweetheart, don't you look beautiful." I looked up to see a guy blocking my path and crazily enough it was Kyle Sternhagen, an actor I'd loved in a TV series years ago. When I was eleven and he played the teenage son on the show, I'd dreamed that someday we would meet and fall in love and get married. Seriously, Kyle and that show were the only things that got me through being eleven and that was before my face was damaged. I hadn't seen him in any shows or movies since, and believe me, I watched for him, wanting another dose of my screen crush. I'd heard he was producing environmental documentaries, and I even watched one on Netflix, but there was no sign of him on the screen except in the credits at the end. As a young girl, I'd longed for him, and like a miracle, here he was saying I looked beautiful. My eleven-year-old self would have jumped with glee. His timing sucked. "Lady in red," he said, "won't you dance with me?"

"Oh I'd love to, but I can't. Maybe another time."

"Another time?" He threw his hands up in mock horror. "Am I being rejected?"

"No, it's not that, it's just I'm looking for a friend." I gazed past him, searching for Russ. I'd settle for Mallory, Jameson, or Layla, since they were all supposed to be together.

"I could be your friend." Kyle grinned and he leaned so close I could smell the liquor on his breath.

I should have turned my back to him and kept going, but I tried one more time to be nice. "I'm really sorry. Normally, I'd love to—"

He grabbed my wrist and grinned flirtatiously. "Just one dance. Then, if you still want to look for your friend, we'll do it together." He grabbed my hand, and I was caught in the current, moving behind him through the crowd and onto the dance floor. Before I knew it, I was pressed up against him, and we were swaying in time to the music. On TV he'd looked so tall, but in real life not so much. Russ was at least three or four inches taller than him. *Russ!* I twisted to see if I could spot him, and Kyle whispered in my ear. "One dance, that's all I ask. And who knows, maybe your friend will spot you."

My tendency to be nice kicked in and I thought, oh the hell with it. I hadn't had much luck searching through the crowd. Maybe Kyle was right and one of my friends might just see me on the dance floor. In my red gown I did stand out.

When the music stopped, I stepped back and Kyle and I clapped politely. "I have to go now," I said, gesturing randomly to the crowd. "Thank you for the dance."

"Wait," he said.

But I didn't wait. I'd already given him too much time. I rushed away, Kyle on my heels. I pushed through the crowd saying, "Excuse me, excuse me!" as I went.

Behind me Kyle called out, "But I didn't get your number!"

In all my eleven-year-old dreaming I'd never once had a scenario where I tried to ditch Kyle Sternhagen. I went around clusters of people drinking champagne and talking. Behind one pillar, a distinguished-looking older man kissed a younger blond woman who looked young enough to be his daughter. But I couldn't let myself get distracted. I pushed forward, zig-zagging my way to the other end of the room.

"Lady in red!"

I made the mistake of glancing back and wound up plowing right into a guy holding a champagne glass. I looked back in time to see the liquid come flying out of his glass drenching his neck and the front of his tux. "Oh no!" I said, stopping. "I'm *so* sorry."

He didn't look much older than me, but he was big. Like steroid big. Like he could bench press a cow. He grunted and said, "Don't worry about it," but his annoyed look contradicted his words. A large wet stain marked the front of his shirt and tie. Champagne dripped off his chin and ran down his neck. He brushed at the front of the tux with his hand as if that would help.

"Here," I grabbed a napkin off a nearby table and started to wipe the champagne dripping down his neck but he stepped back before I'd barely started.

"Stop it!" he yelled, clapping a hand over his neck and letting go of the champagne glass, which shattered as it hit the floor. As he walked angrily away, a shorter man with a gray beard and glasses came up from behind and asked, "What happened?" The guy with the champagne-stained shirt grumbled a response, but I couldn't hear what it was because I was overwhelmed by the hateful feelings I'd picked up when my hand had connected with his skin seconds earlier. The sensation had been brief but powerful. This guy was pure evil. The kind of person who accelerated when he saw a puppy in the middle of the road. Or thought nothing of killing a president and helping to take over a government if it meant he came out on top. He was, I could tell, one of the Associates, which meant that the older man with him was in league with them too. I looked down at the napkin in my hand. Besides being wet, it had a smudge of something that looked like a dark beige cream. Something on his skin had been covered up with thick make-up.

I got a sudden image, remembering when Russ told me about a test the Associates had put him through. He'd passed through a series of rooms, each one with its own challenge. In one room, he went up against two young guys who shared his talent for shooting electricity, and one of them, he'd told me, had a snake tattooed on his neck. On the very same side of the neck that this guy had covered with makeup. If it was the same person, that would explain his reaction.

I was jarred out of my thoughts by a pair of arms wrapped around me in a tight bear hug. "Lady in red, I have found you!" Kyle said, breathing hard.

CHAPTER FORTY-FOUR

RUSS

After seeing David Hofstetter drop to his knees, I thought I'd triggered a heart attack in the man. When he said, "Dammit Russ," I was actually relieved that he swore at me, because if he could speak that forcefully, he was probably going to be okay.

"David! Are you okay?" I asked. Around us people stopped talking to see what the deal was with the guy kneeling on the floor.

He shook his head like a dog after a bath. "Oh man, you've got some zap there, son."

I extended my hand and helped him up.

David rose and brushed off his knees, then spoke to the curious onlookers. "I'm fine, really. Nothing to see here. As you were." They took him at his word and turned away, resuming their drinking and conversation. Given how much champagne was being served it was understandable that the crowd was so mellow.

Jameson and Mallory said their hellos to David, and I introduced Layla to him. After the usual pleasantries, he said,

"If you folks don't mind, I'd like to talk to Russ alone for a minute."

Mallory and Jameson took a few steps back, but Layla pulled me so close that her body melded against mine. "I'm sorry, but Russ was instructed to be with me at all times."

David gave her a winning smile. "This will only take a second. It's personal." He had that pleading puppy dog look that made me think this was about Carly.

She returned his smile. "You can say anything in front of me, isn't that right, Russ?"

Oh, I did hate being in the middle. This reminded me of the time my parents got into a heated argument. When my mom left the room, my dad had said, "Is it me, or is she being completely irrational?" That's when I made a really big mistake. I agreed with him and she overheard me. Now whenever things get testy, Mom sniffs and says, "I guess I'm being irrational." I'd learned my lesson. I didn't want to be in the middle and I resented him for putting me there. Layla's safety trumped everything else this evening. I said, "David, is this about my sister? Because if it is, it'll have to wait."

He hesitated, "Well, it's just that…"

"Oh no, it *is* about Carly."

"Do you have any idea how she'll react when she finds out I'm still alive?" He said all the words in a rush.

Layla shot me a puzzled look, but I didn't want to get into a lengthy explanation. I took her arm and said, "We'll talk about this later."

Layla said, "Oh Russ, show some mercy and talk to the man."

The only way to say it was to just tell him the truth.

"David, I couldn't keep lying to Carly. I already told her that you're still alive. Oh, and I told her you were Frank's dad too."

He had a stricken look on his face. "How did she react?"

I liked David, I really did, but I loved my sister and my nephew a whole lot more. "How do you think she reacted? She was mad and when she got over being mad, she was crushed. All those years." I shook my head. "You know you broke her heart." My words made an impact. He looked suitably punished. I asked, "Anything else you want to know?"

When he didn't respond, I said, "I guess that's it then." We started to walk away, but he recovered and followed us, grabbing my arm. "Just one more thing. Please, just listen. This will only take a few seconds."

I'd gone this far, how could I not listen to just one more thing? Besides, I was starting to feel sorry for him. "Sure thing, David. What is it?"

He had hold of my sleeve and he leaned in to speak near my ear. "If I die before I get to see Carly would you tell her something for me?" I nodded and he continued. "Tell her that I know I made a big mistake. That if I could do it over again, I would have stayed, no matter what. Tell her that I know now that love should always come first. Can you tell her that for me?"

A little dramatic, I thought, but he was heading in the right direction. I said, "Sure, I could tell her that, but I won't need to. You're going to see her soon, David."

"I hope so." When he pulled away I thought I saw the glint of tears in his eyes. He exhaled and said, "Now I need to go back to work."

As he walked away, Layla said, "If you think you won't have to explain what that was all about, you're dead wrong."

CHAPTER FORTY-FIVE

NADIA

I felt Kyle's arms around my shoulders but I didn't pull away. "Help me out a minute, will you?" I asked sweetly. "I need to look for my friend, but I can't see over the crowd."

"Tell me what she looks like and I'll find her," he said eagerly, letting go and putting one hand visor-like over his forehead.

"Nope, I have a better idea. Do this and give me a boost." I demonstrated what I wanted, interlocking my fingers to make a stirrup.

He was just drunk enough to go for it. I stepped into the curve of his fingers and pulled up on his shoulders until I was suspended above the crowd. From his leering grin I could tell that he liked having me pressed against him. I scanned the room, looking from end to end. The dance floor looked less crowded from this angle, and the band members more lively, especially the bandleader who energetically raised and lowered his arms to set the beat.

"Do you see her?" he asked. Where he got the idea my friend was a girl, I didn't know but I didn't correct him.

"Not yet. Still looking."

And then I saw her—Mallory on the other side of the crowd, with her hand tucked into Jameson's elbow. They were both looking intently at something with very serious expressions on their faces. I didn't see Russ or Layla, but they could have been one of the several people nearby facing away from me. "Mallory," I yelled, waving my arm from side to side. "Mallory!"

"You see her?" Kyle asked, his eyes turned up to meet mine. He sounded glad for me.

"Yes." Between the band and the singing, it was noisy. I tried again, this time shouting. "Mallory!" Her head snapped upward and in my direction. I could have sworn she saw me. It was just for a moment though, and then just as quickly she looked away. Was it a trick of my imagination or was she ignoring me? Either way, at least I finally had a handle on where they were.

I watched as Mallory spoke to Jameson and a realization hit me in a good way. She wasn't wearing a necklace, so someone must have taken it from her. Which was good because I'd forgotten to mention it to Nedra before she'd ushered me into the room to try on gowns. It seemed like an important detail to forget and the only excuse I had was that the pressure and lack of sleep was getting to me.

Just as I was about to tell Kyle to put me down, I noticed a commotion about twenty feet away. I didn't see the man fall, but he obviously had. I could only see his protruding legs—black pants and shiny shoe—and the backs of the other people clustered around him. A guy broke out of the circle and screamed, "Someone call 911! My father's had a heart attack!" The crowd gave him space and he shouted again. "We need a doctor." And then he happened to see me suspended above the crowd and his eyes locked with mine. I knew then that it was the guy I bumped into, the one who'd had champagne dashed across the front of his tux. Unlike Mallory, there was no doubt in my mind. He'd seen me and the contempt in his eyes said we weren't friends. A second later he went back to being a concerned son, yelling for help for his father. The anguish in his voice played well to the people around him, some of whom consoled him while others rushed to get help.

I saw the bearded old man more clearly now. He lay on his back, his face pale and his glasses askew. Was that how someone who had a heart attack looked? I didn't know.

Kyle interrupted my thoughts. "You're getting heavy."

I glanced down to see the vein is his forehead prominently protruding. "Just hang on." The heart attack commotion seemed to only be occupying a small back corner of the Bash. In front, the band played on and couples twirled around the dance floor, oblivious to the crisis. The crowd parted as a medical team came through with a rolling gurney. A man, escorted by a Secret Service agent, led the way holding a large medical bag and two guys in scrubs. A doctor with paramedics? The doctor set the bag down and started barking orders to the other guys. The ring of onlookers stepped back, giving them space. I appeared to be the only one in the room that thought this whole scenario was fishy.

"Okay, you can let me down."

Kyle cooperated, lowering me gently and taking hold of my waist to steady me until my feet were on the floor. "There you go," he said with a crooked smile.

"Thanks," I said, and I took off, heading in the direction

where I'd seen Mallory and Jameson. "Wait!" Kyle called after me, but I was through being nice. He'd have to find some other girl to pick up.

I hadn't gotten far when the band stopped playing and the lights brightened. The singer said, "Ladies and gentleman, I give you the President of the United States of America."

The band began playing "Hail to the Chief" and the crowd cheered loudly. President Bernstein walked up the stage steps and over to the microphone. She smiled and held up her hand to silence the crowd.

After the president called her daughter onto the stage, I got my first Bash view of Russ as he traipsed obediently behind her. I cupped my mouth and yelled, "Russ!" but my voice couldn't be heard above the crowd applauding at the sight of the first daughter bounding up the stairs onto the stage. When she said, "My date this evening is the fabulous Russ Becker. Isn't he handsome? Give it up for Russ!" I felt my gut clench and I wasn't sure if it was from jealousy or worry.

All I knew was that I had to warn Russ. I didn't have any power but the power of knowledge. He'd know what to do.

If I could have, I'd have run to the stage, but there was this small matter of four hundred people blocking my way. I pushed through the crowd, slipping through gaps, and moving around couples. As fast as I tried to go, I still only went at the pace of a lazy river raft—agonizingly slow. A few people objected as I shoved my way around them. "Ex*cuse* me!" one man said loudly. I had no time to answer or I would have said, *I'm sorry I bumped your elbow but I'm frantically trying to save the president's life. My apologies. Jerkwad.*

Thinking I might not get there in time made me crazy

with worry. *Think, Nadia, think.* I decided I'd have a clearer path if I moved along the edge of the room, so I veered to the far left side. I was impatient with these people. These beautiful, privileged people. They stood in their tuxes and gorgeous gowns with drinks in hand, oblivious to the danger lurking among them, watching the stage in front, blocking my way. I wanted to yell, to tell them there was an emergency and they should exit the room, but between the applause, the band, and their chattering, I didn't think I'd get heard.

I was moving faster now, keeping my gaze straight ahead and getting more aggressive. When two people standing too close together blocked my path, I used my hands to part them like treading water. I stopped worrying about accidentally stepping on the hem of a dress, or bumping someone's glass; I just went. I left startled people in my wake, and at one point I heard a woman's voice behind me say, "Someone's in a big hurry," and I thought: *you got that right.*

I was making good headway when I came to two men standing shoulder to shoulder. I said, "Excuse me," and gave each one's arm a push then squeezed through the opening and bumped—bam—right into the back of a white-jacketed man. Shocked, I realized I'd happened upon the very scene I wanted to warn Russ about, the Associates posing as father and son. And from the feelings I'd picked up from touching the back of this man's jacket, he was one of them too. I gasped. "Pardon me," I said and took a step back. But the doctor turned and saw me before I could slip away. His eyes narrowed and a sick smile spread across his face. He grabbed my arm forcefully. "Nadia," he said. "What a surprise."

CHAPTER FORTY-SIX

RUSS

With only about an hour left to the evening, I was starting to feel like we might be in the clear, but I wasn't going to let my guard down yet. Layla and her parents had finished receiving guests without any problems, and since then we'd danced, mingled, and had refreshments. A stream of people came up to talk to Layla over the course of the evening and she always introduced them and I shook hands like a good date. Some of the ladies made comments about how cute we were as a couple. Most of them were middle-aged, and except for the actors and singers whose names I already knew, I had trouble keeping track of them. I kept looking for the scenario that had played out in Kevin Adams' homemade comic book, but so far there was nothing. I was also looking for Nadia. Every time I saw someone shyly lurking in the shadows, I thought it might be her, but it never was. It seemed like she wasn't going to get here in time after all. Thank God. She'd be safe.

One more hour and this would be over. One more hour.

When Layla's mother went up on the stage and the band played "Hail to the Chief," I felt my attention go into overdrive. Yes, there were two Secret Service agents located discretely on either side of her, but still she was vulnerable. I knew how quickly someone could get struck down. A bullet flies faster than a hiccup, a lightning bolt crosses the room like a sneeze. One second a person can be standing there just fine, planning what they're going to do the next day. A moment later there is no next day. Someone's death is always a loss, but if the president were killed it would be a national tragedy. No, a worldwide tragedy. I held my breath as she held up her hand to stop the applause.

"This is where she announces it's my birthday," Layla whispered, holding my arm fiercely. "And then I'll have to cut the cake and pose for pictures." Under her breath she made a noise that reminded me of a car crash. "If I were a good girl I'd be up there already." She shot me a rebellious grin.

Layla told me she liked the occasional perks of being the president's daughter—the backstage concert passes, traveling, getting to visit movie sets. But she hated not having any privacy and having to keep up a fake public persona. And she was not looking forward to sharing her birthday with four hundred people even if it was just for fifteen minutes.

The president spoke. "As many of you know, my daughter Layla will be celebrating her nineteenth birthday tomorrow." Polite applause filled the ballroom. Off in the distance, a drunken male yelled, "Happy birthday, Layla! You rock! Woo hoo!"

Layla leaned over and whispered in my ear. "That's Kyle Sternhagen. Every year he gets totally wasted."

When the clapping and laughter subsided, the president said, "Layla? Will you come up and join your father and me on stage?" She lifted her hand to shield her eyes as she searched for her daughter. "Where are you, dear?"

Layla cooperatively raised a hand and called out, "Right here, Mom." She took my arm and pulled me along with her and we headed to the stage. Mr. Bernstein had already joined his wife and they'd linked arms like Ferris Bueller's parents standing over his bed. Off to one side, Vice President Montalbo and his wife held hands and smiled.

The crowd parted as we walked forward. I tried to avoid stepping on her dress while simultaneously staying alert to those around us in case I had to fend off an attack. Layla, who had her paparazzi smile on, greeted people along the way. Mallory and Jameson followed behind us; I could hear Mallory's excited whispering to Jameson. During our training we'd gone over the night's schedule dozens of times. I knew that Layla's cutting of the cake was only symbolic. In the back kitchen were trays full of wrapped cake that would be positioned by the exits for the guests to take home. Layla would take the first slice, taste the frosting, and declare it delicious. The crowd would sing "Happy Birthday," and then the band would play one last song ("Come Fly With Me" was the usual choice, since it was Layla's favorite). Afterward the first family would thank everyone for coming and depart through a secret door located behind the stage. And then the lights would be raised, and the band would pack up their equipment. If the guests didn't get the hint by the time the staff began cleaning up, they would politely be told the building had to be vacated for security reasons.

Layla bounded up the stairs at a remarkably fast clip, given her high heels. I tried to stay behind, but she wouldn't let go of my hand. When we got to the center of the stage, she held my hand up like pronouncing me the winner, then spoke into the microphone, "My date this evening is the fabulous Russ Becker. Isn't he handsome? Give it up for Russ!" As the applause thundered, a warm flush crept over my cheeks. In a few seconds, my reddened face would be evident to everyone there. There was no stopping a blush once it started.

Out of the corner of my mouth, I said, "Thanks, Layla."

"You didn't think you were going to get off easy, did you?" she said, smirking.

Embarrassed, I surveyed the room. From this angle I saw the entire banquet hall, the rows and rows of people standing in front of the stage like concert-goers waiting for the opening chords of their favorite song. But behind them, way in back and off to one side, was something more alarming, something that just looked *wrong*. A group of men clustered around a gurney. I squinted, trying to figure out what was happening. The patient lying on the gurney was the gray-bearded father of the muscle-bound boy, the same pair who caught Layla's attention earlier. A man in a white jacket (a doctor?) was talking to a dark-haired woman in red. It was hard to see what was going on. Why were they just hanging out here? Wouldn't someone sick or injured get rushed to the hospital?

A server wheeled a cart holding a large tiered chocolate cake onto the stage, and President Bernstein said, "Please join me in singing 'Happy Birthday' to Layla." The band leader raised his baton and the room filled with music and the sound of voices singing the familiar tune.

Layla still had her arm linked through mine, but I shook it loose and took a step forward to get a better view of the back of the room.

CHAPTER FORTY-SEVEN

NADIA

The doctor pulled me closer. I tried getting away, my feet scrabbling on the smooth floor, but his firm grip meant I was not going to be going anywhere soon. I was close enough to see every detail: the dark wavy hair and mustache, large plastic rimmed glasses, and the bulbous nose, which I knew to be fake, as were the hair and mustache. He had a stethoscope draped over his neck like a pet python. The white jacket had the name Dr. Michael Mitchard embroidered over the pocket, but I knew this man and he wasn't Dr. Michael Mitchard. "Mr. Specter," I said breathlessly. "Don't do this."

"Oh ho!" he said, close to my ear. "Aren't you turning out to be quite the little pistol?"

"Let me go," I said, thinking quickly. "I didn't see anything. You know I don't have any powers that can hurt you."

Both of the Secret Service agents standing on either side of the gurney turned to look at me. Young guys with a clean cut look and nearly identical suits. They could have been brothers. "Help me," I pleaded. "He won't let me go."

Mr. Specter waved at them to turn around and they did,

showing me without a doubt where their allegiance fell. His hold on my arm was even tighter now. "I can't let you go. You're a liability, Nadia. I underestimated you before, but it's not going to happen again."

I glanced up at the stage. One of the servers had wheeled out a cart holding what looked like a chocolate wedding cake, and Layla was giving an impassioned speech about everything that had happened in her life since her last birthday. All eyes were on Layla. No one seemed to notice the girl in the red dress being held against her will. To buy time, I said, "What do you mean you underestimated me?"

"You're not supposed to be here," he said. "According to my visions, you should be in the morgue back in Edgewood."

"Why would I be in the morgue?" My heart thumped in my chest.

"That's usually what happens to someone whose throat gets slashed by a butcher knife," Mr. Specter said almost cheerfully. He reached out and touched the stitches on my neck and I flinched. "Somehow you've managed to disturb the future space-time continuum. Why didn't your mother get that knife in a little deeper?"

"I kicked her."

"And why would you do that?"

I stared at him dumbfounded. "Because I wanted to live."

"But you didn't before. Hmm…" And almost to himself he said, "I wonder why that's changed?"

On stage, the president asked the audience if they'd join her in singing "Happy Birthday" to her daughter, Layla. In a moment, the noise level in the room was going to build an acoustic wall. If I was going to yell for help, it had to be now.

"Let go of me!" I shouted. My yelling got the attention of the gray bearded man on the gurney. He started to sit up and his fake son pushed him back down, but not before I saw the older man's eyes. I knew those eyes, but I didn't have the luxury of figuring out where I'd seen him before. I kept screaming. "Someone help me!" And then, thinking I might be able to get Russ's attention, I screamed, "Russ, be careful. It's Mr. Specter—," Too late, I felt a needle jab the side of my neck and immediately I lost control of my limbs. It was as if every muscle had instantly become paralyzed. My vision became fuzzy but I felt Mr. Specter catch me right before I collapsed onto the floor.

"She just had a bit too much to drink," he said to those standing around us.

I felt my consciousness fading away. It was happening fast, so fast that if I couldn't do it quickly, it wasn't going to happen at all. *Take me out of my body.*

And just like that I was hovering over my body, watching as Mr. Specter held me in his arms. It was the way people describe near death experiences, their spirit floating above their dead body. But I wasn't dead. At least not yet. And best yet? I could see them but they couldn't see me.

I needed to act quickly, and yet I couldn't help but pause and look at myself for a second. Good grief, I was small. I knew I was shorter than almost everyone else, but really, I had no idea. No wonder Russ had been able to carry me so effortlessly in Peru. And here I'd worried that I was too heavy.

The second thing that hit me was that I was actually beautiful. It didn't hurt that I wore a gorgeous red gown and that my hair was twisted into a sophisticated up-do held in place by a gem-studded headband. Nice accessories and all, but it was my face that was surprising. Even without much makeup my skin was flawless, and I had such nice features—long dark lashes, cute nose, high cheekbones. They'd been there all the time, but I never knew it. I'd been too busy keeping my hood up to hide my hideous skin. I never knew I could look so good. I'd thought if my scars were fixed I would look average and looking average would have been fine with me. I prayed to be average, in fact. I wanted to blend in and be like everyone else, but this girl's face was beyond that. She was gorgeous. If it wasn't me, I would want it to be.

Layla Bernstein might have four hundred people singing "Happy Birthday" to her. She was rich and beautiful and tall and famous, but I no longer envied her. I was exactly who I needed to be. If I got out of this night alive, I would never complain again.

The crowd was getting boisterous now, singing with gusto and raising their glasses to toast Layla. I could hear Kyle Sternhagen over the rest of the voices, making up extra lyrics to the song and adding "cha, cha, cha," during the pauses. He was drunk, but at least he'd have made a suitable witness. I shouldn't have been so quick to ditch him. Now I had no one looking out for me.

And then I saw my savior. A real Secret Service agent strode purposefully onto the scene. The look on his face said he knew something was off. "What's going on here?" he asked, indicating my limp body.

"She just had a little too much to drink," Mr. Specter said, playing the part of Dr. Mitchard. "Tomorrow she'll pay a price, but otherwise she'll be fine."

The agent's eyes narrowed. "Why aren't you transporting the heart attack patient to the hospital?"

"I've determined it was a panic attack. The patient is sta-bilized and waiting for a family member to come pick him up."

"I'm going to need to check on this," he said, shaking his head.

Inwardly I cheered, but before I could make it an all-out celebration one of the fake agents stepped forward. "No need to do that. I've got it covered."

My savior said, "And who might you be?" His voice was indignant. Yes! Their cover was blown and soon a whole squad of Secret Service agents would swoop in and arrest the five of them. An old man accompanied by his so-called son, a fake doctor, and two imitation Secret Service agents. Who in their right mind thought this idea would work?

The fake agent leaned in close and rested his hand on my savior's arm. He said, "Everything here is fine. You're going to walk away now and feel satisfied that you've investigated the situation. If anyone asks, you will assure them that the doctor and his crew were sanctioned by the White House. Do you understand?"

My heart sank as I recognized he was using Mallory's brand of mind control. Would it work?

The agent blinked like he'd suddenly awakened from a long nap. "Yes, I understand."

"Now go and check out the guy who's escorting Layla Bernstein. He seems suspicious. You need to take him out of the room for questioning."

My savior obediently wandered off and didn't even look back. The plane had gone over the island and didn't see me waving for help. He was gone.

On stage the band played an intro and then launched right into "Happy Birthday." The crowd sang along, some of them lifting their glasses to toast Layla.

Even so, I stayed with my body, so I heard the old man on the gurney lift his oxygen mask and say, "Smooth. Now what are you going to do with her?" No one around them could hear his voice, which sounded incredibly feminine. I veered closer and looked beyond the fake beard and mustache, and the matching hair piece. The tux no doubt covered a body girdle hiding this person's true female form. Or maybe there was some kind of padding rounding it all out. I wasn't sure of the details, but I was certain of one thing. Underneath all the deception lurked someone I knew.

Mrs. Whitehouse.

Mr. Specter nodded to one of the Secret Service agents. "Take her, will you?" He handed my body off as easily as if I were a life-sized Raggedy Ann.

"What do you want me to do with her?"

"Do whatever you want," he said. "Just get her out of sight. And whatever you do, make sure it's permanent."

The young guy Russ had called Snake Boy grinned so wide I could see the gold tooth in the back of his mouth. "Let me take her," he said. "I got me a few ideas what to do with her." Oh man, I had a sick, sick feeling about this.

Mr. Specter frowned at Snake Boy. "You're not going anywhere." He gestured to the wheeled base of the gurney. "I'll need you in case the Specteron doesn't work." I could see now that the base was a metal box with tubes coming out of it, one of which was attached to the oxygen mask covering the patient's face. Mr. Specter nudged the box with his foot, where Mrs. Whitehouse, in character as the old man, still lay.

She slapped at his hand. "Careful there. Don't set it off while I'm on top of it."

"I designed this thing myself," Mr. Specter said, absent-mindedly tugging on the stethoscope." Believe me, it won't go off until I activate it. And that's not happening until the official goodnight. And believe me, it will be an official goodnight. Or should I call it the last and *final* goodnight?" He tilted his head toward the stage where the president stood with her husband and daughter. Russ was no longer next to Layla. I rose and scanned the room only to see him moving frantically through the crowd, a tuxedoed salmon trying to swim against the current.

I watched the faux Secret Service agent carry my body out of the hall through swinging doors. My head, still covered in the glimmering headband, drooped over his arm and my legs dangled loosely. I wanted to take action, but I was conflicted. Should I stay and see what Mr. Specter was up to, or follow my own body? Or maybe something else entirely.

I decided. *Take me to Russ Becker.*

CHAPTER FORTY-EIGHT

RUSS

I stood on the stage trying to see what was going on in the back of the room. My breath caught in my chest when the dark-haired woman turned around and I realized it was Nadia and that the doctor had her by the arm. Nadia twisted around and yelled my name, and my heart burst into a million pieces. She needed me and I wasn't there.

She screamed something I couldn't make out and the doctor put his hand up to her neck. Whatever he did caused her to wilt like he'd killed her. Swiftly, he scooped her up before she hit the floor and held her in his arms like a sleeping child.

Adrenaline bursting and heart pounding, I leaped down the stairs. I couldn't get to Nadia fast enough; the ocean of people made it impossible to make any headway. I pushed through the guests. The ones who noticed me, and that seemed to be all of them, looked puzzled.

"The boy's running scared," one man joked.

Three more steps and I heard a woman call out, "What's the matter? Can't handle Layla?"

Layla. Oh no. When I dashed off the stage, I'd only had

one person in mind. Nadia. During training they'd repeatedly stressed the importance of never leaving Layla unprotected and I'd done just that without a second's thought. I'd done the worst thing a bodyguard could do—I'd left my post.

I looked back to see that Jameson had already taken my place by Layla's side. He saw me looking at him, noticed my hesitation, and motioned for me to just go. His gesture said that he had this and I should do what I had to do. I weighed the situation for about a nanosecond. I wasn't sure I could trust him, but it came down to this: I had to. Nothing was more important than Nadia.

I kept going in the direction where I'd last seen Nadia fall limp into the doctor's arms. The image of him hurting her made me burn with anger. With each step I took, the electricity in my body welled up inside of me, building and building, until finally it was so strong, I had to clench my muscles to keep it from spilling out. If I didn't watch it, I'd wind up frying that man alive. I needed to hang on to some semblance of control or I was going to blow up this whole building.

I charged onward with my gaze straight ahead. I kept my words to a minimum. "Move." Startled, most people stepped aside and the ones who didn't were shoved.

"Stop right there."

I glanced up to see a Secret Service agent standing in my path. He'd arrived so suddenly we nearly collided. I pointed to myself. Me? And he nodded, all serious and said, "Don't take another step. You need to come with me for questioning."

I didn't get it. All of the agents had been informed that I was Layla's date, and I'd already passed through security. Why would the Secret Service want to question me?

ABSOLUTION

There was only one explanation. He had to be an imposter planted by the Associates. When he roughly grabbed my elbow, I shook it off and when he reached for something inside his suit coat, I reacted by giving him a jolt of electricity. I tried to keep it small, something less than being tased, but I overshot by a lot. I wasn't touching him at the time, so the charge arced through the air and into his mid-section. Everyone around us who saw the blast stepped back, alarmed. He dropped to his knees and rocked back and forth, trying to contain the pain. I took advantage of the situation and kept moving. The group "Happy Birthday" sing-along had just wrapped up and the applause drowned out the guests cries of alarm. "Someone help this man," a woman screamed.

"Him. He's the one who did this," another woman cried out and even though my back was to her, I knew she was pointing in my direction. I definitely looked like the bad guy here, but I didn't have time to explain. For now my only hope was to get lost in the crowd before the panic spread.

From the front of the room, I heard the singer take to the microphone again. "That was a wonderful rendition of 'Happy Birthday.' And now, if you'll indulge us, the band would like to perform another special piece for Layla's birthday." The band launched into a song I recognized as the Beatles classic birthday song. Luck was with me because the band was so loud it drowned out the outcry behind me.

Twenty feet away from where I'd zapped the agent, I saw the air start to shimmer right in front of my face. Because I knew what would happen next I stopped. Just as I expected, the shimmer took on color and then form. And then it became a perfect holographic image of Nadia. From the startled exclamations of those around me they could see it too,

372

but I couldn't worry about them right now. The joy I felt came out in one word. *Nadia!*

Russ, I don't have much time, so listen carefully.

I shut out the world and concentrated on her, and her alone. *Yes?*

Mr. Specter is here dressed up as a doctor and Mrs. Whitehouse is posing as an old guy who had a heart attack. They're with the Associates and the others with them are Associates too. Some of them look like Secret Service agents.

I know, I encountered one already. He wanted me to go with him for questioning.

That one actually was a Secret Service agent. She shook her head. *Never mind that now. The gurney the patient is lying on is a weapon Mr. Specter invented. He said he improved on Tesla's design. I'm not quite sure how it works but it shoots some kind of deadly particle beam. It's going to go off when the president says good night. You have to leave right now. Right now!*

But what happened to you? Where did they take you?

She said, *I'm fine. Don't worry about me. I need to know you're safe so just leave the building and get as far away as possible. I love you but I have to go!*

But what about everybody else? I thought about the president's family and Mallory and Jameson, all of them unaware of what was about to happen. I thought of Kyle Sternhagen singing drunkenly off key, and all the scientists and artists and everyone else who was present in this room. All the great minds of our day were together in one place. All of them were about to die, and I was going to be a coward and go? That wasn't right.

She shook her head. *You're the only one I'm worried about.*

Be safe. I love you. Her image quivered for a few seconds. *Leave right now. Promise me!*

And then she faded from sight.

CHAPTER FORTY-NINE

NADIA

It killed me to have to pull away from Russ, but I had a bad feeling about what was happening to my body. I concentrated hard and put out a request: *take me to Nadia.* It felt weird to refer to myself in the third person, but it must have been the right thing to do because it worked.

I found myself following the Secret Service imposter as he carried me down a long fluorescent-lit back hallway. My body was completely limp; my head jiggled slightly with each step and my legs swung like pendulums. One of my arms was pressed against his chest, the other, the one wearing the ring Russ had given me, hung loosely in front. Seeing the ring from this angle reminded me of the night I'd received it, and what Russ had said about the continuous spiral pattern—*it symbolizes our interlocking lives and our never-ending love.* Oh, why did I let him go? We should have run away together that night. I could have so easily crawled through that window. It didn't matter where we went after that. We would have figured something out. At least we'd now be safe and together instead of in this impossible situation.

The man carrying my body spoke quietly under his

breath. At first I thought he was talking to himself until I figured out what he was saying. "It's a shame what I have to do to you, pretty girl," he said, looking down at my face. "Such a shame."

He turned a corner and came upon a portly man pushing a mop around the tile floor. When he straightened up, it was easier to see his janitor's blue shirt with the oval name patch that said, "Dean."

"Wet floor. Be careful," Dean said leaning on the mop like it was holding him up.

I feared the imposter agent might kill Dean, but instead the guy said, "Will do, thanks."

"What's with her?" Dean asked, motioning with his head. Up close I saw that he had a day's worth of dark whiskers covering his lower face and the top half of his neck.

"This little lady had a bit too much to drink."

"Ah." Dean gave him an understanding nod. "Good champagne is wasted on those that can't handle their liquor. Me, I could drink all night and never feel a thing."

"I hear you brother." The agent maneuvered around Dean and kept going. "Have a nice night."

"Yeah, you too." Dean sighed and went back to his work.

The agent continued to a service elevator at the end of the hallway. Getting in, he pushed the button for the lowest level and hummed along with the music. A sense of panic overwhelmed me. I'd been too much of a spectator, tagging along with my body, but not doing anything to protect myself. But really what could I do? In this state I couldn't turn on a light switch, much less fend off an attacker. If I were lucky, Russ, my hero, had listened to me and was on his way out of the building. I was on my own.

But. And there was a but and it was a big one. I could show myself to someone else and get them to help me. Who wouldn't want to save an unconscious girl from who knows what kind of horrible thing?

The closest person, proximity wise, was Dean, the janitor. He didn't look particularly muscular, but he was big and he'd have the element of surprise on his side. Yes, he would do.

Take me to Dean.

He was right where we'd left him, still mopping, still sighing. I concentrated on making myself seen, and gave him a mental nudge to lift his head so he could see me. His eyes widened in surprise as I became visible. I said, *Dean, you have to help! The girl you saw being carried—*

I stopped mid-sentence because Dean had started visibly shaking and then it got worse. His face grew white and a wet spot formed around his crotch, spread down his leg and ended in a puddle on the floor between his shoes.

I tried to reassure him. *It's okay. I'm a real person. I'm just astral—*

But he didn't stick around to hear the rest. Instead, he turned and ran, screaming with the high-pitched wail of a little girl. No one would ever believe him, but I suspected he'd be telling this story for the rest of his life.

Take me back to Nadia.

We were in a cleaning supply closet. Shelves on one side held various bottles and jars of cleaning solutions. Leaning against the opposite wall was a jumble of brooms and mops, next to a bucket on wheels. And in the middle of all this there I was, flat on my back on the floor with the fake Secret Service agent kneeling next to me studying my face.

I materialized faster than I ever had before. I willed my astral projected self to fill the closet with my presence. *What do you think you're doing? Get away from me!*

This man did not react in fear like Dean the janitor, but he did look puzzled. "What are you?" he asked.

I couldn't resist. *I'm your worst nightmare.*

He put his hands over his ears, like he was trying to shut out my voice in his head, but I had news for him. Wasn't going to work.

Covering your ears won't help.

Lowering his hands, he said, "I wasn't doing anything to her." He stuck out his chin defiantly. "Nothing at all. Just go away." Pointing to the door, "Be gone. Leave me alone."

And that's when it hit me. He had no idea that the girl on the floor was me. Russ had recognized my likeness when I'd astral projected, and so had Mallory and Jameson, but they knew it was me from the start. This guy didn't have a clue, which gave me a huge advantage. *I'm not going anywhere*, I said. *You need to leave this girl and go or you'll be sorry.*

He shrugged. "No can do," he said. "I've got my orders." He shook off his suit coat and pulled something out of the inside pocket, then fastidiously folded the jacket in two and set it on a nearby shelf. Now I could see that the object in his hand was a knife. He took off the sheath and admired the knife, looking at himself in the reflection of the silver blade.

I was afraid of him. Why wasn't he afraid of me? *Stop.* I made my voice as powerful as I knew how. *Stop right this minute.*

"Or what?" he said, bored. He ran his finger over the blade's jagged edge.

I scrambled to come up with an answer, but I had nothing.

"I thought as much," he said, and then as if, giving himself a pep talk, chanted, "The hallucinations never last. The voices aren't real. The hallucinations never last. The voices aren't real." He took the knife and held it over my neck, like he had a rump roast in front of him and he was deciding where to cut. The stitches from my encounter with my mother's knife stood out on my exposed neck. I could still remember the horror of the blade slicing into my skin and the feeling of blood flowing down my front.

I'm not a hallucination. I said, frantically. *I'm a ghost.*

Now I had his attention. The knife still in his hand, he looked straight at me. "Like a dead person?"

Yes, I'm dead. One of your relatives has sent a message. She says, I thought for a moment, *that she is disappointed in you. She wants you to change your ways.*

His face fell. "Nonny?"

Yes. She says it's not too late. That you're a good boy and you know better. Nonny says you should let go of the past. Terrible things happened to you when you were a little boy, but it wasn't your fault and that doesn't mean you're a bad person. The words poured out of me without any thought on my part. Where was all this coming from?

He whispered, "She always said I was a good boy."

You can still be good and make her proud. Nonny says to put the knife away and leave the girl alone. And from now on, live a good life. Something else popped into my head. *She also says you should go to a doctor and get help for the hallucinations.*

He stood up and pointed with the knife. "I should just leave her here like this?"

Yes. Just go. Leave the building as fast as you can and from now on choose to do the right thing. Make Nonny proud.

CHAPTER FIFTY

RUSS

Nadia had said, *I'm fine. Don't worry about me. I need to know you're safe so just leave the building and get as far away as possible. I love you but I have to go!* And: *Leave right now. Promise me!* But I hadn't promised and I knew I couldn't just run out of the room and leave everyone else behind.

I hesitated, feeling pulled in three directions. Part of me (most of me) wanted to find Nadia. Another part felt like I should go back and protect Layla. But the third part, reaching Mr. Specter and disengaging his machine, had the biggest pull and it was, I knew, the reason I was here.

The band played on, but I knew when the song was over, the president was going to thank everyone for coming and say good-night. According to Nadia, that was when the weapon would be activated. I needed to get to the back of the room and pushing through the crowd took too much time. I had to change my strategy.

"Back off," I yelled. "I need some space." I moved in a circle with my arms outstretched, letting off sparks as I turned.

The people around me responded the way I thought they would.

"Ouch!"

"Ow!"

"What was that?"

"Stop it!"

Those who got shocked instinctively moved away from the pain. After I'd done a full revolution, a circle had cleared around me. Just what I was aiming for. Palms down, I let out an enormous blast, giving the impression of lightning coming off of both hands. The impact pushed me upward and forward. Once I was over the crowd, I realized I was going to fall short of my goal. If the room were empty I could have done another blast and given myself more liftoff, but there were too many people beneath me and someone was bound to be in the way. Killing innocent bystanders was never an option. I grabbed at the draped fabric that decorated the ceiling thinking I'd swing down like in the movies, but it wasn't securely attached and when I fell, it came down with me. The only thing it did was slow my fall, but not by much. Below, spectators screamed as I landed in a crouch and scrambled to keep my balance.

A path had cleared between me and my destination. The patient, Mrs. Whitehouse as a man with a gray beard, stood next to the gurney while the doctor, Mr. Specter, regarded me with amusement. On either side of them stood several young men, including the guy posing as the older man's son. Mr. Specter looked ridiculous in his fake hairpiece, mustache, and glasses. He looked straight at me and over the sound of the music yelled, "You're late, Mr. Becker." The same words he'd use when I used to arrive to his sophomore science class after the bell had rung.

No sooner were the words out of his mouth than the imposter son walked angrily toward me with palms extended. Zaps of electricity shot out of him and pelted me in the chest. It took my breath away. The guy outweighed me by a lot and his rage was intimidating, but his methods were all wrong. I was Russ Becker. At home that meant I was a second child in a middle class family in a small town in Wisconsin. But in a situation like this, it meant I had the upper hand. I'd been called a second gen, but that wasn't technically correct. I wasn't the second generation to experience the lux spiral, but I had been exposed to particles from the lux spiral once as a baby and again when I was fifteen. Every cell in my body had been infused with something special since I was a few months old. And shooting electricity at me was like handing me weapons.

"Woo hoo, how do you like that?" the guy crowed. Between the familiar look and the distinctive voice, I knew who I was dealing with. When the Associates had abducted Frank, they'd made me go through a series of tests before they would release him, and this guy was part of one of those tests. At the time I'd dubbed him Snake Boy because he had a python tattooed on the side of his neck. I'd defeated him and his friend, Wavy Hair, the day of the test, and I could do it again.

"I like it fine, thanks." I sent his electricity right back at him, which took him off guard. He fell to the floor writhing from the impact. The air crackled from the current and onlookers scrambled for the exits.

Now I was the one walking with a vengeance, ready for the

next attacker, an Associate dressed as a Secret Service agent. I realized as he got closer that I'd met him before too. Tonight his hair was slicked down, and he'd cleaned up pretty well in the suit and white shirt, but I would have known Wavy Hair anywhere. One of my worst memories was of him and his buddy knocking me down and repeatedly zapping me with electricity whenever I tried to get up. "Remember me?" I shouted, sparks flying off my hands.

"Meb-be I do." Wavy Hair laughed. "I remember how easy it were to pin you down. Me and my buddy almost had you crying like a little girl."

He threw a lightning bolt toward me and I instinctively ducked. Straightening up, I returned the favor, shooting electricity back at him. He wheeled around, deflecting my shot with one of his own. This was proving to be harder than I thought. From the floor, Snake Boy, screamed something unintelligible. It sounded like he was cheering his friend on.

I recoiled, ready to go again, when something above me whooshed through the air skimming the top of my head. Before I could even react, I saw that it was a thick rope with a tassel heading straight for Wavy Hair. In a matter of seconds, the rope wrapped around him, pinning his arms to his side and whipping around him with such force that he fell to the floor.

In the front of the room the band wound down awkwardly as they *finally* realized something was wrong. One final squawk of a trumpet and the music had silenced. A man yelled, "Everyone take cover!" Panic ensued—men in their tuxedos shielded their dates, everyone scrambling to get out of the room or at least away from me. I glanced up to see that one of the curtains was no longer being held back by its tasseled rope. Jameson cupped his hands over his mouth and yelled from the stage, "You're welcome."

Looking back I saw Mr. Specter flip the top off the gurney and pull out what looked like the nozzle from a gas pump. An enormous roar filled the air as he aimed the nozzle toward the front of the room. A stream of glittering bits moved slowly and deliberately through the air. Was it electricity or a liquid or something else completely? Like glittering confetti, the individual pieces revolved around each other within the deadly particle beam. I'd never seen anything like it. The beam was heading toward the stage where Secret Service agents were escorting the president and her family off the stage.

A collage of words went through my mind all at once.

Nadia telling me I needed to leave and adding, *You're the only one I'm worried about. Be safe. I love you.*

Mr. Bernstein introducing me as *Russ Becker, the miracle maker from Wisconsin.*

Carly saying, *I'm proud of you, Russ. You're doing the right thing even though you know it might not end well.*

And President Bernstein: *I know I can rely on you.*

I knew what I had to do.

CHAPTER FIFTY-ONE

NADIA

When Nonny's grown-up boy left the supply closet, I listened to his footsteps as he walked down the hall. When he broke into a run, I knew he was going to follow the instructions to leave the building as quickly as possible. I didn't think he'd come back, which meant my body was safe enough for now.

Take me to Russ.

I'd hoped to find him in front of the building, or in a cab driving fast and far away, but instead I went to the ballroom where it was complete pandemonium. My heart sank. The elegant soiree was now a disaster scene. Frightened guests yelled and carried on as they pushed to get out. Secret Service agents tried to slow down the stampede to the doors. Russ stood in a clearing as if he were in a bubble. A few feet from him a man was lying on the floor with a thick rope wrapped around his midsection. His feet kicked weakly like a bug who'd been sprayed with insecticide. Behind Russ, another guy was curled in a fetal position on the floor, smoke rising off of him. On the stage in front, the first family was exiting out a door in the back shielded on all sides by protective agents.

And Mr. Specter, still in his Dr. Mitchard disguise, had activated his death ray beam and aimed it at the front of the room. The beam didn't shoot out quickly like in science fiction movies. Instead it moved languidly, sparkling and rotating as it went. It was a beautiful but determined beam, created to search for life then snuff it out. There was no way to get away from it once you were in its path. In a minute, everyone in the front of the room would be obliterated.

Run, Russ! Go. Now!

Russ made no sign of having heard me. Instead, he ejected himself in the air the same way he'd propelled himself onto my roof the night he'd given me the ring. He pushed off the floor using electrical currents from both hands and rose right in the path of the beam. When he met it, he blocked it with his own body. With his arms outstretched, it held him suspended in midair.

Oh, Russ, no…

The death ray's beam reflecting off his body created a light so brilliant I could barely make out the expression on his face. I don't know how long he hung there as a human barricade keeping the beam from going any farther. Even as painful as it was to watch, I couldn't keep my eyes away. Seeing someone you love suffering is the cruelest thing there is. I would have traded places with him like it was nothing, had him safe in another room, while I absorbed all of the Associates' evil, even if it ended my life. But I didn't have that choice.

Everyone in the room was fleeing away from this spectacle, except for three people running toward it. Mallory,

Jameson, and David Hofstetter. David took the lead, holding his arm out to indicate the others should stay back. When they got closer, Mallory gestured to the Associate Jameson had hogtied and cried out, "That one is getting loose." Sure enough, he'd managed to unravel the curtain tieback and was struggling to his feet. David pointed and let loose an electrical charge, small compared to what Russ could do, but enough to subdue the man.

Mr. Specter wrestled with the nozzle trying to direct it away from Russ, but the energy was drawn to Russ now like a flame to fuel. Russ twitched from side to side and I flinched. I'd once been burned with battery acid and thought that was the worst pain a person could ever experience, but this had to be ten times worse. How much more could he take?

David walked right up to Mr. Specter and blasted a lightning bolt at his feet to make a point. "Turn it off right now," he shouted, "or I swear I'll fry you alive."

Mr. Specter didn't even turn his head to look; he was still struggling with the nozzle.

I made myself known in front of him—faster than I'd ever materialized before. There was no way he couldn't see me. Judging from David, Mallory, and Jameson's expressions, each of them could see me too. I screamed in my head. *You have to shut it down. You're killing him.*

Mr. Specter yelled, "I can't turn it off. It won't let me." I wasn't sure if he was responding to me or David, but I heard the desperation in his voice and knew he told the truth. The machine was out of control. There was no stopping it now or ever. I willed my astral projected self to rise up closer to Russ. Even with the bright light I could make out the grimace on his face. It was the look of someone in agony. I didn't want to say good-bye.

I'm here with you, Russ. I love you. I didn't think he heard me so I tried again, keeping in mind that this might be the last opportunity I'd have to tell him how I felt. *I want to thank you. You've changed me in every way. Your love has made me stronger.*

I felt a flicker of something in return. An unspoken message, the way lovers smile at each other across a room.

At that moment, the glare intensified, getting brighter and brighter.

And then, the tide turned.

The room reverberated with a high pitched thrumming sound. The glow coming off of Russ's body spiked, until it was like looking at the sun. And then, a deafening blast filled the room as the ray bounced off Russ and reversed straight toward Mr. Specter and the death ray machine. The impact caused an explosion that shattered the chandeliers. Thick black vapor poured from the spot where Mr. Specter had stood only a moment ago.

Only seconds before the hall had been filled with the sounds of voices crying out, and people running to get to the exits. Now it was as still as death itself.

CHAPTER FIFTY-TWO

RUSS

Spasms of pain wracked my body as the beam held me trapped high above the floor. Worse yet was the psychological torture. The death ray was more than just energy; it was a collection of every negative emotion ever felt by anyone anywhere. I experienced the pain of prisoners of war, the agony of abused children, the loss of a thousand loved ones' deaths. All of the world's collective sorrows. Mired in it, it was hard to imagine why anyone would want to live at all. Life was all so dire and pointless. Nothing good could ever come from being a human being. We were born, we suffered, and then we died.

The word excruciating was invented to describe the physical and emotional pain I felt when suspended by the death ray. Nothing made sense anymore. What was the point of all this again? I didn't have a clue.

It seemed to go on and on. I could have been up there for minutes or hours. I wondered why I thought it was a good idea to leap up and stop the beam. It started as a selfless gesture. I wanted to keep the death ray from harming anyone else, but as I felt it filling every cell in my body, I knew this wasn't a real solution. There would be a saturation point and when that happened, I wouldn't be able to hold it back anymore. Then all of my suffering would be for nothing. It felt like a million burning fishhooks were poking and twisting every inch of my body. I writhed in pain and prayed for it to end. If it was a death ray, why wasn't I dead already?

When I felt Nadia's presence, it was a comfort. I was glad she would go on living long after I was gone. So much of her life had been terrible; she deserved better things to come. But even hearing her say she loved me didn't lessen the anguish. The torment was endless and infinite. I blinked back tears. If I gave in to it, that was the end. I wanted it to be over, but I didn't want my life to end this way.

To offset the pain, I concentrated on Nadia. Her voice rang in my head, the words crystal clear. *Your love has made me stronger.* Nadia had survived so much in her life—the excruciating pain of getting burned by battery acid, the horror of having a scarred face, the isolation of her home life. Whatever happened, she just handled it. I wasn't sure my love had made her stronger. She'd been strong to begin with. If anything, it seemed to me that she'd made me a better person. Or maybe we just brought out the best in each other.

Without even thinking about it, I drew up my strength, and made my body into a shield. A shield that deflected the death ray, sending it back to the machine and its creator.

The explosion was ear-splitting and so violent it made the building shake, but there was no ball of fire, like when a bomb goes off. The chandeliers burst and I heard the clatter of glass slivers as they fell to the floor. The death ray machine exploded and became a dark cloud that covered everything and then dissipated, leaving only wreckage. Without the beam to hold me up I dropped fast. My stomach lurched the same way it did riding a roller coaster. I knew if I landed the wrong way, that would be it for me. I'd braced for a crash landing knowing I would hit hard, so it was a shock to feel myself being caught and lowered gently to the floor. I bent my knees and tried to catch my breath. I was shaky, but alive.

The emergency lights came on almost instantaneously and through the eye-sting of smoke, I saw confusion. A billow of dust blanketed the room. Everyone who'd been standing behind the machine had been struck down. The fabric draping the ceiling was sooty and tattered, and tables and chairs had been knocked over or propelled across the room. Once the dust cleared I saw that the few remaining guests clustered close to the exits, looked shell shocked. Off to one side, a woman whined like a dog in distress.

Behind where the death ray had been, bodies littered the floor. A Secret Service agent lay completely still on the floor behind where the machine had been, his leg bent at an awkward angle. Behind him, Mr. Specter was sprawled on the floor face down with a blanket of soot covering his white jacket and blood pooling around his head. Judging from the amount of blood loss, he had to be dead. He'd started all this, and I'd only been defending everyone else here, but there was still a part of me that wanted to walk away guilt-free. Playing games where opponents died didn't really affect me. In real life, though, it's a horror that can't be described. I knew I would never get these images out of my head. They would haunt me for the rest of my days.

Jameson rushed up to me. "We need to stop them," he said, his voice high-pitched and frantic.

"Stop who?" I looked down to see that Mallory was now

kneeling next to David Hofstetter, pressing a cloth napkin to the front of his bloody shirt. "Are you okay?" I asked, and David grunted something positive in response.

"I've got him," Mallory said, concentrating on putting pressure on the wound. "You guys just do what you need to do."

Jameson snapped his fingers in front of my face. "Focus, Russ. We need to catch Mrs. Whitehouse and that other guy. The fake son."

"Where's Nadia?" I asked, wheeling around.

Jameson grabbed my arm. "You can find Nadia later. We need to go now." Conflicted, I followed him. I wanted an inventory of all the people I cared about—Nadia, Carly, Layla and her parents, Dr. Anton and Rosie. I wanted to know where they were and that they were safe and unharmed. But we were running now, past the stunned guests, who were helping each other to their feet and attending to minor wounds. We left the ballroom, and Jameson glanced back at me. "I'm not sure which way they went, but it's a safe bet they left the building. The two of them ran out while you were up in the air doing your dramatic, save-the-world scene."

Trust Jameson to come up with a comment like that. "I could have died, you know," I said.

"Yes, but you didn't, did you?" He gestured to an exit sign. "I think taking the stairs is a safe bet." He tried the knob, but the door was locked. I motioned for him to step aside, and gave it a blast, blowing it open.

"At least one of us has skills," I said as we went through. We charged down the stairs, down and around from floor to floor, grabbing the railing at each turn.

"Yeah, well you would have fallen on your ass a few minutes ago if not for me."

"That was you?" I thought of my drop from the ceiling and the sensation that a giant pair of arms had caught me on the way down. It didn't feel like Jameson, but I didn't have any other explanation so he had to be speaking the truth. I owed my life to Jameson. What a revelation.

"All me," he said. "So if you're talking about skills, give me some credit."

"Thanks, Jameson."

"You're welcome, pal."

We got to the first floor and burst out of the stairwell. Jameson said, "They'd have to drive out of here. I say we try the back parking lot where the employees park."

"We need to check the front where the valet is," I said. "They'd be in front. Definitely in front."

"Don't you think that would be too obvious?" Jameson said.

"That's why they'd do it," I said, leading the way. There wasn't time to get into it, but my hunch was based on more than that. You'd have to be completely arrogant to show up at the Presidential Black Tie Bash in disguise wheeling in a weapon of annihilation and think you could get away with it. And that's exactly the kind of person who would come and go using the front door with the rest of the guests.

We made our way across the lobby and through the doors that led outside. The front circular walk was crowded with guests waiting for their cars. I overheard one woman say, "I'm surprised the police aren't here taking statements." As we pushed through the crowd, conversations buzzed around us. Judging from what I overheard, everyone here had gotten out before the explosion. They were all clear that *something* had happened, they just couldn't get a handle on what it was. Was it a light show gone wrong, a terrorist attack, an electrical malfunction? When we reached the valet, I asked, "Did you see a short old man with a beard? He was with a young guy, his son?"

Jameson stepped next to me and joined in. "The son is like his size," he said, resting a hand on my shoulder, "but super muscular. Like, even the guy's neck is big."

The valet, a young guy with a blond buzz cut shrugged. "Yeah, I saw 'em. They drove up in a Bentley." He raised his eyebrows. "Nice ride."

"Can you tell us where the car is parked?" Jameson asked.

"It's not parked anywhere; it's right there." Turning around, we followed his outstretched arm and saw a silver Bentley speed past and accelerate down the drive toward the road. "Their chauffeur just picked them up."

Without a word, Jameson and I took off running after the car. Two people rode in the backseat, but it was impossible to see much more than that. The u-shaped drive had a median filled with flowering bushes surrounded by decorative stone. Jameson tried to stop the car by telekinetically winging some of the stones at it while I made a feeble attempt to shoot electricity at the rear wheels, but the fact of the matter was that we were too far out of range.

As we settled back on the curb in defeat, both of us panting breathlessly, Jameson picked at a piece of grass and said, "So close. Man, that was frustrating."

"At least we tried."

He said, "Why didn't you catapult yourself at them?"

"I couldn't do it. Tapped out." I leaned back and stretched my legs. Off in the distance I heard the wail of an ambulance. "Maybe we'll get another chance."

"Yeah I'm sure you'll be seeing Mrs. Whitehouse in the lunch line when you go back to school," Jameson said. "You can take her down while she's spooning out macaroni and cheese."

"The lunch program doesn't serve macaroni and cheese," I said, but I got his point. Chances were good we wouldn't be seeing Mrs. Whitehouse ever again.

CHAPTER FIFTY-THREE

NADIA

The death ray aimed at Russ's chest reversed direction and a second later the machine exploded. I left Russ's side to give Jameson a frantic message. *Catch him!* I said. There was only a fraction of a second, but I have to give Jameson credit—he totally came through, cushioning Russ's fall right before he would have hit the floor.

Russ looked dazed, but okay. Jameson and Mallory got through it too, but David Hofstetter must have been standing too close to the machine, because he'd gotten hit and knocked to the floor. Mallory grabbed a napkin off the floor and knelt down to apply pressure to the wound. As much as I wanted to stick around, I had to see where Mrs. Whitehouse went.

I'd noticed her earlier, still in disguise, slipping out of the ballroom, along with her sham son. This had happened about the same time Russ had thrown himself onto the death ray. While he was risking his life to undo their dirty work, they'd scurried away like rats leaving a sinking ship. So much for loyalty to Mr. Specter. He was the bad guy in all this, but still I felt for him. Having friends betray you was the worst.

But now I had to see where Mrs. Whitehouse and her cohort went. If they had something else planned and were coming back, I wanted to be able to warn Russ and the others. *Take me to Mrs. Whitehouse.*

The two were exiting an elevator and heading toward the front door of the building and I followed right along. The son, a bulky young guy with his neck tattoo now starting to show, had a cell phone to his ear. "Right now. Yes, this minute." There was a pause while he listened to the person on the other end and then he answered. "Aborted. We'll explain later." He ended the call and stuck the phone in his pocket. "He said he's sitting there and he'll pull the car around."

Mrs. Whitehouse didn't say a word. She stopped and looked back at the elevator with teary eyes.

"What are you waiting for?" His eyes shifted from her to the front door and back again. "The deal was if it didn't go as planned, I was out of there. And it didn't go as planned. In a few minutes this place is going to be overrun with uniforms and I'm not gonna be here when that happens."

"But what if Sam's injured and I'm not there to take care of him?" She asked, her voice plaintive.

"Look." The guy lowered his face to hers and spoke in a harsh whisper. "One of two things happened. He's either okay and he'll meet up with us later, or he's dead and it won't help for you to get caught."

At the word dead her lip started quivering, but he didn't notice or didn't care. She gulped as if trying to pull back tears.

He continued, "Now march to the door, and get your act together. I swear I'll leave you behind. I swear, I will walk right out that door," he pointed, "and I will not look back. I am *not* getting pinched because you can't deal. Now move."

She trudged behind him with the enthusiasm of a teenager forced to go on a family outing. Through the swinging glass doors they went and outside where the valet stood at his post. Other patrons were exiting now, all of them buzzing about the odd way the evening had ended. "I bet we read all about it tomorrow," a silver-haired lady in a mink shawl said. "It's probably some kind of preview for a show or movie."

Her portly companion nodded. "A magic act, no doubt."

While she waited, Mrs. Whitehouse stroked her fake beard, and muttered under her breath. "Come on, come on." She craned her neck. "How long does it take to pull a car around?"

"Just relax, *Dad*. He'll be here as soon as he can."

They waited a few more minutes, Mrs. Whitehouse sadly stroking her beard and looking like she was on the edge of losing it, while Snake Boy stood stock still, cool as can be. Behind them, people poured out of the building, chattering away about the spectacle. The new arrivals had seen more and the fear in their voices was evident. They wondered why the authorities weren't there. "Who's in charge here?" one man said. "I'd like to talk to someone in authority."

"How much longer?" Mrs. Whitehouse asked, her eyes wide. "Maybe we should start walking."

"Cool it. Look, that's him."

A large silver vehicle with an impressive front end and distinctive prism headlights circled the drive and pulled up in front of them. The driver, who wore a classic chauffeur's cap, didn't get out to open the door for them. Instead, Mrs.

Whitehouse yanked it open and slid into the back, followed by her fake son. I went along for the ride.

"What the hell happened in there?" I recognized Kevin Adam's voice before the chauffeur even turned around. Usually Kevin had a middle-aged cool thing going for him, but he didn't have it now, and he'd aged about ten years since the last time I'd seen him. His eyes were hangdog tired. His mouth turned down in a disapproving line.

"Just drive," Snake Boy said. "We'll have time to talk later."

As the car sped down the drive, Mrs. Whitehouse noticed something out the back window. "Faster," she cried. "Before they catch up."

Snake Boy and I turned to see Jameson and Russ running behind the car, their arms pumping with every stride. Snake Boy turned and glared. "Unbelievable."

I mentally cheered them on, even as I saw they weren't keeping pace with the car. Russ flung a small lightning bolt in our direction but it fell short. With a tilt of his head, Jameson lifted some pebbles from a planting bed and tossed them after us. They hit the window, but not too forcefully. Ping. Ping. Ping.

"What was that?" Mrs. Whitehouse turned around, her eyes wide. She'd pulled the beard and mustache off and bits of adhesive stuck to her chin.

Snake Boy scoffed. "It's nothing. Just keep going."

The Bentley turned out of the drive and onto the roadway, losing Russ and Jameson who watched helplessly from behind. They'd stopped running. Russ dropped his hands to his side in defeat while Jameson palmed his forehead. Kevin floored it and Russ and Jameson got smaller and smaller until I couldn't see them at all. A few miles out, Kevin took off the chauffeur's hat and ran his hands through his hair, trying to regain his Elvis pompadour. Tears streaked down Mrs. Whitehouse's face. "This wasn't how it was supposed to go," she cried. "Sam and I should be out celebrating right now." She pulled a tissue out of her pocket and blew her nose. "We were going to make a difference. A lot of people talk about it, but we were actually going to do it. We can change the world, is what he always said. The two of us were going to change the world for the better. And not for the glory," she said. "But because someone needed to take charge. Someone smart, someone looking out for the collective. We've planned this for years. We spent ages gaining allies on the inside, anticipating problems, practicing every scenario. And for what?" Her voice was bitter. "For nothing."

"*What* exactly happened?" Kevin asked. "Where's Sam?"

"We had to leave him behind," Snake Boy said. "Don't worry about it, just keep driving."

Mrs. Whitehouse said. "I'll tell you what happened. That damn Russ Becker intercepted the beam so it never reached the target. By all rights it should have killed him but since he was just out there running after the car like a dog, I guess it didn't."

"If he's still alive maybe Sam's okay," Kevin said hopefully. "Then we can all go back to Edgewood and forget this nonsense. Just live a normal life."

"I'm not forgetting anything," Mrs. Whitehouse said, resting her forehead against the window. "No way, no how. I'm remembering every bit of this for the rest of my life."

CHAPTER FIFTY-FOUR

RUSS

Jameson and I only rested for a few minutes before we got up from the curb, brushed ourselves off and headed back. When we got up to where the Bash was held, we found the doors closed, locked, and guarded by beefy security officers. "We need to get into the hall," Jameson said to the guy standing in front of the door we'd used just twenty minutes before.

"This whole area is off limits." The guy folded his arms and I saw that his biceps were the size of Jameson's head.

"Is there someone you can check with?" I asked. "Because I think they'll make an exception for us."

"No exceptions."

"You must have a list. I think you'll find our names on it."

He raised an eyebrow. "You two are somehow special?"

I ignored his sarcasm. "I'm Russ Becker. Maybe you've heard of me? I was Layla Bernstein's date?"

"Layla's gone home and I think you should too. Run along now. Playtime's over."

Jameson and I exchanged a questioning look. Should we try to get past this guy, wait it out, or what? Before we could decide, the door swung open and Dr. Anton stuck his head out. "Russ? Jameson? Oh good, you're back." He spoke to the guard. "They're okay. Let them pass."

Jameson gave the guy a smug grin as we walked by but I didn't bother. "Is the president and her family safe?" I asked.

Dr. Anton nodded. "And the vice president and his wife too. You did it, Russ. Because of you, we've avoided an international incident." He led us further into the room. "Come this way. We were watching on the monitor but by the time we came in you two were gone. We've been looking for you." We stepped over debris, including broken glass, soot, and assorted pieces of metal. On the opposite side, paramedics ratcheted a stretcher up so it could be wheeled out of the room. My sister stood nearby wringing her hands. When Carly saw me, she yelled, "Russ, get over here."

I hurried to her side. The paramedics had pulled a sheet over the body. I knew what was underneath. "David?" I asked.

Carly bit her lip and nodded. "You've got to help him, Russ." She blocked a wheel with her foot so they couldn't move it. "Give my brother a chance. He can fix him."

The two paramedics exchanged a look and then one of them said, "I'm sorry to tell you this, ma'am, but he's gone." He did sound sorry. He sounded very sorry.

She ignored him and pulled me closer. "You can do this." Her voice was ragged. "You *have* to do this."

Dr. Anton spoke to the paramedics. "Hey guys, could we just have a few minutes here to pay our last respects?"

The one who had spoken shrugged. "Sure, okay. We'll take five."

Before they'd even walked out of hearing range, Carly

had uncovered David's face. His eyes were closed and there was a small cut on his forehead, but otherwise he appeared to be fine. "I was just talking to him a few minutes ago. There shouldn't be oxygen deprivation damage or anything yet. Do your thing, Russ."

My heart sank. I had healed people on the brink of death, but I was pretty sure I couldn't raise someone who was already gone. I wasn't God. I was only a high school junior with superpowers. I felt a hand on my shoulder and saw Rosie standing next to me. "Just try," she urged. "Even if it doesn't work, your sister will know that you tried your best."

"Don't just try," Carly said angrily. "Do it."

I held my palms over David and willed the energy to go from my hands to him. I wished that his cells would draw from my energy and jumpstart his heart. I envisioned Carly, Frank, and David as a family and tried pouring the love Frank and Carly would have for David into his still body. I kept wishing and thinking and hoping. Energy. Love. Life. I took the words and channeled them through my hands to David's body.

I glanced up at Carly, took note of her tear-stained face, and tried again. Energy. Love. Life. I knew how to do this.

But none of it worked. David was gone, only a shell remained. I looked up to see Carly wringing her hands. I shook my head. "I'm really sorry, Carly. I'm not getting anything."

"Try harder then," Carly said, and when I shook my head no, her face contorted in anger and she lashed out at me, hitting me over and over again, the flat of her hand against my back. It didn't really hurt, but still I flinched. She cried, "Do it! Do it! Just do it!"

Finally Dr. Anton said, "That's enough," and pulled her away. "Russ can't do it, Carly. If he could, he would." She shook him off and collapsed into the fetal position on the floor, rocking back and forth and wailing. When Rosie tried to place a consoling hand on her shoulder she pushed it away.

"I'm so sorry," I said helplessly. "I can't do anything. It's too late. He's gone."

She looked up, her eyes smudged with makeup. "He was alive a few minutes ago. Where were you then, Russ?" she asked, venom in her voice. "What was so all-fire important that you couldn't be here for me? The one time I needed you and you were gone."

Her words shook me. She was right, I'd let her down, and now David was dead.

Almost like she'd heard my thoughts, Rosie put a comforting hand on my arm. "It's not your fault, Russ. You're only one person, you can't be in more than one place at a time."

"I would have stayed," I said, "but he didn't look that bad off." Even to me it sounded lame. "And Mallory said to go."

The quiet threatened to devour me. I glanced around the room. "Where is Mallory?"

Rosie said, "Mallory is working downstairs right now. They stopped all the folks who witnessed the explosion and she's using her talent to convince them it was just an act, part of tonight's entertainment."

"Is someone watching Mallory to make sure she's doing the right thing?" The fact that Mallory ran toward the death beam and tried to stop Mr. Specter made me believe she was on our side. Still, Nadia had said she couldn't be trusted.

405

Rosie nodded. "The necessary safeguards are in place."

"What about all the people who left before the explosion?" Jameson said. "There were a lot of them outside talking about it."

Carly let out a heartbreaking wail. If I could have, I'd have traded places with David. How could I tell my nephew that his dad died because of me?

Dr. Anton said, "The White House will release an official statement along the lines that the whole thing was an act, a preview of a movie going into production next year. Some of the guests have minor cuts or ripped clothing. That will be attributed to a mechanical malfunction. They'll be given gifts to compensate."

"No guests were killed?" Jameson asked.

"None." Dr. Anton smiled. "Luckily the deaths have been limited to those working for the Associates as well as three Secret Service agents. Brave men who gave their lives for their country."

"You three did well. I'm proud to know you," Rosie said.

I said, "Does anyone know where Nadia is?"

CHAPTER FIFTY-FIVE

NADIA

Poor Russ. I'd witnessed the meltdown Carly had after Russ was unable to bring David back. Even though Russ had already put his own life on the line and saved the country, and maybe even the world, from harm, I could tell he still felt like a failure. When he'd said, "Does anyone know where Nadia is?" his voice sounded so sad, I could have cried for him. And then, of course, I was overjoyed because it meant that he was worried about me and wanted to be with me.

I whispered, *Russ, I'm in the building still unconscious.* I told him I was in a closet in the basement and that I'd guide him. I thought it would be a simple matter. He'd find me, I'd slip back into my body, and we'd be reunited.

Ten minutes later in the supply closet, I watched as Russ cradled me in his arms. He stroked my cheek with one finger, looked up at the astral projected version of me and said, "You're so cold." He turned to look at Dr. Anton, who stood behind me. Jameson, too, had followed him down, and all three of them looked worried.

I started to say I was fine, but I was interrupted by Dr.

Anton who knelt down to check on me. He pressed two fingers to my wrist, frowned and then checked my neck. "Her pulse is really faint," he said.

Russ said, "But the fact that you are getting a pulse means she's okay, right?"

It's probably because I'm projecting, I said, referring to my faint heartbeat. I'd discovered that although Dr. Anton and Jameson could make out my form, I could only talk to one person at a time. Only Russ could hear me.

"She says it's because she's astral projecting."

If the idea that I could astral project was news to Dr. Anton, he wasn't showing it.

Jameson smacked a fist into his hand, like a catcher punching his glove. "So tell her to get back in there already."

"Wait!" Dr. Anton said. "Ask Nadia what they did to her. What's the last thing she remembers?"

A needle to my neck. One quick prick and I felt myself slipping away.

Russ repeated my words, and Dr. Anton nodded. He looked up at me and said, "Nadia, I know it's scary, but you need to slip back in. We'll do whatever we can to try and counteract the damage done by the injection. It may take some time, but we'll have the best minds in the country working on your case. You're in good hands."

Until he said the word damage, I hadn't been afraid at all. I'd assumed the effects of the injection were temporary, something to keep me quiet and out of the way. The thought that I might be permanently damaged never occurred to me. It didn't take much to go from there to thinking I might die. My mind reeled and in seconds I'd imagined my own funeral, my parents sobbing inconsolably, and Russ grieving for a short while before going on and living his life without me. In the future he'd have new girlfriends or a wife, and I would be just a bittersweet memory.

"Don't worry, Nadia," Russ said aloud. "I can heal you."

He sounded so positive that the whole funeral scene faded from my mind. Of course I wasn't going to die. I was sixteen. I had so much more to do.

"Go ahead," he urged, looking from me to my body. "It'll be okay."

Like diving into a pool, I just did it. I added my ethereal form to my human body. It would be okay. Russ said so.

CHAPTER FIFTY-SIX

————•○●○•————

RUSS

Dr. Anton called the paramedics who arrived a few minutes after Nadia slid into her body. I'd expected a change once she went back—that her face would regain its color or her heartbeat would grow stronger—but nothing happened. She was exactly the same. I put my hands over her body and directed my energy into her cells. I added every positive emotion I had, love being foremost, and willed it with every ounce of my being. But just like with David Hofstetter, I failed. "Why isn't it working?" I asked.

Dr. Anton rested a reassuring hand on my shoulder. "It's not a matter of healing her," he said. "Because she's not sick or injured. I suspect that she was given something akin to a paralytic drug. Until we figure it out and give her the antidote, nothing is going to change."

It was so frustrating. I could feel Nadia's energy, but I couldn't connect. The realization washed over me that maybe I'd never be able to find her, that maybe the Associates had paralyzed her permanently, and Nadia was now trapped in some lower depths I'd never be able to reach. I brushed my lips against her cheek and whispered, "Hang in there, Nadia. I love you."

And then the paramedics took over, checking her vitals, moving her onto a rolling stretcher, putting an oxygen mask over her mouth. The three of us moved along with them as they maneuvered down the hall and into the elevator. On the ride up my eyes never left Nadia. Even under the harsh light there was no sign that she'd once had scars covering one side of her face. Now she was perfect inside and out. Thoughts ran through my head. *Please let Nadia be well. Please, please, please. Bring her back to me.*

When the elevator opened on the main floor, Mallory stood, blocking our way. Her face registered surprise. "I was just coming down to find you," she said.

One of the paramedics said, "Miss, could you please step aside?"

Mallory ignored him. "Was Nadia injected with something?" she asked.

Dr. Anton and I simultaneously said, "Yes."

"Then I know how to fix her." She stepped inside the elevator.

Dr. Anton spoke to the paramedics. "Could you just give us a minute?" He held the door open, and made a motion for them to leave. Both of them left without questioning him. I was starting to understand that Dr. Anton was kind of a big deal around here. He pushed the button to close the door, giving us privacy.

Mallory held a hand out. "Russ, I need the necklace I gave you earlier." When I didn't react, she added, "The one in your pocket?"

"You said not to give it back to you no matter what."

"I meant *during* the Bash. It's okay now."

Dr. Anton said, "Go ahead. Give it to her."

I reached into the inside pocket of my suit coat, pulled out the rose necklace and handed it to her. She examined it for a moment, then turned it around. "It has two parts," she said. "When I press on here," she said, pointing, "a needle pops out that can be used to disable someone. If you do the same thing on the other side, another needle pops out that dispenses medication to counteract the first one." Mallory pushed on the top of the rose and a short needle popped out at the base of the rose. "And then you do this." She put the needle against the base of Nadia's neck.

Jameson, Dr. Anton, and I all reacted at once.

"Wait!"

"Stop!"

"Just a minute!"

But she was too fast for us. By the time I'd grabbed her hand, she'd already plunged the needle into Nadia's skin. My heart sank. We had no idea what she'd just injected into Nadia. What if it was more of the same and the added dose killed her?

"You shouldn't have done that," I said. "We don't know what was in that." I was so angry I couldn't stand to look at Mallory, so instead I looked down at Nadia, still and sweet, defenseless against the world.

"I told you what was in it," Mallory said, her eyes wide and innocent. "Why would I do it otherwise?"

"If you gave her the right thing, why didn't it work?" I asked.

"I don't know. Maybe it takes time."

Dr. Anton said, "It would have been better if we could have analyzed the medication before it was administered." He beckoned to Mallory with one curved finger. "If you'd close that up and give it to me, I'd appreciate it." Once she handed it over, he said, "PG officials will want to know how this came into your possession."

Mallory said, "I understand."

Nadia's neck had a tiny puncture mark from where Mallory had poked the needle. I ran my finger over her collar bone while Dr. Anton opened the door and motioned for the paramedics to return. I kept pace with them as they wheeled her out of the elevator and down the hall to the front of the building. I kept my gaze on Nadia the whole time, so I was the first to notice when her eyes fluttered open.

"Hey," I said, smiling down at her. "Welcome back."

CHAPTER FIFTY-SEVEN

RUSS

The Bash had taken a lot out of all of us, so when we finally got on the plane we were more than ready to go home. I was the middle man this time around, in the center seat with Nadia by the window and my sister Carly on the aisle. Once we were in the air, I let out a sigh of relief. We'd all made it safe and sound.

The day before we'd been questioned by some Praetorian Guard officials in a conference room in PGDC. Our old friend Dr. Wentworth was there along with Mitch and Will, but I got the impression that wasn't the full extent of it. They were the ones interviewing us, but others elsewhere were watching us via remote viewing. I could sense a surplus of electricity in the room—microphones, cameras, and cables.

Mallory got the brunt of their questions. I got the idea they weren't entirely convinced that Mallory wasn't an Associate spy, but when Nadia backed up her story by telling them what she saw in Mallory's room that night— Mr. Specter controlling her through the Deleo, they softened. "I was instructed to inject Layla Bernstein," Mallory said. "She'd collapse and the distraction would give them an opening to bring the doctor in with the wheeled gurney with the Specteron..."

"The Specteron?" Mitch asked.

"That's what he called it. It was his invention. A death ray machine."

"Go ahead," Dr. Wentworth urged.

"Well, that's about it. I was supposed to inject Layla but I didn't."

"Instead you gave the necklace to Russ?" Mitch said, prompting her.

"Yes."

"And why would you do that?" he asked.

"So that I wouldn't give in and follow Mr. Specter's orders."

"I see," Dr. Wentworth said, looking over her glasses. "But I think the real question is, *why* didn't you follow Mr. Specter's orders? What kept you from complying?"

Mallory pointed to Nadia and me. "It was them. Nadia astral projected to me and told me not to listen to him. And Russ told me how he fought the Deleo the last time so I knew it could be done."

"I see," Dr. Wentworth said, but she didn't look like she understood at all. "And the vice president—what message did you give him?"

Mallory said, "His loyalties are with the current administration and the Praetorian Guard, of course."

I raised my hand. "I have a question."

"Yes?"

"Did you guys know that Mr. Specter was still alive and that he was the new commander?"

"I'm sorry, Russ, but that's classified information," Dr. Wentworth said. I took that as a no.

In the end they had all of us write out everything that had happened from the minute we'd left Edgewood until the time we were called into the conference room. When we'd signed our statements we were free to go.

After we'd packed up and left PGDC, taking the elevator to the parking structure, Nadia said, "Now I know how Dorothy felt after she had to leave Oz to go home to Kansas." And now we were on the plane, where she rested her head against my shoulder. Her eyes were closed and her breathing slow and relaxed. She'd refused to go to the hospital the previous night, but the doctor had checked her over and given her the okay.

"Is she sleeping?" Carly asked, leaning over.

"Yeah, I think she's pretty tired."

"I think we're all really tired," Carly said.

It was the most she'd spoken to me since I'd failed to bring David back. I saw my opening. "You know Carly, David must have had a feeling that he was going to die. He told me that if he didn't get a chance to talk to you that I should tell you that he realized he made a big mistake and that if he had to do it over again he would have stayed with you, no matter what." There was one more thing, too. What was it? Oh yeah. "He also said that he figured out later that love should always come first."

She sighed. "Thanks Russ, but I know all that. We had a chance to talk for a few minutes before he died. He said he was sorry and that I was the only woman he ever loved. His life insurance policy has me and Frank as beneficiaries, can you believe that?"

"That's something anyway."

Carly shook her head. "Whatever it is, it's not enough. Money can't replace a person. And where do I go from here? It's like I've been waiting years for something to happen, and now I know it's never going to happen."

"I'm sorry."

"I'm sorry too, Russ. I shouldn't have blamed you. It wasn't your fault. Damn Associates."

"Well the good news," I said, "is that Dr. Anton thinks they'll leave me alone now. He said that with the new leadership their focus will shift and that the Praetorian Guard has the upper hand now."

"I hope he's right." She adjusted her seat to recline. "But I tend to think they're like cockroaches. Just when you think you got 'em all, they pop up again."

CHAPTER FIFTY-EIGHT

NADIA

"Nadia," my mother called up the stairs. "Your young man is here."

"Coming," I yelled back. I did one last check. My hair was pinned up, with curly wisps framing my face. My glittery red headband added a nice touch and held everything in place. I double-checked the zipper on the back of my dress, slipped my feet into a pair of red bejeweled shoes, and admired myself in the mirror. I spoke to my reflection, "Not bad. Not bad at all."

When I came down the stairs, I saw from the look on Russ's face that he recognized the dress. I didn't think I was supposed to take my evening gown home with me, but no one asked for it back, so I just tucked it into my suitcase. In the days that followed, sometimes I had to take it out and look at it just to convince myself that it had all been real.

Russ whistled and said, "Wow. You look beautiful."

I curtseyed and said, "Thank you, sir."

"You mind your manners with my daughter," Mom said. She'd been taking her medication and was a lot more reasonable, but no matter how many pills she took, she was never going to be my dream mother.

"Yes, ma'am, I will. I promise."

"And have her home by eleven."

"Certainly."

My dad said, "Oh I think they can stay out later than eleven…"

I saw the look on my mother's face and knew not to push it. "No, Dad, it's okay. If Mom wants me back by eleven, I'll make a point to be home by then."

"If I find out you weren't at the Homecoming Dance you'll be in big trouble," Mom warned, a scowl on her face.

How ridiculous. All she had to do was look at us. We were teenagers in formal wear; if we didn't go to the dance where else would we go?

"I'll show you pictures," I said. And then, before she could come up with anything else, I hurried Russ out the front door. My mother watched through the front window as Russ held the car door open for me. I waved and she let the curtain drop. It wasn't until we turned at the end of my street that I felt completely free. I caught Russ sneaking glances my way and he looked pretty pleased. "What are you thinking about?" I asked.

"I was thinking," he said, "that I can't believe your mom let you go to the dance with me."

"Well, as long as you mind your manners…"

"I think her definition of manners and mine are completely different." He laughed and then his face got serious. "You know, Nadia, you've saved my life a few times now. I don't know how I can ever pay you back."

I reached over and put my hand against his mouth and he kissed it, giving me a shiver of pleasure. I said, "You already have."

ABOUT THE AUTHOR

National best-selling author Karen McQuestion writes books for adults, kids, and teens. Her novels regularly place in the top 100 Kindle books, and each successive novel has added to her ever-growing fan base, making her one of the pre-eminent Amazon Publishing authors. McQuestion lives in Wisconsin with her family and is always working on her next novel. www.karenmcquestion.com

ACKNOWLEDGEMENTS

Many thanks to Kay Bratt, Kay Ehlers, Geri Erickson, Alice L. Kent, Tiffany Lovering, Greg McQuestion, Charlie McQuestion, Maria McQuestion, and Jack McQuestion. Your insights and suggestions have been invaluable and I am grateful.

A personal note from Karen...

If you've enjoyed this novel, I'd love to hear your thoughts in a review. Without readers, a story is a dead thing, just words on a page, so thanks for bringing this one to life! I don't have the words to say how much I appreciate readers like you.

And one other thing: although I've toured the White House and done research, I obviously have no inside knowledge of the Secret Service or security protocol concerning the president. I tried to make the novel as accurate as possible, but there may be errors, and for that I apologize. Hopefully readers can overlook any inaccuracies and still find the story entertaining. If it bothers you too much, try to pretend *Absolution* is fictional, and that people don't actually have superpowers and that there isn't an underground city under Washington D.C.

Made in the USA
Lexington, KY
14 September 2014